Havelock Ellis, Walter Savage Landor

The Pentameron

Havelock Ellis, Walter Savage Landor

The Pentameron

ISBN/EAN: 9783337395834

Printed in Europe, USA, Canada, Australia, Japan

Cover: Foto ©Andreas Hilbeck / pixelio.de

More available books at **www.hansebooks.com**

THE PENTAMERON AND OTHER IMAGINARY CONVERSATIONS BY WALTER SAVAGE LANDOR: EDITED, WITH A PREFACE, BY HAVELOCK ELLIS.

LONDON:

WALTER SCOTT, 24 WARWICK LANE

NEW YORK AND TORONTO:

W. J. GAGE & CO.

1889

CONTENTS.

PREFACE.

THE *Pentameron* and a selection of comparatively late *Imaginary Conversations* (reprinted without any omissions from the edition of 1846) are here brought together. *The Pentameron* belongs to the remarkable triad of books which Landor produced between 1834 and 1837, the others being *The Citation and Examination of William Shakspeare for Deer-stealing*, and the *Pericles and Aspasia.**

These three books vary much both in character and quality. *The Examination of William Shakspeare* is a failure, or, certainly, the nearest approach to a failure in any of Landor's longer writings. It is written with care ; there is a certain stolid unity about it which is impressive when it is looked at as a whole, but at scarcely more than one or two points can we hear Landor's true voice. Sir Thomas Lucy is a portentous Justice Shallow ; Master Silas the Chaplain and Ephraim the Clerk are alike dreary and silly ; while the youthful Shakespeare shows little promise of those eminent abilities which have since attracted so much attention. In painting the humours of a rich and massive nature, a Montaigne or a Porson, Landor was incomparable ; he had not the light hand which is needed to paint the humours of a fool. If it had not been for a faint

* A brief sketch of Landor's life, and an estimate of his position in English literature, will be found in the Introduction by the present writer to the volume of *Imaginary Conversations* in this Series.

sparkle of epigram emitted by the dying Lamb, " Only two
men could have written it, the man who did write it, or he
of whom it was written," *The Examination of William
Shakspeare* would probably never have been mistaken for
a masterpiece.

Pericles and Aspasia is the longest of Landor's works.
It is written in the form of letters between Aspasia,
her friend Cleone, Pericles, Anaxagoras, Alcibiades. Here
Landor enshrined all that he had meditated or imagined of
the glory that was Greece. It possesses a certain unity,
though it is fragmentary and digresses on every side,
sometimes startling us by transparently veiled diatribes
directed at Georgian (scarcely yet Victorian) England, and
we must not look for archæological realism. But here
and there, throughout, we may discover pleasant pictures
of Athenian life, true Landorian jewels of speech and
imagery. The wise and tolerant Pericles, the intelligent
and sympathetic Aspasia, the playful Alcibiades, Sophocles,
Thucydides, Aristophanes, are all brought before us in
those forms in which they had so often appeared to
Landor; while at the end the dying Pericles briefly and
nobly sums up the experiences of a life that had sometimes
seemed as of but a moment's length, " at another time, as
if centuries had passed within it ; for within it have existed
the greater part of those who since the origin of the world
have been the luminaries of the human race."

All three of these works were, for the most part, written
at the Villa Gherardesca, at Fiesole, near Florence, during
the happiest years of Landor's life. This circumstance has
an intimate bearing on the third, *The Pentameron*, for
The Pentameron is written to the praise and glory of
Boccaccio, who was, of all the Continental writers of the
modern world, the one whom Landor most loved and

revered; and it was in the grounds of the Villa Gherardesca
that Boccaccio had in part laid the scene of his *Decameron.*
Thither it was that the ladies and youths of that joyous
band journeyed in the pale dawn, listening to the songs of
the nightingales that seemed to greet them with delight,
and to whose sweet and fresh notes, not willing to be
outdone, they added their own songs that echoed along the
valley; and here, in the intervals of song or of cheerful
repast, under the living arbours by the lake's side, they told
so many of their immortal stories. *

" Be it known," Landor writes to his friend Francis Hare,
" I am master of the very place to which the greatest genius
of Italy, or the Continent, conducted those ladies who told
such pleasant tales in the warm weather, and the very scene
of his *Ninfale.*" In 1829, by the kindness of a wealthy
friend, who lent him the necessary money, Landor had been
enabled to purchase this most enviable piece of property,
and here, with his children, he found endless delight in his
gardens and fountains, his myrtles and pomegranates, his
conservatories for lemons and oranges, and the French fruit
trees he was planting. " I have the best water, the best air,
and the best oil in the world. I have a residence for life,
and literally may sit under my own vine and my own fig-
tree." And, to crown these delights, that divinity of early
days, Ianthe, no longer young, appeared at Florence, and
assisted at the planting operations.

His poems are full of tender and delicious reference to
his " citron groves of Fiesole," and to the little stream,
Affrico—

> " By him made sacred whom alone
> 'Twere not profane to call
> The bard divine ; "

---

* See *Decameron,* beginning of Giornata vii.

to Valdarno below him, the crest of Vallombrosa in the
east—

> " The massy walls at which we gaze,
>   Where, amid songs and village glee,
>   Soars immemorial Fiesole.
>
>   .   .   .   .   .   .
>
>   England, in all thy scenes so fair,
>   Thou canst not show what charmed me there !" *

About the hills of Fiesole Landor wandered alone,
moulding aloud the massive harmonies of his prose, or
meditating on his favourites of the men of old.   Of these,
Boccaccio could, at Fiesole, scarcely fail to be among the
first, and Landor's meditations on the man and his work,
among the scenes in which he had himself lived and
moved, slowly grew into a narrative of conversation and
episode, five days in duration, between Boccaccio and
Petrarch, which, in imitation of its hero's greater
Decameron, was ultimately entitled *The Pentameron.*

Of all Landor's works *The Pentameron* is that which
shows him in the richest and most various ways ; his
tender humanity, his eloquence, his stately humour, his
literary insight, his broad toleration, his imperial instinct
of style, are nowhere so delightfully combined as here.
There is scarcely a single declension from its gracious
and harmonious level ; even on the most purely imaginative side he is here represented at his best in the
allegory which concludes the last day.   Undoubtedly, on
a close examination, we realise clearly, even here, the

---

* Landor's poems are too little known. A judicious selection, in
convenient shape, is much needed, and would form a volume full of
delight for those who care for classic outline and concentration, the
delicate suggestiveness and repose which mark Landor's poems (as
in a considerable degree Matthew Arnold's) and which make them so
interesting a complement to his prose.

very definite limits of Landor's genius. His enthusiastic conception of Boccaccio is sometimes rather vague and uncritical ; his estimate of Dante (delicately as he appreciated the artistic value of lines and passages in his work) is sadly lacking in sympathy and historical insight ; the story which Boccaccio is made to tell, with the notion of substituting it for one of the more outrageous stories of the *Decameron*, is so stupid and pointless that even the most Puritanic of Boccaccio's admirers would hesitate to abolish in its favour the most licentious of the master's tales— whichever it may be. But these blots leave but a slight impression ; our memory dwells on the modest and gentle figure of the great story-teller himself—"the most imaginative and creative genius that our Italy, or indeed our world, hath in any age beheld," as Landor makes Petrarch call him—on the courteous and dignified bearing of that venerable Canon of Holy Church, Laura's lover, as he discourses of Dante with his old friend, or chats graciously with Assuntina, or, having with but two or three efforts mounted his sober steed, rides solemnly to mass, to be received festively by the village youths and maidens, and to set them to dance before service ; on Ser Biagio, the parish priest, and his gently-touched foibles; on the charming little maid, Assuntina, and her lover. It is these who make up a poem full of the fragrance and charm of Fiesole, a poem whose leaves, as Mrs. Browning said, "are too delicious to turn over."

H. E.

THE EDITOR'S INTRODUCTION.

WANTING a bell for my church at San Vivaldo, and hearing that our holy religion is rapidly gaining ground in England, to the unspeakable comfort and refreshment of the Faithful, I bethought myself that I might peradventure obtain such effectual aid, from the piety and liberality of the converts, as well-nigh to accomplish the purchase of one. Desirous moreover of visiting that famous nation, of whose spiritual prosperity we all entertain such animated hopes, now that the clouds of ignorance begin to break and vanish, I resolved that nothing on my part should be wanting to so blessed a consummation. Therefore, while I am executing my mission in regard to the bell, I omit no opportunity of demonstrating how much happier and peacefuller are we who live in unity, than those who, abandoning the household of Faith, clothe themselves with shreds and warm themselves with shavings.

Subsidiary to the aid I solicit, I brought with me, and here lay before the public, translated by the best hand I could afford to engage, " *Certain Interviews of Messer Francesco Petrarca and Messer Giovanni Boccaccio*, etc," which, the booksellers tell me, should be entitled " *The Pentameron*," unless I would return with nothing in my pocket. I am ignorant what gave them this idea of my intent, unless it be my deficiency in the language, for certainly I had come to no such resolution. Assurances are made to me by the intelligent and experienced in such merchandise, that the manuscript is honestly worth from twenty-five to thirty francesconi, or dollars. To such a pitch hath England risen up again, within these few years, after all the expenditure of her protracted war.

Is there any true Italian, above all is there any worthy native of Certaldo or San Vivaldo, who revolveth not in his mind what a surprise and delight it will be to Giovanni in Paradise, the first time he hears, instead of that cracked and jarring tumbril (which must have grated in his ear most grievously ever since its accident, and have often tried his patience), just such another as he was wont to hear when he rode over to join our townspeople at their *festa?* It will do his heart good, and make him think of old times ; and perhaps he may drop a couple of prayers to the Madonna for whoso had a hand in it.

Lest it should be bruited in England or elsewhere, that being in my seventieth year, I have unadvisedly quitted my parish, "*fond of change,*" to use the blessed words of Saint Paul, I am ready to show the certificate of Monsignore, my diocesan, approving of my voyage. Monsignore was pleased to think me capable of undertaking it, telling me that I looked hale, spoke without quavering, and, by the blessing of our lady, had nigh upon half my teeth in their sockets, while, pointing to his own and shaking his head, he repeated the celebrated lines of Horatius Flaccus, who lived in the reign of Augustus, a short time before the Incarnation :—

> " Non ebur, sed horridùm
> Buccâ dehiscit in meâ lacuna ! "

Then, turning the discourse from so melancholy a topic, he was pleased to relate from the inexhaustible stores of his archæological acquirements, that no new bell whatever had been consecrated in his diocese of Samminiato since the year of our Lord 1611 : in which year, on the first Sunday of August, a thunderbolt fell into the belfry of the Duomo, by the negligence of Canonico Malatesta, who, according to history, in his hurry to dine with Conte Geronimo Bardi, at our San Vivaldo, omitted a word in the mass. While he was playing at bowls after dinner on that Sunday, or, as some will have it, while he was beating Ser Matteo Filicaia at backgammon, and the younger men and ladies of those two noble families were bird-catching with the *civetta*, it began to thunder : and, within the evening, intelligence of the thunderbolt was brought to the Canonico. On his return the day following it was remarked, says the chronicler, that the people took off their caps at the distance of only two or three paces, instead of fifteen or twenty, and few stopped who met him : for the rumour had already gone abroad of his omission. He often rode, as usual, to Conte Geronimo's, gammoned Ser Matteo, hooded the *civetta*, limed a twig or two, stood behind the spinette, hummed the next note, turned over the pages of the music-book of the *contessine*, beating time on the chair-back, and showing them what he could do now and then on the *viola di gamba*. Only eight years had elapsed when, in the flower of his age (for he had scarcely seen sixty), he was found dead in his bed, after as hearty and convivial a supper as ever Canonico ate. No warning, no *olio santo*, no viaticum, poor man! Candles he had ; and it was as much as he had, poor sinner! And this also happened in the month of August! Monsignore, in his great liberality, laid no heavy stress on the coincidence ; but merely said,

" Well, Pievano ! a mass or two can do him no harm ; let us hope he stands in need of few more ; but when you happen to have leisure, and nobody else to think about, prythee clap a wet clout on the fire there below in behalf of Canonico Malatesta."

I have done it gratis, and I trust he finds the benefit of it. In the same spirit and by the same authority I gird myself for this greater enterprise. Unable to form a satisfactory opinion on the manuscript, I must again refer to my superior. It is the opinion then of Monsignore, that our five dialogues were written down by neither of the interlocutors, but rather by some intimate, who loved them equally. "For," said Monsignore, "it was the practice of Boccaccio to stand up among his personages, and to take part himself in their discourses. Petrarca, who was fonder of sheer dialogue and had much practice in it, never acquired any dexterity in this species of composition, it being all question and answer, short, snappish, quibbling, and uncomfortable. I speak only of his *Remedies of Adversity and Prosperity*, which indeed leave his wisdom all its wholesomeness, but render it somewhat apt to cleave to the roof of the mouth. The better parts of Homer are in dialogue : and downward from him to Galileo the noblest works of human genius have assumed this form : among the rest I am sorry to find no few heretics and scoffers. At the present day the fashion is over : every man pushes every other man behind him, and will let none speak out but himself.

The *Interviews* took place not within the walls of Certaldo, although within the parish, at Boccaccio's villa. It should be notified to the curious, that about this ancient town, small, deserted, dilapidated as it is, there are several towers and turrets yet standing, one of which belongs to the mansion inhabited in its day by Ser Giovanni. His tomb and effigy are in the church. Nobody has opened the grave to throw light upon his relics ; nobody has painted the marble ; nobody has broken off a foot or a finger to do him honour ; not even an English name is engraven on the face ; although the English hold confessedly the highest rank in this department of literature. In Italy, and particularly in Tuscany, the remains of the illustrious are inviolable ; and, among the illustrious, men of genius hold the highest rank. The arts are more potent than curiosity, more authoritative than churchwardens : what Englishman will believe it ? Well ! let it pass, courteous strangers ! ye shall find me in future less addicted to the marvellous. At present I have only to lay before you an ancient and (doubt it not) an authentic account of what passed between my countrymen, Giovanni and Francesco, before they parted for ever. It seemed probable, at this meeting, that Giovanni would have been called away first ; for heavy and of long continuance had been his infirmity : but he outlived it three whole years. He could not outlive his friend so many months, but followed him to the tomb before he had worn the glossiness off the cloak Francesco in his will bequeathed to him.

We struggle with Death while we have friends around to cheer us ; the moment we miss them we lose all heart for the contest. Pardon my reflection ! I ought to have remembered I am not in my stone pulpit, nor at home

PRETE DOMENICO GRIGI,

Pievano of San Vivaldo.

LONDON, *October* 1, 1836.

THE PENTAMERON.

THE PENTAMERON;

OR,

INTERVIEWS OF MESSER GIOVANNI BOCCACCIO AND MESSER FRANCESCO PETRARCA,

WHEN

SAID MESSER GIOVANNI LAY INFIRM AT HIS VILLETTA HARD BY CERTALDO;

AFTER WHICH THEY SAW NOT EACH OTHER ON OUR SIDE OF PARADISE:

SHOWING HOW THEY DISCOURSED UPON THAT FAMOUS THEOLOGIAN

MESSER DANTE ALIGHIERI,

AND SUNDRY OTHER MATTERS.

EDITED BY PIEVANO D. GRIGI.

THE PENTAMERON.

Boccaccio. Who is he that entered, and now steps so silently and softly, yet with a foot so heavy it shakes my curtains?

Frate Biagio! can it possibly be you?

No more physic for me, nor masses neither, at present.

Assunta! Assuntina! who is it?

Assunta. I can not say, Signor Padrone! he puts his finger in the dimple of his chin, and smiles to make me hold my tongue.

Boccaccio. Fra Biagio! are you come from Samminiato for this? You need not put your finger there. We want no secrets. The girl knows her duty and does her business. I have slept well, and wake better.

[*Raising himself up a little.*

Why? who are you? It makes my eyes ache to look aslant over the sheets; and I can not get to sit quite upright so conveniently; and I must not have the window-shutters opened, they tell me.

Petrarca. Dear Giovanni! have you then been very unwell?

Boccaccio. O that sweet voice! and this fat friendly hand of thine, Francesco!

Thou hast distilled all the pleasantest flowers, and all the wholesomest herbs of spring, into my breast already.

What showers we have had this April, ay! How could you come along such roads? If the devil were my labourer, I would make him work upon these of Certaldo. He would have little time and little itch for mischief ere he had finished them, but would gladly fan himself with an Agnus-castus, and go to sleep all through the carnival.

Petrarca. Let us cease to talk both of the labour and the labourer. You have then been dangerously ill?

Boccaccio. I do not know: they told me I was: and truly a man might be unwell enough, who has twenty masses said for him, and fain sigh when he thinks what he has paid for them. As I hope to be saved, they cost me a *lira* each. Assunta is a good market-girl in eggs, and mutton, and cow-heel; but I would not allow her to argue and haggle about the masses. Indeed she knows best whether they were not fairly worth all that was asked for them, although I could have bought a winter cloak for less money. However, we do not want both at the same time. I did not want the cloak: I wanted *them*, it seems. And yet I begin to think God would have had mercy on me, if I had begged it of him myself in my own house. What think you?

Petrarca. I think he might.

Boccaccio. Particularly if I offered him the sacrifice on which I wrote to you.

Petrarca. That letter has brought me hither.

Boccaccio. You do then insist on my fulfilling my promise, the moment I can leave my bed. I am ready and willing.

Petrarca. Promise! none was made. You only told me that, if it pleased God to restore you to your health again, you are ready to acknowledge his mercy by the holocaust of your *Decameron*. What proof have you that God would exact it? If you could destroy the *Inferno* of Dante, would you?

Boccaccio. Not I, upon my life! I would not promise to burn a copy of it on the condition of a recovery for twenty years.

Petrarca. You are the only author who would not rather demolish another's work than his own; especially if he thought it better: a thought which seldom goes beyond suspicion.

Boccaccio. I am not jealous of anyone : I think admiration pleasanter. Moreover, Dante and I did not come
forward at the same time, nor take the same walks. His
flames are too fierce for you and me : we had trouble
enough with milder. I never felt any high gratification in
hearing of people being damned; and much less would I
toss them into the fire myself. I might indeed have put a
nettle under the nose of the learned judge in Florence,
when he banished you and your family ; but I hardly
think I could have voted for more than a scourging to the
foulest and fiercest of the party.

Petrarca. Be as compassionate, be as amiably irresolute,
toward your own *Novelle*, which have injured no friend of
yours, and deserve more affection.

Boccaccio. Francesco ! no character I ever knew, ever
heard of, or ever feigned, deserves the same affection as
you do ; the tenderest lover, the truest friend, the firmest
patriot, and, rarest of glories ! the poet who cherishes
another's fame as dearly as his own.

Petrarca. If aught of this is true, let it be recorded of me
that my exhortations and intreaties have been successful,
in preserving the works of the most imaginative and
creative genius that our Italy, or indeed our world, hath in
any age beheld.

Boccaccio. I would not destroy his poems, as I told you,
or think I told you. Even the worst of the Florentines,
who in general keep only one of God's commandments,
keep it rigidly in regard to Dante—

> Love them who curse you.

He called them all scoundrels, with somewhat less courtesy
than cordiality, and less afraid of censure for veracity than
adulation : he sent their fathers to hell, with no inclination
to separate the child and parent : and now they are hugging
him for it in his shroud ! Would you ever have suspected
them of being such lovers of justice ?

You must have mistaken my meaning; the thought
never entered my head : the idea of destroying a single

copy of Dante! And what effect would that produce? There must be fifty, or near it, in various parts of Italy.

Petrarca. I spoke of you.

Boccaccio. Of me! My poetry is vile; I have already thrown into the fire all of it within my reach.

Petrarca. Poetry was not the question. We neither of us are such poets as we thought ourselves when we were younger, and as younger men think us still. I meant your *Decameron;* in which there is more character, more nature, more invention, than either modern or ancient Italy, or than Greece, from whom she derived her whole inheritance, ever claimed or ever knew. Would you consume a beautiful meadow because there are reptiles in it; or because a few grubs hereafter may be generated by the succulence of the grass?

Boccaccio. You amaze me: you utterly confound me.

Petrarca. If you would eradicate twelve or thirteen of the *Novelle*, and insert the same number of better, which you could easily do within as many weeks, I should be heartily glad to see it done. Little more than a tenth of the *Decameron* is bad: less than a twentieth of the *Divina Commedia* is good.

Boccaccio. So little?

Petrarca. Let me never seem irreverent to our master.

Boccaccio. Speak plainly and fearlessly, Francesco! Malice and detraction are strangers to you.

Petrarca. Well then: at least sixteen parts in twenty of the *Inferno* and *Purgatorio* are detestable, both in poetry and principle: the higher parts are excellent indeed.

Boccaccio. I have been reading the *Paradiso* more recently. Here it is, under the pillow. It brings me happier dreams than the others, and takes no more time in bringing them. Preparation for my lectures made me remember a great deal of the poem. I did not request my auditors to admire the beauty of the metrical version:

> Osanna sanctus deus Sabbaoth,
> Super-illustrans charitate tuâ
> Felices ignes horum Malahoth,

nor these, with a slip of Italian between two pales of Latin :

> Modicum,* et non videbitis me,
> Et iterum, sorelle mie dilette,
> Modicum, et vos videbitis me.

I dare not repeat all I recollect of

> Pepe Setan, Pepe Setan, aleppe,

as there is no holy-water-sprinkler in the room : and you are aware that other dangers awaited me, had I been so imprudent as to show the Florentines the allusion of our poet. His *gergo* is perpetually in play, and sometimes plays very roughly.

Petrarca. We will talk again of him presently. I must now rejoice with you over the recovery and safety of your prodigal son, the *Decameron*.

Boccaccio. So then, you would preserve at any rate my favourite volume from the threatened conflagration.

Petrarca. Had I lived at the time of Dante, I would have given him the same advice in the same circumstances. Yet how different is the tendency of the two productions ! Yours is somewhat too licentious ; and young men, in whose nature, or rather in whose education and habits, there is usually this failing, will read you with more pleasure than is commendable or innocent. Yet the very time they occupy with you, would perhaps be spent in the midst of those excesses or irregularities, to which the moralist, in his utmost severity, will argue that your pen directs them. Now there are many who are fond of standing on the brink of precipices, and who nevertheless are as cautious as any of falling in. And there are minds desirous of being warmed by description, which without

---

* It may puzzle an Englishman to read the lines beginning with *Modicum*, so as to give the metre. The secret is, to draw out *et* into a dissyllable, et-te, as the Italians do, who pronounce Latin verse, if possible, worse than we, adding a syllable to such as end with a consonant.

this warmth, might seek excitement among the things described.

I would not tell you in health what I tell you in convalescence, nor urge you to compose what I dissuade you from cancelling. After this avowal, I do declare to you, Giovanni, that in my opinion, the very idlest of your tales will do the world as much good as evil; not reckoning the pleasure of reading, nor the exercise and recreation of the mind, which in themselves are good. What I reprove you for, is the indecorous and uncleanly; and these, I trust, you will abolish. Even these, however, may repel from vice the ingenuous and graceful spirit, and can never lead any such toward them. Never have you taken an inhuman pleasure in blunting and fusing the affections at the furnace of the passions; never, in hardening by sour sagacity and ungenial strictures, that delicacy which is more productive of innocence and happiness, more estranged from every track and tendency of their opposites, than what in cold, crude systems hath holden the place and dignity of the highest virtue. May you live, O my friend, in the enjoyment of health, to substitute the facetious for the licentious, the simple for the extravagant, the true and characteristic for the indefinite and diffuse.

Boccaccio. I dare not defend myself under the bad example of any : and the bad example of a great man is the worst defence of all. Since, however, you have mentioned Messer Dante Alighieri, to whose genius I never thought of approaching, I may perhaps have been formerly the less cautious of offending by my levity, after seeing him display as much or more of it in hell itself.

Petrarca. The best apology for Dante, in his poetical character, is presented by the indulgence of criticism, in considering the *Inferno* and *Purgatorio* as a string of *Satires,* part in narrative and part in action ; which renders the title of *Commedia* more applicable. The filthiness of some passages would disgrace the drunkenest horse-dealer ; and the names of such criminals are recorded by the poet as would be forgotten by the hangman in six months. I wish I could expatiate rather on his injudiciousness than on his ferocity, in devising punishments for various crimes ; or rather, than on his malignity in composing catalogues of criminals to inflict them on. Among the rest we find a gang of coiners. He calls by name all the rogues and vagabonds of every city in Tuscany, and curses every city for not sending him more of them. You would fancy that Pisa might have contented him ; no such thing. He hoots,

" Ah Pisa ! scandal to the people in whose fine country *si* means *yes*, why are thy neighbours slack to punish thee ? May Capraia and Gorgona stop up the mouth of the Arno, and drown every soul within thee ! "

Boccaccio. None but a prophet is privileged to swear and curse at this rate, and several of those got broken heads for it.

Petrarca. It did not happen to Dante, though he once was very near it, in the expedition of the exiles to recover the city. Scarcely had he taken breath after this impreca· tion against the Pisans, than he asks the Genoese why such a parcel of knaves as themselves were not scattered over the face of the earth.

Boccaccio. Here he is equitable. I wonder he did not incline to one or other of these rival republics.

Petrarca. In fact, the Genoese fare a trifle better under him than his neighbours the Pisans do.

Boccaccio. Because they have no Gorgona and Capraia to block them up. He can not do all he wishes, but he does all he can, considering the means at his disposal. In like manner Messer Gregorio Peruzzi, when he was tormented by the quarrels and conflicts of Messer Gino Ubaldini's truffle-dog at the next door, and Messer Guidone Fantecchi's shop-dog, whose title and quality are in abeyance, swore bitterly, and called the Virgin and St. Catherine to witness that he would cut off their tails if ever he caught them. His cook, Niccolo Buonaccorsi, hoping to gratify his master, set baits for them, and captured them both in the kitchen. But unwilling to cast hands prematurely on the delinquents, he, after rating them for their animosities and their ravages, bethought himself in what manner he might best conduct his enterprise to a successful issue. He was the rather inclined to due deliberation in these counsels, as they, laying aside their private causes of contention in front of their common enemy, and turning the principal stream of their ill-blood into another channel, agreed in demonstrations which augured no little indocility. Messer Gregorio hath many servants, and moreover all the conveniences which so plenteous a house requires. Among the rest is a long hempen cloth suspended by a roller. Niccolo, in the most favourable juncture, was minded to slip this hempen cloth over the two culprits, whose consciences had made them slink toward the door against which it was fastened. The smell of it was not unsatisfactory to them, and an influx of courage had nearly borne away the worst suspicions. At this instant, while shrewd inquisitiveness and incipient hunger were regaining the ascendancy, Niccolo Buonaccorsi, with all the sagacity and courage, all the promptitude and timeliness of his profession, covered both conspirators in the inextricable folds of the fatal winding-sheet, from which their heads alone emerged. Struggles, and barkings, and exhibitions of teeth, and plunges forward, were equally ineffectual. He continued to twist it about them, until the notes of resentment partook of remonstance and pain : but he told them plainly he would never remit a jot, unless they became more domesticated and reasonable. In this state of exhaustion and contrition he brought them into the presence of Ser Gregorio, who immediately turned round toward the wall, crossed himself, and whispered an *ave.* At ease and happy as he was at the accomplishment of a desire so long cherished, no sooner had he expressed his piety at so gracious a dispensation, than, reverting to the captor and the captured, he was seized with unspeakable consternation. He discovered at once that he had made as rash a vow as Jeptha's. Alas! one of the children of captivity, the truffle-dog, had no tail ! Fortunately for Messer Gregorio, he found a friend among the White Friars, Frate Geppone Pallorco, who told him that when we cannot do a thing promised by vow, whether we fail by moral inability or by physical, we must do the thing nearest it; "which," said Fra Geppone, "hath always been my practice. And now," added this cool, considerate white friar, "a dog may have no tail, and yet be a dog to all intents and purposes, and enable a good Christian to perform anything reasonable he promised in his behalf. Whereupon I would advise you, Messer Gregorio, out of the loving zeal I bear toward the whole family of the Peruzzi, to amerce him of that which, if not tail, is next to tail. Such function, I doubt not, will satisfactorily show the blessed Virgin, and Saint Catherine, your readiness and solicitude to perform the vow solemnly made before those two adorable ladies, your protectresses and witnesses." Ser Gregorio bent his knee at first hearing their names, again at the mention of them in this relation-ship toward him, called for the kitchen knife, and, in absolving his promise, had lighter things to deal with than Gorgona and Capraia.

Petrarca. Giovanni! this will do instead of one among the worst of the hundred : but with little expenditure of labour you may afford us a better.

Our great fellow-citizen, if indeed we may denominate him a citizen who would have left no city standing in Italy, and less willingly his native one, places in the mouth of the devil, together with Judas Iscariot, the defenders of their country, and the best men in it, Brutus and Cassius. Certainly his feeling of patriotism was different from theirs.

I should be sorry to imagine that it subjected him to any harder mouth or worse company than his own, although in a spirit so contrary to that of the two Romans, he threatened us Florentines with the sword of Germans. The two Romans, now in the mouth of the devil, chose rather to lose their lives than to see their country, not under the government of invaders, but of magistrates from their own city placed irregularly over them ; and the laws, not subverted, but administered unconstitutionally. That Frenchmen and Austrians should argue and think in this manner, is no wonder, no inconsistency : that a Florentine, the wisest and greatest of Florentines, should have done it, is portentous.

How merciful is the Almighty, O Giovanni! What an argument is here! how much stronger and more convincing than philosophers could devise or than poets could utter, unless from inspiration, against the placing of power in the hands of one man only, when the highest genius at that time in the world, or perhaps at any time, betrays a disposition to employ it with such a licentiousness of inhumanity.

Boccaccio. He treats Nero with greater civility : yet Brutus and Cassius, at worst, but slew an atheist, while the other rogue flamed forth like the pestilential dog-star, and burnt up the first crop of Christians to light the ruins of Rome. And the artist of these ruins thought no more of his operation than a scene-painter would have done at the theatre.

Petrarca. Historians have related that Rome was consumed by Nero for the purpose of suppressing the rising sect, by laying all the blame on it. Do you think he cared what sect fell or what sect rose? Was he a zealot in religion of any kind? I am sorry to see a lying spirit the most prevalent one, in some among the earliest and firmest holders of that religion which is founded on truth and singleness of intention. There are pious men who believe they are rendering a service to God by bearing false witness in his favour, and who call on the father of lies to hold up his light before the Sun of Righteousness.

We may mistake the exact day when the conflagration began : certain it is, however, that it was in summer : * and it is presumable that the commencement of the persecution was in winter, since Juvenal represents the persecuted as serving for lamps in the streets. Now, as the Romans did not frequent the theatres, nor other places of public entertainment, by night, such conveniences were uncalled for in

* Des Vignolles has calculated that the conflagration began on the 19th of July, in the year 64, and the persecution on the 15th of November.

summer, a season when the people retired to rest betimes, from the same motive as at present, the insalubrity of the evening air in the hot weather. Nero must have been very forbearing if he waited those many months before he punished a gang of incendiaries. Such clemency is unexampled in milder princes.

Boccaccio. But the Christians were not incendiaries, and he knew they were not.

Petrarca. It may be apprehended that, among the many virtuous of the new believers, a few seditious were also to be found, forming separate and secret associations, choosing generals or superiors to whom they swore implicit obedience, and under whose guidance or impulse they were ready to resist, and occasionally to attack, the magistrates, and even the prince ; men aspiring to rule the state by carrying the sword of assassination under the garb of holiness. Such persons are equally odious to the unenlightened and the enlightened, to the arbitrary and the free. In the regular course of justice, their crimes would have been resisted by almost as much severity, as they appear to have undergone from despotic power and popular indignation.

Boccaccio. We will talk no longer about these people. But since the devil has really and *bonâ fide* Brutus and Cassius in his mouth, I would advise him to make the most of them, for he will never find two more such morsels on the same platter. Kings, emperors, and popes, would be happy to partake with him of so delicate and choice a repast : but I hope he has fitter fare for them.

Messer Dante Alighieri does not indeed make the most gentle use of the company he has about him in hell and purgatory. Since, however, he hath such a selection of them, I wish he could have been contented, and could have left our fair Florentines to their own fancies in their dressing-rooms.

"The time," he cries, "is not far distant, when there will be an indictment on parchment, forbidding the impudent young Florentines to show their breasts and nipples."

Now, Francesco, I have been subject all my life to a

strange distemper in the eyes, which no oculist can cure, and which, while it allows me to peruse the smallest character in the very worst female hand, would never let me read an indictment on parchment where female names are implicated, although the letters were a finger in length. I do believe the same distemper was very prevalent in the time of Messer Dante ; and those Florentine maids and matrons who were not afflicted by it, were too modest to look at letters and signatures stuck against the walls.

He goes on, " Was there ever girl among the Moors or Saracens, on whom it was requisite to inflict spiritual or *other* discipline to make her go covered ? "

Some of the *other* discipline, which the spiritual guides were, and are still, in the habit of administering, have exactly the contrary effect to make them go covered, whatsoever may be urged by the confessor.

" If the shameless creatures," he continues, " were aware of the speedy chastisement which Heaven is preparing for them, they would at this instant have their mouths wide open to roar withal."

Petrarca. This is not very exquisite satire, nor much better manners.

Boccaccio. Whenever I saw a pretty Florentine in such a condition, I lowered my eyes.

Petrarca. I am glad to hear it.

Boccaccio. Those whom I could venture to cover, I covered with all my heart.

Petrarca. Humanely done. You might likewise have added some gentle admonition.

Boccaccio. They would have taken anything at my hands rather than that. Truly they thought themselves as wise as they thought me : and who knows but they were, at bottom ?

Petrarca. I believe it may, in general, be best to leave them as we find them.

Boccaccio. I would not say that, neither. Much may be in vain, but something sticks.

Petrarca. They are more amused than settled by anything

we can advance against them, and are apt to make light of the gravest. It is only the hour of reflection that is at last the hour of sedateness and improvement.

Boccaccio. Where is the bell that strikes it?

Petrarca. Fie! fie! Giovanni! This is worse than the indictment on parchment.

Boccaccio. Women like us none the less for joking with them about their foibles. In fact, they take it ill when we cease to do so, unless it is age that compels us. We may give our courser the rein to any extent, while he runs in the common field and does not paw against privacy, nor open his nostrils on individuality. I mean the individuality of the person we converse with, for another's is pure zest.

Petrarca. Surely you cannot draw this hideous picture from your own observation : has any graver man noted it?

Boccaccio. Who would believe your graver men upon such matters? Gout and gravel, bile and sciatica, are the upholsterers that stuff their moral sentences. Crooked and cramp are truths written with chalkstones. When people like me talk as I have been talking, they may be credited. We have no ill-will, no ill-humour, to gratify; and vanity has no trial here at issue. He was certainly born on an unlucky day for his friends, who never uttered any truths but unquestionable ones. Give me food that exercises my teeth and tongue, and ideas that exercise my imagination and discernment.

Petrarca. When you are at leisure, and in perfect health, weed out carefully the few places of your *Decameron* which are deficient in these qualities.

Boccaccio. God willing; I wish I had undertaken it when my heart was lighter. Is there anything else you can suggest for its improvement, in particular or in general?

Petrarca. Already we have mentioned the inconsiderate and indecorous. In what you may substitute hereafter, I would say to you, as I have said to myself, do not be on all occasions too ceremonious in the structure of your sentences.

Boccaccio. You would surely wish me to be round and polished. Why do you smile?

Petrarca. I am afraid these qualities are often of as little advantage in composition as they are corporeally. When action and strength are chiefly the requisites, we may perhaps be better with little of them. The modulations of voice and language are infinite. Cicero has practised many of them ; but Cicero has his favourite swells, his favourite flourishes and cadences. Our Italian language is in the enjoyment of an ampler scope and compass ; and we are liberated from the horrible sounds of *us, am, um, ant, int, unt,* so predominant in the finals of Latin nouns and verbs. We may be told that they give strength to the dialect : we might as well be told that bristles give strength to the boar. In our Italian we possess the privilege of striking off the final vowel from the greater part of masculine nouns, and from the greater part of tenses in the verbs, when we believe they impede our activity and vigour.

Boccaccio. We are as wealthy in words as is good for us ; and she who gave us these, would give us more if needful. In another age it is probable that curtailments will rather be made than additions ; for it was so with the Latin and Greek. Barbaric luxury sinks down into civic neatness, and chaster ornaments fill rooms of smaller dimensions.

Petrarca. Cicero came into possession of the stores collected by Plautus, which he always held very justly in the highest estimation ; and Sallust is reported to have misapplied a part of them. At his death they were scattered and lost.

Boccaccio. I am wiser than I was when I studied the noble orator, and wiser by his means chiefly. In return for his benefits, if we could speak on equal terms together, the novelist with the philosopher, the citizen of Certaldo with the Roman consul, I would fain whisper in his ear, " Escape from rhetoric by all manner of means : and if you must cleave (as indeed you must) to that old shrew, Logic, be no fonder of exhibiting her than you would be of a plain, economical wife. Let her be always busy, never intrusive ; and readier to keep the chambers clean and orderly than to expatiate on their proportions or to display their furniture."

Petrarca. The citizen of Certaldo is fifty-fold more richly endowed with genius than the Roman consul, and might properly——

Boccaccio. Stay! stay! Francesco! or they will shave all the rest of thy crown for thee, and physic thee worse than me.

Petrarca. Middling men, favoured in their lifetime by circumstances, often appear of higher stature than belongs to them ; great men always of lower. Time, the sovran, invests with befitting raiment and distinguishes with proper ensigns the familiars he has received into his eternal habitations : in these alone are they deposited : you must wait for them.

No advice is less necessary to you, than the advice to express your meaning as clearly as you can. Where the purpose of glass is to be seen through, we do not want it tinted nor wavy. In certain kinds of poetry the case may be slightly different ; such, for instance, as are intended to display the powers of association and combination in the writer, and to invite and exercise the compass and comprehension of the intelligent. Pindar and the Attic tragedians wrote in this manner, and rendered the minds of their audience more alert and ready and capacious. They found some fit for them, and made others. Great painters have always the same task to perform. What is excellent in their art can not be thought excellent by many, even of those who reason well on ordinary matters, and see clearly beauties elsewhere. All correct perceptions are the effect of careful practice. We little doubt that a mirror would direct us in the most familiar of our features, and that our hand would follow its guidance, until we try to cut a lock of our hair. We have no such criterion to demonstrate our liability to error in judging of poetry ; a quality so rare that perhaps no five contemporaries ever were masters of it.

Boccaccio. We admire by tradition ; we censure by caprice ; and there is nothing in which we are more

ingenious and inventive. A wrong step in politics sprains a
foot in poetry ; eloquence is never so unwelcome as when
it issues from a familiar voice ; and praise hath no echo but
from a certain distance. Our critics, who know little about
them, would gaze with wonder at anything similar, in our
days, to Pindar and Sophocles, and would cast it aside, as
quite impracticable. They are in the right : for sonnet and
canzonet charm greater numbers. There are others, or may
be hereafter, to whom far other things will afford far higher
gratification.

Petrarca. But our business at present is with prose and
Cicero ; and our question now is, what is Ciceronian ? He
changed his style according to his matter and his hearers.
His speeches to the people vary from his speeches to the
senate. Toward the one he was impetuous and exacting ;
toward the other he was usually but earnest and anxious,
and sometimes but submissive and imploring, yet equally
unwilling, on both occasions, to conceal the labour he had
taken to captivate their attention and obtain success. At
the tribunal of Cæsar, the dictator, he laid aside his costly
armour, contracted the folds of his capacious robe, and
became calm, insinuating, and adulative, showing his spirit
not utterly extinguished, his dignity not utterly fallen, his
consular year not utterly abolished from his memory, but
Rome, and even himself, lowered in the presence of his
judge.

Boccaccio. And after all this, can you bear to think what
I am ?

Petrarca. Complacently and joyfully ; venturing, nevertheless, to offer you a friend's advice.

Enter into the mind and heart of your own creatures :
think of them long, entirely, solely : never of style, never of
self, never of critics, cracked or sound. Like the miles of an
open country, and of an ignorant population, when they are
correctly measured they become smaller. In the loftiest
rooms and richest entablatures are suspended the most
spider-webs ; and the quarry out of which palaces are
erected is the nursery of nettle and bramble.

Boccaccio. It is better to keep always in view such writers as Cicero, than to run after those idlers who throw stones that can never reach us.

Petrarca. If you copied him to perfection, and on no occasion lost sight of him, you would be an indifferent, not to say a bad writer.

Boccaccio. I begin to think you are in the right. Well then, retrenching some of my licentious tales, I must endeavour to fill up the vacancy with some serious and some pathetic.

Petrarca. I am heartily glad to hear of this decision ; for, admirable as you are in the jocose, you descend from your natural position when you come to the convivial and the festive. You were placed among the Affections, to move and master them, and gifted with the rod that sweetens the fount of tears. My nature leads me also to the pathetic ; in which, however, an imbecile writer may obtain celebrity. Even the hard-hearted are fond of such reading, when they are fond of any ; and nothing is easier in the world than to find and accumulate its sufferings. Yet this very profusion and luxuriance of misery is the reason why few have excelled in describing it. The eye wanders over the mass without noticing the peculiarities. To mark them distinctly is the work of genius ; a work so rarely performed, that, if time and space may be compared, specimens of it stand at wider distances than the trophies of Sesostris. Here we return again to the *Inferno* of Dante, who overcame the difficulty. In this vast desert are its greater and its less oasis ; Ugolino and Francesca di Rimini. The peopled region is peopled chiefly with monsters and moschitoes : the rest for the most part is sand and suffocation.

Boccaccio. Ah ! had Dante remained through life the pure solitary lover of Bice, his soul had been gentler, tranquiller, and more generous. He scarcely hath described half the curses he went through, nor the roads he took on the journey : theology, politics, and that barbican of the *Inferno,* marriage, surrounded with its

Selva selvaggia ed aspra e forte.

Admirable is indeed the description of Ugolino, to whoever can endure the sight of an old soldier gnawing at the scalp of an old archbishop.

Petrarca. The thirty lines from

> Ed io sentj,

are unequalled by any other continuous thirty in the whole dominions of poetry.

Boccaccio. Give me rather the six on Francesca: for if in the former I find the simple, vigorous, clear narration, I find also what I would not wish, the features of Ugolino reflected full in Dante. The two characters are similar in themselves; hard, cruel, inflexible, malignant, but, whenever moved, moved powerfully. In Francesca, with the faculty of divine spirits, he leaves his own nature (not indeed the exact representative of theirs) and converts all his strength into tenderness. The great poet, like the original man of the Platonists, is double, possessing the further advantage of being able to drop one half at his option, and to resume it. Some of the tenderest on paper have no sympathies beyond; and some of the austerest in their intercourse with their fellow-creatures, have deluged the world with tears. It is not from the rose that the bee gathers her honey, but often from the most acrid and the most bitter leaves and petals.

> Quando legemmo il disiato viso
>   Esser baciato di cotanto amante,
> Questi, chi mai da me non sia diviso!
>   La bocca mi baciò tutto tremante . . .
> *Galeotto* fù il libro, e chi lo scrisse . . .
>   Quel giorno più non sia vi legemmo avante.

In the midst of her punishment, Francesca, when she comes to the tenderest part of her story, tells it with complacency and delight; and, instead of naming Paolo, which indeed she never has done from the beginning, she now designates him as

> Questi chi mai da me non sia diviso!

Are we not impelled to join in her prayer, wishing them happier in their union?

Petrarca. If there be no sin in it.

Boccaccio. Ay, and even if there be . . . God help us :

What a sweet aspiration in each cesura of the verse! three love-sighs fixed and incorporate! Then, when she hath said

La bocca mi baciò, tutto tremante,

she stops: she would avert the eyes of Dante from her: he looks for the sequel: she thinks he looks severely: she says,

" *Galeotto* is the name of the book,"
fancying by this timorous little flight she has drawn him far enough from the nest of her young loves. No, the eagle beak of Dante and his piercing eyes are yet over her.

" *Galeotto* is the name of the book."

" What matters that? "

" And of the writer."

" Or that either? "

At last she disarms him : but how?

" *That* day we read no more."

Such a depth of intuitive judgment, such a delicacy of perception, exists not in any other work of human genius ; and from an author who, on almost all occasions, in this part of the work, betrays a deplorable want of it.

Petrarca. Perfection of poetry! The greater is my wonder at discovering nothing else of the same order or cast in this whole section of the poem. He who fainted at the recital of Francesca,

And he who fell as a dead body falls,

would exterminate all the inhabitants of every town in Italy! What execrations against Florence, Pistoia, Siena, Pisa, Genoa! what hatred against the whole human race! what exultation and merriment at eternal and immitigable sufferings! Seeing this, I can not but consider the *Inferno* as the most immoral and impious book that ever was written. Yet, hopeless that our country shall ever see again such poetry, and certain that without it our future poets would be more feebly urged forward to excellence, I would have dissuaded Dante from cancelling it, if this had been his intention.   Much however as I admire his vigour and severity of style in the description of Ugolino, I acknowledge with you that I do not discover so much imagination, so much creative power, as in the Francesca. I find indeed a minute detail of probable events : but this is not all I want in a poet : it is not even all I want most in a scene of horror.   Tribunals of justice, dens of murderers, wards of hospitals, schools of anatomy, will afford us nearly the same sensations, if we hear them from an accurate observer, a clear reporter, a skilful surgeon, or an attentive nurse.   There is nothing of sublimity in the horrific of Dante, which there always is in Æschylus and Homer.   If you, Giovanni, had described so nakedly the reception of Guiscardo's heart by Gismonda, or Lorenzo's head by Lisabetta, we could hardly have endured it.

Boccaccio. Prythee, dear Francesco, do not place me over Dante : I stagger at the idea of approaching him.

Petrarca. Never think I am placing you blindly or indiscriminately.   I have faults to find with you, and even here. Lisabetta should by no means have been represented cutting off the head of her lover, *" as well as she could "* with a clasp-knife.   This is shocking and improbable.   She might have found it already cut off by her brothers, in order to bury the corpse more commodiously and expeditiously. Nor indeed is it likely that she should have intrusted it to her waiting-maid, who carried home in her bosom a treasure so dear to her, and found so unexpectedly and so lately.

Boccaccio. That is true : I will correct the oversight. Why do we never hear of our faults until everybody knows them, and until they stand in record against us ?

Petrarca. Because our ears are closed to truth and friendship for some time after the triumphal course of composition.   We are too sensitive for the gentlest touch ; and when we really have the most infirmity, we are angry to be told that we have any.

Boccaccio. Ah Francesco! thou art poet from scalp to heel: but what other would open his breast as thou hast done! They show ostentatiously far worse weaknesses; but the most honest of the tribe would forswear himself on this. Again, I acknowledge it, you have reason to complain of Lisabetta and Gismonda.

Petrarca. They keep the soul from sinking in such dreadful circumstances by the buoyancy of imagination. The sunshine of poetry makes the colour of blood less horrible, and draws up a shadowy and a softening haziness where the scene would otherwise be too distinct. Poems, like rivers, convey to their destination what must without their appliances be left unhandled: these to ports and arsenals, this to the human heart.

Boccaccio. So it is; and what is terror in poetry is horror in prose. We may be brought too close to an object to leave any room for pleasure. Ugolino affects us like a skeleton, by dry bony verity.

Petrarca. We can not be too distinct in our images; but although distinctness, on this and most other occasions, is desirable in the imitative arts, yet sometimes in painting, and sometimes in poetry, an object should not be quite precise. In your novel of Andrevola and Gabriotto, you afford me an illustration.

> Le pareva dal corpo di lui uscire una
> cosa oscura e terribile.

This is like a dream: this *is* a dream. Afterward, you present to us such palpable forms and pleasing colours as may relieve and soothe us.

> Ed avendo molte rose, bianche e vermi-
> glie, colte, perciocche la stagione era.

Boccaccio. Surely you now are mocking me. The roses, I perceive, would not have been there, had it not been the season.

Petrarca. A poet often does more and better than he is

aware at the time, and seems at last to know as little about it as a silkworm knows about the fineness of her thread.

The uncertain dream that still hangs over us in the novel, is intercepted and hindered from hurting us by the spell of the roses, of the white and the red; a word the less would have rendered it incomplete. The very warmth and geniality of the season shed their kindly influence on us; and we are renovated and ourselves again by virtue of the clear fountain where we rest. Nothing of this poetical providence comes to our relief in Dante, though we want it oftener. It would be difficult to form an idea of a poem, into which so many personages are introduced, containing so few delineations of character, so few touches that excite our sympathy, so few elementary signs for our instruction, so few topics for our delight, so few excursions for our recreation. Nevertheless, his powers of language are prodigious; and, in the solitary places where he exerts his force rightly, the stroke is irresistible. But how greatly to be pitied must he be, who can find nothing in paradise better than sterile theology! and what an object of sadness and of consternation, he who rises up from hell like a giant refreshed!

Boccaccio. Strange perversion! A pillar of smoke by day and of fire by night; to guide no one. Paradise had fewer wants for him to satisfy than hell had; all which he fed to repletion. But let us rather look to his poetry than his temper.

Petrarca. We will then.

A good poem is not divided into little panes like a cathedral window; which little panes themselves are broken and blurred, with a saint's coat on a dragon's tail, a doctor's head on the bosom of a virgin martyr, and having about them more lead than glass, and more gloom than colouring. A good satire or good comedy, if it does not always smile, rarely and briefly intermits it, and never rages. A good epic shows us more and more distinctly, at every book of it we open, the features and properties of heroic character, and terminates with accomplishing some momentous action.

A good tragedy shows us that greater men than ourselves have suffered more severely and more unjustly; that the highest human power hath suddenly fallen helpless and extinct; or, what is better to contemplate and usefuller to know, that uncontrolled by law, unaccompanied by virtue, unfollowed by contentment, its possession is undesirable and unsafe. Sometimes we go away in triumph with Affliction proved and purified, and leave her under the smiles of heaven. In all these consummations the object is excellent; and here is the highest point to which poetry can attain. Tragedy has no bye-paths, no resting-places; there is everywhere action and passion. What do we find of this nature, or what of the epic, in the Orpheus and Judith, the Charon and Can della Scala, the Sinon and Maestro Adamo?

Boccaccio. Personages strangely confounded! In this category it required a strong hand to make Pluto and Pepe Satan keep the peace, both having the same pretensions, and neither the sweetest temper.

Petrarca. Then the description of Mahomet is indecent and filthy. Yet Dante is scarcely more disgusting in this place, than he is insipid and spiritless in his allegory of the marriages, between Saint Francesco and Poverty, Saint Dominico and Faith. I speak freely and plainly to you, Giovanni, and the rather, as you have informed me that I have been thought invidious to the reputation of our great poet; for such he is transcendently, in the midst of his imperfections. Such likewise were Ennius and Lucilius in the same period of Roman literature. They were equalled, and perhaps excelled: will Dante ever be, in his native tongue? The past generations of his countrymen, the glories of old Rome, fade before him the instant he springs upward, but they impart a more constant and a more genial delight.

Boccaccio. They have less hair-cloth about them, and smell less cloisterly; yet they are only choristers.

The generous man, such as you, praises and censures with equal freedom, not with equal pleasure: the freedom and the pleasure of the ungenerous are both contracted, and lie only on the left hand.

Petrarca. When we point out to our friends an object in the country, do we wish to diminish it? do we wish to show it overcast? Why then should we in those nobler works of creation, God's only representatives, who have cleared our intellectual sight for us, and have displayed before us things more magnificent than Nature would without them have revealed?

We poets are heated by proximity. Those who are gone warm us by the breath they leave behind them in their course, and *only* warm us: those who are standing near, and just before, fever us. Solitude has kept me uninfected; unless you may hint perhaps that pride was my preservative against the malignity of a worse disease.

Boccaccio. It might well be, though it were not; you having been crowned in the capital of the Christian world.

Petrarca. That indeed would have been something, if I had been crowned for my Christianity, of which I suspect there are better judges in Rome than there are of poetry. I would rather be preferred to my rivals by the two best critics of the age than by all the others; who, if they think differently from the two wisest in these matters, must necessarily think wrong.

Boccaccio. You know that not only the two first, but many more, prefer you; and that neither they, nor any who are acquainted with your character, can believe that your strictures on Dante are invidious or uncandid.

Petrarca. I am borne toward him by many strong impulses. Our families were banished by the same faction: he himself and my father left Florence on the same day, and both left it for ever. This recollection would rather make me cling to him than cast him down. Ill fortune has many and tenacious ties: good fortune has few and fragile ones. I saw our illustrious fellow citizen once only, and when I was a child. Even the sight of such a poet, in early days, is dear to him who aspires to become one, and the memory is always in his favour. The worst I can recollect to have said against his poem to others, is, that the architectural fabric of the *Inferno* is unintelligible without a long study, and only to be understood after distracting our attention from its inhabitants. Its locality and dimensions are at last uninteresting, and would better have been left in their obscurity. The zealots of Dante compare it, for invention, with the infernal regions of Homer and Virgil. I am ignorant how much the Grecian poet invented, how much existed in the religion, how much in the songs and traditions of the people. But surely our Alighieri has taken the same idea, and even made his descent in the same part of Italy, as Æneas had done before. In the *Odyssea* the mind is perpetually relieved by variety of scene and character. There are vices enough in it, but rising from lofty or from powerful passions, and under the veil of mystery and poetry : there are virtues too enough, and human and definite and practicable. We have man, although a shade, in his own features, in his own dimensions : he appears before us neither cramped by systems nor jaundiced by schools ; no savage, no cit, no cannibal, no doctor. Vigorous and elastic, he is such as poetry saw him first ; he is such as poetry would ever see him. In Dante, the greater part of those who are not degraded, are debilitated and distorted. No heart swells here, either for overpowered valour or for unrequited love. In the shades alone, but in the shades of Homer, does Ajax rise to his full loftiness : in the shades alone, but in the shades of Virgil, is Dido the arbitress of our tears.

Boccaccio. I must confess there are nowhere two whole cantos in Dante which will bear a sustained and close comparison with the very worst book of the *Odyssea* or the *Æneid ;* that there is nothing of the same continued and unabated excellence, as Ovid's in the contention for the armour of Achilles ; the most heroic of heroic poetry, and only censurable, if censurable at all, because the eloquence of the braver man is more animated and more persuasive than his successful rival's. I do not think Ovid the best poet that ever lived, but I think he wrote the most of good poetry, and, in proportion to its quantity, the least of bad or indifferent. The *Inferno*, the *Purgatorio*, the *Paradiso*, are pictures from the walls of our churches and chapels and monasteries, some painted by Giotto and Cimabue, some earlier. In several of these we detect not only the cruelty, but likewise the satire and indecency of Dante. Sometimes there is also his vigour and simplicity, but oftener his harshness and meagreness and disproportion. I am afraid the good Alighieri, like his friends the painters, was inclined to think the angels were created only to flagellate and burn us ; and Paradise only for us to be driven out of it. And in truth, as we have seen it exhibited, there is but little hardship in the case.

The opening of the third canto of the *Inferno* has always been much admired. There is indeed a great solemnity in the words of the inscription on the portal of hell : nevertheless, I do not see the necessity for three verses out of six. After

> Per me si va nell' eterno dolore,

it surely is superfluous to subjoin

> Per me si va fra la perduta gente ;

for, beside the *perduta gente*, who else can suffer the eternal woe ? And when the portal has told us that "*Justice moved the high Maker to make it*," surely it might have omitted the notification that his "*divine power*" did it.

> Fecemi la divina potestate.

The next piece of information I wish had been conveyed even in darker characters, so that they never could have been deciphered. The following line is,

> La somma Sapienza e 'l primo Amore.

If God's first love was hell-making, we might almost wish his affections were as mutable as ours are : that is, if holy church would countenance us therein.

Petrarca. Systems of poetry, of philosophy, of government, form and model us to their own proportions. As our systems want the grandeur, the light, and the symmetry of the ancient, we can not hope for poets, philosophers, cr statesmen, of equal dignity. Very justly do you remark that our churches and chapels and monasteries, and even our shrines and tabernacles on the road-side, contain in painting the same punishments as Alighieri hath registered in his poem : and several of these were painted before his birth. Nor surely can you have forgotten that his master, Brunetto Latini, composed one on the same plan.

The Virtues and Vices, and persons under their influence, appear to him likewise in a wood, wherein he, like Dante, is bewildered. Old walls are the tablets both copy : the arrangement is the devise of Brunetto. Our religion is too simple in its verities, and too penurious in its decorations, for poetry of high value. We can not hope or desire that a pious Italian will ever have the audacity to restore to Satan a portion of his majesty, or to remind the faithful that he is a fallen angel.

Boccaccio. No, no, Francesco ; let us keep as much of him down as we can, and as long.

Petrarca. It might not be amiss to remember that even human power is complacent in security, and that Omnipotence is ever omnipotent, without threats and fulminations.

Boccaccio. These, however, are the main springs of sacred poetry, of which I think we already have enough.

Petrarca. But good enough ?

Boccaccio. Even much better would produce less effect than that which has occupied our ears from childhood, and comes sounding and swelling with a mysterious voice from the deep and dark recesses of antiquity.

Petrarca. I see no reason why we should not revert, at times, to the first intentions of poetry. Hymns to the Creator were its earliest efforts.

Boccaccio. I do not believe a word of it, unless He himself was graciously pleased to inspire the singer ; of which we have received no account. I rather think it originated in pleasurable song, perhaps of drunkenness, and resembled the dithyrambic. Strong excitement alone could force and hurry men among words displaced and exaggerated ideas.

Believing that man fell, first into disobedience, next into ferocity and fratricide, we may reasonably believe that war-songs were among the earliest of his intellectual exertions. When he rested from battle he had leisure to think of love ; and the skies and the fountains and the flowers reminded him of her, the coy and beautiful, who fled to a mother from the ardour of his pursuit. In after years he lost a son, his companion in the croft and in the forest : images too grew up there, and rested on the grave. A daughter, who had wondered at his strength and wisdom, looked to him in vain for succour at the approach of death. Inarticulate grief gave way to passionate and wailing words, and Elegy was awakened. We have tears in this world before we have smiles, Francesco ! we have struggles before we have composure ; we have strife and complaints before we have submission and gratitude. I am suspicious that if we could collect the " winged words " of the earliest hymns, we should find that they called upon the Deity for vengeance. Priests and rulers were far from insensible to private wrongs. Chryses in the *Iliad* is willing that his king and country should be enslaved, so that his daughter be sent back to him. David in the *Psalms* is no unimportunate or luke-warm applicant for the discomfiture and extermination of his adversaries : and, among the visions of felicity, none brighter is promised a fortunate warrior, than to dash the infants of his enemy against the stones. The Holy Scriptures teach us that the human race was created on the banks of the Euphrates, and where the river hath several branches. Here the climate is extremely hot ; and men, like birds, in hot climates, never sing well. I doubt whether there was ever a good poet in the whole city and whole plain of Babylon. Egypt had none but such as she imported. Mountainous countries bear them as they bear the more fragrant plants and savoury game. Judæa had hers : Attica reared them among her thyme and hives : and Tuscany may lift her laurels not a span below. Never have the accents of poetry been heard on the fertile banks of the Vistula ; and Ovid taught the borderers of the Danube an indigenous* song in vain.

Petrarca. Orpheus, we hear, sang on the banks of the Hebrus.

Boccaccio. The banks of the Hebrus may be level or rocky, for what I know about them : but the river is represented by the poets as rapid and abounding in whirl-pools ; hence, I presume, it runs among rocks and inequalities. Be this as it may : do you imagine that Thrace in those early days produced a philosophical poet ?

Petrarca. We have the authority of history for it.

Boccaccio. Bad authority too, unless we sift and cross-examine it. Undoubtedly there were narrow paths of commerce, in very' ancient times, from the Euxine to the Caspian, and from the Caspian to the kingdoms of the remoter East. Merchants in those days were not only the most adventurous, but the most intelligent men : and there were ardent minds, uninfluenced by a spirit of lucre, which were impelled by the ardour of imagination into untravelled regions. Scythia was a land of fable, not only to the Greeks, but equally to the Romans. Thrace was a land of fable, we may well believe, to the nearest towns of northern India. I imagine that Orpheus, whoever he was, brought his knowledge from that quarter. We are too apt to fancy that Greece owed everything to the Phœnicians and Egyptians. The elasticity of her mind threw off, or the warmth of her imagination transmuted, the greater part of her earlier acquisitions. She was indebted to Phœnicia for nothing but her alphabet ; and even these signs she modified, and endowed them with a portion of her flexibility and grace.

Petrarca. There are those who tell us that Homer lived before the age of letters in Greece.

---

* Aptaque sunt nostris barbara verba modis.
What are all the other losses of literature in comparison with this ?

Boccaccio. I wish they knew the use of them as well as he did. Will they not also tell us that the commerce of the two nations was carried on without the numerals (and such were letters) by which traders cast up accounts? The Phœnicians traded largely with every coast of the Ægean sea; and among their earliest correspondents were the inhabitants of the Greek maritime cities, insular and continental. Is it credible that Cyprus, that Crete, that Attica, should be ignorant of the most obvious means by which commerce was maintained? or that such means should be restricted to commerce, among a people so peculiarly fitted for social intercourse, so inquisitive, so imaginative, as the Greeks?

Petrarca. Certainly it is not.

Boccaccio. The Greeks were the most creative, the Romans the least creative, of mankind. No Roman ever invented anything. Whence then are derived the only two works of imagination we find among them; the story of the *Ephesian* Matron*, and the story of *Pysche*? Doubtless from some country farther eastward than Phœnicia and Egypt. The authors in which we find these insertions are of little intrinsic worth.

When the Thracians became better known to the Greeks they turned their backs upon them as worn-out wonders, and looked toward the inexhaustible Hyperboreans. Among these too she placed wisdom and the arts, and mounted instruments through which a greater magnitude was given to the stars.

Petrarca. I will remain no longer with you among the Thracians or the Hyperboreans. But in regard to low and level countries, as unproductive of poetry, I entreat you not to be too fanciful nor too exclusive. Virgil was born on the Mincio, and has rendered the city of his birth too celebrated to be mistaken.

---

* One similar, and better conceived, is given by Du Halde from the Chinese. If the fiction of Pysche had reached Greece so early as the time of Plato, it would have caught his attention, and he would have delivered it down to us, however altered.

Boccaccio. He was born in the territory of Mantua, not in the city. He sang his first child's song on the shoulders of the Apennines; his first man's under the shadow of Vesuvius.

I would not assert that a great poet must necessarily be born on a high mountain : no indeed, no such absurdity : but where the climate is hot, the plains have never shown themselves friendly to the imaginative faculties. We surely have more buoyant spirits on the mountain than below, but it is not requisite for this effect that our cradles should have been placed on it.

Petrarca. What will you say about Pindar?

Boccaccio. I think it more probable that he was reared in the vicinity of Thebes than within the walls. For Bœotia, like our Tuscany, has one large plain, but has also many eminences, and is bounded on two sides by hills.

Look at the vale of Capua ! Scarcely so much as a sonnet was ever heard from one end of it to the other ; perhaps the most spirited thing was some Carthaginian glee, from a soldier in the camp of Hannibal. Nature seems to contain in her breast the same milk for all, but feeding one for one aptitude, another for another ; and, as if she would teach him a lesson as soon as he could look about him, she has placed the poet where the air is unladen with the exhalations of luxuriance.

Petrarca. In my delight to listen to you after so long an absence, I have. been too unwary ; and you have been speaking too much for one infirm. Greatly am I to blame, not to have moderated my pleasure and your vivacity. You must rest now : to-morrow we will renew our conversation.

Boccaccio. God bless thee, Francesco ! I shall be talking with thee all night in my slumbers. Never have I seen thee with such pleasure as to-day, excepting when I was deemed worthy by our fellow-citizens of bearing to thee, and of placing within this dear hand of thine, the sentence of recall from. banishment, and when my tears streamed over the ordinance as I read it, whereby thy paternal lands were redeemed from the public treasury.

Again God bless thee! Those tears were not quite exhausted: take the last of them.

SECOND DAY'S INTERVIEW.

Petrarca. How have you slept, Giovanni?

Boccaccio. Pleasantly, soundly, and quite long enough. You too methinks have enjoyed the benefit of riding; for you either slept well or began late. Do you rise in general three hours after the sun!

Petrarca. No indeed.

Boccaccio. As for me, since you would not indulge me with your company an hour ago, I could do nothing more delightful than to look over some of your old letters.

Petrarca. Ours are commemorative of no reproaches, and laden with no regrets. Far from us

> With drooping wing the spell-bound spirit moves
> O'er flickering friendships and extinguisht loves.

Boccaccio. Ay, but as I want no record of your kindness now you are with me, I have been looking over those to other persons, on past occasions. In the Latin one to the tribune, whom the people at Rome usually call Rienzi, I find you address him by the denomination of Nicolaus Laurentii. Is this the right one?

Petrarca. As we Florentines are fond of omitting the first syllable in proper names, calling Luigi *Gigi*, Giovanni *Nanni*, Francesco *Cecco*, in like manner at Rome they say *Renzi* for Lorenzi, and by another corruption it has been pronounced and written Rienzi. Believe me, I should never have ventured to address the personage who held and supported the highest dignity on earth, until I had ascertained his appellation : for nobody ever quite forgave, unless in the low and ignorant, a wrong pronunciation of his name ; the humblest being of opinion that they have one of their own, and one both worth having and worth knowing. Even dogs, they observe, are not miscalled. It would have been as Latin in sound, if not in structure, to write Rientius as Laurentius : but it would certainly have been offensive to a dignitary of his station, as being founded on a sportive and somewhat childish familiarity.

Boccaccio. Ah Francesco! we were a good deal younger in those days ; and hopes sprang up before us like mushrooms : the sun produced them, the shade produced them, every hill, every valley, every busy and every idle hour.

Petrarca. The season of hope precedes but little the season of disappointment. Where the ground is unprepared, what harvest can be expected? Men bear wrongs more easily than irritations ; and the Romans, who had sunk under worse degradation than any other people on record, rose up against the deliverer who ceased to consult their ignorance. I speak advisedly and without rhetoric on the foul depths of their debasement. The Jews, led captive into Egypt and into Babylon, were left as little corrupted as they were found ; and perhaps some of their vices were corrected by the labours that were imposed on them. But the subjugation of the Romans was effected by the depravation of their morals, which the priesthood took away, giving them ceremonies and promises instead. God had indulged them in the exercise of power : first the kings abused it, then the consuls, then the tribunes. One only magistrate was remaining who never had violated it, farther than in petty frauds and fallacies suited to the occasion, not having at present more within his reach. It was now his turn to exercise his functions, and no less grievously and despotically than the preceding had done. For this purpose the Pontifex Maximus needed some slight alterations in the popular belief; and he collected them from that Pantheon which Roman policy had enlarged at every conquest. The priests of Isis had acquired the highest influence in the city : those of Jupiter were jealous that foreign gods should become more than supplementary and subordinate: but as the women in general leaned toward Isis, it was in vain to contest the point, and prudent to adopt a little at a time from the discipline of the shaven brotherhood. The names and titles of the ancient gods had received many additions, and they were often asked which they liked best. Different ones were now given them ; and gradually, here and there, the older dropped into desuetude. Then arose the star in the east ; and all was manifested.

Boccaccio. Ay, ay, but the second company of shepherds sang to a different tune from the first, and put them out. Trumpeters ran in among them, horses neighed, tents waved their pennons, and commanders of armies sought to raise themselves to supreme authority, some by leading the faction of the ancient faith, and some by supporting the recenter. At last the priesthood succeeded to the power of the pretorian guard, and elected, or procured the election of, an emperor. Every man who loved peace and quiet took refuge in a sanctuary, now so efficient to protect him ; and nearly all who had attained a preponderance in wisdom and erudition, brought them to bear against the worn-out and tottering institutions, and finally to raise up the coping-stone of an edifice which overtopped them all.

Petrarca. At present we fly to princes as we fly to caves and arches, and other things of the mere earth, for shelter and protection.

Boccaccio. And when they afford it at all, they afford it with as little care and knowledge. Like Egyptian embalmers, they cast aside the brains as useless or worse, but carefully swathe up all that is viler and heavier, and place it in their painted catacombs.

Petrarca. What Dante saw in his day, we see in ours. The danger is, lest first the wiser, and soon afterward the unwiser, in abhorrence at the presumption and iniquity of the priesthood, should abandon religion altogether, when it is forbidden to approach her without such company.

Boccaccio. Philosophy is but the calix of that plant of paradise, religion. Detach it, and it dies away; meanwh.le the plant itself, supported by its proper nutriment, retains its vigour.

Petrarca. The good citizen and the calm reasoner come at once to the same conclusion : that philosophy can never hold many men together ; that religion can ; and those who without it would not let philosophy, nor law, nor humanity exist. Therefore it is our duty and interest to remove all obstruction from it ; to give it air, light, space, and freedom ; carrying in our hands a scourge for fallacy, a chain for cruelty, and an irrevocable ostracism for riches that riot in the house of God.

Boccaccio. Moderate wealth is quite enough to teach with.

Petrarca. The luxury and rapacity of the church, together with the insolence of the barons, excited that discontent which emboldened Nicolo de Rienzi to assume the station of tribune. Singular was the prudence, and opportune the boldness, he manifested at first. His modesty, his piety, his calm severity, his unbiassed justice, won to him the affections of every good citizen, and struck horror into the fastnesses of every castellated felon. He might by degrees have restored the republic of Rome, had he preserved his moderation : he might have become the master of Italy, had he continued the master of himself : but he allowed the weakest of the passions to run away with him : he fancied he could not inebriate himself soon enough with the intemperance of power. He called for seven crowrs, and placed them successively on his head. He cited Lewis of Bavaria and Charles of Bohemia to appear and plead their causes before him ; and lastly, not content with exasperating and concentrating the hostility of barbarians, he set at defiance the best and highest feelings of his more instructed countrymen, and displayed his mockery of religion and decency by bathing in the porphyry font of the Lateran. How my soul grieved for his defection! How bitterly burst forth my complaints, when he ordered the imprisonment of Stefano Colonna in his ninetieth year!

For these atrocities you know with what reproaches I
assailed him, traitor as he was to the noblest cause that
ever strung the energies of mankind.   For this cause, under
his auspices, I had abandoned all hope of favour and
protection from the pontiff: I had cast into peril, almost
into perdition, the friendship, familiarity, and love of the
Colonnas.   Even you, Giovanni, thought me more rash
than you would say you thought me, and wondered at
seeing me whirled along with the tempestuous triumphs
that seemed mounting toward the Capitol.   It is only in
politics that an actor appears greater by the magnitude of
the theatre ; and we readily and enthusiastically give way
to the deception.   Indeed, whenever a man capable of
performing great and glorious actions is emerging from
obscurity, it is our duty to remove, if we can, all obstruction
from before him ; to increase his scope and his powers, to
extol and amplify his virtues.   This is always requisite, and
often insufficient, to counteract the workings of malignity
round about him.   But finding him afterward false and
cruel, and, instead of devoting himself to the common-
wealth, exhausting it by his violence and sacrificing it to his
vanity, then it behoves us to stamp the foot, and to call in
the people to cast down the idol.   For nothing is so
immoral or pernicious as to keep up the illusion of greatness
in wicked men.   Their crimes, because they have fallen
into the gulf of them, we call misfortunes ; and, amid ten
thousand mourners, grieve only for him who made them so.
Is this reason ? is this humanity ?

Boccaccio. Alas ! it is man.

Petrarca. Can we wonder then that such wretches have
turned him to such purposes ?   The calmness, the sagacity,
the sanctitude of Rienzi, in the ascent to his elevation,
rendered him only the more detestable for his abuse of
power.

Boccaccio. Surely the man grew mad.

Petrarca. Men often give the hand to the madness that
seizes them.   He yielded to pride and luxury : behind them
came jealousy and distrust : fear followed these, and

cruelty followed fear.   Then the intellects sought the
subterfuge that bewildered them ; and an ignoble flight was
precluded by an ignominious death.

Boccaccio. No mortal is less to be pitied, or more to be
detested, than he into whose hands are thrown the fortunes
of a nation, and who squanders them away in the idle
gratification of his pride and his ambition.   Are not these
already gratified to the full by the confidence and deference
of his countrymen ?   Can silks, and the skins of animals,
can hammered metals and sparkling stones,' enhance the
value of legitimate dominion over the human heart ?   Can
a wise man be desirous of having a less wise successor ?
And, of all the world, would he exhibit this inferiority in a
son ?   Irrational as are all who aim at despotism, this is
surely the most irrational of their speculations.   Vulgar
men are more anxious for title and decoration than for
power ; and notice, in their estimate, is preferable to regard.
We ought as little to mind the extinction of such existences
as the dying down of a favourable wind in the prosecution
of a voyage.   They are fitter for the calendar than for
history, and it is well when we find them in last year's.

Petrarca. What a year was Rienzi's last to me !   What
an extinction of all that had not been yet extinguished !
Visionary as was the flash of his glory, there was another
more truly so, which this, my second great loss and sorrow,
opened again before me.

Verona ! loveliest of cities, but saddest to my memory !
while the birds were singing in thy cypresses the earliest
notes of spring, the blithest of hope, the tenderest of desire,
she, my own Laura, fresh as the dawn around her, stood
before me.   It was her transit ; I knew it ere she spake.*

O Giovanni ! the heart that has once been bathed in
love's pure fountain, retains the pulse of youth for ever.
Death can only take away the sorrowful from our affections :
the flower expands ; the colourless film that enveloped it
falls off and perishes.

* This event is related by Petrarca as occurring on the sixth of
April, the day of her decease.

Boccaccio. We may well believe it: and, believing it, let
us cease to be disquieted for their absence who have but
retired into another chamber. We are like those who have
overslept the hour : when we rejoin our friends, there is
only the more joyance and congratulation.   Would we
break a precious vase, because it is as capable of containing
the bitter as the sweet ?   No : the very things which touch
us the most sensibly are those which we should be the
most reluctant to forget.   The noble mansion is most
distinguished by the beautiful images it retains of beings
past away ; and so is the noble mind.

The damps of autumn sink into the leaves and prepare
them for the necessity of their fall : and thus insensibly are
we, as years close round us, detached from our tenacity of
life by the gentle pressure of recorded sorrows.   When the
graceful dance and its animating music are over, and the
clapping of hands (so lately linked) hath ceased ; when
youth and comeliness and pleasantry are departed,

> Who would desire to spend the following day
> Among the extinguisht lamps, the faded wreaths,
> The dust and desolation left behind ?

But whether we desire it or not, we must submit.   He
who hath appointed our days hath placed their contents
within them, and our efforts can neither cast them out nor
change their quality.   In our present mood we will not
dwell too long on this subject, but rather walk forth into the
world, and look back again on the bustle of life.   Neither
of us may hope to exert in future any extraordinary influence
on the political movements of our country, by our presence
or intervention : yet surely it is something to have set at
defiance the mercenaries who assailed us, and to have stood
aloof from the distribution of the public spoils.   I have at
all times taken less interest than you have taken in the
affairs of Rome ; for the people of that city neither are, nor
were of old, my favourites.

It appears to me that there are spots accursed, spots
doomed to eternal sterility ; and Rome is one of them.   No

gospel announces the glad tidings of resurrection to a fallen nation. Once down, and down for ever. The Babylonians, the Macedonians, the Romans, prove it. Babylon is a desert, Macedon a den of thieves, Rome (what is written as an invitation on the walls of her streets) one vas: *immondezzaio*, morally and substantially.

Petrarca. The argument does not hold good throughout. Persia was conquered : yet Persia, long afterward sprang up again with renovated strength and courage, and Sapor mounted his war-horse from the crouching neck of Valentinian. In nearly all the campaigns with the Romans she came off victorious : none of her kings or generals were ever led in triumph to the Capitol ; but several Roman emperors lay prostrate on their purple in the fields of Parthia. Formidable at home, victorious over friends and relatives, their legions had seized and subdivided the arable plains of Campania and the exuberant pastures of the Po ; but the glebe that bordered the Araxes was unbroken by them. Persia, since those times, has passed through many vicissitudes, of defeat and victory, of obscurity and glory : and why may not our country ? Let us take hopes where we can find them, and raise them where we find none.

Boccaccio. In. some places we may ; in others, the fabric of hopes is too arduous an undertaking. When I was in Rome nothing there reminded me of her former state, until I saw a goose in the grass under the Capitoline hill. This perhaps was the only one of her inhabitants that had not degenerated. Even the dogs looked sleeply, mangy, suspicious, perfidious, and thievish. The goose meanwhile was making his choice of herbage about triumphal arches and monumental columns, and picking up worms ; the surest descendants, the truest representatives, and enjoying the inalienable succession, of the Cæsars. This is all that goose or man can do at Rome. She, I think, will be the last city to rise from the dead.

Petrarca. There is a trumpet, and on earth, that shall awaken even her.

Boccaccio. I should like to live and be present.

Petrarca. This can not be expected. But you may live many years, and see many things to make you happy. For you will not close the doors too early in the evening of existence against the visits of renovating and cheerful thoughts, which keep our lives long up, and help them to sink at last without pain or pressure.

Boccaccio. Another year or two perhaps, with God's permission. Fra Biagio felt my pulse on Wednesday, and cried, "Courage! Ser Giovanni! there is no danger of Paradise yet: the Lord forbid!"

"Faith!" said I, "Fra Biagio! I hope there is not. What with prayers and masses, I have planted a foot against my old homestead, and will tug hard to remain where I am."

"A true soldier of the faith!" quoth Fra Biagio, and drank a couple of flasks to my health. Nothing else, he swore to Assunta, would have induced him to venture beyond one; he hating all excesses, they give the adversary such advantage over us; although God is merciful and makes allowances.

Petrarca. Impossible as it is to look far and with pleasure into the future, what a privilege is it, how incomparably greater than any other that genius can confer, to be able to direct the backward flight of fancy and imagination to the recesses they most delighted in; to be able, as the shadows lengthen in our path, to call up before us the youth of our sympathies in all their tenderness and purity!

Boccaccio. Mine must have been very pure, I suspect, for I am sure they were very tender. But I need not call them up; they come readily enough of their own accord; and I find it perplexing at times to get entirely rid of them. Sighs are very troublesome when none meet them half-way. The worst of mine now are while I am walking uphill. Even to walk upstairs, which used occasionally to be as pleasant an exercise as any, grows sadly too much for me. For which reason I lie here below; and it is handier too for Assunta.

Petrarca. Very judicious and considerate. In high

situations, like Certaldo and this villetta, there is no danger from fogs or damps of any kind. The skylark yonder seems to have made it her first station in the air.

Boccaccio. To welcome thee, Francesco !

Petrarca. Rather say, to remind us both of our Dante. All the verses that ever were written on the nightingale are scarcely worth the beautiful triad of this divine poet on the lark.

> La lodoletta che in aere si spazia,
> Prima cantando, e poi tace contenta
> Dell' ultima dolcezza che la sazia.

In the first of them do not you see the twinkling of her wings against the sky ? As often as I repeat them my ear is satisfied, my heart (like hers) contented.

Boccaccio. I agree with you in the perfect and unrivalled beauty of the first ; but in the third there is a redundance. Is not *contenta* quite enough, without *che la sazia?* The picture is before us, the sentiment within us, and behold ! we kick when we are full of manna.

Petrarca. I acknowledge the correctness and propriety of your remark ; and yet beauties in poetry must be examined as carefully as blemishes, and even more ; for we are more easily led away by them, although we do not dwell on them so long. We two should never be accused, in these days, of malevolence to Dante, if the whole world heard us. Being here alone, we may hazard our opinions even less guardedly, and set each other right as we see occasion.

Boccaccio. Come on then ; I will venture. I will go back to find fault ; I will seek it even in Francesca.

To hesitate, and waver, and turn away from the subject, was proper and befitting in her. The verse, however, in no respect satisfies me. Anyone would imagine from it that *Galeotto* was really both the title of the book and the name of the author ; neither of which is true. Galeotto, in the *Tavola Ritonda*, is the person who interchanges the correspondence between Lancilotto and Ginevra. The appellation is now become the generic of all men whose business it is to promote the success of others in illicit love. Dante was stimulated in his satirical vein, when he attributed to Francesca a ludicrous expression, which she was very unlikely in her own nature, and greatly more so in her state of suffering, to employ or think of, whirled round as she was incessantly with her lover. Neither was it requisite to say, "the book was a Galeotto, and so was the author," when she had said already that a passage in it had seduced her. Omitting this unnecessary and ungraceful line, her confusion and her delicacy are the more evident, and the following comes forth with fresh beauty. In the commencement of her speech I wish these had likewise been omitted,

" E cio sa il tuo dottore ;"

since he knew no more about it than anybody else. As we proceed, there are passages in which I can not find my way, and where I suspect the poet could not show it me. For instance, is it not strange that Briareus should be punished in the same way as Nimrod, when Nimrod sinned against the living God, and when Briareus attempted to overthrow one of the living God's worst antagonists, Jupiter? an action which our blessed Lord, and the doctors of the holy church, not only attempted, but (to their glory and praise for evermore) accomplished.

Petrarca. Equally strange that Brutus and Cassius (a remark which escaped us in our mention of them yesterday) should be placed in the hottest pit of hell for slaying Cæsar, and that Cato, who would have done the same thing with less compunction, should be appointed sole guardian and governor of purgatory.

Boccaccio. What interest could he have made to be promoted to so valuable a post, in preference to doctors, popes, confessors, and fathers? Wonderful indeed! and they never seemed to take it much amiss.

Petrarca. Alighieri not only throws together the most opposite and distant characters, but even makes Jupiter and our Saviour the same person.

E se lecito m' è, o sommo *Giove !*
Che fosti in terra per noi *crocifisso.*

Boccaccio. Jesus Christ ought no more to be called
Jupiter than Jupiter ought to be called Jesus Christ.

Petrarca. In the whole of the *Inferno* I find only the
descriptions of Francesca and of Ugolino at all admirable.
Vigorous expressions there are many, but lost in their
application to base objects ; and insulated thoughts in high
relief, but with everything crumbling round them.　Propor-
tionally to the extent, there is a scantiness of poetry, if
delight is the purpose or indication of it.　Intensity shows
everywhere the powerful master : and yet intensity is not
invitation.　A great poet may do everything but repel us.
Established laws are pliant before him : nevertheless his
office hath both its duties and its limits.

Boccaccio. The simile in the third canto, the satire at the
close of the fourth, and the description at the commencement of the eighth, if not highly admirable, are what no
ordinary poet could have produced.

Petrarca. They are streaks of light in a thunder-cloud.
You might have added the beginning of the twenty-seventh,
in which the poetry of itself is good, although not excellent,
and the subject of it assuages the weariness left on us, after
passing through so many holes and furnaces, and under-
going the dialogue between Simon and Master Adam.

Boccaccio. I am sorry to be reminded of this.　It is like
the brawl of the two fellows in Horace's *Journey to
Brundusium.*　They are the straitest parallels of bad wit
and bad poetry that ancient and modern times exhibit.
Ought I to speak so sharply of poets who elsewhere have
given me so great delight ?

Petrarca. Surely you ought.　No criticism is less beneficial to an author or his reader than one tagged with
favour and tricked with courtesy.　The gratification of our
humours is not the intent and scope of criticism, and those
who indulge in it on such occasions are neither wise nor
honest.

Boccaccio. I never could see why we should designedly

and prepensely give to one writer more than his due, to another less. If we offer an honest man ten crowns when we owe him only five, he is apt to be offended. The perfumer and druggist weigh out the commodity before them to a single grain. If they do it with odours and powders, should not we attempt it likewise, in what is either the nutriment or the medicine of the mind? I do not wonder that Criticism has never yet been clear-sighted and expert among us: I do, that she has never been dispassionate and unprejudiced. There are critics who, lying under no fear of a future state in literature, and all whose hope is for the present day, commit injustice without compunction. Every one of these people has some favourite object for the embraces of his hatred, and a figure of straw will never serve the purpose. He must throw his stone at what stands out; he must twitch the skirt of him who is ascending. Do you imagine that the worst writers of any age were treated with as much asperity as you and I? No, Francesco! give the good folks their due: they are humaner to their fellow-creatures.

Petrarca. Disregarding the ignorant and presumptuous, we have strengthened our language by dipping it afresh in its purer and higher source, and have called the Graces back to it. We never have heeded how Jupiter would have spoken, but only how the wisest men would, and how words follow the movements of the mind. There are rich and copious veins of mineral in regions far remote from commerce and habitations: these veins are useless: so are those writings of which the style is uninviting and inaccessible, through its ruggedness, its chasms, its points, its perplexities, its obscurity. There are scarcely three authors, beside yourself, who appear to heed whether any guest will enter the gate, quite satisfied with the consciousness that they have stores within. Such wealth, in another generation, may be curious, but cannot be current. When a language grows up all into stalk, and its flowers begin to lose somewhat of their character, we must go forth into the open fields, through the dingles, and among the mountains, for fresh seed. Our ancestors did this, no very long time ago. Foremost in zeal, in vigour and authority, Alighieri took on himself the same patronage and guardianship of our adolescent dialect, as Homer of the Greek : and my Giovanni hath since endowed it so handsomely, that additional bequests, we may apprehend, will only corrupt its principles, and render it lax and lavish.

Boccaccio. Beware of violating those canons of criticism you have just laid down. We have no right to gratify one by misleading another, nor, when we undertake to show the road, to bandage the eyes of him who trusts us for his conductor. In regard to censure, those only speak ill who speak untruly, unless a truth be barbed by malice and aimed by passion. To be useful to as many as possible is the especial duty of a critic, and his utility can only be attained by rectitude and precision. He walks in a garden which is not his own ; and he neither must gather the blossoms to embellish his discourse, nor break the branches to display his strength. Rather let him point to what is out of order, and help to raise what is lying on the ground.

Petrarca. Auditors, and readers in general, come to hear or read, not your opinion delivered, but their own repeated. Fresh notions are as disagreeable to some as fresh air to others ; and this inability to bear them is equally a symptom of disease. Impatience and intolerance are sure to be excited at any check to admiration in the narratives of Ugolino and of Francesca: nothing is to be abated: they are not only to be admirable, but entirely faultless.

Boccaccio. You have proved to me that, in blaming our betters, we ourselves may sometimes be unblamed. When authors are removed by death beyond the reach of irritation at the touch of an infirmity, we best consult their glory by handling their works comprehensively and unsparingly. Vague and indefinite criticism suits only slight merit, and presupposes it. Lineaments irregular and profound as Dante's are worthy of being traced with patience and fidelity. In the charts of our globe we find distinctly marked the promontories and indentations, and oftentimes the direction of unprofitable marshes and impassable sands and wildernesses : level surfaces are unnoted. I would not detract one atom from the worth of Dante ; which can not be done by summing it up exactly, but may be by negligence in the computation.

Petrarca. Your business, in the lectures; is not to show his merits, but his meaning ; and to give only so much information as may be given without offence to the factious. Whatever you do beyond, is for yourself, your friends, and futurity.

Boccaccio. I may write more lectures, but never shall deliver them in person as the first. Probably, so near as I am to Florence, and so dear as Florence hath always been to me, I shall see that city no more. The last time I saw it, I only passed through. Four years ago, you remember, I lost my friend Acciaioli. Early in the summer of the preceding, his kindness had induced him to invite me again to Naples, and I undertook a journey to the place where my life had been too happy. There are many who pay dearly for sunshine early in the season : many, for pleasure in the prime of life. After one day lost in idleness at Naples, if intense and incessant thoughts (however fruitless) may be called so, I proceeded by water to Sorento, and thence over the mountains to Amalfi. Here, amid whatever is most beautiful and most wonderful in scenery, I found the Seniscalco. His palace, his gardens, his terraces, his woods, abstracted his mind entirely from the solicitudes of state; and I was gratified at finding in the absolute ruler of a kingdom, the absolute master of his time. Rare felicity ! and he enjoyed it the more after the toils of business and the intricacies of policy. His reception of me was most cordial. He showed me his long avenues of oranges and citrons : he helped me to mount the banks of slippery short herbage, whence we could look down on their dark masses, and their broad irregular belts, gemmed with golden fruit and sparkling flowers. We stood high above them, but not above their fragrance, and sometimes we wished the breeze to bring us it, and sometimes to carry a part of it away : and the breeze came and went as if obedient to our volition.   Another day he conducted me farther from the palace, and showed me, with greater pride than I had ever seen in him before, the pale-green olives, on little smooth plants, the first year of their bearing.   " I will teach my people here," said he, "to make as delicate oil as any of our Tuscans." We had feasts among the caverns : we had dances by day under the shade of the mulberries, by night under the lamps of the arcade : we had music on the shore and on the water.

When next I stood before him, it was afar from these. Torches flamed through the pine-forest of the Certosa : priests and monks led the procession : the sound of the brook alone filled up the intervals of the dirge : and other plumes than the dancers' waved round what was Acciaiol..

Petrarca. Since in his family there was nobody who, from education or pursuits or consanguinity, could greatly interest him ; nobody to whom so large an accumulation of riches would not rather be injurious than beneficial, and place rather in the way of scoffs and carpings than exalt to respectability ; I regret that he omitted to provide for the comforts of your advancing years.

Boccaccio. The friend would not spoil the philosopher. Our judgment grows the stronger by the dying-down of our affections.

Petrarca. With a careful politician and diplomatist all things find their places but men : and yet he thinks he has niched it nicely, when, as the gardener is left in the garden, the tailor on his board at the casement, he leaves the author at his desk : to remove him would put the world in confusion.

Boccaccio. Acciaioli knew me too well to suppose we could serve each other : and his own capacity was amply sufficient for all the exigencies of the state.   Generous,*

---

* This sentiment must be attributed to the gratitude of Boccaccio, not to the merits of Acciaioli, who treated him unworthily.

kind, constant soul! the emblazoned window throws now its rich mantle over him, moved gently by the vernal air of Marignole, or, as the great chapel-door is opened to some visitor of distinction, by the fresh eastern .breeze from the valley of the Elsa. We too (mayhap) shall be visited in the same condition; but in a homelier edifice, but in a humbler sepulchre, but by other and far different guests. While they are discussing and sorting out our merits, which are usually first discovered among the nettles in the church-yard, we will carry this volume with us, and show Dante what we have been doing.

Petrarca. We have each of us had our warnings: indeed all men have them : and not only at our time of life, but almost every day of their existence. They come to us even in youth; although, like the lightnings that are said to play incessantly, in the noon and in the morning and throughout the year, we seldom see and never look for them. Come, as you proposed, let us now continue with our Dante.

Ugolino relates to him his terrible dream, in which he fancied that he had seen Gualando, Sismondi, and Lan-franco, killing his children : and he says that, when he awakened, he heard them moan in their sleep. In such circumstances, his awakening ought rather to have removed the impression he laboured under; since it showed him the vanity of the dream, and afforded him the consolation that the children were alive. Yet he adds immediately, what, if he were to speak it at all, he should have deferred,

"You are very cruel if you do not begin to grieve, considering what my heart presaged to me; and, if you do not weep at it, what is it you are wont to weep at?"

Boccaccio. Certainly this is ill-timed; and the conference would indeed be better without it anywhere.

Petrarca. Farther on, in whatever way we interpret

Poscia più che 'l dolor potè 'l digiuno,

the poet falls sadly from his sublimity.

Boccaccio. If the fact were as he mentions, he should

have suppressed it, since we had already seen the most pathetic in the features, and the most horrible in the stride, of Famine. Gnawing, not in hunger, but in rage and revenge, the archbishop's skull, is, in the opinion of many, rather ludicrous than tremendous.

Petrarca. In mine, rather disgusting than ludicrous : but Dante (we must whisper it) is the great master of the disgusting. When the ancients wrote indecently and loosely, they presented what either had something alluring or something laughable about it, and, if they disgusted, it was involuntarily. Indecency is the most shocking in deformity. We call indecent, while we do not think it, the nakedness of the Graces and the Loves.

Boccaccio. When we are less barbarous we shall become more familiar with them, more tolerant of sliding beauty, more hospitable to erring passion, and perhaps as indulgent to frailty as we are now to ferocity. I wish I could find in some epitaph, "he loved so many:" it is better than, "he killed so many." Yet the world hangs in admiration over this ; you and I should be found alone before the other.

Petrarca. Of what value are all the honours we can expect from the wisest of our species, when even the wisest hold us lighter in estimation than those who labour to destroy what God delighted to create, came on earth to ransom, and suffered on the cross to save! Glory then, glory can it be, to devise with long study, and to execute with vast exertions, what the fang of a reptile or the leaf of a weed accomplishes in an hour? Shall anyone tell me, that the numbers sent to death or to wretchedness make the difference, and constitute the great? Away then from the face of nature as we see her daily! away from the interminable varieties of animated creatures! away from what is fixed to the earth and lives by the sun and dew! Brute inert matter does it: behold it in the pestilence, in the earthquake, in the conflagration, in the deluge!

Boccaccio. Perhaps we shall not be liked the better for what we ourselves have written : yet I do believe we shall be thanked for having brought to light, and for having sent into circulation, the writings of other men. We deserve as much, were it only that it gives people an opportunity of running over us, as ants over the images of gods in orchards, and of reaching by our means the less crude fruits of less ungenial days. Be this as it may, we have spent our time well in doing it, and enjoy (what idlers never can) as pleasant a view in looking back as forward.

Now do tell me, before we say more of the *Paradiso,* what can I offer in defence of the Latin scraps from litanies and lauds, to the number of fifty or thereabout?

Petrarca. Say nothing at all, unless you can obtain some Indulgences for repeating them.

Boccaccio. And then such verses as these, and several score of no better :

> I credo ch' ei credette ch' io credessi.
> O Jacomo, dicea, di sant Andrea.
> Come Livio scrisse, che non erra.
> Nel quale un cinque cento dieci e cinque.
> Mille ducento con sessanta sei.
> Pepe Satan, Pepe Satan, Pepè.
> Raffael mai *amec, zabe, almi.*
> Non avria pur dell orlo fatto *crich.*

Petrarca. There is no occasion to look into and investigate a puddle; we perceive at first sight its impurity; but it is useful to analyse, if we can, a limpid and sparkling water, in which the common observer finds nothing but transparency and freshness: for in this, however the idle and ignorant ridicule our process, we may exhibit what is unsuspected, and separate what is insalubrious. We must do then for our poet that which other men do for themselves; we must defend him by advancing the best authority for something as bad or worse; and although it puzzle our ingenuity, yet we may almost make out in quantity, and quite in quality, our spicilege from Virgil himself. If younger men were present, I would admonish and exhort them to abate no more of their reverence for the Roman poet on the demonstration of his imperfections,

than of their love for a parent or guardian who had walked
with them far into the country, and had shown them its
many beauties and blessings, on his lassitude or his
debility. Never will such men receive too much homage.
He who can best discover their blemishes, will best appreciate their merit, and most zealously guard their honour.
The flippancy with which genius is often treated by
mediocrity, is the surest sign of a prostrate mind's incon-
tinence and impotence. It will gratify the national pride
of our Florentines, if you show them how greatly the nobler
parts of their fellow-citizen excel the loftiest of his Mantuan
guide.

Boccaccio. Of Virgil?

Petrarca. Even so.

Boccaccio. He had no suspicion of his equality with this
prince of Roman poets, whose footsteps he follows with
reverential and submissive obsequiousness.

Petrarca. Have you never observed that persons of high
rank universally treat their equals with deference ; and that
ill-bred ones are often smart and captious? Even their
words are uttered with a brisk and rapid air, a tone higher
than the natural, to sustain the factitious consequence and
vapouring independence they assume. Small critics and
small poets take all this courage when they licentiously shut
out the master; but Dante really felt the veneration he
would impress. Suspicion of his superiority he had none
whatever, nor perhaps have you yourself much more.

Boccaccio. I take all proper interest in my author ; I am
sensible to the duties of a commentator ; but in truth I
dare hardly entertain that exalted notion. I should have
the whole world against me.

Petrarca. You must expect it for *any* exalted notion ; for
anything that so startles a prejudice as to arouse a suspicion
that it may be dispelled. You must expect it if you throw
open the windows of infection. Truth is only unpleasant
in its novelty. He who first utters it, says to his hearer,
"You are less wise than I am." Now who likes this?

Boccaccio. But surely if there are some very high places

in our Alighieri, the inequalities are perpetual and vast; whereas the regularity, the continuity, the purity of Virgil, are proverbial.

Petrarca. It is only in literature that what is proverbial is suspicious; and mostly in poetry. Do we find in Dante, do we find in Ovid, such tautologies and flatnesses as these?

> Quam si dura silex . . *aut stet Marpessia cautes*
> Majus adorta nefas . . *majoremque orsa furorem.*
> Arma *amens* capio . . nec *sat rationis* in armis.
> Superatne . . *et vescetur aura*
> *Ætheria . . neque adhuc credelibus occubat umbris?*
> Omnes . . cœlicolas . . omnes supera alta tenentes.
> Scuta *latentia condunt.*
> Has inter voces . . *media inter talia verba.*
> Finem dedit . . *ore loquendi.*
> Insonuere cavæ . . *sonitumque dedere cavernæ.*
> *Ferro* accitam . . crebrisque *bipennibus.*
> Nec nostri generis puerum . . *nec sanguinis.*

Boccaccio. These things look very ill in Latin; and yet they had quite escaped my observation. We often find, in the *Psalms of David,* one section of a sentence placed as it were in symmetry with another, and not at all supporting it by presenting the same idea. It is a species of piety to drop the nether lip in admiration; but in reality it is not only the modern taste that is vitiated; the ancient is little less so, although differently. To say over again what we have just ceased to say, with nothing added, nothing improved, is equally bad in all languages and all times.

Petrarca. But in these repetitions we may imagine one part of the chorus to be answering another part opposite.

Boccaccio. Likely enough. However, you have ransacked poor Virgil to the skin, and have stripped him clean.

Petrarca. Of all who have ever dealt with *Winter,* he is the most frost-bitten. Hesiod's description of the snowy season is more poetical and more formidable. What do you think of these icicles?—

> Œraque dissiliunt vulgo; *vestesque rigescunt!*

Boccaccio. Wretched falling-off.

Petrarca. He comes close enough presently.

> Stiriaque hirsutis dependent horrida barbis.

We will withdraw from the Alps into the city.   And now are you not smitten with reverence at seeing

> Romanos rerum dominos ; *gentemque togatam ?*

> The masters of the world   . and *long-tailed coats !*

Come to Carthage.   What a recommendation to a beautiful queen does Æneas offer, in himself and his associates !

> *Lupi ceu*
> *Raptores ;* atrâ in nebulâ, quos *improba ventris*
> Exegit cæcos rabies ! ´

Ovid is censured for his

> *Consiliis* non *curribus* utere nostris.

Virgil never for

> *Inceptoque* et *sedibus* hæret in iisdem.

The same in its quality, but more forced.

The affectation of Ovid was light and playful ; Virgil's was wilful, perverse, and grammatistical.   Are we therefore to suppose that every hand able to elaborate a sonnet may be raised up against the majesty of Virgil ?   Is ingratitude so rare and precious, that we should prefer the exposure of his faults to the enjoyment of his harmony ?   He first delivered it to his countrymen in unbroken links under the form of poetry, and consoled them for the eloquent tongue that had withered on the Rostra.   It would be no difficult matter to point out at least twenty bad passages in the *Æneid,* and a proportionate number of worse in the *Georgics.*   In your comparison of poet with poet, the defects as well as the merits of each ought to be placed side by side. This is the rather to be expected, as Dante professes to be Virgil's disciple. You may easily show that his humility no more became him than his fierceness.

Boccaccio. You have praised the harmony of the Roman poet. Now in single verses I think our poetry is sometimes more harmonious than the Latin, but never in whole sentences. Advantage could perhaps be taken of our metre if we broke through the stanza. Our language is capable, I think, of all the vigour and expression of the Latin ; and, in regard to the pauses in our versification, in which chiefly the harmony of metre consists, we have greatly the advantage. What, for instance, is more beautiful than your

> Solo . . e pensoso . . i piu deserti campi
> Vo . . misurando . . a passi tardi . . e lenti.

Petrarca. My critics have found fault with the *lenti*, calling it an expletive, and ignorant that equally in Italian and Latin the word signifies both *slow* and *languid*, while *tardi* signifies *slow* only.

Boccaccio. Good poetry, like good music, pleases most people, but the ignorant and inexpert lose half its pleasures, the invidious lose them all. What a paradise lost is here !

Petrarca. If we deduct the inexpert, the ignorant, and the invidious, can we correctly say it pleases most people ? But either my worst compositions are the most admired, or the insincere and malignant bring them most forward for admiration, keeping the others in the back-ground ! Sonnetteers, in consequence, have started up from all quarters.

Boccaccio. The sonnet seems peculiarly adapted to the languor of a melancholy and despondent love, the rhymes returning and replying to every plaint and every pulsation. Our poetasters are now converting it into the penfold and pound of stray thoughts and vagrant fancies. No sooner have they collected in their excursions as much matter as they conveniently can manage, than they seat themselves down and set busily to work, punching it neatly out with a clever cubic stamp of fourteen lines in diameter.

Petrarca. A pretty sonnet may be written on a lambkin or a parsnep, there being room enough for truth and tenderness on the edge of a leaf or the tip of an ear ; but a great poet must clasp the higher passions breast high, and compel them in an authoritative tone to answer his interrogatories.

We will now return again to Virgil, and consider in what relation he stands to Dante. Our Tuscan and Homer are never inflated.

Boccaccio. Pardon my interruption ; but do you find that Virgil is ? Surely he has always borne the character of the most chaste, the most temperate, the most judicious among the poets.

Petrarca. And will not soon lose it. Yet never had there swelled, in the higher or the lower regions of poetry, such a gust as here, in the exordium of the *Georgics :*

> Tuque adeo, quem mox quæ sint habitura deorum
> Concilia incertum est, urbisne invisere, Cæsar,
> Terrarumque velis curam, et te maximus orbis
> Auctorem frugum ? . .

Boccaccio. Already forestalled !
Petrarca.

> . . . tempestatumque potentem.

Boccaccio. Very strange coincidence of opposite qualifications.
Petrarca.

> Accipiat, cingens maternâ tempora myrto :
> An deus immensi venias maris. . . .

Boccaccio. Surely he would not put down Neptune ?
Petrarca.

> . . ac tua nautæ
> Numina sola colant : *tibi serviat ultima Thule.* ·

Boccaccio. Catch him up ! catch him up ! uncoil the whole of the vessel's rope ! never did man fall overboard so unluckily, or sink so deep on a sudden.

Petrarca.

> Teque sibi generum Tethys *emat omnibus undis ?*

Boccaccio. Nobody in his senses would bid against her : what indiscretion ! and at her time of life too !

> Tethys then really, most gallant Cæsar !
> If you would only condescend to please her,
> With all her waves would your good graces buy,
> And you should govern all the Isle of Skie.

Petrarca.

> Anne novum *tardis* sidus te mensibus addas ?

Boccaccio. For what purpose ?   If the months were *slow,* he was not likely to mend their speed by mounting another passenger.   But the vacant place is such an inviting one !

Petrarca.

> Qua locus Erigonen inter Chelasque sequentes
> Panditur.

Boccaccio. Plenty of room, sir !

Petrarca.

> . . . ipse tibi jam brachia contrahit ardens,
> Scorpius. . . .

Boccaccio. I would not incommode him ; I would beg him to be quite at his ease.

Petrarca.

> . . . et cœli justâ plus parte reliquit.
> Quicquid eris (nam te nec sperent Tartara regem
> Nec tibi regnandi veniet tam dira cupido,
> Quamvis Elysios miretur Græcia campós,
> Nec repetita sequi curet Proserpina matrem).

Boccaccio. Was it not enough to have taken all Varro's invocation, much enlarged, without adding these verses to the other twenty-three ?

Petrarca. Vainly will you pass through the later poets of the empire, and look for the like extravagance and bombast. Tell me candidly your opinion, not of the quantity but of the quality.

Boccaccio. I had scarcely formed one upon them before. Honestly and truly, it is just such a rumbling rotundity as might have been blown, with much ado, if Lucan and Nero had joined their pipes and puffed together into the same bladder. I never have admired, since I was a school-boy, the commencement or the conclusion of the *Georgics ;* an unwholesome and consuming fungus at the foot of the tree, a withered and loose branch at the summit.

Boccaccio. Virgil and Dante are altogether so different, that, unless you will lend me your whole store of ingenuity, I shall never bring them to bear one upon the other.

Petrarca. Frequently the points of comparison are salient in proportion as the angles of similitude recede : and the absence of a quality in one man usually makes us recollect its presence in another ; hence the comparison is at the same time natural and involuntary. Few poets are so different as Homer and Virgil, yet no comparison has been made oftener. Ovid, although unlike Homer, is greatly more like him than Virgil is ; for there is the same facility, and apparently the same negligence, in both. The great fault in the *Metamorphoses* is in the plan, as proposed in the argument,

primaque ab origine mundi
In mea *perpetuum* deducere tempora carmen.

Had he divided the more interesting of the tales, and omitted all the transformations, he would have written a greater number of exquisite poems than any author of Italy or Greece. He wants on many occasions the gravity of Virgil ; he wants on all the variety of cadence ; but it is a very mistaken notion that he either has heavier faults or

more numerous.   His natural air of levity, his unequalled
and unfailing ease, have always made the contrary opinion
prevalent.   Errors and faults are readily supposed, in
literature as in life, where there is much gaiety : and the
appearance of ease, among those who never could acquire
or understand it, excites a suspicion of negligence and
faultiness.   Of all the ancient Romans, Ovid had the
finest imagination ; he likewise had the truest tact in judging the poetry of his contemporaries and predecessors.
Compare his estimate with Quintilian's of the same writers,
and this will strike you forcibly.   He was the only one of
his countrymen who could justly appreciate the labours of
Lucretius.

> Carmina sublimis tunc sunt peritura Lucreti,
> Exitio terras quum dabit una dies.

And the kindness with which he rests on all the others,
shows a benignity of disposition which is often lamentably
deficient in authors who write tenderly upon imaginary
occasions.

I begin to be inclined to your opinion in regard to the
advantages of our Italian versification.   It surely has a
greater variety, in its usual measure, than the Latin, in
dactyls and spondees.   We admit several feet into ours :
the Latin, if we believe the grammarians, admits only two
into the heroic; and at least seven verses in every ten
conclude with a dissyllabic word.

Boccaccio. We are taught indeed that the final foot of an
hexameter is always a spondee : but our ears deny the
assertion, and prove to us that it never is, any more than it
is in the Italian.   In both the one and the other the last
foot is uniformly a trochee in pronunciation.   There is only
one species of Latin verse which ends with a true inflexible
spondee, and this is the *scazon*.   Its name of the *limper* is
but little prepossessing, yet the two most beautifu¹ and most
perfect poems of the language are composed n it—the
Miser Catulle and the *Sirmio*.

Petrarca. This is likewise my opinion of those two little golden images, which however are insufficient to ra se Catullus on an equality with Virgil : nor would twenty such. Amplitude of dimensions is requisite to constitute the greatness of a poet, besides his symmetry of form and his richness of decoration. We have conversed more than once together on the defects and oversights of the correct and elaborate Mantuan, but never without the expression of our gratitude for the exquisite delight he has afforded us. We may forgive him his Proteus and his Pollio ; but we can not well forbear to ask him, how Æneas came to know that Acragas was *formerly* the sire of high-mettled steeds, even if such had been the fact? But such was only the fact a thousand years afterwards, in the reign of Gelon.

Boccaccio. Was it *then ?* Were the horses of Gelon and Theron and Hiero, of Agrigentine or Sicilian breed ? The country was never celebrated for a race adapted to chariots ; such horses were mostly brought from Thessaly, and probably some from Africa. I do not believe there was ever a fine one in Italy before the invasion of Pyrrhus. No doubt, Hannibal introduced many. Greece herself, I suspect, was greatly indebted to the studs of Xerxes for the noblest of her prizes on the Olympic plain. In the kingdom of Naples I have observed more horses of high blood than in any other quarter of Italy. It is there that Pyrrhus and Hannibal were stationary : and, long after these, the most warlike of men, the Normans, took posses-sion of the country. And the Normans would have horses worthy of their valour, had they unyoked them from the chariot of the sun. Subduers of France, of Sicily, of Cyprus, they made England herself accept their laws.

Virgil, I remember, in the *Georgics,* has given some directions in the choice of horses. He speaks unfavourably of the white : yet painters have been fond of representing the leaders of armies mounted on them. And the reason is quite as good as the reason of a writer on husbandry, Cato or Columella, for choosing a house-dog of a contrary colour : it being desirable that a general should be as conspicuous as possible, and a dog, guarding against thieves, as invisible.

I love beyond measure in Virgil his kindness toward dumb creatures. Although he represents his Mezentius as a hater of the Gods, and so inhuman as to fasten dead bodies to the living, and violates in him the unity of character more than character was ever violated before, we treat as impossible all he has been telling us of his atrocities, when we hear his allocution to Rhœbus.

Petrarca. The dying hero, for hero he is trancendently above all the others in the *Æneid*, is not only the kindest father, not only the most passionate in his grief for Lausus, but likewise gives way to manly sorrows for the mute companion of his warfare.

> Rhœbe diu, res si qua diu mortalibus usquam,
> Viximus.

Here the philosophical reflection addressed to the worthy quadruped, on the brief duration of human and equine life, is ill applied. It is not the thought for the occasion ; it is not the thought for the man. He could no more have uttered it than Rhœbus could have appreciated it. This is not however quite so great an absurdity as the tender apostrophe of the monster Proteus to the dead Eurydice. Beside, the youth of Lausus, and the agility and strength of Mezentius, as exerted in many actions just before his fall, do not allow us to suppose that he who says to his horse,

> Diu viximus,

had passed the meridian of existence.

Boccaccio. Francesco ! it is a pity you had no opportunity of looking into the mouth of the good horse Rhœbus : perhaps his teeth had not lost all their marks.

Petrarca. They would have been lost upon me, though horses' mouths to the intelligent are more trustworthy than many others.

Boccaccio. I have always been of opinion that Virgil is inferior to Homer, not only in genius, but in judgment, and to an equal degree at the very least. I shall never dare to employ half your suggestions in our irritable city, for fear of raising up two new factions, the Virgilians and the Dantists.

Petrarca. I wish in good truth and seriousness you could raise them, or anything like zeal for genius, with whomsoever it might abide.

Boccaccio. You really have almost put me out of conceit with Virgil.

Petrarca. I have done a great wrong then both to him and you. Admiration is not the pursuivant to all the steps even of an admirable poet; but respect is stationary. Attend him where the ploughman is unyoking the sorrowful ox from his companion dead at the furrow; follow him up the arduous ascent where he springs beyond the strides of Lucretius; and close the procession of his glory with the coursers and cars of Elis.

THIRD DAY'S INTERVIEW.

It being now the Lord's day, Messer Francesco thought it meet that he should rise early in the morning and bestir himself, to hear mass in the parish church at Certaldo. Whereupon he went on tiptoe, if so weighty a man could indeed go in such a fashion, and lifted softly the latch of Ser Giovanni's chamber-door, that he might salute him ere he departed, and occasion no wonder at the step he was about to take. He found Ser Giovanni fast asleep, with the missal wide open across his nose, and a pleasant smile on his genial joyous mouth. Ser Francesco leaned over the couch, closed his hands together, and, looking with even more than his usual benignity, said in a low voice,

"God bless thee, gentle soul! the mother of purity and innocence protect thee!"

He then went into the kitchen, where he found the girl Assunta, and mentioned his resolution. She informed him that the horse had eaten his * two beans, and was as strong as a lion and as ready as a lover. Ser Francesco patted her on the cheek, and called her *semplicetta!* She was overjoyed at this honour from so great a man, the bosom-friend of her good master, whom she had always thought the greatest man in the world, not excepting Monsignore, until he told her he was only a dog confronted with Ser Francesco. She tripped alertly across the paved court into the stable, and took down the saddle and bridle from the farther end of the rack. But Ser Francesco, with his natural politeness, would not allow her to equip his palfrey.

"This is not the work for maidens," said he; "return to the house, good girl!"

She lingered a moment, then went away; but, mistrusting the dexterity of Ser Francesco, she stopped and turned back again, and peeped through the half-closed door, and heard sundry sobs and wheezes round about the girth. Ser Francesco's wind ill seconded his intention; and, although he had thrown the saddle valiantly and stoutly in its station, yet the girths brought him into extremity. She entered again, and dissembling the reason, asked him whether he would not take a small beaker of the sweet white wine before he set out, and offered to girdle the horse while his Reverence bitted and bridled him. Before any answer could be returned, she had begun. And having now satisfactorily executed her undertaking, she felt irrepressible delight and glee at being able to do what Ser Francesco had failed in. He was scarcely more successful with his allotment of the labour; found unlooked-for intricacies and complications in the machinery, wondered that human wit could not simplify it, and declared that the animal had

* Literally, *due fave*, the expression on such occasions to signify a small quantity.

never exhibited such restiveness before. In fact, he never had experienced the same grooming. At this conjuncture, a green cap made its appearance, bound with straw-coloured ribbon, and surmounted with two bushy sprigs of hawthorn, of which the globular buds were swelling, and some bursting, but fewer yet open. It was young Simplizio Nardi, who sometimes came on the Sunday morning to sweep the court-yard for Assunta.

"O! this time you are come just when you were wanted," said the girl.

"Bridle, directly, Ser Francesco's horse, and then go away about your business."

The youth blushed, and kissed Ser Francesco's hand, begging his permission. It was soon done. He then held the stirrup; and Ser Francesco, with scarcely three efforts, was seated and erect on the saddle. The horse, however, had somewhat more inclination for the stable than for the expedition; and, as Assunta was handing to the rider his long ebony staff, bearing an ivory caduceus, the quadruped turned suddenly round. Simplizio called him *bestiaccia !* and then, softening it, *poco garbato !* and proposed to Ser Francesco that he should leave the bastone behind, and take the crab-switch he presented to him, giving at the same time a sample of its efficacy, which covered the long grizzle hair of the worthy quadruped with a profusion of pink blossoms, like embroidery. The offer was declined; but Assunta told Simplizio to carry it himself, and to walk by the side of Ser Canonico quite up to the church-porch, having seen what a sad, dangerous beast his reverence had under him.

With perfect good will, partly in the pride of obedience to Assunta, and partly to enjoy the renown of accompanying a canon of holy church, Simplizio did as she enjoined.

And now the sound of village bells, in many hamlets and convents and churches out of sight, was indistinctly heard, and lost again; and at last the five of Certaldo seemed to crow over the faintness of them all. The freshness of the

morning was enough of itself to excite the spirits of youth;
a portion of which never fails to descend on years that are
far removed from it, if the mind has partaken in innocent
mirth while it was its season and its duty to enjoy it.
Parties of young and old passed the canonico and his
attendant with mute respect, bowing and bare-headed; for
that ebony staff threw its spell over the tongue, which the
frank and hearty salutation of the bearer was inadequate to
break.   Simplizio, once or twice, attempted to call back
an intimate of the same age with himself; but the utmost
he could obtain was a *riveritissimo !* and a genuflexion to
the rider.   It is reported that a heart-burning rose up from
it in the breast of a cousin, some days after, too distinctly
apparent in the long-drawn appellation of *Gnor** Simplizio.

Ser Francesco moved gradually forward, his steed picking
his way along the lane, and looking fixedly on the stones
with all the sobriety of a mineralogist.   He himself was
well satisfied with the pace, and told Simplizio to be
sparing of the switch, unless in case of a hornet or a gadfly.
Simplizio smiled, toward the hedge, and wondered at the
condescension of so great a theologian and astrologer, in
joking with him about the gadflies and hornets in the
beginning of April.   "Ah! there are men in the world
who can make wit out of anything!" said he to himself.

As they approached the walls of the town, the whole
country was pervaded by a stirring and diversified air of
gladness.   Laughter and songs and flutes and viols, inviting
voices and complying responses, mingled with merry bells
and with processional hymns, along the woodland paths and
along the yellow meadows.   It was really the *Lord's Day*,
for he made his creatures happy in it, and their hearts were
thankful.   Even the cruel had ceased from cruelty; and the
rich man alone exacted from the animal his daily labour.
Ser Francesco made this remark, and told his youthful
guide that he had never been before where he could not
walk to church on a Sunday; and that nothing should
persuade him to urge the speed of his beast, on the seventh

---

* Contraction of *signor*, customary in Tuscany.

day, beyond his natural and willing foot's-pace. He reached the gates of Certaldo more than half an hour before the time of service, and he found laurels suspended over them, and being suspended; and many pleasant and beautiful faces were protruded between the ranks of gentry and clergy who awaited him. Little did he expect such an attendance; but Fra Biagio of San Vivaldo, who himself had offered no obsequiousness or respect, had scattered the secret of his visit throughout the whole country. A young poet, the most celebrated in the town, approached the canonico with a long scroll of verses, which fell below the knee, beginning,

How shall we welcome our illustrious guest?

To which Ser Francesco immediately replied, "Take your favourite maiden, lead the dance with her, and bid all your friends follow; you have a good half-hour for it."

Universal applauses succeeded, the music struck up, couples were instantly formed. The gentry on this occasion led out the cittadinanza, as they usually do in the villeggiatura, rarely in the carnival, and never at other times. The elder of the priests stood round in their sacred vestments, and looked with cordiality and approbation on the youths, whose hands and arms could indeed do much, and did it, but whose active eyes could rarely move upward the modester of their partners.

While the elder of the clergy were thus gathering the fruits of their liberal cares and paternal exhortations, some of the younger looked on with a tenderer sentiment, not unmingled with regret. Suddenly the bells ceased; the figure of the dance was broken; all hastened into the church; and many hands that joined on the green, met together at the font, and touched the brow reciprocally with its lustral waters, in soul-devotion.

After the service, and after a sermon a good church-hour in length to gratify him, enriched with compliments from all authors, Christian and Pagan, informing him at the conclusion that, although he had been crowned in the Capitol, he must die, being born mortal, Ser Francesco rode homeward. The sermon seemed to have sunk deeply into him, and even into the horse under him, for both of them nodded, both snorted, and one stumbled. Simplizio was twice fain to cry,

"Ser Canonico! Riverenza! in this country if we sleep before dinner it does us harm. There are stones in the road, Ser Canonico, loose as eggs in a nest, and pretty nigh as thick together, huge as mountains."

"Good lad!" said Ser Francesco, rubbing his eyes, "toss the biggest of them out of the way, and never mind the rest."

The horse, although he walked, shuffled almost into an amble as he approached the stable, and his master looked up at it with nearly the same contentment. Assunta had been ordered to wait for his return, and cried,

"O Ser Francesco! you are looking at our long apricot, that runs the whole length of the stable and barn, covered with blossoms as the old white hen is with feathers. You must come in the summer, and eat this fine fruit with Signor Padrone. You can not think how ruddy and golden and sweet and mellow it is. There are peaches in all the fields, and plums, and pears, and apples, but there is not another apricot for miles and miles. Ser Giovanni brought the stone from Naples before I was born: a lady gave it to him when she had eaten only half the fruit off it: but perhaps you may have seen her, for you have ridden as far as Rome, or beyond. Padrone looks often at the fruit, and eats it willingly; and I have seen him turn over the stones in his plate, and choose one out from the rest, and put it into his pocket, but never plant it."

"Where is the youth?" inquired Ser Francesco.

"Gone away," answered the maiden.

"I wanted to thank him," said the Canonico.

"May I tell him so?" asked she.

"And give him," continued he, holding a piece of silver . . .

"I will give him something of my own, if he goes on and behaves well," said she: "but Signor Padrone would drive

him away for ever, I am sure, if he were tempted in an evil
hour to accept a quattrino, for any service he could render
the friends of the house."

Ser Francesco was delighted with the graceful animation
of this ingenuous girl, and asked her, with a little curiosity,
how she could afford to make him a present.

"I do not intend to make him a present," she replied:
"but it is better he should be rewarded by me," she blushed
and hesitated, "or by Signor Padrone," she added, "than
by your reverence. He has not done half his duty yet; not
half. I will teach him: he is quite a child; four months
younger than me."

Ser Francesco went into the house, saying to himself at
the doorway,

"Truth, innocence, and gentle manners, have not yet left
the earth. There are sermons that never make the ears
weary. I have heard but few of them, and come from
church for this."

Whether Simplizio had obeyed some private signal from
Assunta, or whether his own delicacy had prompted him to
disappear, he was now again in the stable, and the manger
was replenished with hay. A bucket was soon after heard
ascending from the well; and then two words, "Thanks,
Simplizio."

When Petrarca entered the chamber, he found Boccaccio
with his breviary in his hand, not looking into it indeed, but
repeating a thanksgiving in an audible and impassioned
tone of voice. Seeing Ser Francesco, he laid the book
down beside him, and welcomed him.

"I hope you have an appetite after 'your ride," said he,
"for you have sent home a good dinner before you."

Ser Francesco did not comprehend him, and expressed it
not in words but in looks.

"I am afraid you will dine sadly late to-day: noon has
struck this half-hour, and you must wait another, I doubt.
However, by good luck, I had a couple of citrons in the
house, intended to assuage my thirst if the fever had
continued. This being over, by God's mercy, I will try

(please God!) whether we two greyhounds can not be a match for a leveret."

" How is this ? " said Ser Francesco.

" Young Marc-Antonio Grilli, the cleverest lad in the parish at noosing any wild animal, is our patron of the feast. He has wanted for many a day to say something in the ear of Matilda Vercelli. Bringing up the leveret to my bedside, and opening the lips, and cracking the knuckles, and turning the foot round to show the quality and quantity of the hair upon it, and to prove that it really and truly was a leveret, and might be eaten without offence to my teeth, he informed me that he had left his mother in the yard, ready to dress it for me; she having been cook to the prior. He protested he owed the *crowned martyr* a forest of leverets, boars, deers, and everything else within them, for having commanded the most backward girls to dance directly. Whereupon he darted forth at Matilda, saying, ' The *crowned martyr* orders it,' seizing both her hands, and swinging her round before she knew what she was about. He soon had an opportunity of applying a word, no doubt as dexterously as hand or foot ; and she said submissively, but seriously, and almost sadly, ' Marc-Antonio, now all the people have seen it, they will think it.'

"And, after a pause,

" ' I am quite ashamed : and so should you be : are not you now ? '

" The others had run into the church. Matilda, who scarcely had noticed it, cried suddenly,

" ' O Santissima ! we are quite alone.'

" ' Will you be mine ? ' cried he, enthusiastically.

" ' O ! they will hear you in the church,' replied she.

" ' They shall, they shall,' cried he again, as loudly.

" ' If you will only go away.'

" ' And then ? '

" ' Yes, yes, indeed.'

" ' The Virgin hears you : fifty saints are witnesses.'

" ' Ah ! they know you made me : they will look kindly on us.'

" He released her hand : she ran into the church, doubling her veil (I will answer for her) at the door, and kneeling as near it as she could find a place.

" ' By St. Peter,' said Marc-Antonio, 'if there is a leveret in the wood, the *crowned martyr* shall dine upon it this blessed day.' And he bounded off, and set about his occupation. I inquired what induced him to designate you by such a title. He answered, that everybody knew you had received the crown of martyrdom at Rome, between the pope and antipope, and had performed many miracles, for which they had canonised you, and that you wanted only to die to become a saint."

The leveret was now served up, cut into small pieces, and covered with a rich tenacious sauce, composed of sugar, citron, and various spices. The appetite of Ser Francesco was contagious. Never was dinner more enjoyed by two companions, and never so much by a greater number. One glass of a fragrant wine, the colour of honey, and unmixed with water, crowned the repast. Ser Francesco then went into his own chamber, and found, on his ample mattress, a cool, refreshing sleep, quite sufficient to remove all the fatigues of the morning ; and Ser Giovanni lowered the pillow against which he had seated himself, and fell into his usual repose. Their separation was not of long continuance : and, the religious duties of the Sabbath having been performed, a few reflections on literature were no longer interdicted.

Boccaccio. How happens it, O Francesco ! that nearly at the close of our lives, after all our efforts and exhortations, we are standing quite alone in the extensive fields of literature ? We are only like to *scoria* struck from the anvil of the gigantic Dante. We carry our fire along with us in our parabola, and, behold ! it falls extinguished on the earth.

Petrarca. Courage ! courage ! we have hardly yet lighted the lamp and shown the way.

Boccaccio. You are a poet ; I am only a commentator, and must soothe my own failures in the success of my master.

I can not but think again and again, how fruitlessly the bravest have striven to perpetuate the ascendancy or to establish the basis of empire, when Alighieri hath fixed a language for thousands of years, and for myriads of men ; a language far richer and more beautiful than our glorious Italy ever knew before, in any of her regions, since the Attic and the Dorian contended for the prize of eloquence on her southern shores. Eternal honour, eternal veneration, to him who raised up our country from the barbarism that surrounded her ! Remember how short a time before him, his master Brunetto Latini wrote in French ; prose indeed ; but whatever has enough in it for poetry, has enough for prose out of its shreds and selvages.

Petrarca. Brunetto ! Brunetto ! it was not well done in thee. An Italian, a poet, write in French ! What human ear can tolerate its nasty nasalities ? what homely intellect be satisfied with its bare-bone poverty ? By good fortune we have nothing to do with it in the course of our examination. Several things in Dante himself you will find more easy to explain than to excuse. You have already given me a specimen of them, which I need not assist you in rendering more copious.

Boccaccio. There are certainly some that require no little circumspection. Difficult as they are to excuse, the difficulty lies more on the side of the clergy than the laity.

Petrarca. I understand you. The *gergo* of your author has always a reference to the court of the Vatican. Here he speaks in the dark : against his private enemies he always is clear and explicit.

Unless you are irresistibly pressed into it, give no more than two, or at most three lectures, on the verse which, I predict, will appear to our Florentines the cleverest in the poem.

Che vel viso degli uomini legge O M O.

Boccaccio. We were very near a new civil war about the interpretation of it.

Petrarca. Foolisher questions have excited general ones. What, I wonder, rendered you all thus reasonable at last?

Boccaccio. The majority, which on few occasions is so much in the right, agreed with me that the two eyes are signified by the two vowels, the nose by the centre of the consonant, and the temples by its exterior lines.

Petrarca. In proceeding to explore the Paradise more minutely, I must caution you against remarking to your audience, that, although the nose is between the eyes, the temples are not, exactly. An observation which, if well established, might be resented as somewhat injurious to the Divinity of the *Commedia.*

Boccaccio. With all its flatnesses-and swamps, many have preferred the *Paradiso* to the other two sections of the poem.

Petrarca. There is as little in it of very bad poetry, or we may rather say, as little of what is no poetry at all, as in either, which are uninviting from an absolute lack of interest and allusion, from the confusedness of the ground-work, the indistinctness of the scene, and the paltriness (in great measure) of the agents. If we are amazed at the number of Latin verses in the *Inferno* and *Purgatorio,* what must we be at their fertility in the *Paradiso,* where they drop on us in ripe clusters through every glen and avenue ! We reach the conclusion of the sixteenth canto before we come in sight of poetry, or more than a glade with a gleam upon it. Here we find a description of Florence in her age of innocence : but the scourge of satire sounds in our ears before we fix the attention.

Boccaccio. I like the old Ghibelline best in the seventeenth, where he dismisses the doctors, corks up the Latin, ceases from psalmody, looses the arms of Calfucci and Arigucci, sets down Caponsacco in the market, and gives us a stave of six verses which repays us amply for our heaviest toils and sufferings.

Tu lascierai ogni cosa diletta, etc.

But he soon grows weary of tenderness and sick of sorrow,

and returns to his habitual exercise of throwing stones and calling names.

Again we are refreshed in the twentieth.   Here we come to the simile : here we look up and see his lark, and are happy and lively as herself.   Too soon the hard fingers of the master are round our wrists again : we are dragged into the school, and are obliged to attend the divinity-examination, which the poet undergoes from Saint Simon-Peter. He acquits himself pretty well, and receives a handsome compliment from the questioner, who, "*inflamed with love*," acknowledges he has given "*a good account of the coinage, both in regard to weight and alloy.*"

"Tell me," continues he, "have you any of it in your pocket ?"

"Yea," replies the scholar, "and so shining and round that I doubt not what mint it comes from."

Saint Simon-Peter does not take him at his word for it, but tries to puzzle and pose him with several hard queries. He answers both warily and wittily, and grows so contented with his examining master, that, instead of calling him, "*a sergeant of infantry*," as he did before, he now entitles him "*the baron.*"

I must consult our bishop ere I venture to comment on these two verses :

> Credo una essenza, si una e si trina
> Che sofferà congiunto *sunt et este,*

as, whatever may peradventure lie within them, they are hardly worth the ceremony of being burnt alive for, although it should be at the expense of the Church.

Petrarca. I recommend to you the straightforward course; but I believe I must halt a little, and advise you to look about you.   If you let people see that there are so many faults in your author, they will reward you, not according to your merits, but according to its defects.   On celebrated writers, when we speak in public, it is safer to speak magnificently than correctly.   Therefore be not too cautious in leading your disciples, and in telling them, here you may step securely, here you must mind your footing : for a florin will drop out of your pocket at every such crevice you stop to cross.

Boccaccio. The room is hardly light enough to let me see whether you are smiling : but, being the most ingenuous soul alive, and by no means the least jocose one, I suspect it. My office is, to explain what is difficult, rather than to expatiate on what is beautiful or to investigate what is amiss. If those who invite me to read the lectures, mark out the topics for me, nothing is easier than to keep within them. Yet with how true and entire a pleasure shall I point out to my fellow-citizens such a glorious tract of splendour as there is in the single line,

> Cio ch'io vedevo mi sembrava un riso
> Dell' universo !

With what exultation shall I toss up my gauntlet into the balcony of proud Antiquity, and cry, *Descend! Contend!*

I have frequently heard your admiration of this passage, and therefore I dwell on it the more delighted. Beside, we seldom find anything in our progress that is not apter to excite a very different sensation. School-divinity can never be made attractive to the Muses ; nor will Virgil and Thomas Aquinas ever cordially shake hands. The unrelenting rancour against the popes is more tedious than unmerited : in a poem I doubt whether we would not rather find it unmerited than tedious. For, of all the sins against the spirit of poetry, this is the most unpardonable. Something of our indignation, and a proportion of our scorn, may fairly be detached from the popes, and thrown on the pusillanimous and perfidious who suffered such excrescences to shoot up, exhausting and poisoning the soil they sprang from.

Petrarca. I do not wonder they make Saint Peter "redden," as we hear they do, but I regret that they make him stammer,

> Quegli che usurpa in terra il luogo mio,
> Il luogo mio, il luogo mio, etc.

Alighieri was not the first catholic who taught us that the papacy is usurpation, nor will he be (let us earnestly hope) the last to inculcate so evident a doctrine.

Boccaccio. Canonico of Parma! Canonico of Parma! you make my hair stand on end. But since nobody sees it beside yourself, prythee tell me how it happens that an infallible pope should denounce as damnable the decision of another infallible pope, his immediate predecessor? Giovanni the twenty-second, whom you knew intimately, taught us that the souls of the just could not enjoy the sight of God until after the day of universal judgment. But the doctors of theology at Paris, and those learned and competent clerks, the kings of France and Naples, would not allow him to die before he had swallowed the choke-pear they could not chew. The succeeding pope, who called himself an ass, in which infallibility was less wounded, and neither king nor doctor carped at it (for not only was he one, but as truth-telling a beast as Balaam's), condemned this error, as indeed well he might, after two kings had set their faces against it.• But on the whole, the thing is ugly and perplexing. That they were both infallible we know; and yet they differed! Nay, the former differed from himself, and was pope all the while; of course infallible! Well, since we may not solve the riddle, let us suppose it is only a mystery the more, and be thankful for it.

Petrarca. That is best.

Boccaccio. I never was one of those who wish for ice to slide upon in summer. Being no theologian, I neither am nor desire to be sharp-sighted in articles of heresy : but it is reported that there are among Christians some who hesitate to worship the Virgin.

Petrarca. Few, let us hope.

Boccaccio. Hard hearts! Imagine her, in her fifteenth year, fondling the lovely babe whom she was destined to outlive! destined to see shedding his blood, and bowing his head in agony. Can we ever pass her by and not say from our hearts :

" O thou whose purity had only the stain of compassionate tears upon it ! blessings, blessings on thee ! "

I never saw her image but it suspended my steps on the highway of the world, discoursed with me, softened and chastened me, showing me too clearly my unworthiness by the light of a reproving smile.

Petrarca. Woe betide those who cut off from us any source of tenderness, and shut out from any of our senses the access to devotion !

Beatrice, in the place before us, changes colour too, as deeply as ever she did on earth ; for Saint Peter, in his passion, picks up and flourishes some very filthy words. He does not recover the use of his reason on a sudden ; but, after a long and bitter complaint that faith and innocence are only to be found in little children ; and that the child moreover who loves and listens to its mother while it lisps, wishes to see her buried when it can speak plainly ; he informs us that this corruption ought to excite no wonder, since the human race must of necessity go astray, not having any one upon earth to govern it.

Boccaccio. Is not this strange though ; from the mouth of one inspired? We are taught that there never shall be wanting a head to govern the church ; could Saint Peter say that it *was* wanting? I feel my catholicism here touched to the quick. However, I am resolved not to doubt : the more difficulties I find, the fewer questions I raise : the saints must settle it, as well as they can, among themselves.

Petrarca. They are nearer the fountain of truth than we are ; and I am confident Saint Paul was in the right.

Boccaccio. I do verily believe he may have been, although at Rome we might be in jeopardy for saying it. Well is it for me that my engagement is to comment on Alighieri's *Divina Commedia* instead of his treatise *De Monarchiâ.* He says bold things there, and sets apostles and popes together by the ears. That is not the worst. He would destroy what is and should be, and would establish what never can nor ought to be.

Petrarca. If a universal monarch could make children good universally, and keep them as innocent when they grow up as when they were in the cradle, we might wish him upon his throne to-morrow. But Alighieri, and those others who have conceived such a prodigy, seem to be unaware that what they would establish for the sake of unity, is the very thing by which this unity must be demolished. For, since universal power does not confer on its possessor universal intelligence, and since a greater number of the cunning could and would assemble round him, he must (if we suppose him like the majority and nearly the totality of his class) appoint a greater proportion of such subjects to the management and control of his dominions. Many of them would become the rulers of cities and of provinces in which they have no connexions or affinities, and in which the preservation of character is less desirable to them than the possession of power. The operations of injustice, and the opportunities of improvement, would be alike concealed from the monarch in the remoter parts of his territories; and every man of high station would exercise more authority than he.

Boccaccio. Casting aside the impracticable scheme of universal monarchy, if kings and princes there must be, even in the midst of civility and letters, why can not they return to European customs, renouncing those Asiatic practices which are become enormously prevalent? why can not they be contented with such power as the kings of Rome and the lucumons of Etruria were contented with? But forsooth they are wiser! and such customs are obsolete! Of their wisdom I shall venture to say nothing, for nothing, I believe, is to be said of it, but the customs are not obsolete in other countries. They have taken deep root in the north, and exhibit the signs of vigour and vitality. Unhappily, the weakest men always think they least want help; like the mad and the drunk. Princes and geese are fond of standing on one leg, and fancy it (no doubt) a position of gracefulness and security, until the cramp seizes them on a sudden: then they find how helpless they are,

and how much better it would have been if they had
employed all the support at their disposal.

Petrarca. When the familiars of absolute princes taunt
us, as they are wont to do, with the only apophthegm they
ever learnt by heart, namely, that it is better to be ruled by
one master than by many, I quite agree with them ; unity
of power being the principle of republicanism, while the
principle of despotism is division and delegation. In the
one system, every man conducts his own affairs, either
personally or through the agency of some trustworthy
representative, which is essentially the same : in the other
system, no man, in quality of citizen, has any affairs of his
own to conduct : but a tutor has been as much set over
him as over a lunatic, as little with his option or consent,
and without any provision, as there is in the case of the
lunatic, for returning reason. Meanwhile, the spirit of
republics is omnipresent in them, as active in the particles
as in the mass, in the circumference as in the centre.
Eternal it must be, as truth and justice are, although not
stationary. Yet when we look on Venice and Genoa, on
the turreted Pisa and our own fair Florence, and many
smaller cities self-poised in high serenity ; when we see
what edifices they have raised, and then glance at the
wretched habitations of the slaves around, the Austrians,
the French, and other fierce restless barbarians ; difficult is
it to believe that the beneficent God, who smiled upon
these our labours, will ever in his indignation cast them
down, a helpless prey to such invaders.

Morals and happiness will always be nearest to perfection
in small communities, where functionaries are appointed by
as numerous a body as can be brought together of the
industrious and intelligent, who have observed in what
manner they superintend their families, and converse with
their equals and dependents. Do we find that farms are
better cultivated for being large? is your neighbour friendlier
for being powerful? is your steward honester and more
attentive for having a mortgage on your estate or a claim to
a joint property in your mansion ? Yet well-educated men

are seen about the streets, so vacant and delirious, as to fancy that a country can only be well governed by somebody who never saw and will never see a twentieth part of it, or know a hundredth part of its necessities; somebody who has no relationships in it, no connexions, no remembrances.   A man without soul and sympathy is alone to be the governor of men!   Giovanni! our Florentines are, beyond all others, a treacherous, tricking, mercenary race. What in the name of heaven will become of them, if ever they listen to these ravings; if ever they lose, by their cowardice and dissensions, the crust of salt that keeps them from putrescency, their freedom?

Boccaccio. Alas! I dare hardly look out sometimes, lest I see before me the day when German and Spaniard will split them down the back and throw them upon the coals. Sad thought! here we will have done with it.   We can not help them: we have made the most of them, like the good tailor who, as Dante says, cuts his coat according to his cloth.

Petrarca. Do you intend, if they should call upon you again, to give them occasionally some of your strictures on his prose writings?

Boccaccio. It would not be expedient.   Enough of his political sentiments is exhibited, in various places of his poem, to render him unacceptable to one party; and enough of his theological, or rather his ecclesiastical, to frighten both.   You and I were never passionately fond of the papacy, to which we trace in great measure the miseries of our Italy, its divisions and its corruptions, the substitution of cunning for fortitude, and of creed for conduct.   He burst into indignation at the sight of this, and, because the popes took away our Christianity, he was so angry he would throw her freedom after it.   Any thorn in the way is fit enough to toss the tattered rag on.   A German king will do; Austrian or Bavarian, Swabian, or Switzer.   And, to humiliate us more and more, and render us the laughing-stock of our household, he would invest the intruder with the title of Roman emperor.   What! it is not enough then that he assumes it! We must invite him, forsooth, to accept it at our hands!

Petrarca. Let the other nations of Europe be governed by their hereditary kings and feudal princes: it is more accordant with those ancient habits which have not yet given way to the blandishment of literature and the pacific triumph of the arts: but let the states of Italy be guided by their own citizens. May nations find out by degrees that the next evil to being conquered is to conquer, and that he who assists in making slaves gives over at last by becoming one!

Boccaccio. Let us endure a French pope, or any other, as well as we can; there is no novelty in his being a stranger. The Romans at all times picked up recruits from the thieves, gods, and priests, of all nations. Dante is wrong I suspect, in imagining the popes to be infidels; and, no doubt, they would pay for indulgences as honestly as they sell them, if there were anybody at hand to receive the money. But who in the world ever thought of buying the cap he was wearing on his own head? Popes are no such triflers. After all, an infidel pope (and I do not believe there are three in a dozen) is less noxious than a sanguinary soldier, be his appellation what it may, if his power is only limited by his will. My experience has however taught me, that where there is a great mass of power concentrated, it will always act with great influence on the secondary around it. Whether pope or emperor or native king occupy the most authority within the Alps, the barons will range themselves under his banner, apart from the citizens. Venice, who appears to have received by succession the political wisdom of republican Rome, has less political enterprise: and the jealousies of her rivals will always hold them back, or greatly check them, from any plan suggested by her for the general good.

Petrarca. It appears to be the will of Providence that power and happiness shall never co-exist. Whenever a state becomes powerful, it becomes unjust; and injustice leads it first to the ruin of others, and next, and speedily, to its own. We, whose hearts are republican, are dazzled by looking so long and so intently at the eagles, and standards, and golden letters, S. P. Q. R. We are reluctant to admit that the most wretched days of ancient Rome were the days of her most illustrious men ; that they began amid the triumphs of Scipio, when the Gracchi perished, and reached the worst under the dictatorship of Cæsar, when perished Liberty herself. A milder and better race was gradually formed by Grecian instruction. Vespasian, Titus, Nerva, Trajan, the Antonines, the Gordians, Tacitus, Probus, in an almost unbroken series, are such men as never wore the diadem in other countries ; and Rome can show nothing comparable to them in the most renowned and virtuous of her earlier consuls. Humanity would be consoled in some degree by them, if their example had sunk into the breasts of the governed. But ferocity is unsoftened by sensuality ; and the milk of the wolf could always be traced in the veins of the effeminated Romans.

Petrarca. That is true: and they continue to this day less humane than any other people of Italy. The better part of their character has fallen off from them ; and in courage and perseverance they are far behind the Venetians and Ligurians. These last, a scanty population, were hardly to be conquered by Rome in the plenitude of her power, and with all her confederates : for which reason they were hated by her beyond all other nations. To gratify the pride and malice of Augustus, were written the verses :

Vane Ligur ! frustraque animis elate superbis,
Nequicquam patrias tentasti lubricus artes.

Since that time, the inhabitants of Genoa and Venice have been enriched with the generous blood of the Lombards. This little tribe on the Subalpine territory, and the Norman on the Apulian, demonstrate to us, by the rapidity and extension of their conquests, that Italy is an over-ripe fruit, ready to drop from the stalk under the feet of the first insect that alights on it.

Boccaccio. The Germans, although as ignorant as the French, are less cruel, less insolent and rapacious. The French have a separate claw for every object of appetite or passion, and a spring that enables them to seize it. The desires of the German are overlaid with food and extinguished with drink, which to others are stimulants and incentives. The German loves to see everything about him orderly and entire, however coarse and common : the nature of the Frenchman is to derange and destroy everything. Sometimes when he has done so, he will reconstruct and refit it in his own manner, slenderly and fantastically ; oftener leaving it in the middle, and proposing to lay the foundation when he has pointed the pinnacles and gilt the weathercock.

Petrarca. There is no danger that the French will have a durable footing in this or any other country. Their levity is more intolerable than German pressure, their arrogance than German pride, their falsehood than German rudeness, and their vexations than German exaction.

Boccaccio. If I must be devoured, I have little choice between the bear and the panther. May we always see the creatures at a distance and across the grating. The French will fondle us, to show us how vastly it is our interest to fondle them ; watching all the while their opportunity ; looking mild and half-asleep ; making a dash at last ; and laying bare and fleshless the arm we extend to them, from shoulder-blade to wrist.

Petrarca. No nation, grasping at so much, ever held so little, or lost so soon what it had inveigled. Yet France is surrounded by smaller and by apparently weaker states, which she never ceases to molest and invade. Whatever she has won, and whatever she has lost, has been alike won and lost by her perfidy ; the characteristic of the people from the earliest ages, and recorded by a succession of historians, Greek and Roman.

Boccaccio. My father spent many years among them, where also my education was completed ; yet whatever I have seen, I must acknowledge, corresponds with whatever

599

I have read, and corroborates in my mind the testimony of tradition. Their ancient history is only a preface to their later. Deplorable as is the condition of Italy, I am more contented to share in her sufferings than in the frothy festivities of her frisky neighbour.

Petrarca. So am I: but we must never deny or dissemble the victories of the ancient Gauls, many traces of which are remaining; not that a nation's glory is the greener for the ashes it has scattered in the season of its barbarism.

Boccaccio. The Cisalpine regions were indeed both invaded and occupied by them; yet, from inability to retain the acquisition, how inconsiderable a part of the population is Gaulish! Long before the time of Cæsar, the language was Latin throughout: the soldiers of Marius swept away the last dregs and stains on the ancient hearth. Nor is there in the physiognomy of the people the slightest indication of the Gaul, as we perceive by medals and marbles. These would surely preserve his features; because they can only be the memorials of the higher orders, which of course would have descended from the conquerors. They merged early and totally in the original mass: and the countenances in Cisalpine busts are as beautiful and dignified as our other Italian races.

Petrarca. The French imagine theirs are too.

Boccaccio. I heartily wish them the full enjoyment of their blessings, real or imaginary: but neither their manners nor their principles coincide with ours, nor can a reasonable hope be entertained of benefit in their alliance. Union at home is all we want, and vigilance to perpetuate the better of our institutions.

Petrarca. The land, O Giovanni, of your early youth, the land of my only love, fascinates us no longer. Italy is our country; and not ours only, but every man's, wherever may have been his wanderings, wherever may have been his birth, who watches with anxiety the recovery of the Arts, and acknowledges the supremacy of Genius. Beside, it is in Italy at last that all our few friends are resident. Yours were left behind you at Paris in your adolescence, if indeed any friendship can exist between a Florentine and a Frenchman: mine at Avignon were Italians, and older for the most part than myself. Here we know that we are beloved by some, and esteemed by many. It indeed gave me pleasure the first morning as I lay in bed, to overhear the fondness and earnestness which a worthy priest was expressing in your behalf.

Boccaccio. In mine?

Petrarca. Yes indeed: what wonder?

Boccaccio. A worthy priest?

Petrarca. None else, certainly.

Boccaccio. Heard in bed! dreaming, dreaming; ay?

Petrarca. No indeed: my eyes and ears were wide open.

Boccaccio. The little parlour opens into your room. But what priest could that be? Canonico Casini? He only comes when we have a roast of thrushes, or some such small matter at table: and this is not the season; they are pairing. Plover eggs might tempt him hitherward. If he heard a plover he would not be easy, and would fain make her drop her oblation before she had settled her nest.

Petrarca. It is right and proper that you should be informed who the clergyman was, to whom you are under an obligation.

Boccaccio. Tell me something about it, for truly I am at a loss to conjecture.

Petrarca. He must unquestionably have been expressing a kind and ardent solicitude for your eternal welfare. The first words I heard on awakening were these:

"Ser Giovanni, although the best of masters . . ."

Boccaccio. Those were Assuntina's.

Petrarca. . . . "may hardly be quite so holy (not being priest or friar) as your Reverence."

She was interrupted by the question, "What conversation holdeth he?"

She answered:

"He never talks of loving our neighbour with all our heart, all our soul, and all our strength, although he often gives away the last loaf in the pantry."

Boccaccio. It was she! Why did she say that? the slut!

Petrarca. "He doth well," replied the confessor. "Of the church, of the brotherhood, that is, of me, what discourses holdeth he?"

I thought the question an indiscreet one; but confessors vary in their advances to the seat of truth.

She proceeded to answer:

"He never said anything about the power of the church to absolve us, if we should happen to go astray a little in good company, like your Reverence."

Here, it is easy to perceive, is some slight ambiguity. Evidently she meant to say, by the seduction of "bad" company, and to express that his Reverence had asserted his power of absolution; which is undeniable.

Boccaccio. I have my version.

Petrarca. What may yours be?

Boccaccio. Frate Biagio; broad as daylight; the whole frock round!

I would wager a flask of oil against a turnip, that he laid another trap for a penance. Let us see how he went on. I warrant, as he warmed, he left off limping in his paces, and bore hard upon the bridle.

Petrarca. "Much do I fear," continued the expositor, "he never spoke to thee, child, about another world."

There was a silence of some continuance.

"Speak!" said the confessor.

"No indeed he never did, poor Padrone!" was the slow and evidently reluctant avowal of the maiden; for, in the midst of the acknowledgment her sighs came through the crevices of the door: then, without any farther interrogation, and with little delay, she added,

"But he often makes this look like it."

Boccaccio. And now, if he had carried a holy scourge, it would not have been on his shoulders that he would have laid it.

Petrarca. Zeal carries men often too far afloat; and confessors in general wish to have the sole steerage of the conscience. When she told him that your benignity made this world another heaven, he warmly and sharply answered,

"It is only we who ought to do that."

"Hush," said the maiden; and I verily believe she at that moment set her back against the door, to prevent the sounds from coming through the crevices, for the rest of them seemed to be just over my night-cap. "Hush," said she, in the whole length of that softest of all articulations, "There is Ser Francesco in the next room : he sleeps long into the morning, but he is so clever a clerk, he may understand you just the same. I doubt whether he thinks Ser Giovanni in the wrong for making so many people quite happy ; and if he should, it would grieve me very much to think he blamed Ser Giovanni."

"Who is Ser Francesco?" he asked, in a low voice.

"Ser Canonico," she answered.

"Of what Duomo?" continued he.

"Who knows?" was the reply; "but he is Padrone's heart's friend, for certain."

"Cospetto di Bacco! It can then be no other than Petrarca. He makes rhymes and love like the devil. Don't listen to him, or you are undone. Does he love you too, as well as Padrone?" he asked, still lowering his voice.

"I can not tell that matter," she answered, somewhat impatiently; "but I love him."

"To my face!" cried he, smartly.

"To the Santissima!" replied she, instantaneously; "for have not I told your Reverence he is Padrone's true hearts friend! And are not you my confessor, when you come on purpose?"

"True, true!" answered he; "but there are occasions when we are shocked by the confession, and wish it made less daringly."

"I was bold ; but who can help loving him who loves my good Padrone?" said she, much more submissively.

Boccaccio. Brave girl, for that !

Dog of a Frate! They are all of a kidney; all of a kennel. I would dilute their meal well and keep them low.

They should not waddle and wallop in every hollow lane, nor loll out their watery tongues at every wash-pool in the parish. We shall hear, I trust, no more about Fra Biagio in the house while you are with us. Ah! were it then for life.

Petrarca. The man's prudence may be reasonably doubted, but it were uncharitable to question his sincerity. Could a neighbour, a religious one in particular, be indifferent to the welfare of Boccaccio, or any belonging to him?

Boccaccio. I do not complain of his indifference. Indifferent! no, not he. He might as well be, though. My Villetta here is my castle: it was my father's; it was his father's. Cowls did not hang to dry upon the same cord with caps in their *podere;* they shall not in mine. The girl is an honest girl, Francesco, though I say it. Neither she nor any other shall be befooled and bamboozled under my roof. Methinks Holy Church might contrive some improvement upon confession.

Petrarca. Hush! Giovanni! But, it being a matter of discipline, who knows but she might.

Boccaccio. Discipline! ay, ay, ay! faith and troth there are some who want it.

Petrarca. You really terrify me. These are sad surmises.

Boccaccio. Sad enough: but I am keeper of my hand-maiden's probity.

Petrarca. It could not be kept safer.

Boccaccio. I wonder what the Frate would be putting into her head?

Petrarca. Nothing, nothing: be assured.

Boccaccio. Why did he ask her all those questions?

Petrarca. Confessors do occasionally take circuitous ways to arrive at the secrets of the human heart.

Boccaccio. And sometimes they drive at it, methinks, a whit too directly. He had no business to make remarks about me.

Petrarca. Anxiety.

Boccaccio. 'Fore God, Francesco, he shall have more of that; for I will shut him out the moment I am again up and stirring, though he stand but a nose's length off. I have no fear about the girl ; no suspicion of her. He might whistle to the moon on a frosty night, and expect as reasonably her descending. Never was a man so entirely at his ease as I am about that; never, never. She is adamant; a bright sword now first unscabbarded; no breath can hang about it. A seal of beryl, of chrysolite, of ruby; to make impressions (all in good time and proper place though) and receive none : incapable, just as they are, of splitting, or cracking, or flawing, or harbouring dirt. Let him mind that. Such, I assure you, is that poor little wench, Assuntina.

Petrarca. I am convinced that so well-behaved a young creature as Assunta——

Boccaccio. Right! Assunta is her name by baptism ; we usually call her Assuntina, because she is slender, and scarcely yet full-grown, perhaps : but who can tell?

As for those friars, I never was a friend to impudence : I hate loose suggestions. In girls' minds you will find little dust but what is carried there by gusts from without. They seldom want sweeping ; when they do, the broom should be taken from behind the house-door, and the master should be the sacristan.

. . . Scarcely were these words uttered when Assunta was heard running up the stairs ; and the next moment she rapped. Being ordered to come in, she entered with a willow twig in her hand, from the middle of which willow twig (for she held the two ends together) hung a fish, shining with green and gold.

" What hast there, young maiden?" said Ser Francesco.

" A fish, Riverenza!" answered she. " In Tuscany we call it *tinca.*"

Petrarca. I too am a little of a Tuscan.

Assunta. Indeed! well, you really speak very like one, but only more sweetly and slowly. I wonder how you can keep up with Signor Padrone—he talks fast when he is in health ; and you have made him so. Why did not you come before? Your Reverence has surely been at Certaldo in time past.

Petrarca. Yes, before thou wert born.

Assunta. Ah sir ! it must have been long ago then.

Petrarca. Thou hast just entered upon life.

Assunta. I am no child.

Petrarca. What then art thou ?

Assunta. I know not : I have lost both father and mother ; there is a name for such as I am.

Petrarca. And a place in heaven.

Boccaccio. Who brought us that fish, Assunta ? hast paid for it ? there must be seven pounds : I never saw the like.

Assunta. I could hardly lift up my apron to my eyes with it in my hand. Luca, who brought it all the way from the Padule, could scarcely be entreated to eat a morsel of bread or sit down.

Boccaccio. Give him a flask or two of our wine ; he will like it better than the sour puddle of the plain.

Assunta. He is gone back.

Bocoaccio. Gone ! who is he, pray ?

Assunta. Luca, to be sure.

Boccaccio. What Luca ?

Assunta. Dominedio ! O Riverenza ! how sadly must Ser Giovanni, my poor padrone, have lost his memory in this cruel long illness ! he can not recollect young Luca of the Bientola, who married Maria.

Boccaccio. I never heard of either, to the best of my knowledge.

Assunta. Be pleased to mention this in your prayers to-night, Ser Canonico ! May Our Lady soon give him back his memory ! and everything else she has been pleased (only in play, I hope) to take away from him ! Ser Francesco, you must have heard all over the world how Maria Gargarelli, who lived in the service of our paroco, somehow was outwitted by Satanasso. Monsignore thought the paroco had not done all he might have done against his whiles and craftiness, and sent his Reverence over to the monastery in the mountains, Laverna yonder, to make him look sharp ; and there he is yet.

And now does Signor Padrone recollect ?

Boccaccio. Rather more distinctly.

Assunta. Ah me! Rather more distinctly! have patience, Signor Padrone! I am too venturous, God help me! But, Riverenza, when Maria was the scorn or the abhorrence of everybody else, excepting poor Luca Sabbatini, who had always cherished her, and excepting Signor Padrone, who had never seen her in his lifetime . . . for paroco Snello said he desired no visits from any who took liberties with Holy Church . . . as if Padrone did! Luca one day came to me out of breath, with money in his hand for our duck. Now it so happened that the duck, stuffed with noble chestnuts, was going to table at that instant. I told Signor Padrone.

Boccaccio. Assunta, I never heard thee repeat so long and tiresome a story before, nor put thyself out of breath so. Come, we have had enough of it.

Petrarca. She is mortified : pray let her proceed.

Boccaccio. As you will.

Assunta. I told Signor Padrone how Luca was lamenting that Maria was seized with an *imagination.*

Petrarca. No wonder then she fell into misfortune, and her neighbours and friends avoided her.

Assunta. Riverenza! how can you smile ? Signor Padrone! and you too ? You shook your head and sighed at it when it happened. The Demonio, who had caused all the first mischief, was not contented until he had given her the *imagination.*

Petrarca. He could not have finished his work more effectually.

Assunta. He was balked, however. Luca said,

"She shall not die under her wrongs, please God!"

I repeated the words to Signor Padrone . . . He seems to listen, Riverenza! and will remember presently . . . and Signor Padrone cut away one leg for himself, clean forgetting all the chestnuts inside, and said sharply, "Give the bird to Luca ; and, hark ye, bring back the minestra."

Maria loved Luca with all her heart, and Luca loved

Maria with all his : but they both hated paroco Snello for such neglect about the evil one. And even Monsignore, who sent for Luca on purpose, had some difficulty in persuading him to forbear from choler and discourse. For Luca, who never swears, swore bitterly that the devil should play no such tricks again, nor alight on girls napping in the parsonage. Monsignore thought he intended to take violent possession, and to keep watch there himself without consent of the incumbent. "I will have no scandal," said Monsignore; so there was none. Maria, though she did indeed, as I told your Reverence, love her Luca dearly, yet she long refused to marry him, and cried very much at last on the wedding-day, and said, as she entered the porch,

"Luca ! it is not yet too late to leave me."

He would have kissed her, but her face was upon his shoulder.

Pievano Locatelli married them, and gave them his blessing : and going down from the altar, he said before the people, as he stood on the last step, "Be comforted, child ! be comforted ! God above knows that thy husband is honest, and that thou art innocent." Pievano's voice trembled, for he was an aged and holy man, and had walked two miles on the occasion. Pulcheria, his governante, eighty years old, carried an apronful of lilies to bestrew the altar ; and partly from the lilies, and partly from the blessed angels who (although invisible) were present, the church was filled with fragrance. Many who heretofore had been frightened at hearing the mention of Maria's name, ventured now to walk up toward her ; and some gave her needles, and some offered skeins of thread, and some ran home again for pots of honey.

Boccaccio. And why didst not thou take her some trifle ?

Assunta. I had none.

Boccaccio. Surely there are always such about the premises.

Assunta. Not mine to give away.

Boccaccio. So then at thy hands, Assunta, she went

off not overladen. Ne'er a bone-bodkin out of thy bravery, ay ?

Assunta. I ran out knitting, with the woodbine and syringa in the basket for the parlour. I made the basket, . . . I and . . . but myself chiefly, for boys are loiterers.

Boccaccio. Well, well : why not bestow the basket, together with its rich contents ?

Assunta. I am ashamed to say it . . . I covered my half-stocking with them as quickly as I could, and ran after her, and presented it. Not knowing what was under the flowers, and never minding the liberty I had taken, being a stranger to her, she accepted it as graciously as possible, and bade me be happy.

Petrarca. I hope you have always kept her command.

Assunta. Nobody is ever unhappy here, except Fra Biagio, who frets sometimes : but that may be the walk ; or he may fancy Ser Giovanni to be worse than he really is.

. . . Having now performed her mission and concluded her narrative, she bowed, and said,

"Excuse me, Riverenza ! excuse me, Signor Padrone ! my arm aches with this great fish."

Then, bowing again, and moving her eyes modestly toward each, she added, "with permission !" and left the chamber.

"About the Sposina," after a pause began Ser Francesco : "about the Sposina, I do not see the matter clearly."

"You have studied too much for seeing all things clearly," answered Ser Giovanni ; "you see only the greatest. In fine, the devil, on this count, is acquitted by acclamation ; and the paroco Snello eats lettuce and chicory up yonder at Laverna. He has mendicant friars for his society every day ; and snails, as pure as water can wash and boil them, for his repast on festivals. Under this discipline, if they keep it up, surely one devil out of legion will depart from him."

FOURTH DAY'S INTERVIEW.

Petrarca. Do not throw aside your *Paradiso* for me.
Have you been reading it again so early?

Boccaccio. Looking into it here and there. I had spare
time before me.

Petrarca. You have coasted the whole poem, and your
boat's bottom now touches ground. But tell me what you
think of Beatrice.

Boccaccio. I think her in general more of the seraphic
doctor than of the seraph. It is well she retained her
beauty where she was, or she would scarcely be tolerable
now and then. And yet, in other parts, we forget the
captiousness in which Theology takes delight, and feel our
bosoms refreshed by the perfect presence of the youthful
and innocent Bice.

There is something so sweetly sanctifying in pure love.

Petrarca.

> Pure love? there is no other ; nor shall be,
> Till the worse angels hurl the better down
> And heaven lie under hell : if God is one
> And pure, so surely love is pure and one.

Boccaccio. You understand it better than I do : you must
have your own way.

Above all, I have been admiring the melody of the
cadence in this portion of the *Divina Commedia.* Some
of the stanzas leave us nothing to desire in facility and
elegance.

Alighieri grows harmonious as he grows humane, and
does not, like Orpheus, play the better with the beasts
about him.

Petrarca. It is in Paradise that we might expect his tones
to be tried and modulated.

Boccaccio. None of the imitative arts should repose on
writhings and distortions. Tragedy herself, unless she lead
from Terror to Pity, has lost her way.

Petrarca. What then must be thought of a long and crowded work, whence Pity is violently excluded, and where Hatred is the first personage we meet, and almost the last we part from?

Boccaccio. Happily the poet has given us here a few breezes of the morning, a few glimpses of the stars, a few similes of objects to which we have been accustomed among the amusements or occupations of the country. Some of them would be less admired in a meaner author, and are welcome here chiefly as a variety and relief to the mind, after a long continuance in a painful posture. Have you not frequently been pleased with a short quotation of verses in themselves but indifferent, from finding them in some tedious dissertation? and especially if they carry you forth a little into the open air.

Petrarca. I am not quite certain whether, if the verses were indifferent, I should willingly exchange the prose for them ; bad prose being less wearisome than bad poetry : so much less indeed, that the advantage of the exchange might fail to balance the account.

Boccaccio. Let me try whether I can not give you an example of such effect, having already given you the tedious dissertation.

Petrarca. Do your worst.

Boccaccio. Not that neither, but bad enough.

THE PILGRIM'S SHELL.

Under a tuft of eglantine, at noon,
I saw a pilgrim loosen his broad shell
To catch the water off a stony tongue ;
Medusa's it might be, or Pan's, erewhile,
For the huge head was shapeless, eaten out
By time and tempest here, and here embost
With clasping tangles of dark maidenhair.
   " How happy is thy thirst ! how soon assuaged !
How sweet that coldest water this hot day ! "
Whispered my thoughts ; not having yet observ'd
His shell so shallow and so chipt around.
Tall though he was, he held it higher, to meet
The sparkler at its outset : with fresh leap,

Vigorous as one just free upon the world,
Impetuous too as one first checkt, with stamp
Heavy as ten such sparklers might be deemed,
Rusht it amain, from cavity and rim
And rim's divergent channels, and dropt thick
(Issuing at wrist and elbow) on the grass.
The pilgrim shook his head, and fixing up
His scallop,
    " There is something yet," said he,
" Too scanty in this world for my desires ! "

Petrarca. O Giovanni! these are better thoughts and opportuner than such lonely places formerly supplied us with. The whispers of rose-bushes were not always so innocent : under the budding and under the full-blown we sometimes found other images : sometimes the pure fountain failed in bringing purity to the heart.

Unholy fire sprang up in fields and woods;
The air that fann'd it came from solitudes.

If our desires are worthy ones and accomplished, we rejoice in after-time; if unworthy and unsuccessful, we rejoice no less at their discomfiture and miscarriage. We can not have all we wish for. Nothing is said oftener, nothing earlier, nothing later. It begins in the arms with the chidings of the nurse; it will terminate with the milder voice of the physician at the death-bed. But although everybody has heard and most have said it, yet nobody seems to have said or considered, that it is much, very much, to be able to form and project our wishes; that, in the voyage we take to compass and turn them to account, we breathe freely and hopefully; and that it is chiefly in the stagnation of port we are in danger of disappointment and disease.

Boccaccio. The young man who resolves to conquer his love, is only half in earnest or has already half conquered it. But fields and woods have no dangers now for us. I may be alone until doomsday, and loose thoughts will be at fault if they try to scent me.

Petrarca. When the rest of our smiles have left us, we may smile at our immunities. There are indeed, for nearly all,

> Rocks on the shore wherefrom we launch on life,
> Before our final harbour rocks again,
> And (narrow sun-paced plains sailed swiftly by)
> Eddies and breakers all the space between.

Yet Nature preserves her sedater charms for us both and I doubt whether we do not enjoy them the more, by exemption from solicitations and distractions. We are not old while we can hear and enjoy, as much as ever,

> The lonely bird, the bird of even-song,
> When, catching one far call, he leaps elate,
> In his full fondness drowns it, and again
> The shrill shrill glee through Serravalle rings.

Boccaccio. The nightingale is a lively bird to the young and joyous, a melancholy one to the declining and pensive. He has notes for every ear; he has feelings for every bosom; and he exercises over gentle souls a wider and more welcome dominion than any other creature. If I must not offer you my thanks, for bringing to me such associations as the bed-side of sickness is rarely in readiness to supply; if I must not declare to you how pleasant and well placed are your reflections on our condition; I may venture to remark on the nightingale, that our Italy is the only country where this bird is killed for the market. In no other is the race of Avarice and Gluttony so hard run. What a triumph for a Florentine, to hold under his fork the most delightful being in all animated nature! the being to which every poet, or nearly every one, dedicates the first fruits of his labours. A cannibal who devours his enemy, through intolerable hunger, or, what he holds as the measure of justice and of righteousness, revenge, may be viewed with less abhorrence than the heartless gormandiser, who casts upon his loaded stomach the little breast that has poured delight on thousands.

Petrarca. The English, I remember Ser Geoffreddo*
telling us, never kill singing-birds nor swallows.

Boccaccio. Music and hospitality are sweet and sacred
things with them , and well may they value their few warm
days, out of which, if the produce is not wine and oil, they
gather song and garner sensibility.

Petrarca. Ser Geoffreddo felt more pleasure in the
generosity and humanity of his countrymen, than in the
victories they had recently won, with incredibly smaller
numbers, over their boastful enemy.

Boccaccio. I know not of what nation I could name so
amusing a companion as Ser Geoffreddo.   The Englishman
is rather an island than an islander; bluff, stormy, rude,
abrupt, repulsive, inaccessible.   We must not however hold
back or dissemble the learning, and wisdom, and courtesy,
of the better.   While France was without one single man
above a dwarf in literature, and we in Italy had only a small
sprinkling of it, Richard de Bury was sent ambassador to
Rome by King Edward.   So great was his learning, that he
composed two grammars, one Greek, one Hebrew ; neither
of which labours had been attempted by the most industrious
and erudite of those who spoke the languages : he likewise
formed so complete a library as belongs only to the Byzan-
tine emperors.   This prelate came into Italy attended by
Ser Geoffreddo, in whose company we spent, as you
remember, two charming evenings at Arezzo.

Petrarca. What wonderful things his countrymen have
been achieving in this century !

Boccaccio. And how curious it is to trace them up into their
Norwegian coves and creeks three or four centuries back !

Petrarca. Do you think it possible that Norway, which
never could maintain sixty thousand† male adults, was
capable of sending, from her native population, a sufficient
force of warriors to conquer the best province of France,

---

* Chaucer.

† With the advantages of her fisheries, which did not exist in the
age of Petrarca, and of her agriculture, which probably is quintupled
since, Norway does not contain at present the double of the number.

and the whole of England ? And you must deduct from these sixty thousand, the aged, the artisans, the cultivators, and the clergy, together with all the dependents of the church : which numbers, united, we may believe amounted to above one half.

Boccaccio. That she could embody such an army from her own very scanty and scattered population ; no, indeed : but if you recollect that a vast quantity of British had been ejected by incursions of Picts, and that also there had been on the borders a general insurrection against the Romans, and against those of half-blood (which is always the case in a rebellion of the Aboriginals), and if you believe, as I do, that the ejected Romans of the coast at least, became pirates, and were useful to the Scandinavians, by introducing what was needful of their arts and saleable of their plunder, taking in exchange their iron and timber, you may readily admit as a probability, that by the display of spoils and the spirit of enterprise, they encouraged, headed, and carried into effect the invasion of France, and subsequently of England. The English gentlemen of Norman descent have neither blue eyes, in general, nor fair complexions, differing in physiognomy altogether both from the Belgic race and the Norwegian. Beside, they are remarkable for a sedate and somewhat repulsive pride, very different from the effervescent froth of the one, and the sturdy simplicity of the other. Ser Geoffreddo is not only the greatest genius, but likewise the most amiable of his nation. He gave his thoughts and took yours with equal freedom. His country-men, if they give you any, throw them at your head ; and, if they receive any, cast them under their feet before you. Courtesy is neither a quality of native growth, nor communicable to them. Their rivals, the French, are the best imitators in the world ; the English the worst ; particularly under the instruction of the Graces. They have many virtues, no doubt ; but they reserve them for the benefit of their families, or of their enemies ; and they seldom take the trouble to unpack them in their short intercourse abroad.

Petrarca. Ser Geoffreddo, I well remember, was no less remarkable for courtesy than for cordiality.

Boccaccio. He was really as attentive and polite toward us as if he had made us prisoners. It is on that occasion the English are most unlike their antagonists and themselves. What an evil must they think it to be vanquished ! when, struggling with their bashfulness and taciturnity, they become so solicitous and inventive in raising the spirits of the fallen. The Frenchman is ready to truss you on his rapier, unless you acknowledge the perfection of his humanity, and to spit in your face, if you doubt for a moment the delicacy of his politeness. The Englishman is almost angry if you mention either of these as belonging to him, and turns away from you that he may not hear it.

Petrarca. Let us felicitate ourselves that we rarely are forced to witness his self-affliction.

Boccaccio. In palaces, and especially the pontifical, it is likely you saw the very worst of them : indeed there are few in any country of such easy, graceful, unaffected manners as our Italians. We are warmer at the extremities than at the heart: sunless nations have central fires. The Englishman is more gratified when you enable him to show you a fresh kindness, than when you remind him of a past one ; and he forgets what he has conferred as readily as we forget what we have received. In our civility, in our good-nature, in our temperance, in our frugality, none excel us ; and greatly are we in advance of other men, in the arts, in the sciences, in the culture, in the application, and in the power of intellect. Our faculties are perfect, with the sole exception of memory; and our memory is only deficient in its retentiveness of obligation.

Petrarca. Better had it failed in almost all its other functions. Yet, if our countrymen presented any flagrant instances of ingratitude, Alighieri would have set apart a *bolga* for their reception.

Boccaccio. When I correct and republish my *Commentary*, I must be as careful to gratify, as my author was to affront them. I know, from the nature of the Florentines and of the Italians in general, that in calling on me to produce one, they would rather I should praise indiscriminately than parsimoniously. And respect is due to them for repairing, by all the means in their power, the injustice their fathers committed; for enduring in humility his resentment; and for investing him with public honours, as they would some deity who had smitten them. Respect is due to them, and I will offer it, for placing their greatness on so firm a plinth, for deriving their pride from so wholesome a source, and for declaring to the world that the founder of a city is less than her poet and instructor.

Petrarca. In the precincts of those lofty monuments, those towers and temples, which have sprung up amid her factions, the name of Dante is heard at last, and heard with such reverence as only the angels or the saints inspire.

Boccaccio. There are towns so barbarous, that they must be informed by strangers of their own great man, when they happen to have produced one; and would then detract from his merits, that they might not exhibit their awkwardness in doing him honour, or their shame in withholding it. There are such; but not in Italy. I have seen youths standing and looking with seriousness, and indeed with somewhat of veneration, on the broad and low stone bench, to the south of the cathedral, where Dante sat to enjoy the fresh air in summer evenings; and where Giotto, in conversation with him, watched the scaffolding rise higher and higher up his gracefullest of towers. It was truly a bold action, when a youngster pushed another down on the poet's seat. The suprised one blushed and struggled, as those do who unwittingly have been drawn into a penalty (not lightened by laughter) for having sitten in the imperial or the papal chair.

Petrarca. These are good signs, and never fallacious. In the presence of such young persons we ought to be very cautious how we censure a man of genius. One expression of irreverence may eradicate what demands the most attentive culture, may wither the first love for the fair and

noble, and may shake the confidence of those who are
about to give the hand to a guidance less liable to error.
We have ever been grateful to the Deity, for saving us from
among the millions swept away by the pestilence, which
depopulated the cities of Italy, and ravaged the whole of
Europe : let us be equally grateful for an exemption as
providential and as rare in the world of letters ; an exemption from that *Plica Polonica* of invidiousness, which infests
the squalider of poetical heads, and has not always spared
those which ought to have been cleanlier.

Boccaccio. Critics are indignant if we are silent, and
petulant if we complain. You and I are so kindly and
considerate in regard to them, that we rather pat their
petulance than prick up their indignation. Marsyas, while
Apollo was flaying him leisurely and dexterously, with all
the calmness of a god, shortened his upper lip prodigiously,
and showed how royal teeth are fastened in their gums :
his eyes grew blood-shot, and expanded to the size of
rock-melons, though naturally, in length and breadth, as
well as colour, they more resembled a well-ripened bean-
pod. And there issued from his smoking breast, and shook
the leaves above it, a rapid irregular rush of yells and howl-
ings. Remarking so material a change in his countenance
and manners, a satyr, who was much his friend and deeply
interested in his punishment, said calmly, " Marsyas !
Marsyas ! is it thou who criest out so unworthily ? If thou
couldst only look down from that pleasant, smooth, shady
beech-tree, thou wouldst have the satisfaction of seeing that
thy skin is more than half drawn off thee : it is hardly worth
while to make a bustle about it now."

Petrarca. Every Marsyas hath his consoling satyr. Probably when yours was flayed, he was found out to be a
good musician, by those who recommended the flaying
and celebrated the flayer. Among authors, none hath so
many friends as he who is just now dead, and had the
most enemies last week. Those who were then his
adversaries are now sincerely his admirers, for moving out
of the way, and leaving one name less in the lottery. And

yet, poor souls! the prize will never fall to them. There is something sweet and generous in the tone of praise, which captivates an ingenuous mind, whatever may be the subject of it; while propensity to censure not only excites suspicion of malevolence, but reminds the hearer of what he can not disentangle from his earliest ideas of vulgarity. There being no pleasure in thinking ill, it is wonderful there should be any in speaking ill. You, my friend, can find none of it: but every step you are about to take in the revisal of your Lectures, will require much caution. Aware you must be that there are many more defects in our author than we have touched or glanced at: principally, the loose and shallow foundation of so vast a structure; its unconnectedness; its want of manners, of passion, of action, consistently and uninterruptedly at work toward a distinct and worthy purpose; and lastly (although less importantly as regards the poetical character) that splenetic temper, which seems to grudge brightness to the flames of hell, to delight in deepening its gloom, in multiplying its miseries, in accumulating weight upon depression, and building labyrinths about perplexity.

Boccaccio. Yet, O Francesco! when I remember what Dante had suffered and was suffering from the malice and obduracy of his enemies; when I feel (and how I do feel it!) that you also have been following up his glory through the same paths of exile; I can rest only on what is great in him, and the exposure of a fault appears to me almost an inhumanity.

The first time I ever walked to his villa on the Mugnone, I felt a vehement desire to enter it; and yet a certain awe came upon me, as about to take an unceremonious and an unlawful advantage of his absence. While I was hesitating, its inhabitant opened the gate, saluted, and invited me. My desire vanished at once; and although the civility far exceeded what a stranger as I was, and so young a stranger too, could expect, or what probably the more illustrious owner would have vouchsafed, the place itself and the disparity of its occupier made me shrink from it in sadness, and stand before him almost silent. I believe I should do the same at the present day.

Petrarca. With such feelings, which are ours in common, there is little danger that we should be unjust toward him; and, if ever our opinions come before the public, we may disregard the petulance and aspersions of those whom nature never constituted our judges, as she did us of Dante. It is our duty to speak with freedom; it is theirs to listen with respect.

Boccaccio. History would come much into the criticism, and would perform the most interesting part in it. But I clearly see how unsafe it is to meddle with the affairs of families: and every family in Florence is a portion of the government, or has been lately. Every one preserves the annals of the republic; the facts being nearly the same, the inferences widely diverging, the motives utterly dissimilar. A strict examination of Dante would involve the bravest and most intelligent; and the court of Rome, with its royal agents, would persecute them as conspirators against religion, against morals, against the peace, the order, the existence of society. When studious and quiet men get into power, they fancy they can not show too much activity, and very soon prove, by exerting it, that they can show too little discretion. The military, the knightly, the baronial, are spurred on to join in the chase; but the fleshers have other names and other instincts.

Petrarca. Posterity will regret that many of those allusions to persons and events, which we now possess in the pages of Dante, have not reached her. Among the ancients there are few poets who more abound in them than Horace does, and yet we feel certain that there are many which are lost to us.

Boccaccio. I wonder you did not mention him before. Perhaps he is no favourite with you.

Petrarca. Why can not we be delighted with an author, and even feel a predilection for him, without a dislike to others? An admiration of Catullus or Virgil, of Tibullus or Ovid, is never to be heightened by a discharge of bile on Horace.

Boccaccio. The eyes of critics, whether in commending or carping, are both on one side, like a turbot's.

Petrarca. There are some men who delight in heating themselves with wine, and others with headstrong froward-ness. These are resolved to agitate the puddle of their blood by running into parties, literary or political, and espouse a champion's cause with such ardour that they run against everything in their way. Perhaps they never knew or saw the person, or understood his merits : what matter? No sooner was I about to be crowned, than it was predicted by these astrologers, that Protonatory Nerucci and Cavallerizzo Vuotasacchetti (two lampooners, whose hands had latterly been kept from their occupation by drawing gold-embroidered gloves on them) would be rife in the mouths of men after my name had fallen into oblivion.

Boccaccio. I never heard of them before.

Petrarca. So much the better for them, and none the worse for you. Vuotasacchetti had been convicted of filching in his youth ; and Nerucci was so expert a logician, and so rigidly economical a moralist, that he never had occasion for veracity.

Boccaccio. The upholders of such gentry are like little girls with their dolls : they must clothe them, although they strip every other doll in the nursery. It is reported that our Giotto, a great mechanician as well as architect and painter, invented a certain instrument by which he could contract the dimensions of any head laid before him. But these gentlemen, it appears, have improved upon it, and not only can contract one, but enlarge another.

Petrarca. He could perform his undertaking with admir-able correctness and precision ; can they theirs?

Boccaccio. I never heard they could : but well enough for their customers and their consciences.

Petrarca. I see then no great accuracy is required.

Boccaccio. If they heard you they would think you very dull.

Petrarca. They have always thought me so : and, if they change their opinion, I shall begin to think so myself.

Boccaccio. They have placed themselves just where, if we were mischievous, we might desire to see them. We have no power to make them false and malicious, yet they become so the moment they see or hear of us, and thus sink lower than our force could ever thrust them. Pigs, it is said, driven into a pool beyond their depth, cut their throats by awkward attempts at swimming. We could hardly wish them worse luck, although each had a devil in him. Come, let us away; we shall find a purer stream and pleasanter company on the Sabine farm.

Petrarca. We may indeed think the first ode of little value, the second of none, until we come to the sixth stanza.

Boccaccio. Bad as are the first and second, they are better than that wretched one, sounded so lugubriously in our ears at school, as the masterpiece of the pathetic; I mean the ode addressed to Virgil on the death of Quinctilius Varus.

Præcipe lugubres
Cantus, Melpomene, cui liquidam pater
Vocem cum citharâ dedit.

Did he want anyone to help him to cry? What man immersed in grief cares a quattrino about Melpomene, or her father's fairing of an artificial cuckoo and a gilt guitar? What man, on such an occasion, is at leisure to amuse himself with the little plaster images of Pudor and Fides, of Justitia and Veritas, or disposed to make a comparison of Virgil and Orpheus? But if Horace had written a thousand-fold as much trash, we are never to forget that he also wrote

Cœlo tonantem, etc.,

in competition with which ode, the finest in the Greek language itself has, to my year, too many low notes, and somewhat of a wooden sound. And give me• *Vixi puellis*, and give me *Quis multa gracilis*, and as many more as you please; for there are charms in nearly all of them. It now occurs to me that what is written, or interpolated,

Acer et *Mauri* peditis cruentum
Vultus in hostem,

should be *manci;* a foot soldier *mutilated*, but looking with indignant courage at the trooper who inflicted the wound. The Mauritanians were celebrated only for their cavalry. In return for my suggestion, pray tell me what is the meaning of

Obliquo laborat
Lympha fugax trepidare rivo.

Petrarca. The moment I learn it you shall have it. *Laborat trepidare I lympha rivo I fugax* too! *Fugacity* is not the action for hard work, or *labour*.

Boccaccio. Since you can not help me out, I must give up the conjecture, it seems, while it has cost me only half a century. Perhaps it may be *curiosa felicitas*.

Petrarca. There again! Was there ever such an unhappy (not to say absurd) expression! And this from the man who wrote the most beautiful sentence in all latinity.

Boccaccio. What is that?

Petrarca. I am ashamed of repeating it, although in itself it is innocent. The words are :

Gratias ago languori tuo, quo diutius sub
umbrâ voluptatis lusimus.

Boccaccio. Tear out this from the volume; the rest, both prose and poetry, may be thrown away. In the *Dinner of Nasidienus*, I remember the expression *nosse laboro ; I am anxious to know :* this expedites the solution but little. In the same piece there is another odd expression :

Tum in lecto quôque *videres*
Stridere secretâ divisos aure *susurros.*

Petrarca. I doubt Horace's felicity in the choice of words, being quite unable to discover it, and finding more evidences of the contrary than in any contemporary or preceding poet; but I do not doubt his infelicity in his *transpositions* of them, in which certainly he is more remarkable than whatsoever writer of antiquity. How simple, in comparison, are Catullus* and Lucretius in the structure of their sentences! but the most simple and natural of all are Ovid and Tibullus. Your main difficulty lies in another road : it consists not in making explanations, but in avoiding them. Some scholars will assert that everything I have written in my sonnets is allegory or allusion ; others will deny that anything is ; and similarly of Dante. It was known throughout Italy that he was the lover of *Beatrice* Porticari. He has celebrated her in many compositions ; in prose and poetry, in Latin and Italian. Hence it became the safer for him afterward to introduce her as an allegorical personage, in opposition to the *Meretrice ;* under which appellation he (and I subsequently) signified the Papacy. Our great poet wandered among the marvels of the Apocalypse, and fixed his eyes the most attentively on the words,

Veni, et ostendam tibi sponsam, uxorem Agni.

He, as you know, wrote a commentary on his *Commedia* at the close of his Treatise *de Monarchiâ.* But he chiefly aims at showing the duties of pope and emperor, and explaining such parts of the poem as manifestly relate to them. The Patarini accused the pope of despoiling and defiling the church ; the Ghibellines accused him of defrauding and rebelling against the emperor ; Dante enlists both under his flaming banner, and exhibits the *Meretrice* stealing from *Beatrice* both the *divine* and the *august* chariot ; the church and empire. Grave critics will protest their inability to follow you through such darkness, saying you are not worth the trouble, and they must give you up. If Laura and Fiametta were allegorical, they could inspire no tenderness in our readers, and little interest. But, alas ! these are no longer the days to dwell on them.

* Except " Non ita me divi vera gemunt juêrint."

Let human art exert her utmost force,
Pleasure can rise no higher than its source ;
And there it ever stagnates where the ground
Beneath it, O Giovanni ! is unsound.

Boccaccio. You have given me a noble quaternion ; for
which I can only offer you such a string of beads as I am
used to carry about with me.   Memory, they say, is the
mother of the Muses : this is her gift, not theirs.

DEPARTURE FROM FIAMETTA.

When go I must, as well she knew,
And neither yet could say adieu,
Sudden was my Fiametta's fear
To let me see or feel a tear.
It could but melt my heart away,
Nor add one moment to my stay.
But it was ripe and would be shed . . .
So from her cheek upon my head
It, falling on the neck behind,
Hung on the hair she oft had twined.
Thus thought she, and her arm's soft strain
Claspt it, and down it fell again.

Come, come, bear your disappointment, and forgive my
cheating you in the exchange !   Ah Francesco ! Francesco !
well may you sigh ; and I too ; seeing we can do little now
but make verses and doze, and want little but medicine and
masses, while Fra Biagio is merry as a lark, and half master
of the house.   Do not look so grave upon me for remember-
ing so well another state of existence.   He who forgets
his love may still more easily forget his friendships.   I am
weak, I confess it, in yielding my thoughts to what returns
no more ; but you alone know my weakness.

Petrarca. We have loved ;* and so fondly as we believe
none other ever did ; and yet, although it was in youth,

* The tender and virtuous Shenstone, in writing the most beautiful
of epitaphs, was unaware how near he stood to Petrarca.   Hei
quanto minus est cum aliis versari quàm tui meminisse,

Pur mi consola che morir per lei
Meglio è che gioir d'altra.

Giovanni, it was not in the earliest white dawn, when we almost shrink from its freshness, when everything is pure and quiet, when little of earth is seen, and much of heaven. It was not so with us; it was with Dante. The little virgin Beatrice Porticari breathed all her purity into his boyish heart, and inhaled it back again; and if war and disaster, anger and disdain, seized upon it in her absence, they never could divert its course nor impede its destination. Happy the man who carries love with him in his opening day! he never loses its freshness in the meridian of life, nor its happier influence in the later hour. If Dante enthroned his Beatrice in the highest heaven, it was Beatrice who conducted him hither. Love, preceding passion, ensures, sanctifies, and I would say survives it, were it not rather an absorption and transfiguration into its own most perfect purity and holiness.

Boccaccio. Up! up! look into that chest of letters, out of which I took several of yours to run over yesterday morning. All those of a friend whom we have lost, to say nothing of a tenderer affection, touch us sensibly, be the subject what it may. When, in taking them out to read again, we happen to come upon him in some pleasant mood, it is then the dead man's hand is at the heart. Opening the same paper long afterward, can we wonder if a tear has raised its little island in it? Leave me the memory of all my friends, even of the ungrateful! They must remind me of some kind feeling; and perhaps of theirs; and for that very reason they deserve another. It was not my fault if they turned out less worthy than I hoped and fancied them. Yet half the world complains of ingratitude, and the remaining half of envy. Of the one I have already told you my opinion, and heard yours; and the other we may surely bear with quite as much equanimity. For rarely are we envied, until we are so prosperous that envy is rather a familiar in our train than an enemy who waylays us. If we saw nothing of such followers and outriders, and no scabbard with our initials upon it, we might begin to doubt our station.

Petrarca. Giovanni, you are unsuspicious, and would scarcely see a monster in a minotaur. It is well, however, to draw good out of evil, and it is the peculiar gift of an elevated mind. Nevertheless, you must have observed, although with greater curiosity than concern, the slipperiness and tortuousness of your detractors.

Boccaccio. Whatever they detract from me, they leave more than they can carry away. Beside, they always are detected.

Petrarca. When they are detected, they raise themselves up fiercely, as if their nature were erect and they could reach your height.

Boccaccio. Envy would conceal herself under the shadow and shelter of contemptuousness, but she swells too huge for the den she creeps into. Let her lie there and crack, and think no more about her. The people you have been talking of can find no greater and no other faults in my writings than I myself am willing to show them, and still more willing to correct. There are many things, as you have just now told me, very unworthy of their company.

Petrarca. He who has much gold is none the poorer for having much silver too. When a king of old displayed his wealth and magnificence before a philosopher, the philosopher's exclamation was :

" How many things are here which I do not want ! "

Does not the same reflection come upon us, when we have laid aside our compositions for a time, and look into them again more leisurely? Do we not wonder at our own profusion, and say like the philosopher,

" How many things are here which I do not want ! "

It may happen that we pull up flowers with weeds ; but better this than rankness. We must bear to see our first-born despatched before our eyes, and give them up quietly.

Boccaccio. The younger will be the most reluctant. There are poets among us who mistake in themselves the freckles of the hay-fever for beauty-spots. In another half century their volumes will be inquired after; but only for the sake of cutting out an illuminated letter from the title-page, or of transplanting the willow at the end, that hangs so prettily over the tomb of Amaryllis. If they wish to be healthy and vigorous, let them open their bosoms to the breezes of Sunium; for the air of Latium is heavy and overcharged. Above all, they must remember two admonitions; first, that sweet things hurt digestion; secondly, that great sails are ill adapted to small vessels. What is there lovely in poetry unless there be moderation and composure? Are they not better than the hot, uncontrollable harlotry of a flaunting, dishevelled enthusiasm? Whoever has the power of creating, has likewise the inferior power of keeping his creation in order. The best poets are the most impressive, because their steps are regular; for without regularity there is neither strength nor state. Look at Sophocles, look at Æschylus, look at Homer.

Petrarca. I agree with you entirely to the whole extent of your observations; and, if you will continue, I am ready to lay aside my Dante for the present.

Boccaccio. No, no; we must have him again between us: there is no danger that he will sour our tempers.

Petrarca. In comparing his and yours, since you forbid me to declare all I think of your genius, you will at least allow me to congratulate you as being the happier of the two.

Boccaccio. Frequently, where there is great power in poetry, the imagination makes encroachments on the heart, and uses it as her own. I have shed tears on writings which never cost the writer a sigh, but which occasioned him to rub the palms of his hands together, until they were ready to strike fire, with satisfaction at having overcome the difficulty of being tender.

Petrarca. Giovanni! are you not grown satirical?

Boccaccio. Not in this. It is a truth as broad and glaring as the eye of the Cyclops. To make you amends for your shuddering, I will express my doubt, on the other hand, whether Dante felt all the indignation he threw into his poetry. We are immoderately fond of warming ourselves; and we do not think, or care, what the fire is composed of. Be sure it is not always of cedar, like Circe's.* Our Alighieri had slipt into the habit of vituperation; and he thought it fitted him; so he never left it off.

Petrarca. Serener colours are pleasanter to our eyes and more becoming to our character. The chief desire in every man of genius is to be thought one; and no fear or apprehension lessens it. Alighieri, who had certainly studied the gospel, must have been conscious that he not only was inhumane, but that he betrayed a more vindictive spirit than any pope or prelate who is enshrined within the fretwork of his golden grating.

Boccaccio. Unhappily, his strong talon had grown into him, and it would have pained him to suffer amputation. This eagle, unlike Jupiter's, never loosened the thunderbolt from it under the influence of harmony.

Petrarca. The only good thing we can expect in such minds and tempers, is good poetry: let us at least get that; and, having it, let us keep and value it. If you had never written some wanton stories, you would never have been able to show the world how much wiser and better you grew afterward.

Boccaccio. Alas! if I live, I hope to show it. You have raised my spirits: and now, dear Francesco! do say a couple of prayers for me, while I lay together the materials of a tale; a right merry one, I promise you. Faith! it shall amuse you, and pay decently for the prayers; a good honest litany-worth. I hardly know whether I ought to have a nun in it: do you think I may?

Petrarca. Can not you do without one?

Boccaccio. No; a nun I must have: say nothing against her; I can more easily let the abbess alone. Yet Frate

---

* Dives inaccessis ubi Solis filia lucis
Urit odoratam nocturna in lumina cedrum.   *Æn.*

Biagio* . . . that Frate Biagio, who never came to visit me but when he thought I was at extremities or asleep . . . Assuntina! are you there?

Petrarca. No; do you want her?

Boccaccio. Not a bit. That Frate Biagio has heightened my pulse when I could not lower it again. The very devil is that Frate for heightening pulses. And with him I shall now make merry . . . God willing . . . in God's good time . . . should it be his divine will to restore me! which I think he has begun to do miraculously. I seem to be within a frog's leap of well again; and we will presently have some rare fun in my *Tale of the Frate.*

Petrarca. Do not openly name him.

Boccaccio. He shall recognise himself by one single expression. He said to me, when I was at the worst, "Ser Giovanni! it would not be much amiss (with permission!) if you begin to think (at any spare time) just a morsel, of eternity."

"Ah! Fra Biagio!" answered I, contritely, "I never heard a sermon of yours but I thought of it seriously and uneasily, long before the discourse was over."

"So must all," replied he, "and yet few have the grace to own it."

Now mind, Francesco! if it should please the Lord to

---

* Our San Vivaldo is enriched by his deposit. In the church, on the fifth flagstone from before the high altar, is this inscription:

HIC SITUS EST,
BEATAM IMMORTALITATEM EXPECTANS,
D. BLASIUS DE BLASIIS,
HUJUS CŒNOBII ABBAS,
SINGULARI VIR CHARITATE,
MORIBUS INTEGERRIMIS,
REI THEOLOGICÆ NEC NON PHYSICÆ
PERITISSIMUS.
ORATE PRO ANIMA EJUS.

To the word *orate* have been prefixed the letters PL, the aspiration, no doubt, of some friendly monk; although Monsignore thinks it susceptible of two interpretations; the other he reserves *in petto.*

Domenico Grigi.

call me unto him, I say, *The Nun and Fra Biagio* will be found, after my decease, in the closet cut out of the wall, behind yon Saint Zacharias in blue and yellow.

Well done! well done! Francesco. I never heard any man repeat his prayers so fast and fluently. Why! how many (at a guess) have you repeated? Such is the power of friendship, and such the habit of religion! They have done me good: I feel myself stronger already. To-morrow I think I shall be able, by leaning on that stout maple stick in the corner, to walk half over my podere.

Have you done? have you done?

Petrarca. Be quiet: you may talk too much.

Boccaccio. I can not be quiet for another hour; so, if you have any more prayers to get over, stick the spur into the other side of them: they must verily speed, if they beat the last.

Petrarca. Be more serious, dear Giovanni.

Boccaccio. Never bid a convalescent be more serious: no, nor a sick man neither. To health it may give that composure which it takes away from sickness. Every man will have his hours of seriousness; but, like the hours of rest, they often are ill chosen and unwholesome. Be assured, our heavenly Father is as well pleased to see his children in the playground as in the school-room. He has provided both for us, and has given us intimations when each should occupy us.

Petrarca. You are right, Giovanni! but we know which bell is heard the most distinctly. We fold our arms at the one, try the cooler part of the pillow, and turn again to slumber; at the first stroke of the other, we are beyond our monitors. As for you, hardly Dante himself could make you grave.

Boccaccio. I do not remember how it happened that we slipped away from his side. One of us must have found him tedious.

Petrarca. If you were really and substantially at his side, he would have no mercy on you.

Boccaccio. In sooth, our good Alighieri seems to have had

601

the appetite of a dogfish or shark, and to have bitten the harder the warmer he was. I would not voluntarily be under his manifold rows of dentals. He has an incisor to every saint in the calendar. I should fare, methinks, like Brutus and the Archbishop. He is forced to stretch himself, out of sheer listlessness, in so idle a place as Purgatory : he loses half his strength in Paradise : Hell alone makes him alert and lively : there he moves about and threatens as tremendously as the serpent that opposed the legions on their march in Africa. He would not have been contented in Tuscany itself, even had his enemies left him unmolested. Were I to write on his model a tripartite poem, I think it should be entitled, *Earth, Italy, and Heaven.*

Petrarca. You will never give yourself the trouble.

Boccaccio. I should not succeed.

Petrarca. Perhaps not : but you have done very much, and may be able to do very much more.

Boccaccio. Wonderful is it to me, when I consider that an infirm and helpless creature, as I am, should be capable of laying thoughts up in their cabinets of words, which Time, as he rushes by, with the revolutions of stormy and destructive years, can never move from their places. On this coarse mattress, one among the homeliest in the fair at Impruneta, is stretched an old burgess of Certaldo, of whom perhaps more will be known hereafter than we know of the Ptolemies and the Pharaohs ; while popes and princes are lying as unregarded as the fleas that are shaken out of the window. Upon my life, Francesco ! to think of this is enough to make a man presumptuous.

Petrarca. No, Giovanni ! not when the man thinks justly of it, as such a man ought to do, and must. For, so mighty a power over Time, who casts all other mortals under his, comes down to us from a greater ; and it is only if we abuse the victory that it were better we had encountered a defeat. Unremitting care must be taken that nothing soil the monuments we are raising : sure enough we are that nothing can subvert, and nothing but our negligence, or worse than negligence, efface them. Under the glorious lamp entrusted to your vigilance, one among the lights of the world, which the ministering angels of our God have suspended for his service, let there stand, with unclosing eyes, Integrity, Compassion, Self-denial.

Boccaccio. These are holier and cheerfuller images than Dante has been setting up before us. I hope every thesis in dispute among his theologians will be settled ere I set foot among them. I like Tuscany well enough : it answers all my purposes for the present : and I am without the benefit of those preliminary studies which might render me a worthy auditor of incomprehensible wisdom.

Petrarca. I do not wonder you are attached to Tuscany. Many as have been your visits and adventures in other parts, you have rendered it pleasanter and more interesting than any : and indeed we can scarcely walk in any quarter from the gates of Florence, without the recollection of some witty or affecting story related by you. Every street, every farm, is peopled by your genius : and this population can not change with seasons or with ages, with factions or with incursions. Ghibellines and Guelphs will have been contested for only by the worms, long before the *Decameron* has ceased to be recited on our banks of blue lilies and under our arching vines. Another plague may come amidst us ; and something of a solace in so terrible a visitation would be found in your pages, by those to whom letters are a refuge and relief.

Boccaccio. I do indeed think my little bevy from Santa Maria Novella would be better company on such an occasion, than a devil with three heads, who diverts the pain his claws inflicted, by sticking his fangs in another place.

Petrarca. This is atrocious, not terrific nor grand. Alighieri is grand by his lights, not by his shadows ; by his human affections, not by his infernal. As the minutest sands are the labours of some profound sea, or the spoils of some vast mountain, in like manner his horrid wastes and wearying minutenesses are the chafings of a turbulent spirit, grasping the loftiest things and penetrating the deepest, and moving and moaning on the earth in loneliness and sadness.

Boccaccio. Among men he is what among waters is

> The strange, mysterious, solitary Nile.

Petrarca. Is that his verse? I do not remember it.

Boccaccio. No, it is mine for the present: how long it may continue mine I can not tell. I never run after those who steal my apples: it would only tire me: and they are hardly worth recovering when they are bruised and bitten, as they are usually. I would not stand upon my verses: it is a perilous boy's trick, which we ought to leave off when we put on square shoes. Let our prose show what we are, and our poetry what we have been.

Petrarca. You would never have given this advice to Alighieri.

Boccaccio. I would never plough porphyry; there is ground fitter for grain. Alighieri is the parent of his system, like the sun, about whom all the worlds are but particles thrown forth from him. We may write little things well, and accumulate one upon another; but never will any be justly called a great poet unless he has treated a great subject worthily. He may be the poet of the lover and of the idler, he may be the poet of green fields or gay society; but whoever is this can be no more. A throne is not built of birds'-nests, nor do a thousand reeds make a trumpet.

Petrarca. I wish Alighieri had blown his on nobler occasions.

Boccaccio. We may rightly wish it: but, in regretting what he wanted, let us acknowledge what he had: and never forget (which we omitted to mention) that he borrowed less from his predecessors than any of the Roman poets from theirs. Reasonably may it be expected that almost all who follow will be greatly more indebted to antiquity, to whose stores we, every year, are making some addition.

Petrarca. It can be held no flaw in the title-deeds of

genius, if the same thoughts re-appear as have been exhibited long ago. The indisputable sign of defect should be looked for in the proportion they bear to the unquestionably original. There are ideas which necessarily must occur to minds of the like magnitude and materials, aspect and temperature. When two ages are in the same phasis, they will excite the same humours, and produce the same coincidences and combinations. In addition to which, a great poet may really borrow : he may even condescend to an obligation at the hand of an equal or inferior : but he forfeits his title if he borrows more than the amount of his own possessions. The nightingale himself takes somewhat of his song from birds less glorified : and the lark, having beaten with her wing the very gates of heaven, cools her breast among the grass. The lowlier of intellect may lay out a table in their field, at which table the highest one shall sometimes be disposed to partake : want does not compel him. Imitation, as we call it, is often weakness, but it likewise is often sympathy.

Boccaccio. Our poet was seldom accessible in this quarter. Invective picks up the first stone on the wayside, and wants leisure to consult a forerunner.

Petrarca. Dante (original enough everywhere) is coarse and clumsy in this career. Vengeance has nothing to do with comedy, nor properly with satire. The satirist who told us that Indignation made his verses* for him, might have been told in return that she excluded him thereby from the first class, and thrust him among the rhetoricians and declaimers. Lucretius, in his vituperation, is graver and more dignified than Alighieri. Painful; to see how tolerant is the atheist, how intolerant the catholic : how anxiously the one removes from among the sufferings of Mortality, her last and heaviest, the fear of a vindictive Fury pursuing her shadow across rivers of fire and tears; how laboriously the other brings down Anguish and Despair, even when Death has done his work. How grateful the one is to that beneficent philosopher who made

* Facit indignatio versum. *Juv.*

him at peace with himself, and tolerant and kindly toward his fellow-creatures! how importunate the other that God should forego his divine mercy, and hurl everlasting torments both upon the dead and the living!

Boccaccio. I have always heard that Ser Dante was a very good man and sound catholic: but Christ forgive me if my heart is oftener on the side of Lucretius!* Observe, I say, my heart; nothing more. I devoutly hold to the sacraments and the mysteries: yet somehow I would rather see men tranquillised than frightened out of their senses, and rather fast asleep than burning. Sometimes I have been ready to believe, as far as our holy faith will allow me, that it were better our Lord were nowhere, than torturing in his inscrutable wisdom, to all eternity, so many myriads of us poor devils, the creatures of his hands. Do not cross thyself so thickly, Francesco! nor hang down thy nether lip so loosely, languidly, and helplessly; for I would be a good catholic, alive or dead. But, upon my conscience, it goes hard with me to think it of him, when I hear that woodlark yonder, gushing with joyousness, or when I see the beautiful clouds, resting so softly one upon another, dissolving . . . and not damned for it. Above all, I am slow to apprehend it, when I remember his great goodness vouchsafed to me, and reflect on my sinful life heretofore, chiefly in summer time, and in cities, or their vicinity. But I was tempted beyond my strength; and I fell as any man might do. However, this last illness, by God's grace, has well nigh brought me to my right mind again in all such matters: and if I get stout in the present month, and can hold out the next without sliding, I do verily think I am safe, or nearly so, until the season of beccaficoes.

Petrarca. Be not too confident!

Boccaccio. Well, I will not be.

Petrarca. But be firm.

Boccaccio. Assuntina! what! are you come in again?

Assunta. Did you or my master call me, Riverenza?

---

* Qy. How much of Lucretius (or Petronius or Catullus, before cited) was then known? *Remark by Monsignore.*

Petrarca. No, child !

Boccaccio. O ! get you gone ! get you gone ! you little rogue you !

Francesco, I feel quite well. Your kindness to my playful creatures in the *Decameron* has revived me, and has put me into good-humour with the greater part of them. Are you quite certain the Madonna`will not expect me to keep my promise? You said you were: I need not ask you again. I will accept the whole of your assurances, and half your praises.

Petrarca. To represent so vast a variety of personages so characteristically as you have done, to give the wise all their wisdom, the witty all their wit, and (what is harder to do advantageously) the simple all their simplicity, requires a genius such as you alone possess. Those who doubt it are the least dangerous of your rivals.

FIFTH DAY'S INTERVIEW.

IT being now the last morning that Petrarca could remain with his friend, he resolved to pass early into his bed-chamber. Boccaccio had risen, and was standing at the open window, with his arms against it. Renovated health sparkled in the eyes of the one; surprise and delight and thankfulness to heaven, filled the other's with sudden tears. He clasped Giovanni, kissed his flaccid and sallow cheek, and falling on his knees, adored the Giver of life, the source of health to body and soul. Giovanni was not unmoved : he bent one knee as he leaned on the shoulder of Francesco, looking down into his face, repeating his words, and adding,

"Blessed be thou, O Lord ! who sendest me health again ! and blessings on thy messenger who brought it."

He had slept soundly ; for ere he closed his eyes he had

unburdened his mind of its freight, not only by employing the prayers appointed by Holy Church, but likewise by ejaculating; as sundry of the fathers did of old. He acknowledged his contrition for many trangressions, and chiefly for uncharitable thoughts of Fra Biagio : on which occasion he turned fairly round on his couch, and leaning his brow against the wall, and his body being in a becomingly curved position, and proper for the purpose, he thus ejaculated :

"Thou knowest, O most Holy Virgin ! that never have I spoken to handmaiden at this villetta, or within my mansion at Certaldo, wantonly or indiscreetly, but have always been, inasmuch as may be, the guardian of innocence ; deeming it better, when irregular thoughts assailed me, to ventilate them abroad than to poison the house with them. And if, sinner as I am, I have thought uncharitably of others, and more especially of Fra Biagio, pardon me, out of thy exceeding great mercies ! And let it not be imputed to me, if I have kept, and may keep hereafter, an eye over him, in wariness and watchfulness ; not otherwise. For thou knowest, O Madonna ! that many who have a perfect and unwavering faith in thee, yet do cover up their cheese from the nibblings of vermin."

Whereupon, he turned round again, threw himself on his back at full length, and feeling the sheets cool, smooth, and refreshing, folded his arms, and slept instantaneously. The consequence of his wholesome slumber was a calm alacrity : and the idea that his visitor would be happy at seeing him on his feet again, made him attempt to get up : at which he succeeded, to his own wonder. And it was increased by the manifestation of his strength in opening the casement, stiff from being closed, and swelled by the continuance of the rains. The morning was warm and sunny : and it is known that on this occasion he composed the verses below :

My old familiar cottage-green !
I see once more thy pleasant sheen ;
The gossamer suspended over
Smart celandine by lusty clover ;

And the last blossom of the plum
Inviting her first leaves to come ;
Which hang a little back, but show
'Tis not their nature to say no.
I scarcely am in voice to sing
How graceful are the steps of Spring ;
And ah ! it makes me sigh to look
How leaps along my merry brook,
The very same to-day as when
He chirrupt first to maids and men.

Petrarca. I can rejoice at the freshness of your feelings :
but the sight of the green turf reminds me rather of its
ultimate use and destination.

For many serves the parish pall,
The turf in common serves for all.

Boccaccio. Very true ; and, such being the case, let us
carefully fold it up, and lay it by until we call for it.

Francesco, you made me quite light-headed yesterday.
I am rather too old to dance either with Spring, as I have
been saying, or with Vanity : and yet I accepted her at
your hand as a partner. In future, no more of comparisons
for me ! You not only can do me no good, but you can
leave me no pleasure : for here I shall remain the few days
I have to live, and shall see nobody who will be disposed
to remind me of your praises. Beside, you yourself will get
hated for them. We neither can deserve praise nor receive
it with impunity.

Petrarca. Have you never remarked that it is into quiet
water that children throw pebbles to disturb it ? and that it
is into deep caverns that the idle drop sticks and dirt ?
We must expect such treatment.

Boccaccio. Your admonition shall have its wholesome
influence over me, when the fever your praises have excited
has grown moderate.

. . . After the conversation on this topic and various
others had continued some time, it was interrupted by a
visitor. The clergy and monkery at Certaldo had never
been cordial with Messer Giovanni, it being suspected that

certain of his *Novelle* were modelled on originals in their orders.   Hence, although they indeed both professed and felt esteem for Canonico Petrarca, they abstained from expressing it at the villetta.   But Frate Biagio of San Vivaldo was (by his own appointment) the friend of the house; and, being considered as very expert in pharmacy, had, day after day, brought over no indifferent store of simples, in ptisans, and other refections, during the continuance of Ser Giovanni's ailment.   Something now moved him to cast about in his mind whether it might not appear dutiful to make another visit.   Perhaps he thought it possible that, among those who peradventure had seen him lately on the road, one or other might expect from him a solution of the questions, What sort of person was the *crowned martyr?* whether he carried a palm in his hand? whether a seam was visible across the throat? whether he wore a ring over his glove, with a chrysolite in it, like the bishops, but representing the city of Jerusalem and the judgment-seat of Pontius Pilate?   Such were the reports; but the inhabitants of San Vivaldo could not believe the Certaldese, who, inhabiting the next township to them, were naturally their enemies. Yet they might believe Frate Biagio, and certainly would interrogate him accordingly.   He formed his determination, put his frock and hood on, and gave a curvature to his shoe, to evince his knowledge of the world, by pushing the extremity of it with his breast-bone against the corner of his cell.   Studious of his figure and of his attire, he walked as much as possible on his heels, to keep up the reformation he had wrought in the workmanship of the cordwainer. On former occasions he had borrowed a horse, as being wanted to hear confession or to carry medicines, which might otherwise be too late.   But, having put on an entirely new habiliment, and it being the season when horses are beginning to do the same, he deemed it prudent to travel on foot.   Approaching the villetta, his first intention was to walk directly into his patient's room : but he found it impossible to resist the impulses of pride, in showing

Assunta his rigid and stately frock, and shoes rather of the equestrian order than the monastic. So he went into the kitchen where the girl was at work, having just taken away the remains of the breakfast.

"Frate Biagio!" cried she, "is this you? Have you been sleeping at Conte Jeronimo's?"

"Not I," replied he.

"Why!" said she, "those are surely his shoes! Santa Maria! you must have put them on in the dusk of the morning, to say your prayers in! Here! here! take these old ones of Signor Padrone, for the love of God! I hope your Reverence met nobody."

Frate. What dost smile at?

Assunta. Smile at! I could find in my heart to laugh outright, if I only were certain that nobody had seen your Reverence in such a funny trim. Riverenza! put on these.

Frate. Not I indeed.

Assunta. Allow me then?

Frate. No, nor you.

Assunta. Then let me stand upon yours, to push down the points.

. . . Frate Biagio now began to relent a little, when Assunta, who had made one step toward the project, bethought herself suddenly, and said,

"No; I might miss my footing. But, mercy upon us! what made you cramp your Reverence with those ox-yoke shoes? and strangle your Reverence with that hang-dog collar?"

"If you must know," answered the Frate, reddening, "it was because I am making a visit to the Canonico of Parma. I should like to know something about him : perhaps you could tell me?"

Assunta. Ever so much.

Frate. I thought no less : indeed I knew it. Which goes to bed first?

Assunta. Both together.

Frate. Demonio! what dost mean?

Assunta. He tells me never to sit up waiting, but to say my prayers and dream of the Virgin.

Frate. As if it was any business of his! Does he put out his lamp himself?

Assunta. To be sure he does: why should not he? what should he be afraid of? It is not winter: and beside, there is a mat upon the floor, all round the bed, excepting the top and bottom.

Frate. I am quite convinced he never said anything to make you blush. Why are you silent?

Assunta. I have a right.

Frate. He did then? ay? Do not nod your head: that will never do. Discreet girls speak plainly.

Assunta. What would you have?

Frate. The truth; the truth; again, I say, the truth.

Assunta. He *did* then.

Frate. I knew it! The most dangerous man living!

Assunta. Ah! indeed he is! Signor Padrone said so.

Frate. He knows him of old: he warned you, it seems.

Assunta. Me! He never said it was I who was in danger.

Frate. He might: it was his duty.

Assunta. Am I so fat? Lord! you may feel every rib. Girls who run about as I do, slip away from apoplexy.

Frate. Ho! ho! that is all, is it?

Assunta. And bad enough too! that such good-natured men should ever grow so bulky; and stand in danger, as Padrone said they both do, of such a seizure?

Frate. What? and art ready to cry about it? Old folks can not die easier: and there are always plenty of younger to run quick enough for a confessor. But I must not trifle in this manner. It is my duty to set your feet in the right way: it is my bounden duty to report to Ser Giovanni all irregularities I know of, committed in his domicile. I could indeed, and would, remit a trifle, on hearing the worst. Tell me now, Assunta! tell me, you little angel! did you . . . we all may, the very best of us may, and do . . . sin, my sweet?

Assunta. You may be sure I do not: for whenever I sin I run into church directly, although it snows or thunders: else I never could see again Padrone's face, or any one's.

Frate. You do not come to me.

Assunta. You live at San Vivaldo.

Frate. But when there is sin so pressing I am always ready to be found. You perplex, you puzzle me. Tell me at once how he made you blush.

Assunta. Well then!

Frate. Well then! you did not hang back so before him. I lose all patience.

Assunta. So famous a man! . . .

Frate. No excuse in that.

Assunta. So dear to Padrone . . .

Frate. The more shame for him!

Assunta. Called me . . .

Frate. And *called* you, did he! the traitorous swine!

Assunta. Called me . . . *good girl.*

Frate. Psha! the wenches, I think, are all mad: but few of them in this manner.

. . . Without saying another word, Fra Biagio went forward and opened the bedchamber-door, saying, briskly,

"Servant! Ser Giovanni! Ser Canonico! most devoted! most obsequious! I venture to incommode you. Thanks to God, Ser Canonico, you are looking well for your years. They tell me you were formerly (who would believe it?) the handsomest man in Christendom, and worked your way glibly, yonder at Avignon.

"Capperi! Ser Giovanni! I never observed that you were sitting bolt-upright in that long-backed arm-chair, instead of lying abed. Quite in the right. I am rejoiced at such a change for the better. Who advised it?"

Boccaccio. So many thanks to Fra Biagio! I not only am sitting up, but have taken a draught of fresh air at the window, and every leaf had a little present of sunshine for me.

There is one pleasure, Fra Biagio, which I fancy you never have experienced, and I hardly know whether I ought to wish it you; the first sensation of health after a long confinement.

Frate. Thanks! infinite! I would take any man's word for that, without a wish to try it. Everybody tells me I am exactly what I was a dozen years ago; while, for my part, I see everybody changed: those who ought to be much about my age, even those . . . Per Bacco! I told them my thoughts when they had told me theirs; and they were not so agreeable as they used to be in former days.

Boccaccio. How people hate sincerity.

Cospetto! why, Frate! what hast got upon thy toes? Hast killed some Tartar and tucked his bow into one, and torn the crescent from the vizier's tent to make the other match it? Hadst thou fallen in thy mettlesome expedition (and it is a mercy and a miracle thou didst not) those sacrilegious shoes would have impaled thee.

Frate. It was a mistake in the shoemaker. But no pain or incommodity whatsoever could detain me from paying my duty to Ser Canonico, the first moment I heard of his auspicious arrival, or from offering my congratulations to Ser Giovanni, on the annunciation that he was recovered and looking out of the window. All Tuscany was standing on the watch for it, and the news flew like lightning. By this time it is upon the Danube.

And pray, Ser Canonico, how does Madonna Laura do?

Petrarca. Peace to her gentle spirit! she is departed.

Frate. Ay, true. I had quite forgotten: that is to say, I recollect it. You told us as much, I think, in a poem on her death. Well, and do you know! our friend Giovanni here is a bit of an author in his way.

Boccaccio. Frate! you confuse my modesty.

Frate. Murder will out. It is a fact, on my conscience. Have you never heard anything about it, Canonico? Ha! we poets are sly fellows: we can keep a secret.

Boccaccio. Are you quite sure you can?

Frate. Try, and trust me with any. I am a confessional

on legs: there is no more a whisper in me than in a woolsack.

I am in feather again, as you see; and in tune, as you shall hear.

April is not the month for moping. Sing it lustily.

Boccaccio. Let it be your business to sing it, being a Frate; I can only recite it.

Frate. Pray do then.

Boccaccio.

> Frate Biagio! sempre quando
> Quà tu vieni cavalcando,
> Pensi che le buone strade
> Per il mondo sien ben rade;
> E, di quante sono brutte,
> La più brutta è tua di tutte.
> Badi, non cascare sulle
> Graziosissime fanciulle,
> Che con capo dritto, alzato,
> Uova portano al mercato.
> Pessima mi pare l'opra
> Rovesciarle sottosopra.
> Deh! scansando le erte e sassi,
> Sempre con premura passi.
> Caro amico! Frate Biagio!
> Passi pur, ma passi adagio.*

Frate. Well now really, Canonico, for one not exactly one of us, that canzone of Ser Giovanni has merit; has not

* Avendo io fatto comparire nel nostro idioma toscano, e senza traduzione, i leggiadri versi sopra stampati, chiedo perdono da chi legge. Non potei, badando con dovuta premura ai miei interessi ed a quelli del proposito mio, non potei, dico, far di meno; stanteche una riunione de' critici, i più vistosi del Regno unito d'Inghilterra ed Irlanda, avrà con unanimità dichiarato, che nessuno, di quanti esistono i mortali, saprà mai indovinare la versione. Stimo assai il traduttore; lavora per poco, e agevolmente; mi pare piutosto galantuomo; non c'è male; ma poeta poco felice poi. Parlano que' Signori critici riveritissimi di certi poemetti e frammenti già da noi ammessi in questo volume, ed anche di altri del medesimo autore forse originali, e restano di avviso commune, che non vi sia neppure una sola parola veramente da intendersi; che il senso (chi sa?) sarà di *ateisimo,* ovvero di *alto tradimento.* Che *questo* non lo sia, nè palsesamente nè occultamente, fermo col proprio pugno. *Domenico Grigi.*

it ? I did not ride, however, to-day ; as you may see by the lining of my frock. But *plus non vitiat;* ay, Canonico ! About the roads he is right enough ; they are the devil's own roads ; that must be said for them.

Ser Giovanni ! with permission ; your mention of eggs in the canzone, has induced me to fancy I could eat a pair of them. The hens lay well now : that white one of yours is worth more than the goose that laid the golden : and you have a store of others, her equals or betters: we have none like them at poor St. Vivaldo. *A riverderci, Ser Giovanni! Schiavo ! Ser Canonico ! mi commandino.*

. . . Fra Biagio went back into the kitchen, helped himself to a quarter of a loaf, ordered a flask of wine, and, trying several eggs against his lips, selected seven, which he himself fried in oil, although the maid offered her services. He never had been so little disposed to enter into conver- sation with her ; and, on her asking him how he found her master, he replied, that in bodily health Ser Giovanni, by his prayers and ptisans, had much improved, but that his faculties were wearing out apace. "He may now run in the same couples with the Canonico : they can not catch the mange one of the other : the one could say nothing to the purpose, and the other nothing at all. The whole conversation was entirely at my charge," added he. "And now, Assunta, since you press it, I will accept the service of your master's shoes. How I shall ever get home I don't know." He took the shoes off the handles of the bellows, where Assunta had placed them out of her way, and tucking one of his own under each arm, limped toward St. Vivaldo.

The unwonted attention to smartness of apparel, in the only article wherein it could be displayed, was suggested to Frate Biagio by hearing that Ser Francesco, accustomed to courtly habits and elegant society, and having not only small hands, but small feet, usually wore red slippers in the morning. Fra Biagio had scarcely left the outer door, than he cordially cursed Ser Francesco for making such a fool of him, and wearing slippers of black list. "These canonicoes," said he, "not only lie themselves, but teach everybody else to do the same. He has lamed me for life : I burn as if I had been shod at the blacksmith's forge."

The two friends said nothing about him, but continued the discourse which his visit had interrupted.

Petrarca. Turn again, I entreat you, to the serious ; and do not imagine that because by nature you are inclined to playfulness, you must therefore write ludicrous things better. Many of your stories would make the gravest men laugh, and yet there is little wit in them.

Boccaccio. I think so myself ; though authors, little disposed as they are to doubt their possession of any quality they would bring into play, are least of all suspicious on the side of wit. You have convinced me. I am glad to have been tender, and to have written tenderly : for I am certain it is this alone that has made you love me with such affection.

Petrarca. Not this alone, Giovanni ! but this principally. I have always found you kind and compassionate, liberal and sincere, and when Fortune does not stand very close to such a man, she leaves only the more room for Friendship.

Boccaccio. Let her stand off then, now and for ever ! To my heart, to my heart, Francesco ! preserver of my health, my peace of mind, and (since you tell me I may claim it) my glory.

Petrarca. Recovering your strength you must pursue your studies to complete it. What can you have been doing with your books ? I have searched in vain this morning for the treasury. Where are they kept ? Formerly they were always open. I found only a short manuscript, which I suspect is poetry, but I ventured not on looking into it, until I had brought it with me and laid it before you.

Boccaccio. Well guessed ! They are verses written by a gentleman who resided long in this country, and who much regretted the necessity of leaving it. He took great delight in composing both Latin and Italian, but never kept a copy of them latterly, so that these are the only ones I could obtain from him. Read : for your voice will improve them.

TO MY CHILD CARLINO.

Carlino ! what art thou about, my boy ?
Often I ask that question, though in vain,
For we are far apart : ah ! therefore 'tis
I often ask it ; not in such a tone
As wiser fathers do, who know too well.
Were we not children, you and I together?
Stole we not glances from each other's eyes ?
Swore we not secrecy in such misdeeds?
Well could we trust each other.   Tell me then
What thou art doing.   Carving out thy name,
Or haply mine, upon my favourite seat,
With the new knife I sent thee over sea ?
Or hast thou broken it, and hid the hilt
Among the myrtles, starr'd with flowers, behind?
Or under that high throne whence fifty lilies
(With sworded tuberoses dense around)
Lift up their heads at once, not without fear
That they were looking at thee all the while.

Does Cincirillo follow thee about ?
Inverting one swart foot suspensively,
And wagging his dread jaw at every chirp
Of bird above him on the olive-branch ?
Frighten him then away ! 'twas he who slew
Our pigeons, our white pigeons peacock-tailed,
That fear'd not you and me . . . alas, nor him !
I flattened his striped sides along my knee,
And reasoned with him on his bloody mind,
Till he looked blandly, and half-closed his eyes
To ponder on my lecture in the shade.
I doubt his memory much, his heart a little,
And in some minor matters (may I say it ?)
Could wish him rather sager.   But from thee
God hold back wisdom yet for many years !
Whether in early season or in late
It always comes high-priced.   For thy pure breast
I have no lesson ; it for me has many.
Come throw it open then !   What sports, what cares
(Since there are none too young for these) engage
Thy busy thoughts ?   Are you again at work,

Walter and you, with those sly labourers,
Geppo, Giovanni, Cecco, and Poeta,
To build more solidly your broken dam
Among the poplars, whence the nightingale
Inquisitively watch'd you all day long?
I was not of your council in the scheme,
Or might have saved you silver without end,
And sighs too without number. Art thou gone
Below the mulberry, where that cold pool
Urged to devise a warmer, and more fit
For mighty swimmers, swimming three abreast?
Or art thou panting in this summer noon
Upon the lowest step before the hall,
Drawing a slice of watermelon, long
As Cupid's bow, athwart thy wetted lips
(Like one who plays Pan's pipe) and letting drop
The sable seeds from all their separate cells,
And leaving bays profound and rocks abrupt,
Redder than coral round Calypso's cave.

Petrarca. There have been those anciently who would have been pleased with such poetry, and perhaps there may be again. I am not sorry to see the Muses by the side of childhood, and forming a part of the family. But now tell me about the books.

Boccaccio. Resolving to lay aside the more valuable of those I had collected or transcribed, and to place them under the guardianship of richer men, I locked them up together in the higher story of my tower at Certaldo. You remember the old tower?

Petrarca. Well do I remember the hearty laugh we had together (which stopped us upon the staircase) at the calculation we made, how much longer you and I, if we continued to thrive as we had thriven latterly, should be able to pass within its narrow circle. Although I like this little villa much better, I would gladly see the place again, and enjoy with you, as we did before, the vast expanse of woodlands and mountains and maremma; frowning fortresses inexpugnable; and others more prodigious for their ruins; then below them, lordly abbeys, overcanopied with stately trees and girded with rich luxuriance; and towns that seem approaching them to do them honour, and villages nestling close at their sides for sustenance and protection.

Boccaccio. My disorder, if it should keep its promise of leaving me at last, will have been preparing me for the accomplishment of such a project. Should I get thinner and thinner at this rate, I shall soon be able to mount not only a turret or a belfry, but a tube of macarone,* while a Neapolitan is suspending it for deglutition.

What I am about to mention, will show you how little you can rely on me! I have preserved the books, as you desired, but quite contrary to my resolution : and, no less contrary to it, by your desire I shall now preserve the *Decameron.* In vain had I determined not only to mend in future, but to correct the past ; in vain had I prayed most fervently for grace to accomplish it, with a final aspiration to Fiametta that she would unite with your beloved Laura, and that, gentle and beatified spirits as they are, they would breathe together their purer prayers on mine. See what follows.

Petrarca. Sigh not at it. Before we can see all that follows from their intercession, we must join them again. But let me hear anything in which they are concerned.

Boccaccio. I prayed ; and my breast, after some few tears, grew calmer. Yet sleep did not ensue until the break of morning, when the dropping of soft rain on the leaves of the fig-tree at the window, and the chirping of a little bird, to tell another there was shelter under them, brought me repose and slumber. Scarcely had I closed my eyes, if indeed time can be reckoned any more in sleep than in heaven, when my Fiametta seemed to have led me into the meadow. You will see it below you: turn away that branch : gently ! gently ! do not break it ; for the little bird sat there.

Petrarca. I think, Giovanni, I can divine the place.

* This is valuable, since it shows that *macarone* (here called *pasta*) was invented in the time of Boccaccio ; so are the letters of Petrarca, which inform us equally in regard to *spectacles.* Ad *ocularium* (occhiali) mihi confugiendum esset auxilium.   *Domenico Grigi.*

Although this fig-tree, growing out of the wall between the cellar and us, is fantastic enough in its branches, yet that other which I see yonder, bent down and forced to crawl along the grass by the prepotency of the young shapely walnut-tree, is much more so. It forms a seat, about a cubit above the ground, level and long enough for several.

Boccaccio. Ha! you fancy it must be a favourite spot with me, because of the two strong forked stakes wherewith it is propped and supported!

Petrarca. Poets know the haunts of poets at first sight ; and he who loved Laura . . . O Laura! did I say he who *loved* thee? . . . hath whisperings where those feet would wander which have been restless after Fiametta.

Boccaccio. It is true, my imagination has often conducted her thither ; but there in this chamber she appeared to me more visibly in a dream.

" Thy prayers have been heard, O Giovanni," said she.

I sprang to embrace her.

" Do not spill the water! Ah! you have spilt a part of it."

I then observed in her hand a crystal vase. A few drops were sparkling on the sides and running down the rim : a few were trickling from the base and from the hand that held it.

" I must go down to the brook," said she, "and fill it again as it was filled before."

What a moment of agony was this to me! Could I be certain how long might be her absence? She went : I was following : she made a sign for me to turn back : I disobeyed her only an instant : yet my sense of disobedience, increasing my feebleness and confusion, made me lose sight of her. In the next moment she was again at my side, with the cup quite full. I stood motionless : I feared my breath might shake the water over. I looked her in the face for her commands . . . and to see it . . . to see it so calm, so beneficent, so beautiful. I was forgetting what I had prayed for, when she lowered her head, tasted of the cup, and gave it me. I drank ; and suddenly sprang forth before me, many groves and palaces and gardens, and their statues and their avenues, and their labyrinths of alaternus and bay, and alcoves of citron, and watchful loopholes in the retirements of impenetrable pomegranate.   Farther off, just below where the fountain slipt away from its marble hall and guardian gods, arose, from their beds of moss and drosera and darkest grass, the sisterhood of oleanders, fond of tantalising with their bosomed flowers and their moist and pouting blossoms the little shy rivulet, and of covering its face with all the colours of the dawn.   My dream expanded and moved forward.   I trod again the dust of Posilipo, soft as the feathers in the wings of Sleep.   I emerged on Baia; I crossed her innumerable arches; I loitered in the breezy sunshine of her mole; I trusted the faithful seclusion of her caverns, the keepers of so many secrets; and I reposed on the buoyancy of her tepid sea. Then Naples, and her theatres and her churches, and grottoes and dells and forts and promontories, rushed forward in confusion, now among soft whispers, now among sweetest sounds, and subsided, and sank, and disappeared. Yet a memory seemed to come fresh from every one: each had time enough for its tale, for its pleasure, for its reflection, for its pang.   As I mounted with silent steps the narrow staircase of the old palace, how distinctly did I feel against the palm of my hand the coldness of that smooth stone-work, and the greater of the cramps of iron in it !

"Ah me ! is this forgetting?" cried I anxiously to Fiametta.

"We must recall these scenes before us," she replied: "such is the punishment of them.   Let us hope and believe that the apparition, and the compunction which must follow it, will be accepted as the full penalty, and that both will pass away almost together."

I feared to lose anything attendant on her presence: I feared to approach her forehead with my lips: I feared to touch the lily on its long wavy leaf in her hair, which filled my whole heart with fragrance.   Venerating, adoring, I bowed my head at last to kiss her snow-white robe, and trembled

at my presumption. And yet the effulgence of her countenance vivified while it chastened me. I loved her . . . I
must not say *more* than ever . . . *better* than ever; it was
Fiametta who had inhabited the skies. As my hand
opened toward her,

"Beware!" said she, faintly smiling; "beware, Giovanni! Take only the crystal; take it, and drink again."

"Must all be then forgotten?" said I sorrowfully.

"Remember your prayer and mine, Giovanni. Shall
both have been granted . . . O how much worse than in
vain?"

I drank instantly; I drank largely. How cool my bosom
grew; how could it grow so cool before her! But it was
not to remain in its quiescency; its trials were not yet over.
I will not, Francesco! no, I may not commemorate the
incidents she related to me, nor which of us said, "I blush
for having loved *first;*" nor which of us replied, "Say
least, say *least*, and blush again."

The charm of the words (for I felt not the encumbrance
of the body nor the acuteness of the spirit) seemed to
possess me wholly. Although the water gave me strength
and comfort, and somewhat of celestial pleasure, many
tears fell around the border of the vase as she held it
up before me, exhorting me to take courage, and inviting
me with more than exhortation to accomplish my deliver-
ance. She came nearer, more tenderly, more earnestly;
she held the dewy globe with both hands, leaning forward,
and sighed and shook her head, drooping at my pusil-
lanimity. It was only when a ringlet had touched the rim,
and perhaps the water (for a sunbeam on the surface could
never have given it such a golden hue) that I took courage,
clasped it, and exhausted it. Sweet as was the water, sweet
as was the serenity it gave me . . . alas! that also which it
moved away from me was sweet!

"This time you can trust me alone," said she, and
parted my hair, and kissed my brow. Again she went
toward the brook: again my agitation, my weakness, my
doubt, came over me: nor could I see her while she raised

the water, nor knew I whence she drew it. When she returned, she was close to me at once: she smiled: her smile pierced me to the bones: it seemed an angel's. She sprinkled the pure water on me; she looked most fondly; she took my hand; she suffered me to press hers to my bosom; but, whether by design I can not tell, she let fall a few drops of the chilly element between.

"And now, O my beloved!" said she, "we have consigned to the bosom of God our earthly joys and sorrows. The joys can not return, let not the sorrows. These alone would trouble my repose among the blessed.

"Trouble thy repose! Fiametta! Give me the chalice!" cried I . . . "not a drop will I leave in it, not a drop."

"Take it!" said that soft voice. "O now most dear Giovanni! I know thou hast strength enough; and there is but little . . . at the bottom lies our first kiss."

"Mine! didst thou say, beloved one? and is that left thee still?"

"*Mine*, said she, pensively; and as she abased her head, the broad leaf of the lily hid her brow and her eyes; the light of heaven shone through the flower."

"O Fiametta! Fiametta!" cried I in agony, "God is the God of mercy, God is the God of love . . . can I, can I ever?" I struck the chalice against my head, unmindful that I held it; the water covered my face and my feet. I started up, not yet awake, and I heard the name of Fiametta in the curtains.

Petrarca. Love, O Giovanni, and life itself, are but dreams at best. I do think

> Never so gloriously was Sleep attended
> As with the pageant of that heavenly maid.

But to dwell on such subjects is sinful. The recollection of them, with all their vanities, brings tears into my eyes.

Boccaccio. And into mine too . . . they were so very charming.

Petrarca. Alas, alas! the time always comes when we must regret the enjoyments of our youth.

Boccaccio. If we have let them pass us.

Petrarca. I mean our indulgence in them.

Boccaccio. Francesco! I think you must remember Raffaellino degli Alfani.

Petrarca. Was it Raffaellino who lived near San Michele in Orto?

Boccaccio. The same. He was an innocent soul, and fond of fish. But whenever his friend Sabbatelli sent him a trout from Pratolino, he always kept it until next day or the day after, just long enough to render it unpalatable. He then turned it over in the platter, smelt at it closer, although the news of its condition came undeniably from a distance, touched it with his forefinger, solicited a testimony from the gills which the eyes had contradicted, sighed over it, and sent it for a present to somebody else. Were I a lover of trout as Raffaellino was, I think I should have taken an opportunity of enjoying it while the pink and crimson were glittering on it.

Petrarca. Trout, yes.

Boccaccio. And all other fish I could encompass.

Petrarca. O thou grave mocker! I did not suspect such slyness in thee: proof enough I had almost forgotten thee.

Boccaccio. Listen! listen! I fancied I caught a footstep in the passage. Come nearer; bend your head lower, that I may whisper a word in your ear. Never let Assunta hear you sigh. She is mischievous: she may have been standing at the door: not that I believe she would be guilty of any such impropriety: but who knows what girls are capable of! She has no malice, only in laughing; and a sigh sets her windmill at work, van over van, incessantly.

Petrarca. I should soon check her. I have no notion . . .

Boccaccio. After all, she is a good girl . . . a trifle of the wilful. She must have it that many things are hurtful to me . . . reading in particular . . . it makes people so odd. Tina is a small matter of the madcap . . . in her own particular way . . . but exceedingly discreet, I do assure you, if they will only leave her alone.

I find I was mistaken, there was nobody.

Petrarca. A cat perhaps.

Boccaccio. No such thing. I order him over to Certaldo while the birds are laying and sitting : and he knows by experience, favourite as he is, that it is of no use to come back before he is sent for. Since the first impetuosities of youth, he has rarely been refractory or disobliging. We have lived together now these five years, unless I miscalculate ; and he seems to have learnt something of my manners, wherein violence and enterprise by no means predominate. I have watched him looking at a large green lizard ; and, their eyes being opposite and near, he has doubted whether it might be pleasing to me if he began the attack ; and their tails on a sudden have touched one another at the decision.

Petrarca. Seldom have adverse parties felt the same desire of peace at the same moment, and none ever carried it more simultaneously and promptly into execution.

Boccaccio. He enjoys his *otium cum dignitate* at Certaldo : there he is my castellan, and his chase is unlimited in those domains. After the doom of relegation is expired, he comes hither at midsummer. And then if you could see his joy ! His eyes are as deep as a well, and as clear as a fountain : he jerks his tail into the air like a royal sceptre, and waves it like the wand of a magician. You would fancy that, as Horace with his head, he was about to smite the stars with it. There is ne'er such another cat in the parish ; and he knows it, a rogue ! We have rare repasts together in the bean-and-bacon time, although in regard to the bean he sides with the philosopher of Samos ; but after due examination. In cleanliness he is a very nun ; albeit in that quality which lies between cleanliness and godliness, there is a smack of Fra Biagio about him. What is that book in your hand ?

Petrarca. My breviary.

Boccaccio. Well, give me mine too . . . there, on the little table in the corner, under the glass of primroses. We can do nothing better.

Petrarca. What prayer were you looking for? let me find it.

Boccaccio. I don't know how it is: I am scarcely at present in a frame of mind for it. We are of one faith: the prayers of the one will do for the other: and I am sure, if you omitted my name, you would say them all over afresh. I wish you could recollect in any book as dreamy a thing to entertain me as I have been just repeating. We have had enough of Dante: I believe few of his beauties have escaped us: and small faults, which we readily pass by, are fitter for small folks, as grubs are the proper bait for gudgeons.

Petrarca. I have had as many dreams as most men. We are all made up of them, as the webs of the spider are particles of her own vitality. But how infinitely less do we profit by them! I will relate to you, before we separate, one among the multitude of mine, as coming the nearest to the poetry of yours, and as having been not totally useless to me. Often have I reflected on it; sometimes with pensiveness, with sadness never.

Boccaccio. Then, Francesco, if you had with you as copious a choice of dreams as clustered on the elm-trees where the Sibyl led Æneas, this, in preference to the whole swarm of them, is the queen dream for me.

Petrarca. When I was younger I was fond of wandering in solitary places, and never was afraid of slumbering in woods and grottoes. Among the chief pleasures of my life, and among the commonest of my occupations, was the bringing before me such heroes and heroines of antiquity, such poets and sages, such of the prosperous and the unfortunate, as most interested me by their courage, their wisdom, their eloquence, or their adventures. Engaging them in the conversation best suited to their characters, I knew perfectly their manners, their steps, their voices: and often did I moisten with my tears the models I had been forming of the less happy.

Boccaccio. Great is the privilege of entering into the studies of the intellectual; great is that of conversing with the guides of nations, the movers of the mass, the regulators of the unruly will, stiff, in its impurity and rust, against the finger of the Almighty Power that formed it : but give me, Francesco, give me rather the creature to sympathise with ; apportion me the sufferings to assuage. Ah, gentle soul ! thou wilt never send them over to another ; they have better hopes from thee.

Petrarca. We both alike feel the sorrows of those around us. He who suppresses or allays them in another, breaks many thorns off his own ; and future years will never harden fresh ones.

My occupation was not always in making the politician talk politics, the orator toss his torch among the populace, the philosopher run down from philosophy to cover the retreat or the advances of his sect ; but sometimes in devising how such characters must act and discourse, on subjects far remote from the beaten track of their career. In like manner the philologist, and again the dialectician, were not indulged in the review and parade of their trained bands, but, at times, brought forward to show in what manner and in what degree external habits had influenced the conformation of the internal man. It was far from unprofitable to set passing events before past actors, and to record the decisions of those whose interests and passions are unconcerned in them.

Boccaccio. This is surely no easy matter. The thoughts are in fact your own, however you distribute them.

Petrarca. All can not be my own ; if you mean by *thoughts* the opinions and principles I should be the most desirious to inculcate. Some favourite ones perhaps may obtrude too prominently, but otherwise no misbehaviour is permitted them : reprehension and rebuke are always ready, and the offence is punished on the spot.

Boccaccio. Certainly you thus throw open, to its full extent, the range of poetry and invention ; which can not but be very limited and sterile, unless where we find displayed much diversity of character as disseminated by nature, much peculiarity of sentiment as arising from position,

marked with unerring skill through every shade and grada-
tion; and finally and chiefly, much intertexture and intensity
of passion. You thus convey to us more largely and expeditiously the stores of your understanding and imagination,
than you ever could by sonnets or canzonets, or sinewless
and sapless allegories.

But weightier works are less captivating. If you had
published any such as you mention, you must have waited
for their acceptance. Not only the fame of Marcellus, but
every other,

Crescit occulto velut arbor ævo;

and that which makes the greatest vernal shoot is apt to
make the least autumnal. Authors in general who have
met celebrity at starting, have already had their reward;
always their utmost due, and often much beyond it. We
can not hope for both celebrity and fame: supremely
fortunate are the few who are allowed the liberty of choice
between them. We two prefer the strength that springs
from exercise and toil, acquiring it gradually and slowly:
we leave to others the earlier blessing of that sleep which
follows enjoyment. How many at first sight are enthusiastic in their favour! Of these how large a portion come
away empty-handed and discontented! like idlers who visit
the seacoast, fill their pockets with pebbles bright from the
passing wave, and carry them off with rapture. After a
short examination at home, every streak seems faint and
dull, and the whole contexture coarse, uneven, and gritty:
first one is thrown away, then another; and before the
week's end the store is gone, of things so shining and
wonderful.

Petrarca. Allegory, which you named with sonnets and
canzonets, had few attractions for me, believing it to be the
delight in general of idle, frivolous, inexcursive minds, in
whose mansions there is neither hall nor portal to receive
the loftier of the Passions. A stranger to the Affections,
she holds a low station among the handmaidens of Poetry,
being fit for little but an apparition in a mask. I had

reflected for some time on this subject, when, wearied with the length of my walk over the mountains, and finding a soft old molehill, covered with grey grass, by the way-side, I laid my head upon it, and slept. I can not tell how long it was before a species of dream or vision came over me.

Two beautiful youths appeared beside me; each was winged; but the wings were hanging down, and seemed ill adapted to flight. One of them, whose voice was the softest I ever heard, looking at me frequently, said to the other,

"He is under my guardianship for the present: do not awaken him with that feather."

Methought, hearing the whisper, I saw something like the feather on an arrow; and then the arrow itself; the whole of it, even to the point; although he carried it in such a manner that it was difficult at first to discover more than a palm's length of it: the rest of the shaft, and the whole of the barb, was behind his ankles.

"This feather never awakens anyone," replied he, rather petulantly; "but it brings more of confident security, and more of cherished dreams, than you without me are capable of imparting."

"Be it so!" answered the gentler . . . "none is less inclined to quarrel or dispute than I am. Many whom you have wounded greviously, call upon me for succour. But so little am I disposed to thwart you, it is seldom I venture to do more for them than to whisper a few words of comfort in passing. How many reproaches on these occasions have been cast upon me for indifference and infidelity! Nearly as many, and nearly in the same terms, as upon you!"

"Odd enough that we, O Sleep! should be thought so alike!" said Love, contemptuously. "Yonder is he who bears a nearer resemblance to you: the dullest have observed it." I fancied I turned my eyes to where he was pointing, and saw at a distance the figure he designated. Meanwhile the contention went on uninterruptedly. Sleep was slow in asserting his power or his benefits. Love recapitulated them ; but only that he might assert his own above them. Suddenly he called on me to decide, and to choose my patron. Under the influence, first of the one, then of the other, I sprang from repose to rapture, I alighted from rapture on repose . . . and knew not which was sweetest. Love was very angry with me, and declared he would cross me throughout the whole of my existence. Whatever I might on other occasions have thought of his veracity, I now felt too surely the conviction that he would keep his word. At last, before the close of the altercation, the third Genius had advanced, and stood near us. I can not tell how I knew him, but I knew him to be the Genius of Death. Breathless as I was at beholding him, I soon became familiar with his features. First they seemed only calm ; presently they grew contemplative ; and lastly beautiful : those of the Graces themselves are less regular, less harmonious, less composed. Love glanced at him unsteadily, with a countenance in which there was somewhat of anxiety, somewhat of disdain ; and cried, " Go away ! go away ! nothing that thou touchest, lives."

"Say rather, child ! " replied the advancing form, and advancing grew loftier and statelier. "Say rather that nothing of beautiful or of glorious lives its own true life until my wing hath passed over it."

Love pouted, and rumpled and bent down with his forefinger the stiff short feathers on his arrow-head; but replied not. Although he frowned worse than ever, and at me, I dreaded him less and less, and scarcely looked toward him. The milder and calmer Genius, the third, in proportion as I took courage to contemplate him, regarded me with more and more complacency. He held neither flower nor arrow, as the others did ; but, throwing back the clusters of dark curls that overshadowed his countenance, he presented to me his hand, openly and benignly. I shrank on looking at him so near, and yet I sighed to love him. He smiled, not without an expression of pity, at perceiving my diffidence, my timidity : for I remembered how soft was the hand of Sleep, how warm and entrancing was Love's. By degrees, I became ashamed of my ingratitude; and turning my face away, I held out my arms, and felt my neck within his. Composure strewed and allayed all the throbbings of my bosom; the coolness of freshest morning breathed around; the heavens seemed to open above me; while the beautiful cheek of my deliverer rested on my head. I would now have looked for those others; but knowing my intention by my gesture, he said, consolatorily,

"Sleep is on his way to the Earth, where many are calling him; but it is not to these he hastens; for every call only makes him fly farther off. Sedately and gravely as he looks, he is nearly as capricious and volatile as the more arrogant and ferocious one."

"And Love!" said I, "whither is he departed? If not too late, I would propitiate and appease him."

"He who can not follow me, he who can not overtake and pass me," said the Genius, "is unworthy of the name, the most glorious in earth or heaven. Look up! Love is yonder, and ready to receive thee."

I looked: the earth was under me: I saw only the clear blue sky, and something brighter above it.

PIEVANO GRIGI TO THE READER.

BEFORE I proceeded on my mission, I had a final audience of Monsignore, in which I asked his counsel, whether a paper sewed and pasted to the *Interviews*, being the substance of an intended *Confession*, might, according to the *Decretals*, be made public. Monsignore took the subject into his consideration, and assented. Previously to the solution of this question, he was graciously pleased to discourse on Boccaccio, and to say, "I am happy to think he died a good catholic, and contentedly."

"No doubt, Monsignore!" answered I, "for when he was on his death-bed, or a little sooner, the most holy man in Italy admonished him terribly of his past transgressions, and frightened him fairly into Paradise."

"Pievano!" said Monsignore, "it is customary in the fashionable literature of our times to finish a story in two manners. The most approved is, to knock on the head every soul that has been interesting you: the second is, to put the two youngest into bed together, promising the same treatment to another couple, or more. Our forefathers were equally zealous about those they dealt with. Every pagan turned Christian : every loose woman had bark to grow about her, as thick and astringent as the ladies had in Ovid's Metamorphoses ; and the gallants, who had played false with them, were driven mad by the monks at their death-bed. I neither hope nor believe that poor Boccaccio gave way to their importunities, but am happy in thinking that his decease was as tranquil as his life was inoffensive. He was not exempt from the indiscretions of youth : he allowed his imagination too long a dalliance with his passions ; but malice was never found among them. Let us then, in charity to him and to ourselves, be persuaded that such a pest as this mad zealot had no influence over him—

> Nè turbò il tuono di nebbiosa mente
> Acqua si limpida e ridente.*

I can not but break into verse, although no poet, while I am thinking of him. Such men as he would bring over more to our good-natured, honest old faith again than fifty monks with scourges at their shoulders."

"Ah, Monsignore!" answered I, "could I but hope to be humbly instrumental in leading back the apostate church to our true catholic, I should be the happiest man alive."

"God forbid you should be without the hope!" said

---

* Nor did the thunderings of a cloudy mind
Trouble so limpid and serene a water.

Monsignore. "The two chief differences now are; with ours, that we must not eat butcher's meat on a Friday; with the Anglican, that they must not eat baked meat on a Sunday. Secondly, that *we* say, *Come, and be saved;* the Anglican says, *Go, and be damned.*"

Since the exposition of Monsignore, the Parliament has issued an Act of Grace in regard to eating. One article says:

"Nobody shall eat on a Sunday roast, or baked, or other hot victuals whatsoever, unless he goes to church in his own carriage; if he goes thither in any other than his own, be he halt or blind, he shall be subject to the penalty of twenty pounds. Nobody shall dance on a Sunday, or play music, unless he also be able to furnish three *écarté* tables at the least, and sixteen wax-lights."

I write from memory; but if the wording is inexact, the sense is accurate. Nothing can be more gratifying to a true Catholic than to see the amicable game played by his bishops with the Anglican. The Catholic never makes a false move. His fish often slips into the red square, marked *Sunday*, but the shoulder of mutton can never get into its place, marked *Friday:* it lies upon the table, and nobody dares touch it. Alas! I am forgetting that this is purely an English game, and utterly unknown among us, or indeed in any other country under heaven.

To promote still farther the objects of religion, as understood in the Universities and the Parliament, it was proposed that public prayers should be offered up for rain on every Sabbath-day, the more effectually to encompass the provisions of the Bill. But this clause was cancelled in the Committee, on the examination of a groom, who deposed that a coach-horse of his master's, the Bishop of London, was touched in the wind, and might be seriously a sufferer: "*for the bishop,*" said he, "*is no better walker than a goose.*"

There is, moreover, great and general discontent in the lower orders of the clergy, that some should be obliged to serve a couple of churches, and perhaps a jail or hospital to boot, for a stipend of a hundred pounds, and even less, while others are incumbents of pluralities, doing no duty at all, and receiving three or four thousands. It is reported that several of the more fortunate are so utterly shameless as to liken the Church to a Lottery-office, and to declare that, unless there were great prizes, no man in his senses would enter into the service of our Lord. I myself have read with my own eyes this declaration, but I hope the signature is a forgery. What is certain is, that the emoluments of the bishopric of London are greater than the united revenue of *twelve* cardinals; that they are amply sufficient for the board, lodging, and education of *three hundred* young men destined to the ministry; and that they might relieve from famine, rescue from sin, and save, perhaps, from eternal punishment, *three thousand fellow-creatures yearly*. On a narrow inspection of one manufacturing town in England, I deliver it as my firm opinion that it contains more crime and wretchedness than all the four continents of our globe. If these enormous masses of wealth had been fairly sub-divided and carefully expended, if a more numerous and a more efficient clergy had been appointed, how very much of sin and sorrow had been obviated and allayed! Ultimately the poor will be driven to desperation, there being no check upon them, no guardian over them; and the eyes of the sleeper, it is to be feared, will be opened by pincers. In the midst of such woes, originating in her iniquities and aggravated by her supineness, the Church of England, the least reformed church in Christendom, and the most opposite to the institutions of the State, boasts of being the purest member of the Reformation. Shocked at such audacity and impudence, the conscientious and pious, not only of her laity but also of her clergy, fall daily off from her, and, resigning all hope of parks and palaces, embrace the cross.

Never since the Reformation (so called) have our prospects been so bright as at the present day. Our own prelates, and those of the English church, are equally at work to the same effect; and the Catholic clergy will come into possession of their churches with as little change in the temporals as in the spirituals. It is the law of the land that the church can not lose her rights and possessions by lapse of time; impossible then that she should lose it by fraud and fallacy. Although the bishops of England, regardless of their vocations and vows, have, by deceit and falsehood, obtained Acts of Parliament, under sanction of which they have severed from their sees, and made over to their families, the possessions of the episcopacy, it can not be questioned that what has been wrongfully alienated will be rightfully restored. No time, no trickery, no subterfuge can conceal it. The exposure of such thievery in such eminent stations, worse and more shameful than any on the Thames or in the lowest haunts of villany and prostitution, and of attempts to seize from their poorer brethren a few decimals to fill up a deficiency in many thousands, has opened wide the eyes of England. Consequently, there are religious men who resort from all quarters to the persecuted mother they had so long abandoned. God at last has made his enemies perform his work; and the English prelates, not indeed on the stool of repentance, as would befit them, but thrust by the scorner into his uneasy chair, are mending with scarlet silk, and seaming with threads of gold, the copes and dalmatics of their worthy predecessors. I am overjoyed in declaring to my townsmen that the recent demeanour of these prelates, refractory and mutinous as it has been (in other matters) to the government of their patron the king, has ultimately (by joining the malcontents in abolishing the favourite farce of religious freedom, and in forbidding roast meat and country air on the Sabbath) filled up my subscription for the bell of San Vivaldo.

Salve Regina Cœli!

PRETE DOMENICO GRIGI.

LONDON, *June* 17*th*, 1837.

———

HEADS OF CONFESSION; A MONTHFUL.

Printed and published Superiorum Licentiâ.

March 14. Being ill at ease, I cried, "Diavolo! I wish that creaking shutter was at thy bedroom instead of mine, old fellow!" Assuntina would have composed me, showing me how wrong it was. Perverse; and would not acknowledge my sinfulness to her. I said she had nothing to do with it; which vexed her.

March 23. Reproved Assuntina, and called her *ragazzaccia!* for asking of Messer Piero Pimperna half the evening's milk of his goat. Very wrong in me; it being impossible she should have known that Messer Piero owed me four *lire* since . . . I forget when.

March 31. It blowing tramontana, I was ruffled: suspected a feather in the minestra: said the rice was as black as a coal. Sad falsehood! made Assuntina cry . . . . Saracenic doings.

Recapitulation. Shameful all this month; I did not believe such bad humour was in me.

Reflection. The devil, if he can not have his walk one way, will take it another; never at a fault. Manifold proof; poor sinner!

April 2. Thought uncharitably of Fra Biagio. The Frate took my hand, asking me to confess, reminding me that I had not confessed since the 3rd of March, although I was so sick and tribulated I could hardly stir. Peevish; said, "Confess yourself; I won't; I am not minded; you will find those not far off who . . ." and then I dipped my head under the coverlet, and saw my error.

April 6. Whispers of Satanasso; pretty clear! A sprinkling of vernal thoughts, much too advanced for the season. About three hours before sunset Francesco came. Forgot my prayers; woke at midnight; recollected, and did not say them. Might have told him; never occurred that, being a Canonico, he could absolve me ; now gone again these three days, this being the fourteenth. Must unload ere heavier-laden. Gratiæ plena ! have mercy upon me !

THE TRANSLATOR'S REMARKS

On the Alleged Jealousy of Boccaccio and Petrarca.

AMONG the most heinous crimes that can be committed against society is the

temerati crimen amici,

and no other so loosens the bonds by which it is held together. Once, and only once in my life, I heard it defended by a person of intellect and integrity. It was the argument of a friendly man, who would have invalidated the fact; it was the solicitude of a prompt and dexterous man, holding up his hat to cover the shame of genius. I have indeed had evidence of some who saw nothing extraordinary or amiss in these filchings and twitchings ; but there are persons whose thermometer stands higher by many degrees at other points than honour. There are insects on the shoals and sands of literature, shrimps which must be half-boiled before they redden ; and there are blushes (no doubt) in certain men, of which the precious vein lies so deep that it could hardly be brought to light by cordage and windlass. Meanwhile their wrathfulness shows itself at once by a plashy and puffy superficies, with an exuberance of coarse rough stuff upon it, and is ready to soak our shoes with its puddle at the first pressure.

"Thou shalt not bear false witness against thy neighbour" is a commandment which the literary cast down from over their communion-table to nail against the doors of the commonalty, with a fist and forefinger pointing at it. Although the depreciation of any work is dishonest, the attempt is more infamous when committed against a friend. The calumniator on such occasions may in some measure err from ignorance, or from inadequate information, but nothing can excuse him if he speaks contemptuously. It is impossible to believe that such writers as Boccaccio and Petrarca could be widely erroneous in each other's merits ; no less incredible is it that, if they did err at all, they would openly avow a disparaging opinion. This baseness was reserved for days when the study opens into the market-place, when letters are commodities, and authors chapmen. Yet even upon their stalls, where an antique vase would stand little chance with a noticeable piece of blue-and-white crockery, and shepherds and sailors and sunflowers in its circumference, it might be heartily and honestly derided; but less probably by the fellow-villager of the vendor, with whom he had been playing at quoits every day of his life. When an ill-natured story is once launched upon the world, there are many who are careful that it shall not soon founder. Thus the idle and inconsiderate rumour, which has floated through ages, about the mutual jealousy of Boccaccio and Petrarca, finds at this day a mooring in all quarters. Never were two men so perfectly formed for friendship; never were two who fulfilled so completely that happy destination. True it is, the studious and exact Petrarca had not elaborated so entirely to his own satisfaction his poem, *Africa*, as to submit it yet to the inspection of Boccaccio, to whom unquestionably he would have been delighted to show it the moment he had finished it. He died, and left it incomplete. We have, it must be acknowledged, the authority of Petrarca himself, that he never had read the *Decameron* through, even to the last year of his life, when he had been intimate with Boccaccio four-and-twenty. How easy would it have been for him to dissemble this fact! how certainly would any man have dissembled it who doubted of his own heart or of his friend's! I must request the liberty of adducing his whole letter, as already translated.

"I have only run over your *Decameron,* and therefore I am not capable of forming a true judgment of its merit: but upon the whole it has given me a great deal of pleasure. *The freedoms in it are excusable; from having been written in youth, from the subjects it treats of, and from the persons for whom it was designed.* Among a great number of gay and witty jokes, there are however many grave and serious sentiments. I did as most people do: I paid most atttention to the beginning and the end. Your description of the people in the Plague is very true and pathetic: and the touching story of Griseldis has *been ever since laid up in my memory, that I may relate it in my conversations with my friends.* A friend of mine at Padua, a man of wit and knowledge, undertook to read it aloud; but he had scarcely got through half of it, when his tears prevented him going on. He attempted it a second time; but his sobs and sighs obliged him to desist. Another of my friends determined on the same venture; and, having read it from beginning to end, without the least alteration of voice or gesture, he said, on returning the book,

" 'It must be owned this is an affecting history, and I should have wept could I have believed it true; but there never was and never will be a woman like Griseldis.' "

Here was the termination of Petrarca's literary life: he closed it with the last words of this letter; which are, "Adieu, my friends! adieu my correspondence." Soon afterward he was found dead in his library, with his arm leaning on a book. In the whole of this composition, what a carefulness and solicitude to say everything that could gratify his friend; with what ingenuity are those faults not palliated but *excused* (his own expression) which must nevertheless have appeared very grievous ones to the purity of Petrarca.

But why did not Boccaccio send him his *Decameron* long before? Because there never was a more perfect gentleman, a man more fearful of giving offence, a man more sensitive to the delicacy of friendship, or more deferential to sanctity of character. He knew that the lover of Laura could not amuse his hours with mischievous or idle passions; he knew that he rose at midnight to repeat his matins, and never intermitted them. On what succeeding hour could he venture to seize? with what countenance could he charge it with the levities of the world? Perhaps the Recluse of Arqua, the visitor of old Certaldo, read at last the *Decameron*, only that he might be able the better to defend it. And how admirably has the final stroke of his indefatigable pen effected the purpose! Is this the jealous rival? Boccaccio received the last testimony of unaltered friendship in the month of Octobei 1373, a few days after the writer's death. December was not over when they met in heaven : and never were two gentler spirits united there.

The character of Petrarca shows itself in almost every one of his various works. Unsuspicious, generous, ardent in study, in liberty, in love, with a self-complacence which in less men would be vanity, but arising in him from the general admiration of a noble presence, from his place in the interior of a heart which no other could approach or merit, and from the homage of all who held the principalities of Learning in every part of Europe.

Boccaccio is only reflected in full from a larger mass of compositions : yet one letter is quite sufficient to display the beauty and purity of his mind. It was written from Venice, when finding there not Petrarca whom he expected to find, but Petrarca's daughter, he describes to the father her modesty, grace, and cordiality in his reception. The imagination can form to itself nothing more lovely than this picture of the gentle Ermissenda : and Boccaccio's delicacy and gratitude are equally affecting. No wonder that Petrarca, in his will, bequeathed to his friend a sum the quintuple in amount of that which he bequeathed to his only brother, whom however he loved tenderly. Such had been, long before their acquaintance, the celebrity of Petrarca, such the honours conferred on him wherever he resided or appeared, that he never thought of equality or rivalry. And such was Boccaccio's reverential modesty, that, to the very close of his life, he called Petrarca his master. Immeasurable as was his own superiority, he no more thought himself the equal of Petrarca than Dante (in whom the superiority was almost as great) thought himself Virgil's. These, I believe, are the only instances on record where poets have been very tenaciously erroneous in the estimate of their own inferiority. The same observation can not be made so confidently on the decisions of contemporary critics. Indeed, the balance in which works of the highest merit are weighed vibrates long before it is finally adjusted. Even the most judicious men have formed injudicious opinions on the living and the recently deceased. Bacon and Hooker could not estimate Shakespeare, nor could Taylor and Barrow give Milton his just award. Cowley and Dryden were preferred to both, by a great majority of the learned. Many, although they believe they discover in a contemporary the qualities which elevate him above the rest, yet hesitate to acknowledge it; part, because they are fearful of censure for singularity; part, because they differ from him in politics or religion; and part, because they delight in hiding, like dogs and foxes, what they can at any time surreptitiously draw out for their sullen solitary repast. Such persons have little delight in the glory of our country, and would hear with disapprobation and moroseness it has produced four men so pre-eminently great, that no name, modern or ancient, excepting Homer, can stand very near the lowest: these are, Shakespeare, Bacon, Milton, and Newton. Beneath the least of these (if anyone can tell which is least) are Dante and Aristoteles, who are unquestionably the next.* Out of Greece and England, Dante is the only man of the first order; such he is, with all his imperfections. Less ardent and energetic, but having no less at command the depths of thought and treasures of fancy, beyond him in

* We can speak only of those whose works are extant. Democritus and Anaxagoras were perhaps the greatest in discovery and invention.

variety, animation, and interest, beyond him in touches
of nature and truth of character, is Boccaccio. Yet he
believed his genius was immeasurably inferior to Alighieri's;
and it would have surprised and pained him to find himself
preferred to his friend Petrarca; which indeed did not
happen in his lifetime. So difficult is it to shake the tenure
of long possession, or to believe that a living man is as
valuable as an old statue, that for five hundred years
together the critics held Virgil far above his obsequious but
high-souled scholar, who now has at least the honour of
standing alone, if not first. Milton and Homer may be
placed together: on the continent Homer will be seen at
the right hand; in England, Milton. Supreme, above all,
immeasurably supreme, stands Shakespeare. I do not
think Dante is any more the equal of Homer than Hercules
is the equal of Apollo. Though Hercules may display
more muscles, yet Apollo is the powerfuller without any
display of them at all. Both together are just equivalent
to Milton, shorn of his *Sonnets,* and of his *Allegro* and
Penseroso; the most delightful of what (wanting a better
name) we call *lyrical* poems. But in the contemplation of
these prodigies we must not lose the company we entered
with. Two contemporaries so powerful in interesting our
best affections, as Giovanni and Francesco, never existed
before or since. Petrarca was honoured and beloved by all
conditions. He collated with the student and investigator,
he planted with the husbandman, he was the counsellor of
kings, the reprover of pontiffs, and the pacificator of
nations. Boccaccio, who never had occasion to sigh for
solitude, never sighed *in* it: there was his station, there his
studies, there his happiness. In the vivacity and versatility
of imagination, in the narrative, in the descriptive, in the
playful, in the pathetic, the world never saw his equal, until
the sunrise of our Shakespeare. Ariosto and Spenser may
stand at no great distance from him in the shadowy and
unsubstantial; but multiform Man was utterly unknown to
them. The human heart, through all its foldings, vibrates
to Boccaccio.

OTHER IMAGINARY CONVERSATIONS.

OTHER IMAGINARY CONVERSATIONS.

DANTE AND BEATRICE.

Dante. When you saw me profoundly pierced with love, and reddening and trembling, did it become you, did it become you, you whom I have always called *the most gentle Bice*, to join in the heartless laughter of those girls around you? Answer me. Reply unhesitatingly. Requires it so long a space for dissimulation and duplicity? Pardon! pardon! pardon! My senses have left me; my heart being gone, they follow.

Beatrice. Childish man! pursuing the impossible.

Dante. And was it this you laughed at? We can not touch the hem of God's garment; yet we fall at his feet and weep.

Beatrice. But weep not, gentle Dante! fall not before the weakest of his creatures, willing to comfort, unable to relieve you. Consider a little. Is laughter at all times the signal or the precursor of derision? I smiled, let me avow it, from the pride I felt in your preference of me; and if I laughed, it was to conceal my sentiments. Did you never cover sweet fruit with worthless leaves? Come, do not drop again so soon so faint a smile. I will not have you grave, nor very serious. I pity you; I must not love you: if I might, I would.

Dante. Yet how much love is due to me, O Bice, who have loved you, as you well remember, even from your tenth year.   But it is reported, and your words confirm it, that you are going to be married.

Beatrice. If so, and if I could have laughed at that, and if my laughter could have estranged you from me, would you blame me?

Dante. Tell me the truth.

Beatrice. The report is general.

Dante. The truth! the truth!   Tell me, Bice.

Beatrice. Marriages, it is said, are made in heaven.

Dante. Is heaven then under the paternal roof?

Beatrice. It has been to me hitherto.

Dante. And now you seek it elsewhere.

Beatrice. I seek it not.   The wiser choose for the weaker.   Nay, do not sigh so.   What would you have, my grave pensive Dante?   What can I do?

Dante. Love me.

Beatrice. I always did.

Dante. Love me?   O bliss of heaven!

Beatrice. No, no, no!   Forbear!   Men's kisses are always mischievous and hurtful; everybody says it.   If you truly loved me, you would never think of doing so.

Dante. Nor even this!

Beatrice. You forget that you are no longer a boy; and that it is not thought proper at your time of life to continue the arm at all about the waist.   Beside, I think you would better not put your head against my bosom; it beats too much to be pleasant to you.   Why do you wish it? why fancy it can do you any good?   It grows no cooler; it seems to grow even hotter.   O! how it burns!   Go, go; it hurts me too: it struggles, it aches, it sobs.   Thank you, my gentle friend, for removing your brow away; your hair is very thick and long; and it began to heat me more than you can imagine.   While it was there, I could not see your face so well, nor talk with you so quietly.

Dante. O! when shall we talk quietly in future?

Beatrice. When I am married.   I shall often come to visit my father.   He has always been solitary since my mother's death, which happened in my infancy, long before you knew me.

Dante. How can he endure the solitude of his house when you have left it?

Beatrice. The very question I asked him.

Dante. You did not then wish to . . . to . . . go away?

Beatrice. Ah no! It is sad to be an outcast at fifteen.

Dante. An outcast?

Beatrice. Forced to leave a home.

Dante. For another?

Beatrice. Childhood can never have a second.

Dante. But childhood is now over.

Beatrice. I wonder who was so malicious as to tell my father that? He wanted me to be married a whole year ago.

Dante. And, Bice, you hesitated?

Beatrice. No; I only wept. He is a dear good father. I never disobeyed him but in those wicked tears; and they ran the faster the more he reprehended them.

Dante. Say, who is the happy youth?

Beatrice. I know not who ought to be happy if you are not.

Dante. I?

Beatrice. Surely you deserve all happiness.

Dante. Happiness! any happiness is denied me. Ah, hours of childhood! bright hours! what fragrant blossoms ye unfold! what bitter fruits to ripen!

Beatrice. Now can not you continue to sit under that old fig-tree at the corner of the garden? It is always delightful to me to think of it.

Dante. Again you smile: I wish I could smile too.

Beatrice. You were usually more grave than I, although very often, two years ago, you told me I was the graver. Perhaps I *was* then indeed; and perhaps I ought to be now: but really I must smile at the recollection, and make you smile with me.

Dante. Recollection of what in particular?

Beatrice. Of your ignorance that a fig-tree is the brittlest of trees, especially when it is in leaf; and moreover of

604

your tumble, when your head was just above the wall, and your hand (with the verses in it) on the very coping-stone. Nobody suspected that I went every day to the bottom of our garden, to hear you repeat your poetry on the other side ; nobody but yourself ; you soon found me out. But on that occasion I thought you might have been hurt ; and I clambered up our high peach-tree in the grass-plot nearest the place ; and thence I saw Messer Dante, with his white sleeve reddened by the fig-juice, and the seeds sticking to it pertinaciously, and Messer blushing, and trying to conceal his calamity, and still holding the verses. They were all about me.

. *Dante.* Never shall any verse of mine be uttered from my lips, or from the lips of others, without the memorial of Bice.

Beatrice. Sweet Dante ! in the purity of your soul shall Bice live ; as (we are told by the goatherds and foresters) poor creatures have been found preserved in the serene and lofty regions of the Alps, many years after the breath of life had left them. Already you rival Guido Cavalcante and Cino da Pistoja : you must attempt, nor perhaps shall it be vainly, to surpass them in celebrity.

Dante. If ever I am above them . . . and I must be . . . I know already what angel's hand will have helped me up the ladder. Beatrice, I vow to heaven, shall stand higher than Selvaggia, high and glorious and immortal as that name will be. You have given me joy and sorrow ; for the worst of these (I will not say the least) I will confer on you all the generations of our Italy, all the ages of our world. But first (alas, from me you must not have it !) may happiness, long happiness, attend you !

Beatrice. Ah ! those words rend your bosom ! why should they ?

Dante. I could go away contented, or almost contented, were I sure of it. Hope is nearly as strong as despair, and greatly more pertinacious and enduring. You have made me see clearly that you never can be mine in this world : but at the same time, O Beatrice ! you have made me see quite as clearly that you may and must be mine in another.

I am older than you: precedency is given to age, and not
to worthiness, in our way to heaven. I will watch over
you; I will pray for you when I am nearer to God, and
purified from the stains of earth and mortality. He will
permit me to behold you, lovely as when I left you. Angels
in vain should call me onward.

Beatrice. Hush, sweetest Dante! hush!

Dante. It is there where I shall have caught the first
glimpse of you again, that I wish all my portion of Paradise
to be assigned me; and there, if far below you, yet within
the sight of you, to establish my perdurable abode.

Beatrice. Is this piety? Is this wisdom? O Dante!
And may not I be called away first?

Dante. Alas! alas! how many small feet have swept off
the early dew of life, leaving the path black behind them!
But to think that you should go before me! It almost
sends me forward on my way, to receive and welcome you.
If indeed, O Beatrice, such should be God's immutable
will, sometimes look down on me when the song to Him is
suspended. Oh! look often on me with prayer and pity;
for there all prayers are accepted, and all pity is devoid of
pain. Why are you silent?

Beatrice. It is very sinful not to love all creatures in the
world. But is it true, O Dante! that we always love those
the most who make us the most unhappy?

Dante. The remark, I fear, is just.

Beatrice. Then, unless the Virgin be pleased to change
my inclinations, I shall begin at last to love my betrothed;
for already the very idea of him renders me sad, wearisome,
and comfortless. Yesterday he sent me a bunch of violets.
When I took them up, delighted as I felt at that sweetest
of odours, which you and I once inhaled together. . . .

Dante. And only once.

Beatrice. You know why. Be quiet now, and hear me.
I dropped the posy; for around it, hidden by various kinds
of foliage, was twined the bridal necklace of pearls. O
Dante! how worthless are the finest of them (and there are
many fine ones) in comparison with those little pebbles, some

of which (for perhaps I may not have gathered up all) may be still lying under the peach-tree, and some (do I blush to say it?) under the fig. Tell me not who threw these, nor for what. But you know you were always thoughtful, and sometimes reading, sometimes writing, and sometimes forgetting me, while I waited to see the crimson cap, and the two bay-leaves I fastened in it, rise above the garden-wall. How silently you are listening, if you do listen!

Dante. Oh! could my thoughts incessantly and eternally dwell among these recollections, undisturbed by any other voice . . . undistracted by any other presence! Soon must they abide with me alone, and be repeated by none but me . . . repeated in the accents of anguish and despair! Why could you not have held in the sad home of your heart that necklace and those violets?

Beatrice. My Dante! we must all obey. . . . I my father, you your God. He will never abandon you.

Dante. I have ever sung, and will for ever sing, the most glorious of His works: and yet, O Bice! He abandons me, He casts me off; and He uses your hand for this infliction.

Beatrice. Men travel far and wide, and see many on whom to fix or transfer their affections; but we maidens have neither the power nor the will. Casting our eyes on the ground, we walk along the straight and narrow road prescribed for us; and, doing this, we avoid in great measure the thorns and entanglements of life. We know we are performing our duty; and the fruit of this knowledge is contentment. Season after season, day after day, you have made me serious, pensive, meditative, and almost wise. Being so little a girl, I was proud that you, so much taller, should lean on my shoulder to overlook my work. And greatly more proud was I when in time you taught me several Latin words, and then whole sentences, both in prose and verse, pasting a strip of paper over, or obscuring with impenetrable ink, those passages in the poets which were beyond my comprehension, and might perplex me. But proudest of all was I when you began to reason with me. What will now be my pride if you are convinced by the first arguments I ever have opposed to you ; or if you only take them up and try if they are applicable. Certainly do I know (indeed, indeed I do) that even the patience to consider them will make you happier. Will it not then make me so ? I entertain no other wish. Is not this true love ?

Dante. Ah, yes ! the truest, the purest, the least perishable, but not the sweetest. Here are the rue and hyssop ; but where the rose ?

Beatrice. Wicked must be whatever torments you : and will you let love do it ? Love is the gentlest and kindest breath of God. Are you willing that the Tempter should intercept it, and respire it polluted into your ear ? Do not make me hesitate to pray to the Virgin for you, nor tremble lest she look down on you with a reproachful pity. To her alone, O Dante ! dare I confide all my thoughts. Lessen not my confidence in my only refuge.

Dante. God annihilate a power so criminal ! O, could my love flow into your breast with hers ! It should flow with equal purity.

Beatrice. You have stored my little mind with many thoughts ; dear because they are yours, and because they are virtuous. May I not, O my Dante ! bring some of them back again to your bosom ; as the *Contadina* lets down the string from the cottage-beam in winter, and culls a few bunches of the soundest for the master of the vineyard ? You have not given me glory that the world should shudder at its eclipse. To prove that I am worthy of the smallest part of it, I must obey God ; and, under God, my father. Surely the voice of Heaven comes to us audibly from a parent's lips. You will be great, and, what is above all greatness, good.

Dante. Rightly and wisely, my sweet Beatrice, have you spoken in this estimate. Greatness is to goodness what gravel is to porphyry : the one is a moveable accumulation, swept along the surface of the earth ; the other stands fixt and solid and alone, above the violence of war and of the tempest ; above all that is residuous of a wasted world. Little men build up great ones ; but the snow colossus soon melts : the good stand under the eye of God ; and therefore stand.

Beatrice. Now you are calm and reasonable, listen to me Bice. You must marry.

Dante. Marry ?

Beatrice. Unless you do, how can we meet again unreservedly ? Worse, worse than ever ! I can not bear to see those large heavy tears following one another, heavy and slow as nuns at the funeral of a sister. Come, I will kiss off one, if you will promise me faithfully to shed no more. Be tranquil, be tranquil ; only hear reason. There are many who know you ; and all who know you must love you. Don't you hear me ? Why turn aside ? and why go farther off ? I will have that hand. It twists about as if it hated its confinement. Perverse and peevish creature ! you have no more reason to be sorry than I have ; and you have many to the contrary which I have not. Being a man, you are at liberty to admire a variety, and to make a choice. Is that no comfort to you ?

Dante.

> Bid this bosom cease to grieve ?
> Bid these eyes fresh objects see ?
> Where's the comfort to believe
> None might once have rivall'd me ?
> What ! my freedom to receive ?
> Broken hearts, are they the free ?
> For another can I live
> When I may not live for thee ?

Beatrice. I will never be fond of you again if you are so violent. We have been together too long, and we may be noticed.

Dante. Is this our last meeting ? If it is . . . and that it is, my heart has told me . . . you will not, surely you will not refuse . . .

Beatrice. Dante ! Dante ! they make the heart sad after : do not wish it. · But prayers . . . O, how much better are they ! how much quieter and lighter they render it ! They carry it up to heaven with them ; and those we love are left behind no longer.

FRA FILIPPO LIPPI AND POPE EUGENIUS THE FOURTH.

Eugenius. Filippo! I am informed by my son Cosimo de' Medici of many things relating to thy life and actions, and among the rest, of thy throwing off the habit of a friar. Speak to me as to a friend. Was that well done?

Filippo. Holy Father! it was done most unadvisedly.

Eugenius. Continue to treat me with the same confidence and ingenuousness; and, beside the remuneration I intend to bestow on thee for the paintings wherewith thou hast adorned my palace, I will remove with my own hand the heavy accumulation of thy sins, and ward off the peril of fresh ones, placing within thy reach every worldly solace and contentment.

Filippo. Infinite thanks, Holy Father! from the innermost heart of your unworthy servant, whose duty and wishes bind him alike and equally to a strict compliance with your paternal commands.

Eugenius. Was it a love of the world and its vanities that induced thee to throw aside the frock?

Filippo. It was indeed, Holy Father! I never had the courage to mention it in confession among my manifold offences.

Eugenius. Bad! bad! Repentance is of little use to the sinner, unless he pour it from a full and overflowing heart into the capacious ear of the confessor. Ye must not go straightforward and bluntly up to your Maker, startling him with the horrors of your guilty conscience. Order, decency, time, place, opportunity, must be observed.

Filippo. I have observed the greater part of them : time, place, and opportunity.

Eugenius. That is much. In consideration of it, I hereby absolve thee.

Filippo. I feel quite easy, quite new-born.

Eugenius. I am desirous of hearing what sort of feelings thou experiencest, when thou givest loose to thy intractable and unruly wishes. Now, this love of the world, what can it mean? A love of music, of dancing, of riding? What in short is it in thee?

Filippo. Holy Father! I was ever of a hot and amorous constitution.

Eugenius. Well, well! I can guess, within a trifle, what that leads unto. I very much disapprove of it, whatever it may be. And then? and then? Prythee go on: I am inflamed with a miraculous zeal to cleanse thee.

Filippo. I have committed many follies, and some sins.

Eugenius. Let me hear the sins; I do not trouble my head about the follies; the Church has no business with them. The state is founded on follies, the Church on sins. Come then, unsack them.

Filippo. Concupiscence is both a folly and a sin. I felt more and more of it when I ceased to be a monk, not having (for a time) so ready means of allaying it.

Eugenius. No doubt. Thou shouldst have thought again and again before thou strippedst off the cowl.

Filippo. Ah! Holy Father! I am sore at heart. I thought indeed how often it had held two heads together under it, and that stripping it off was double decapitation. But compensation and contentment came, and we were warm enough without it.

Eugenius. I am minded to reprove thee gravely. No wonder it pleased the Virgin, and the saints about her, to permit that the enemy of our faith should lead thee captive into Barbary.

Filippo. The pleasure was all on their side.

Eugenius. I have heard a great many stories both of males and females who were taken by Tunisians and Algerines: and although there is a sameness in certain parts of them, my especial benevolence toward thee, worthy

Filippo, would induce me to lend a vacant ear to thy report. And now, good Filippo, I could sip a small glass of muscatel or Orvieto, and turn over a few bleached almonds, or essay a smart dried apricot at intervals, and listen while thou relatest to me the manners and customs of that country, and particularly as touching thy own adversities. First, how wast thou taken?

Filippo. I was visiting at Pesaro my worshipful friend the canonico Andrea Paccone, who delighted in the guitar, played it skilfully, and was always fond of hearing it well accompanied by the voice. My own instrument I had brought with me, together with many gay Florentine songs, some of which were of such a turn and tendency, that the canonico thought they would sound better on water, and rather far from shore, than within the walls of the canonicate. He proposed then, one evening when there was little wind stirring, to exercise three young abbates* on their several parts, a little way out of hearing from the water's edge.

Eugenius. I disapprove of exercising young abbates in that manner.

Filippo. Inadvertently, O Holy Father! I have made the affair seem worse than it really was. In fact, there were only two genuine abbates; the third was Donna Lisetta, the good canonico's pretty niece, who looks so archly at your Holiness when you bend your knees before her at bed-time.

Eugenius. How? Where?

Filippo. She is the angel on the right-hand side of the Holy Family, with a tip of amethyst-coloured wing over a basket of figs and pomegranates. I painted her from memory: she was then only fifteen, and worthy to be the niece of an archbishop. Alas! she never will be: she plays and sings among the infidels, and perhaps would eat a landrail on a Friday as unreluctantly as she would a roach.

Eugenius. Poor soul! So this is the angel with the

* Little boys, wearing clerical habits, are often called *abbati*.

amethyst-coloured wing? I thought she looked wanton: we must pray for her release . . . from the bondage of sin. What followed in your excursion?

Filippo. Singing, playing, fresh air, and plashing water, stimulated our appetites. We had brought no eatable with us but fruit and thin *marzopane*, of which the sugar and rose-water were inadequate to ward off hunger; and the sight of a fishing-vessel between us and Ancona, raised our host immoderately. "Yonder smack," said he, "is sailing at this moment just over the very best sole-bank in the Adriatic. If she continues her course and we run toward her, we may be supplied, I trust in God, with the finest fish in Christendom. Methinks I see already the bellies of those magnificent sole bestar the deck, and emulate the glories of the orient sky." He gave his orders with such a majestic air, that he looked rather like an admiral than a priest.

Eugenius. How now, rogue! Why should not the churchman look majestically and courageously? I myself have found occasion for it, and exerted it.

Filippo. The world knows the prowess of your Holiness.

Eugenius. Not mine, not mine, Filippo! but His who gave me the sword and the keys, and the will and the discretion to use them. I trust the canonico did not misapply his station and power, by taking the fish at any unreasonably low price; and that he gave his blessing to the remainder, and to the poor fishermen and to their nets.

Filippo. He was angry at observing that the vessel, while he thought it was within hail, stood out again to sea.

Eugenius. He ought to have borne more manfully so slight a vexation.

Filippo. On the contrary, he swore bitterly he would have the master's ear between his thumb and forefinger in another half-hour, and regretted that he had cut his nails in the morning lest they should grate on his guitar. "They may fish well," cried he, "but they can neither sail nor row; and, when I am in the middle of that tub of theirs, I will teach them more than they look for." Sure enough he was

in the middle of it at the time he fixed : but it was by aid
of a rope about his arms, and the end of another laid lustily
on his back and shoulders. "Mount, lazy long-chined
turnspit, as thou valuest thy life," cried Abdul the corsair,
"and away for Tunis." If silence is consent, he had it.
The captain, in the Sicilian dialect, told us we might talk
freely, for he had taken his siesta. "Whose guitars are
those?" said he. As the canonico raised his eyes to
heaven and answered nothing, I replied, "Sir, one is mine :
the other is my worthy friend's there." Next he asked the
canonico to what market he was taking those young slaves,
pointing to the abbates. The canonico sobbed and could
not utter one word. I related the whole story ; at which
he laughed. He then took up the music, and commanded
my reverend guest to sing an air peculiarly tender, invoking
the compassion of a nymph, and calling her cold as ice.
Never did so many or such profound sighs accompany it.
When it ended, he sang one himself in his own language,
on a lady whose eyes were exactly like the sicmitars of
Damascus, and whose eyebrows met in the middle like the
cudgels of prize-fighters. On the whole she resembled both
sun and moon, with the simple difference that she never
allowed herself to be seen, lest all the nations of the earth
should go to war for her, and not a man be left to breathe
out his soul before her. This poem had obtained the prize
at the University of Fez, had been translated into the
Arabic, the Persian, and the Turkish languages, and was
the favourite lay of the corsair. He invited me lastly to
try my talent. I played the same air on the guitar, and
apologised for omitting the words, from my utter ignorance
of the Moorish. Abdul was much pleased, and took the
trouble to convince me that the poetry they conveyed,
which he translated literally, was incomparably better than
ours. "Cold as ice !" he repeated, scoffing : "anybody
might say that who had seen Atlas : but a genuine poet
would rather say, 'Cold as a lizard or a lobster.'" There
is no controverting a critic who has twenty stout rowers,
and twenty well-knotted rope-ends. Added to which, he

seemed to know as much of the matter as the generality of those who talk about it. He was gratified by my attention and edification, and thus continued: " I have remarked in the songs I have heard, that these wild woodland creatures of the west, these nymphs, are a strange fantastical race. But are your poets not ashamed to complain of their inconstancy? whose fault is that? If ever it should be my fortune to take one, I would try whether I could not bring her down to the level of her sex; and if her inconstancy caused any complaints, by Allah! they should be louder and shriller than ever rose from the throat of Abdul." I still thought it better to be a disciple than a commentator.

Eugenius. If we could convert this barbarian and detain him awhile at Rome, he would learn that women and nymphs (and inconstancy also) are one and the same. These cruel men have no lenity, no suavity. They who do not as they would be done by, are done by very much as they do. Women will glide away from them like water; they can better bear two masters than half one; and a new metal must·be discovered before any bars are strong enough to confine them. But proceed with your narrative.

Filippo. Night had now closed upon us. Abdul placed the younger of the company apart, and after giving them some boiled rice, sent them down into his own cabin. The sailors, observing the consideration and distinction with which their master had treated me, were civil and obliging. Permission was granted me, at my request, to sleep on deck.

Eugenius. What became of your canonico?

Filippo. The crew called him a conger, a priest, and a porpoise.

Eugenius. Foul-mouthed knaves! could not one of these terms content them? On thy leaving Barbary was he left behind?

Filippo. Your Holiness consecrated him, the other day, Bishop of Macerata.

Eugenius. True, true; I remember the name, Saccone. How did he contrive to get off?

Filippo. He was worth little at any work ; and such men are the quickest both to get off and to get on. Abdul told me he had received three thousand crowns for his ransom.

Eugenius. He was worth more to him than to me. I received but two first-fruits, and such other things as of right belong to me by inheritance. The bishopric is passably rich : he may serve thee.

Filippo. While he was a canonico he was a jolly fellow ; not very generous ; for jolly fellows are seldom that ; but he would give a friend a dinner, a flask of wine or two in preference, and a piece of advice as readily as either. I waited on Monsignor at Macerata, soon after his elevation.

Eugenius. He must have been heartily glad to embrace his companion in captivity, and the more especially as he himself was the cause of so grievous a misfortune.

Filippo. He sent me word he was so unwell he could not see me. "What ! " said I to his valet, "is Monsignor's complaint in his eyes ? " The fellow shrugged up his shoulders and walked away. Not believing that the message was a refusal to admit me, I went straight upstairs, and finding the door of an ante-chamber half open, and a chaplain milling an egg-posset over the fire, I accosted him. The air of familiarity and satisfaction he observed in me left no doubt in his mind that I had been invited by his patron. "Will the man never come ? " cried his lordship. "Yes, Monsignor ! " exclaimed I, running in and embracing him ; "behold him here ! " He started back, and then I first discovered the wide difference between an old friend and an egg-posset.

Eugenius. Son Filippo ! thou hast seen but little of the world, and art but just come from Barbary. Go on.

Filippo. "Fra Filippo ! " said he gravely, "I am glad to see you. I did not expect you just at present : I am not very well : I had ordered a medicine and was impatient to take it. If you will favour me with the name of your inn, I will send for you when I am in a condition to receive you ; perhaps within a day or two." "Monsignor ! " said I, "a

change of residence often gives a man a cold, and oftener a
change of fortune. Whether you caught yours upon deck
(where we last saw each other), from being more exposed
than usual, or whether the mitre holds wind, is no question
for me, and no concern of mine."

Eugenius. A just reproof, if an archbishop had made it.
On uttering it, I hope thou kneeledst and kissedst his
hand.

Filippo. I did not indeed.

Eugenius. Oh ! there wert thou greatly in the wrong.
Having, it is reported, a good thousand crowns yearly of
patrimony, and a canonicate worth six hundred more, he
might have attempted to relieve thee from slavery, by
assisting thy relatives in thy redemption.

Filippo. The three thousand crowns were the uttermost
he could raise, he declared to Abdul, and he asserted that
a part of the money was contributed by the inhabitants of
Pesaro. "Do they act out of pure mercy ?" said he. "Ay,
they must, for what else could move them in behalf of
such a lazy, unserviceable street-fed cur ?" In the morning,
at sunrise, he was sent aboard. And now, the vessel being
under weigh, "I have a letter from my lord Abdul," said
the master, "which, being in thy language, two fellow
slaves shall read unto thee publicly." They came forward
and began the reading. "Yesterday I purchased these two
slaves from a cruel, unrelenting master, under whose lash
they have laboured for nearly thirty years. I hereby give
orders that five ounces of my own gold be weighed out to
them." Here one of the slaves fell on his face ; the
other lifted up his hands, praised God, and blessed his
benefactor.

Eugenius. The pirate ? the unconverted pirate ?

Filippo. Even so. "Here is another slip of paper for
thyself to read immediately in my presence," said the
master. The words it contained were, "Do thou the same,
or there enters thy lips neither food nor water until thou
landest in Italy. I permit thee to carry away more than
double the sum : I am no suttler : I do not contract for

thy sustenance." The canonico asked of the master whether he knew the contents of the letter ; he replied, no. "Tell your master, lord Abdul, that I shall take them into consideration." "My lord expected a much plainer answer, and commanded me, in case of any such as thou hast delivered, to break this seal." He pressed it to his forehead and then broke it. Having perused the characters reverentially, "Christian ! dost thou consent ? " The canonico fell on his knees, and overthrew the two poor wretches who, saying their prayers, had remained in the same posture before him quite unnoticed. "Open thy trunk and take out thy money-bag, or I will make room for it in thy bladder." The canonico was prompt in the execution of the command. The master drew out his scales, and desired the canonico to weigh with his own hand five ounces. He groaned and trembled : the balance was unsteady. "Throw in another piece : it will not vitiate the agreement," cried the master. It was done. Fear and grief are among the thirsty passions, but add little to the appetite. It seemed however as if every sigh had left a vacancy in the stomach of the canonico. At dinner the cook brought him a salted bonito, half an ell in length ; and in five minutes his Reverence was drawing his middle finger along the white backbone, out of sheer idleness, until were placed before him some as fine dried locusts as ever provisioned the tents of Africa, together with olives the size of eggs and colour of bruises, shining in oil and brine. He found them savoury and pulpy, and, as the last love supersedes the foregoing, he gave them the preference, even over the delicate locusts. When he had finished them, he modestly requested a can of water. A sailor brought a large flask, and poured forth a plentiful supply. The canonico engulfed the whole, and instantly threw himself back in convulsive agony. "How is this ? " cried the sailor. The master ran up and, smelling the water, began to buffet him, exclaiming, as he turned round to all the crew, "How came this flask here ? " All were innocent. It appeared however that it was a flask of mineral water, strongly sulphureous, taken out of a Neapolitan vessel, laden with a great abundance of it for some hospital in the Levant. It had taken the captor by surprise in the same manner as the canonico. He himself brought out instantly a capacious stone jar covered with dew, and invited the sufferer into the cabin. Here he drew forth two richly-cut wine-glasses, and, on filling one of them, the outside of it turned suddenly pale, with a myriad of indivisible drops, and the senses were refreshed with the most delicious fragrance. He held up the glass between himself and his guest, and looking at it attentively, said, "Here is no appearance of wine; all I can see is water. Nothing is wickeder than too much curiosity: we must take what Allah sends us, and render thanks for it, although it fall far short of our expectations. Beside, our prophet would rather we should even drink wine than poison." The canonico had not tasted wine for two months: a longer abstinence than ever canonico endured before. He drooped: but the master looked still more disconsolate. "I would give whatever I possess on earth rather than die of thirst," cried the canonico. "Who would not?" rejoined the captain, sighing and clasping his fingers. "If it were not contrary to my commands, I could touch at some cove or inlet." "Do, for the love of Christ!" exclaimed the canonico. "Or even sail back," continued the captain. "O Santa Vergine!" cried in anguish the canonico. "Despondency," said the captain, with calm solemnity, "has left many a man to be thrown overboard: it even renders the plague, and many other disorders, more fatal. Thirst too has a powerful effect in exasperating them. Overcome such weaknesses, or I must do my duty. The health of the ship's company is placed under my care; and our lord Abdul, if he suspected the pest, would throw a Jew, or a Christian, or even a bale of silk, into the sea: such is the disinterestedness and magnanimity of my lord Abdul." "He believes in fate; does he not?" said the canonico. "Doubtless: but he says it is as much fated that he should throw into the sea a fellow who is infected, as that the fellow should have ever been so." "Save me, O save me!" cried the canonico, moist as if the spray had pelted him. "Willingly, if possible," answered calmly the master. "At present I can discover no certain symptoms; for sweat, unless followed by general prostration, both of muscular strength and animal spirits, may be cured without a hook at the heel." "Giesu-Maria!" ejaculated the canonico."

Eugenius. And the monster could withstand that appeal ?

Filippo. It seems so. The renegade who related to me, on my return, these events as they happened, was very circumstantial. He is a Corsican, and had killed many men in battle, and more out; but is (he gave me his word for it) on the whole an honest man.

Eugenius. How so? honest? and a renegade?

Filippo. He declared to me that, although the Mahomedan is the best religion to live in, the Christian is the best to die in; and that, when he has made his fortune, he will make his confession, and lie snugly in the bosom of the Church.

Eugenius. See here the triumphs of our holy faith ! The lost sheep will be found again.

Filippo. Having played the butcher first.

Eugenius. Return we to that bad man, the master or captain, who evinced no such dispositions.

Filippo. He added, "The other captives, though older men, have stouter hearts than thine." "Alas! they are longer used to hardships," answered he. "Dost thou believe, in thy conscience," said the captain, "that the water we have aboard would be harmless to them ? for we have no other; and wine is costly; and our quantity might be insufficient for those who can afford to pay for it." "I will answer for their lives," replied the canonico. "With thy own?" interrogated sharply the Tunisian. "I must not tempt God," said, in tears, the religious man. "Let us be plain," said the master. "Thou knowest thy money is safe; I myself counted it before thee when I brought it from the scrivener's; thou hast sixty broad gold pieces; wilt thou be answerable, to the whole amount of them, for the

lives of thy two countrymen if they drink this water?" "O
Sir! said the canonico, "I will give it, if, only for these few
days of voyage, you vouchsafe me one bottle dâily of that
restorative wine of Bordeaux. The other two are less
liable to the plague : they do not sorrow and sweat as I do.
They are spare men. There is enough of me to infect a
fleet with it ; and I can not bear to think of being anywise
the cause of evil to my fellow-creatures." "The wine is
my patron's," cried the Tunisian ; " he leaves everything at
my discretion : should I deceive him?" "If he leaves
everything at your discretion," observed the logician of
Pesaro, "there is no deceit in disposing of it." The master
appeared to be satisfied with the argument. "Thou shalt
not find me exacting," said he ; "give me the sixty pieces,
and the wine shall be thine." At a signal, when the
contract was agreed to, the two slaves entered, bringing a
hamper of jars. "Read the contract before thou signest,"
cried the master. He read. "How is this? how is this?
*Sixty golden ducats to the brothers Antonio and Bernabo
Panini, for wine received from them?*" The aged men
tottered under the stroke of joy ; and Bernabo, who would
have embraced his brother, fainted.

On the morrow there was a calm, and the weather was
extremely sultry. The canonico sat in his shirt on deck,
and was surprised to see, I forget which of the brothers,
drink from a goblet a prodigious draught of water.
"Hold!" cried he angrily ; "you may eat instead ; but
putrid or sulphureous water, you have heard, may produce
the plague, and honest men be the sufferers by your folly
and intemperance." They assured him the water was
tasteless, and very excellent, and had been kept cool in the
same kind of earthen jars as the wine. He tasted it, and
lost his patience. It was better, he protested, than any
wine in the world. They begged his acceptance of the jar
containing it. But the master, who had witnessed at a
distance the whole proceeding, now advanced, and, placing
his hand against it, said sternly, "Let him have his own."
Usually, when he had emptied the second bottle, a desire

of converting the Mahometans came over him : and they showed themselves much less obstinate and refractory than they are generally thought. He selected those for edification who swore the oftenest and the loudest by the Prophet ; and he boasted in his heart of having overcome, by precept and example, the stiffest tenet of their abominable creed. Certainly they drank wine, and somewhat freely. The canonico clapped his hands, and declared that even some of the apostles had been more pertinacious recusants of the faith.

Eugenius. Did he so? Cappari! I would not have made him a bishop for twice the money if I had known it earlier. Could not he have left them alone? Suppose one or other of them did doubt and persecute, was he the man to blab it out among the heathen?

Filippo. A judgment, it appears, fell on him for so doing. A very quiet sailor, who had always declined his invitations, and had always heard his arguments at a distance and in silence, being pressed and urged by him, and reproved somewhat arrogantly and loudly, as less docile than his messmates, at last lifted up his leg behind him, pulled off his right slipper, and counted deliberately and distinctly thirty-nine sound strokes of the same, on the canonico's broadest tablet, which (please your holiness) might be called, not inaptly, from that day, the tablet of memory. In vain he cried out. Some of the mariners made their moves at chess and waved their left hands as if desirous of no interruption ; others went backward and forward about their business, and took no more notice than if their messmate was occupied in caulking a seam or notching a flint. The master himself, who saw the operation, heard the complaint in the evening, and lifted up his shoulders and eyebrows, as if the whole were quite unknown to him. Then, acting as judge-advocate, he called the young man before him and repeated the accusation. To this the defence was purely interrogative. " Why would he convert me? I never converted him." Turning to his spiritual guide, he said, " I quite forgive thee : nay, I am ready to appear in thy favour, and to declare that, in general, thou hast been more decorous than people of thy faith and profession usually are, and hast not scattered on deck that inflammatory language which I, habited in the dress of a Greek, heard last Easter. I went into three churches; and the preachers in all three denounced the curse of Allah on every soul that differed from them a tittle. They were children of perdition, children of darkness, children of the devil, one and all. It seemed a matter of wonder to me, that, in such numerous families and of such indifferent parentage, so many slippers were kept under the heel. Mine, in an evil hour, escaped me: but I quite forgive thee. After this free pardon I will indulge thee with a short specimen of my preaching. I will call none of you a generation of vipers, as ye call one another; for vipers neither bite nor eat during many months of the year: I will call none of you wolves in sheep's clothing; for if ye are, it must be acknowledged that the clothing is very clumsily put on. You priests, however, take people's souls aboard whether they will or not, just as we do your bodies: and you make them pay much more for keeping these in slavery than we make you pay for setting you free body and soul together. You declare that the precious souls, to the especial care of which Allah has called and appointed you, frequently grow corrupt, and stink in his nostrils. Now, I invoke thy own testimony to the fact: thy soul, gross as I imagine it to be from the greasy wallet that holds it, had no carnal thoughts whatsoever, and that thy carcase did not even receive a fly-blow, while it was under my custody. Thy guardian angel (I speak it in humility) could not ventilate thee better. Nevertheless, I should scorn to demand a single maravedi for my labour and skill, or for the wear and tear of my pantoufle. My reward will be in Paradise, where a Houri is standing in the shade, above a vase of gold and silver fish, with a kiss on her lip, and an unbroken pair of green slippers in her hand for me." Saying which, he took off his foot again, the one he had been using, and showed the sole of it, first to the master, then to all the crew, and declared it had become (as they might see) so smooth and oily by the application, that it was dangerous to walk on deck in it.

Eugenius. See ! what notions these creatures have, both of their fool's paradise and of our holy faith ! The seven sacraments, I warrant you, go for nothing ! Purgatory, purgatory itself, goes for nothing !

Filippo. Holy Father ! we must stop thee. *That* does not go for nothing, however.

Eugenius. Filippo ! God forbid I should suspect thee of any heretical taint ; but this smells very like it. If thou hast it now, tell me honestly. I mean, hold thy tongue. Florentines are rather lax. Even Son Cosimo might be stricter : so they say : perhaps his enemies. The great always have them abundantly, beside those by whom they are served, and those also whom they serve. Now would I give a silver rose with my benediction on it, to know of a certainty what became of those poor creatures the abbates. The initiatory rite of Mahometanism is most diabolically malicious. According to the canons of our catholic Church, it disqualifies the neophyte for holy orders, without going so far as adapting him to the choir of the pontificial chapel. They limp ; they halt.

Filippo. Beatitude ! which of them ?

Eugenius. The unbelievers : they surely are found wanting.

Filippo. The unbelievers too ?

Eugenius. Ay, ay, thou half renegade ! Couldst not thou go over with a purse of silver, and try whether the souls of these captives be recoverable ? Even if they should have submitted to such unholy rites, I venture to say they have repented.

Filippo. The devil is in them if they have not.

Eugenius. They may become again as good Christians as before.

Filippo. Easily, methinks.

Eugenius. Not so easily ; but by aid of Holy Church in the administration of indulgences.

Filippo. They never wanted those, whatever they want.

Eugenius. The corsair then is not one of those ferocious creatures which appear to connect our species with the lion and panther.

Filippo. By no means, Holy Father! He is an honest man; so are many of his countrymen, bating the sacrament.

Eugenius. Bating! poor beguiled Filippo! Being unbaptised, they are only as the beasts that perish : nay worse : for the soul being imperishable, it must stick to their bodies at the last day, whether they will or no, and must sink with it into the fire and brimstone.

Filippo. Unbaptised! why, they baptise every morning.

Eugenius. Worse and worse! I thought they only missed the stirrup; I find they overleap the saddle. Obstinate blind reprobates! of whom it is written . . . of whom it is written . . . of whom, I say, it is written . . . as shall be manifest before men and angels in the day of wrath.

Filippo. More is the pity! for they are hospitable, frank, and courteous. It is delightful to see their gardens, when one has not the weeding and irrigation of them. What fruit! what foliage! what trellises! what alcoves! what a contest of rose and jessamine for supremacy in odour! of lute and nightingale for victory in song! And how the little bright ripples of the docile brooks, the fresher for their races, leap up against one another, to look on! and how they chirrup and applaud, as if they too had a voice of some importance in these parties of pleasure that are loth to separate.

Eugenius. Parties of pleasure! birds, fruits, shallow-running waters, lute-players, and wantons! Parties of pleasure! and composed of these! Tell me now, Filippo, tell me truly, what complexion in general have the discreeter females of that hapless country.

Filippo. The colour of an orange-flower, on which an over-laden bee has left a slight suffusion of her purest honey.

Eugenius. We must open their eyes.

Filippo. Knowing what excellent hides the slippers of this people are made of, I never once ventured on their less perfect theology, fearing to find it written that I should be a-bed on my face the next fortnight. My master had expressed his astonishment that a religion so admirable as ours was represented should be the only one in the world the precepts of which are disregarded by all conditions of men. "Our Prophet," said he, "our Prophet ordered us to go forth and conquer; we did it: yours ordered you to sit quiet and forbear; and, after spitting in his face, you threw the order back into it, and fought like devils."

Eugenius. The barbarians talk of our Holy Scriptures as if they understood them perfectly. The impostor they follow has nothing but fustian and rhodomontade in his impudent lying book from beginning to end. I know it, Filippo, from those who have contrasted it, page by page, paragraph by paragraph, and have given the knave his due.

Filippo. Abdul is by no means deficient in a good opinion of his own capacity and his Prophet's all-sufficiency, but he never took me to task about my faith or his own.

Eugenius. How wert thou mainly occupied?

Filippo. I will give your Holiness a sample both of my employments and of his character. He was going one evening to a country-house, about fifteen miles from Tunis; and he ordered me to accompany him. I found there a spacious garden, over-run with wild flowers and most luxuriant grass, in irregular tufts, according to the dryness or the humidity of the spot. The clematis overtopped the lemon and orange trees; and the perennial pea sent forth here a pink blossom, here a purple, here a white one, and, after holding (as it were) a short conversation with the humbler plants, sprang up about an old cypress, played among its branches, and mitigated its gloom. White pigeons, and others in colour like the dawn of day, looked down on us and ceased to coo, until some of their companions, in whom they had more confidence, encouraged them loudly from remoter boughs, or alighted on the shoulders of Abdul, at whose side I was standing. A few of them examined me in every position their inquisitive eyes could take; displaying all the advantages of their versatile necks, and pretending querulous fear in the midst of petulant approaches.

Eugenius. Is it of pigeons thou art talking, O Filippo? I hope it may be.

Filippo. Of Abdul's pigeons. He was fond of taming all creatures; men, horses, pigeons, equally: but he tamed them all by kindness. In this wilderness is an edifice not unlike our Italian chapter-houses built by the Lombards, with long narrow windows, high above the ground. The centre is now a bath, the waters of which, in another part of the inclosure, had supplied a fountain, at present in ruins, and covered by tufted canes, and by every variety of aquatic plants. The structure has no remains of roof: and, of six windows, one alone is unconcealed by ivy. This had been walled up long ago, and the cement in the inside of it was hard and polished. "Lippi!" said Abdul to me, after I had long admired the place in silence, "I leave to thy superintendence this bath and garden. Be sparing of the leaves and branches: make paths only wide enough for me. Let me see no mark of hatchet or pruning-hook, and tell the labourers that whoever takes a nest or an egg shall be impaled."

Eugenius. Monster! so then he would really have impaled a poor wretch for eating a bird's egg? How disproportionate is the punishment to the offence!

Filippo. He efficiently checked in his slaves the desire of transgressing his command. To spare them as much as possible, I ordered them merely to open a few spaces, and to remove the weaker trees from the stronger. Meanwhile I drew on the smooth blank window the figure of Abdul and of a beautiful girl.

Eugenius. Rather say handmaiden : choicer expression ; more decorous.

Filippo. Holy Father! I have been lately so much out of practice, I take the first that comes in my way. Handmaiden I will use in preference for the future.

Eugenius. On then! and God speed thee!

Filippo. I drew Abdul with a blooming handmaiden. One of his feet is resting on her lap, and she is drying the ankle with a saffron robe, of which the greater part is fallen in doing it. That she is a bondmaid is discernible, not only by her occupation, but by her humility and patience, by her loose and flowing brown hair, and by her eyes expressing the timidity at once of servitude and of fondness. The countenance was taken from fancy, and was the loveliest I could imagine: of the figure I had some idea, having seen it to advantage in Tunis. After seven days Abdul returned. He was delighted with the improvement made in the garden. I requested him to visit the bath. "We can do nothing to that," answered he impatiently. "There is no sudatory, no dormitory, no dressing-room, no couch. Sometimes I sit an hour there in the summer, because I never found a fly in it—the principal curse of hot countries, and against which plague there is neither prayer nor amulet, nor indeed any human defence." He went away into the house. At dinner he sent me from his table some quails and ortolans, and tomatoes and honey and rice, beside a basket of fruit covered with moss and bay-leaves, under which I found a verdino fig, deliciously ripe, and bearing the impression of several small teeth, but certainly no reptile's.

Eugenius. There might have been poison in them, for all that.

Filippo. About two hours had passed, when I heard a whirr and a crash in the windows of the bath (where I had dined and was about to sleep), occasioned by the settling and again the flight of some pheasants. Abdul entered. "Beard of the Prophet! what hast thou been doing? That is myself! No, no, Lippi! thou never canst have seen her: the face proves it: but those limbs! thou hast divined them aright: thou hast had sweet dreams then! Dreams are large possessions: in them the possessor may cease to possess his own. To the slave, O Allah! to the slave is permitted what is not his! . . . I burn with anguish to think how much . . . yea, at that very hour. I would not another should, even in a dream. . . . But, Lippi! thou never canst have seen above the sandal?" To which I answered, "I never have allowed my eyes to look even on that. But if any one of my lord Abdul's fair slaves resembles, as they surely must all do, in duty and docility, the figure I have represented, let it express to him my congratulation on his happiness." "I believe," said he, "such representations are forbidden by the Koran; but as I do not remember it, I do not sin. There it shall stay, unless the angel Gabriel comes to forbid it." He smiled in saying so.

Eugenius. There is hope of this Abdul. His faith hangs about him more like oil than pitch.

Filippo. He inquired of me whether I often thought of those I loved in Italy, and whether I could bring them before my eyes at will. To remove all suspicion from him, I declared I always could, and that one beautiful object occupied all the cells of my brain by night and day. He paused and pondered, and then said, "Thou dost not love deeply." I thought I had given the true signs. "No, Lippi! we who love ardently, we, with all our wishes, all the efforts of our souls, can not bring before us the features which, while they were present, we thought it impossible we ever could forget. Alas! when we most love the absent, when we most desire to see her, we try in vain to bring her image back to us. The troubled heart shakes and confounds it, even as ruffled waters do with shadows. Hateful things are more hateful when they haunt our sleep: the lovely flee away, or are changed into less lovely."

Eugenius. What figures now have these unbelievers?

Filippo. Various in their combinations as the letters or the numerals; but they all, like these, signify something. Almeida (did I not inform your Holiness?) has large hazel eyes . . .

Eugenius. Has she? thou never toldest me that. Well, well! and what else has she? Mind! be cautious! use decent terms.

Filippo. Somewhat pouting lips.

Eugenius. Ha! ha! What did they pout at?

Filippo. And she is rather plump than otherwise.

Eugenius. No harm in that.

Filippo. And moreover is cool, smooth, and firm as a nectarine gathered before sunrise.

Eugenius. Ha! ha! do not remind me of nectarines. I am very fond of them; and this is not the season! Such females as thou describest are said to be among the likeliest to give reasonable cause for suspicion. I would not judge harshly, I would not think uncharitably; but, unhappily, being at so great a distance from spiritual aid, peradventure a desire, a suggestion, an inkling . . . ay? If she, the lost Almeida, came before thee when her master was absent . . . which I trust she never did. . . . But those flowers and shrubs and odours and alleys and long grass and alcoves, might strangely hold, perplex, and entangle, two incautious young persons . . . ay?

Filippo. I confessed all I had to confess in this matter the evening I landed.

Eugenius. Ho! I am no candidate for a seat at the rehearsal of confessions: but perhaps my absolution might be somewhat more pleasing and unconditional. Well! well! since I am unworthy of such confidence, go about thy business . . . paint! paint!

Filippo. Am I so unfortunate as to have offended your Beatitude?

Eugenius. Offend *me*, man! who offends *me?* I took an interest in thy adventures, and was concerned lest thou mightest have sinned; for by my soul! Filippo! those are the women that the devil hath set his mark on.

Filippo. It would do your Holiness's heart good to rub it out again, wherever he may have had the cunning to make it.

Eugenius. Deep! deep!

Filippo. Yet it may be got at; she being a Biscayan by birth, as she told me, and not only baptised, but going by sea along the coast for confirmation, when she was captured,

Eugenius. Alas ! to what an imposition of hands was this tender young thing devoted !   Poor soul !

Filippo. I sigh for her myself when I think of her.

Eugenius. Beware lest the sigh be mundane, and lest the thought recur too often.   I wish it were presently in my power to examine her myself on her condition.   What thinkest thou ?   Speak.

Filippo. Holy Father ! she would laugh in your face.

Eugenius. So lost !

Filippo. She declared to me she thought she should have died, from the instant she was captured until she was comforted by Abdul : but that she was quite sure she should if she were ransomed.

Eugenius. Has the wretch then shaken her faith ?

Filippo. The very last thing he would think of doing. Never did I see the virtue of resignation in higher perfection than in the laughing, light-hearted Almeida.

Eugenius. Lamentable !   Poor lost creature ! lost in this world and in the next.

Filippo. What could she do ? how could she help herself?

Eugenius. She might have torn his eyes out, and have died a martyr.

Filippo. Or have been bastinaded, whipped, and given up to the cooks and scullions for it.

Eugenius. Martyrdom is the more glorious the greater the indignities it endures.

Filippo. Almeida seems unambitious.   There are many in our Tuscany who would jump at the crown over those sloughs and briars, rather than perish without them : she never sighs after the like.

Eugenius. Nevertheless, what must she witness ! what abominations ! what superstitions !

Filippo. Abdul neither practises nor exacts any other superstition than ablutions.

Eugenius. Detestable rites ! without our authority.   I venture to affirm that, in the whole of Italy and Spain, no convent of monks or nuns contains a bath ; and that the worst inmate of either would shudder at the idea of observing such a practice in common with the unbeliever. For the washing of the feet indeed we have the authority of the earlier Christians; and it may be done; but solemnly and sparingly. Thy residence among the Mahometans, I am afraid, hath rendered thee more favourable to them than beseems a Catholic, and thy mind, I do suspect, sometimes goes back into Barbary unreluctantly.

Filippo. While I continued in that country, although I was well treated, I often wished myself away, thinking of my friends in Florence, of music, of painting, of our villegiatura at the vintage-time; whether in the green and narrow glades of Pratolino, with lofty trees above us, and little rills unseen, and little bells about the necks of sheep and goats, tinkling together ambiguously; or amid the grey quarries, or under the majestic walls of modern Fiesole; or down in the woods of the Doccia, where the cypresses are of such a girth that, when a youth stands against one of them, and a maiden stands opposite, and they clasp it, their hands at the time do little more than meet. Beautiful scenes, on which Heaven smiles eternally, how often has my heart ached for you! He who hath lived in this country can enjoy no distant one. He breathes here another air; he lives more life; a brighter sun invigorates his studies, and serener stars influence his repose. Barbary hath also the blessing of climate; and although I do not desire to be there again, I feel sometimes a kind of regret at leaving it. A bell warbles the more mellifluously in the air when the sound of the stroke is over, and when another swims out from underneath it, and pants upon the element that gave it birth. In like manner the recollection of a thing is frequently more pleasing than the actuality; what is harsh is dropped in the space between. There is in Abdul a nobility of soul on which I often have reflected with admiration. I have seen many of the highest rank and distinction, in whom I could find nothing of the great man, excepting a fondness for low company, and an aptitude to shy and start at every spark of genius or virtue that sprang up above or before them. Abdul was solitary, but affable : he was proud, but patient and complacent. I

ventured once to ask him how the master of so rich a house
in the city, of so many slaves, of so many horses and mules,
of such corn-fields, of such pastures, of such gardens, woods,
and fountains, should experience any delight or satisfaction
in infesting the open sea, the high-road of nations. Instead
of answering my question, he asked me in return whether I
would not respect any relative of mine who avenged his
country, enriched himself by his bravery, and endeared to
him his friends and relatives by his bounty. On my reply
in the affirmative, he said that his family had been deprived
of possessions in Spain much more valuable than all the
ships and cargoes he could ever hope to capture, and that
the remains of his nation were threatened with ruin and
expulsion. "I do not fight," said he "whenever it suits the
convenience, or gratifies the malignity, or the caprice of two
silly, quarrelsome princes, drawing my sword in perfectly
good-humour, and sheathing it again at word of command,
just when I begin to get into a passion. No; I fight on
my own account; not as a hired assassin, or still baser
journeyman."

Eugenius. It appears then really that the Infidels have
some semblances of magnanimity and generosity?

Filippo. I thought so when I turned over the many
changes of fine linen; and I was little short of conviction
when I found at the bottom of my chest two hundred
Venetian zecchins.

Eugenius. Corpo di Bacco! Better things, far better
things, I would fain do for thee, not exactly of this description; it would excite many heart-burnings. Information
has been laid before me, Filippo, that thou art attached to a
certain young person, by name Lucrezia, daughter of
Francesco Buti, a citizen of Prato.

Filippo. I acknowledge my attachment: it continues.

Eugenius. Furthermore, that thou hast offspring by her.

Filippo. Alas! 'tis undeniable.

Eugenius. I will not only legitimatise the said offspring by
motu proprio and rescript to consistory and chancery . . .

Filippo. Holy Father! Holy Father! For the love of

the Virgin, not a word to consistory or chancery of the two hundred zecchins. As I hope for salvation, I have but forty left, and thirty-nine would not serve them.

Eugenius. Fear nothing. Not only will I perform what I have promised, not only will I give the strictest order that no money be demanded by any officer of my courts, but, under the seal of Saint Peter, I will declare thee and Lucrezia Buti man and wife.

Filippo. Man and wife !

Eugenius. Moderate thy transport.

Filippo. O Holy Father ! may I speak ?

Eugenius. Surely she is not the wife of another ?

Filippo. No, indeed.

Eugenius. Nor within the degrees of consanguinity and affinity ?

Filippo. No, no, no. But . . . man and wife ! Consistory and chancery are nothing to this fulmination.

Eugenius. How so ?

Filippo. It is man and wife the first fortnight, but wife and man ever after. The two figures change places : the unit is the decimal and the decimal is the unit.

Eugenius. What, then, can I do for thee ?

Filippo. I love Lucrezia; let me love her ; let her love me. I can make her at any time what she is not; I could never make her again what she is.

Eugenius. The only thing I can do then is to promise I will forget that I have heard anything about the matter. But, to forget it, I must hear it first.

Filippo. In the beautiful little town of Prato, reposing in its idleness against the hill that protects it from the north, and looking over fertile meadows, southward to Poggio Cajano, westward to Pistoja, there is the convent of Santa Margarita. I was invited by the sisters to paint an altar-piece for the chapel. A novice of fifteen, my own sweet Lucrezia, came one day alone to see me work at my Madonna. Her blessed countenance had already looked down on every beholder lower by the knees. I myself who made her could almost have worshipped her.

Eugenius. Not while incomplete; no half-virgin will do.

Filippo. But there knelt Lucrezia! there she knelt! first looking with devotion at the Madonna, then with admiring wonder and grateful delight at the artist. Could so little a heart be divided? 'Twere a pity! There was enough for me; there is never enough for the Madonna. Resolving on a sudden that the object of my love should be the object of adoration to thousands, born and unborn, I swept my brush across the maternal face, and left a blank in heaven. The little girl screamed; I pressed her to my bosom.

Eugenius. In the chapel?

Filippo. I knew not where I was; I thought I was in Paradise.

Eugenius. If it was not in the chapel, the sin is venial. But a brush against a Madonna's mouth is worse than a beard against her votary's.

Filippo. I thought so too, Holy Father!

Eugenius. Thou sayest thou hast forty zecchins; I will try in due season to add forty more. The fisherman must not venture to measure forces with the pirate. Farewell! I pray God, my son Filippo, to have thee alway in His holy keeping.

TASSO AND CORNELIA.

Tasso. She is dead, Cornelia! she is dead!

Cornelia. Torquato! my Torquato! after so many years of separation do I bend once more your beloved head to my embrace?

Tasso. She is dead!

Cornelia. Tenderest of brothers! bravest and best and most unfortunate of men! What, in the name of heaven . so bewilders you?

Tasso. Sister! sister! sister! I could not save her.

Cornelia. Certainly it was a sad event; and they who are out of spirits may be ready to take it for an evil omen. At this season of the year the vintagers are joyous and negligent.

Tasso. How! what is this?

Cornelia. The little girl was crushed, they · say, by a wheel of the car laden with grapes, as she held out a handful of vine-leaves to one of the oxen. And did you happen to be there just at the moment?

Tasso. So then the little too can suffer! the ignorant, the indigent, the unaspiring! Poor child She was kind-hearted, else never would calamity have befallen her.

Cornelia. I wish you had not seen the accident.

Tasso. I see it? I? I saw it not. No other is crushed where I am. The little girl died for her kindness! Natural death!

Cornelia. Be calm, be composed, my brother!

Tasso. You would not require me to be composed or calm if you comprehended a thousandth part of my sufferings.

Cornelia. Peace! peace! we know them all.

Tasso. Who has dared to name them? Imprisonment, derision, madness.

Cornelia. Hush! sweet Torquato! If ever these existed, they are past.

Tasso. You do think they are sufferings? ay?

Cornelia. Too surely.

Tasso. No, not too surely: I will not have that answer. They would have been; but Leonora was then living. Unmanly as I am! did I complain of them? and while she was left me?

Cornelia. My own Torquato! is there no comfort in a sister's love? Is there no happiness but under the passions? Think, O my brother, how many courts there are in Italy: are the princes more fortunate than you? Which among them all loves truly, deeply, and virtuously? Among them all is there anyone, for his genius, for his generosity, for his gentleness, ay, for his mere humanity, worthy to be beloved?

Tasso. Princes! talk to me of princes! How much cross-grained wood a little gypsum covers! a little carmine quite beautifies! Wet your forefinger with your spittle; stick a broken gold-leaf on the sinciput; clip off a beggar's beard to make it tresses; kiss it; fall down before it; worship it. Are you not irradiated by the light of its countenance! Princes! princes! Italian princes! Estes! What matters that costly carrion? Who thinks about it? *(After a pause.)* She is dead! She is dead!

Cornelia. We have not heard it here.

Tasso. At Sorrento you hear nothing but the light surges of the sea, and the sweet sprinkles of the guitar.

Cornelia. Suppose the worst to be true.

Tasso. Always, always.

Cornelia. If she ceases, as then perhaps she must, to love and to lament you, think gratefully, contentedly, devoutly, that her arms had clasped your neck before they were crossed upon her bosom, in that long sleep which you have rendered placid, and from which your harmonious voice shall once more awaken her. Yes, Torquato! her bosom had throbbed to yours, often and often, before the organ-peal shook the fringes round the catafalc. Is not this much, from one so high, so beautiful?

Tasso. Much? yes; for abject me. But I did so love her! so love her!

Cornelia. Ah! let the tears flow : she sends you that balm from heaven.

Tasso. So love her did poor Tasso! Else, O Cornelia, it had indeed been much. I thought, in the simplicity of my heart, that God was as great as an emperor, and could bestow and had bestowed on me as much as the German had conferred or could confer on his vassal. No part of my insanity was ever held in such ridicule as this. And yet the idea cleaves to me strangely, and is liable to stick to my shroud.

Cornelia. Woe betide the woman who bids you to forget that woman who has loved you : she sins against her sex. Leonora was unblameable. Never think ill of her for what you have suffered.

Tasso. Think ill of her? I? I? I? No; those we love, we love for everything; even for the pain they have given us. But she gave me none; it was where she was not that pain was.

Cornelia. Surely, if love and sorrow are destined for companionship, there is no reason why the last comer of the two should supersede the first.

Tasso. Argue with me, and you drive me into darkness. I am easily persuaded and led on while no reasons are thrown before me. With these you have made my temples throb again. Just Heaven! dost thou grant us fairer fields, and wider, for the whirlwind to lay waste? ·Dost thou build us up habitations above the street, above the palace, above the citadel, for the Plague to enter and carouse in? Has not my youth paid its dues, paid its penalties? Can not our griefs come first, while we have strength to bear them? The fool! the fool! who thinks it a misfortune that his love is unrequited. Happier young man! look at the violets until thou drop asleep on them. Ah! but thou must awake!

Cornelia. O heavens! what must you have suffered! for a man's heart is sensitive in proportion to its greatness.

Tasso. And a woman's?

Cornelia. Alas! I know not; but I think it can be no other.   Comfort thee, comfort thee, dear Torquato!

Tasso. Then do not rest thy face upon my arm; it so reminds me of her.   And thy tears too! they melt me into her grave.

Cornelia. Hear you not her voice as it appeals to you, saying to you, as the priests around have been saying to *her*, Blessed soul! rest in peace?

Tasso. I heard it not; and yet I am sure she said it.   A thousand times has she repeated it, laying her head on my heart to quiet it, simple girl!   She told it to rest in peace... and she went from me!   Insatiable love! ever self-torturer, never self-destroyer! the world, with all its weight of miseries, can not crush thee, can not keep thee down. Generally men's tears, like the droppings of certain springs, only harden and petrifiy what they fall on; but mine sank deep into a tender heart, and were its very blood.   Never will I believe she has left me utterly.   Oftentimes, and long before her departure, I fancied we were in heaven together.   I fancied it in the fields, in the gardens, in the palace, in the prison.   I fancied it in the broad daylight, when my eyes were open, when blessed spirits drew around me that golden circle which one only of earth's inhabitants could enter.   Oftentimes in my sleep also I fancied it; and sometimes in the intermediate state, in that serenity which breathes about the transported soul, enjoying its pure and perfect rest, a span below the feet of the Immortal.

Cornelia. She has not left you; do not disturb her peace by these repinings.

Tasso. She will bear with them.   Thou knowest not what she was, Cornelia; for I wrote to thee about her while she seemed but human.   In my hours of sadness, not only her beautiful form, but her very voice bent over me.   How girlish in the gracefulness of her lofty form! how pliable in her majesty! what composure at my petulance and reproaches! what pity in her reproofs! Like the air that angels breathe in the metropolitan temple of the Christian world, her soul at every season preserved one temperature. But it was when she could and did love me! Unchanged must ever be the blessed one who has leaned in fond security on the unchangeable. The purifying flame shoots upward, and is the glory that encircles their brows when they meet above.

Cornelia. Indulge in these delightful thoughts, my Torquato! and believe that your love is and ought to be imperishable as your glory. Generations of men move forward in endless procession to consecrate and commem.- orate both. Colour-grinders and gilders, year after year, are bargained with to refresh the crumbling monuments and tarnished decorations of rude, unregarded royalty, and to fasten the nails that cramp the crown upon its head. Meanwhile, in the laurels of my Torquato there will always be one leaf above man's reach, above time's wrath and injury, inscribed with the name of Leonora.

Tasso. O Jerusalem! I have not then sung in vain the Holy Sepulchre.

Cornelia. After such devotion of your genius, you have undergone too many misfortunes.

Tasso. Congratulate the man who has had many, and may have more. I have had, I have, I can have, one only.

Cornelia. Life runs not smoothly at all seasons, even with the happiest; but after a long course, the rocks subside, the views widen, and it flows on more equably at the end.

Tasso. Have the stars smooth surfaces? No, no; but how they shine!

Cornelia. Capable of thoughts so exalted, so far above the earth we dwell on, why suffer any to depress and anguish you?

Tasso. Cornelia, Cornelia! the mind has within its temples and porticoes and palaces and towers: the mind has under it, ready for the course, steeds brighter than the sun and stronger than the storm; and beside them stand winged chariots, more in number than the Psalmist hath attributed to the Almighty. The mind, I tell thee again, hath its hundred gates, compared whereto the Theban are but willow wickets ; and all those hundred gates can genius throw open. But there are some that groan heavily on their hinges, and the hand of God alone can close them.

Cornelia. Torquato has thrown open those of his holy temple ; Torquato hath stood, another angel, at his tomb ; and am I the sister of Torquato ? Kiss me, my brother, and let my tears run only from my pride and joy l Princes have bestowed knighthood on the worthy and unworthy ; thou hast called forth those princes from their ranks, pushing back the arrogant and presumptuous of them like intrusive varlets, and conferring on the bettermost crowns and robes, imperishable and unfading.

Tasso. I seem to live back into those days. I feel the helmet on my head ; I wave the standard over it : brave men smile upon me ; beautiful maidens pull them gently back by the scarf, and will not let them break my slumber, nor undraw the curtain. Corneliolina ! . . .

Cornelia. Well, my dear brother ! why do you stop so suddenly in the midst of them ? They are the pleasantest and best company, and they make you look quite happy and joyous.

Tasso. Corneliolina, dost thou remember Bergamo ? What city was ever so celebrated for honest and valiant men, in all classes, or for beautiful girls l There is but one class of those : Beauty is above all ranks ; the true Madonna, the patroness and bestower of felicity, the queen of heaven.

Cornelia. Hush, Torquato, hush ! talk not so.

Tasso. What rivers, how sunshiny and revelling, are the Brembo and the Serio l What a country the Valtellina! I went back to our father's house, thinking to find thee again, my little sister ; thinking to kick away thy ball of yellow silk as thou wast stooping for it, to make thee run after me and beat me. I woke early in the morning ; thou wert grown up and gone. Away to Sorrento : I knew the road : a few strides brought me back : here I am. To-morrow, my Cornelia, we will walk together, as we used to do, into the cool and quiet caves on the shore ; and we will catch the little breezes as they come in and go out again on the backs of the jocund waves.

Cornelia. We will indeed to-morrow ; but before we set out we must take a few hours' rest, that we may enjoy our ramble the better.

Tasso. Our Sorrentines, I see, are grown rich and avaricious. They have uprooted the old pomegranate hedges, and have built high walls to prohibit the wayfarer from their vineyards.

Cornelia. I have a basket of grapes for you in the book-room that overlooks our garden.

Tasso. Does the old twisted sage-tree grow still against the window ?

Cornelia. It harboured too many insects at last, and there was always a nest of scorpions in the crevice.

Tasso. O ! what a prince of a sage-tree ! And the well too, with its bucket of shining metal, large enough for the largest cocomero* to cool in it for dinner.

Cornelia. The well, I asure you, is as cool as ever.

Tasso. Delicious ! delicious ! And the stonework round it, bearing no other marks of waste then my pruning-hook and dagger left behind ?

Cornelia. None whatever.

Tasso. White in that place no longer ; There has been time enough for it to become all of one colour : grey, mossy, half-decayed.

Cornelia. No, no ; not even the rope has wanted repair.

Tasso. Who sings yonder ?

Cornelia. Enchanter ! No sooner did you say the word cocomero than here comes a boy carrying one upon his head.

Tasso. Listen ! listen ! I have read in some book or other those verses long ago. They are not unlike my *Aminta.* The very words !

* Water-melon.

Cornelia. Purifier of love, and humaniser of ferocity, how many, my Torquato, will your gentle thoughts make happy!

Tasso. At this moment I almost think I am one among them.*

Cornelia. Be quite persuaded of it. Come, brother, come with me. You shall bathe your heated brow and weary limbs in the chamber of your childhood. It is there we are always the most certain of repose. The boy shall sing to you those sweet verses; and we will reward him with a slice of his own fruit.

Tasso. He deserves it; cut it thick.

Cornelia. Come then, my truant! Come along, my sweet smiling Torquato!

Tasso. The passage is darker than ever. Is this the way to the little court? Surely those are not the steps that lead

---

* The miseries of Tasso arose not only from the imagination and the heart. In the metropolis of the Christian world, with many admirers and many patrons, bishops, cardinals, princes, he was left destitute, and almost famished. These are his own words : "*Appena* in questo stato ho comprato *due meloni :* e benche io sia stato *quasi sempre infermo,* molte volte mi sono contentato del : manzo e la ministra di latte o di zucca, *quando ho potuto averne,* mi e stata in vece di delizie." In another part he says that he was unable to pay the carriage of a parcel. No wonder ; if he had not wherewithal to buy enough of zucca for a meal. Even had he been in health and appetite, he might have satisfied his hunger with it for about five farthings, and have left half for supper. And now a word on his insanity. Having been so imprudent not only as to make it too evident in his poetry that he was the lover of Leonora, but also to signify (not very obscurely) that his love was returned, he much perplexed the Duke of Ferrara, who, with great discretion, suggested to him the necessity of feigning madness. The lady's honour required it from a brother ; and a true lover, to convince the world, would embrace the project with alacrity. But there was no reason why the seclusion should be in a dungeon, or why exercise and air should be interdicted. This cruelty, and perhaps his uncertainty of Leonora's compassion, may well be imagined to have produced at last the malady he had feigned. But did Leonora love Tasso as a man would be loved? If we wish to do her honour, let us hope it : for what greater glory can there be, than to have estimated at the full value so exalted a genius, so affectionate and so generous a heart!

down toward the bath ?   O yes ! we are right ; I smell
the lemon-blossoms.   Beware of the old wilding that bears
them ; it may catch your veil; it may scratch your fingers !
Pray, take care : it has many thorns about it.   And now,
Leonora ! you shall hear my last verses !   Lean your ear a
little toward me ; for I must repeat them softly under this
low archway, else others may hear them too.   Ah ! you
press my hand once more.   Drop it, drop it ! or the verses
will sink into my breast again, and lie there silent !   Good
girl !

> Many, well I know, there are
> Ready in your joys to share,
> And (I never blame it) you
> Are almost as ready too.
> But when comes the darker day,
> And those friends have dropt away,
> Which is there among them all
> You should, if you could, recall ?
> One who wisely loves and well
> Hears and shares the griefs you tell ;
> Him you ever call apart
> When the springs o'erflow the heart ;
> For you know that he alone
> Wishes they were *but* his own.
> Give, while these he may divide,
> Smiles to all the world beside.

Cornelia. We are now in the full light of the chamber ;
can not you remember it, having looked so intently all
around ?

Tasso. O sister ! I could have slept another hour.   You
thought I wanted rest : why did you waken me so early ?
I could have slept another hour or longer.   What a dream !
But I am calm and happy.

Cornelia. May you never more be otherwise !   Indeed,
he can not be whose last verses are such as those.

Tasso. Have you written any since that morning ?

Cornelia. What morning ?

Tasso. When you caught the swallow in my curtains, and
trod upon my knees in catching it, luckily with naked feet.
The little girl of thirteen laughed at the outcry of her

brother Torquatino, and sang without a blush her earliest lay.

Cornelia. I do not recollect it.

Tasso. I do.

> Rondinello ! rondinello !
> Tu sei nero, ma sei bello.
> Cosa fà se tu sei nero ?
> Rondinello ! sei il primiero
> De' volanti, palpitanti,
> (E vi sono quanti quanti !)
> Mai tenuto a questo petto,
> E perciò sei il mio diletto.*

Cornelia. Here is the cocomero; it can not be more insipid. Try it.

Tasso. Where is the boy who brought it? where is the boy who sang my Aminta? Serve him first; give him largely. Cut deeper; the knife is too short: deeper; mia brava Corneliolina! quite through all the red, and into the middle of the seeds. Well done!

---

* The author wrote the verses first in English, but he found it easy to write them better in Italian: they stood in the text as below: they only do for a girl of thirteen :—

> Swallow ! swallow ! though so jetty
> Are your pinions, you are pretty :
> And what matter were it though
> You were blacker than a crow ?
> Of the many birds that fly
> (And how many pass me by !)
> You're the first I ever prest,
> Of the many, to my breast :
> Therefore it is very right
> You should be my own delight.

PRINCESS MARY AND PRINCESS ELIZABETH.

Mary. My dear dear sister! it is long, very long, since we met.

Elizabeth. Methinks it was about the time they chopped off our uncle Seymour's head for him. Not that he was *our* uncle though . . . he was only Edward's.

Mary. The Lord Protector, if not your uncle, was always doatingly fond of you; and he often declared to me, even within your hearing, he thought you very beautiful.

Elizabeth. He said as much of you, if that is all; and he told me why . . . "*not to vex me*" . . . as if, instead of vexing me, it would not charm me. I beseech your Highness, is there anything remarkable or singular in thinking me . . . what he thought me?

Mary. No, indeed; for so you are. But why call me *Highness?* drawing back and losing half your stature in the circumference of the curtsey.

Elizabeth. Because you are now, at this blessed hour, my lawful queen.

Mary. Hush, prythee hush! The parliament has voted otherwise.

Elizabeth. They would chouse you.

Mary. What would they do with me?

Elizabeth. Trump you.

Mary. I am still at a loss.

Elizabeth. Bamboozle you.

Mary. Really, my dear sister, you have been so courted by the gallants, that you condescend to adopt their language, in place of graver.

Elizabeth. Cheat you then . . . will that do?

Mary. Comprehensibly.

Elizabeth. I always speak as the thing spoken of requires. To the point.   Would our father have minded the caitiffs?

Mary. Naming our father, I should have said, *our father now in bliss;* for surely he must be; having been a rock of defence against the torrent of irreligion.

Elizabeth. Well; in bliss or out, there, here, or anywhere, would he, royal soul! have minded parliament?   No such fool he.   There were laws before there were parliaments; and there were kings before there were laws.   Were I in your Majesty's place (God forbid the thought should ever enter my poor weak head, even in a dream!) I would try the mettle of my subjects: I would mount my horse, and head them.

Mary. Elizabeth! you were always a better horsewoman than I am: I should be ashamed to get a fall among the soldiers.

Elizabeth. Pish! Pish! it would be among knights and nobles . . . the worst come to the worst.   Lord o' mercy! do you think they never saw such a thing before?

Mary. I must hear of no resistance to the powers that be.   Besides, I am but a weak woman.

Elizabeth. I do not see why women should be weak, unless they like.

Mary. Not only the Commons, but likewise the peers, have sworn allegiance.

Elizabeth. Did you ever in your lifetime, in any chronicle or commentary, read of any parliament that was not as ready to be forsworn as to swear?

Mary. Alas!

Elizabeth. If ever you did, the book is a rare one, kept in an out-of-the-way library, in a cedar chest all to itself, with golden locks and amber seals thereto.

Mary. I would not willingly think so ill of men.

Elizabeth. For my part, I can't abide 'em.   All that can be said, is, some are not so bad as others.   You smile, and deem the speech a silly and superfluous one.   We may live, sister Mary, to see and acknowledge that it is not quite so sure and flat a verity as it now appears to us. I never come near a primrose but I suspect an adder under it; and the sunnier the day the more misgivings.

Mary. But we are now, by the settlement of the monarchy, farther out of harm's way than ever.

Elizabeth. If the wench has children to-morrow, as she may have, they will inherit.

Mary. No doubt they would.

Elizabeth. No doubt? I will doubt: and others shall doubt too. The heirs of my body . . . yours first . . . God prosper them! Parliament may be constrained to retrace its steps. One half sees no harm in taking bribes, the other no guilt in taking fright. Corruption is odious and costly : but, when people have yielded to compulsion, conscience is fain to acquiesce. Men say they were forced, and what is done under force is invalid.

Mary. There was nothing like compulsion.

Elizabeth. Then let there be. Let the few yield to the many, and all to the throne. Now is your time to stir. The furnace is mere smut, and no bellows to blow the embers. Parliament is without a leader. Three or four turnspits are crouching to leap upon the wheel ; but, while they are snarling and snapping one at another, what becomes of the roast? Take them by the scruff, and out with 'em. The people will applaud you. They want bread within doors, and honesty without. They have seen enough of partisans and parliaments.

Mary. We can not do without one.

Elizabeth. Convoke it then : but call it with sound of trumpet. Such a body is unlikely to find a head. There is little encouragement for an honest knight or gentleman to take the station. The Commons slink away with lowered shoulders, and bear hateful compunction against the very names and memory of those braver men, who, in dangerous times and before stern authoritative warlike sovrans, supported their pretensions. Kings, who peradventure would have strangled such ringleaders, well remember and

well respect them : their fellows would disown their bene-
factors and maintainers. Kings abominate their example ;
clowns would efface the images on their sepulchres. What
forbearance on our part can such knaves expect, or what
succour from the people ?

Mary. What is done is done.

Elizabeth. Oftentimes it is easier to undo than to do.
I should rather be glad than mortified at what has been
done yonder. In addition to those churls and chapmen in
the lower house, there are also among the peers no few who
voted most audaciously.

Mary. The majority of them was of opinion that the
Lady Jane should be invested with royal state and dignity.

Elizabeth. The majority ! So much the better . . . so
much the better, say I. I would find certain folk who
should make sharp inquest into their title-deeds, and spell
the indentures syllable by syllable. Certain lands were
granted for certain services ; which services have been
neglected. I would not in such wise neglect the lands in
question, but annex them to my royal domains.

Mary. Sister ! sister ! you forget that the Lady Jane
Gray (as was) is now queen of the realm.

Elizabeth. Forget it indeed ! The vile woman ! I am
minded to call her as such vile women are called out of
doors.

Mary. Pray abstain ; not only forasmuch as it would be
unseemly in those sweet, slender, delicate lips of yours, but
also by reason that she is adorned with every grace and
virtue, bating (which indeed outvalues them all) the true
religion. Sister ! I hope and believe I in this my speech
have given you no offence : for your own eyes, I know, are
opened. Indeed, who that is not wilfully blind can err in
so straight a road, even if so gentle and so sure a guidance
were wanting ? The mind, sister, the mind itself must
be crooked which deviates a hair's breadth. Ay, that
intelligent nod would alone suffice to set my bosom quite at
rest thereupon. Should it not ?

Elizabeth. It were imprudent in me to declare my real

opinion at this juncture. We must step warily when we walk among cockatrices. I am barely a saint; indeed far from it; and I am much too young to be a martyr. But that odious monster, who pretends an affection for reformation, and a reverence for learning, is counting the jewels in the crown, while you fancy she is repeating her prayers, or conning her Greek.

Sister Mary! as God is in heaven, I hold nothing so detestable in a woman as hypocrisy. Add thereunto, as you fairly may, avarice, man-hunting, lasciviousness. The least atom of the least among these vices is heavy enough to weigh down the soul to the bottomless pit.

Mary. Unless divine grace——

Elizabeth. Don't talk to me. Don't spread the filth fine.

Now could not that empty fool, Dudley, have found some other young person of equal rank with Mistress Jane, and of higher beauty? Not that any other such, pretty as the boy is, would listen to his idle discourse.

And, pray, who are these Dudleys? The first of them was made a man of by our grandfather. And what was the man after all? Nothing better than a huge smelting-pot, with a commodious screw at the colder end of the ladle.

I have no patience with the bold harlotry.

Mary. I see you have not, sister!

Elizabeth. No, nor have the people. They are on tip-toe for rising in all parts of the kingdom.

Mary. What can they do? God help them!

Elizabeth. Sister Mary! good sister Mary! did you say *God help them?* I am trembling into a heap. It is well you have uttered such works to safe and kindred ears. If they should ever come whispered at the Privy Council, it might end badly.

I believe my visit hath been of as long continuance as may seem befitting. I must be gone.

Mary. Before your departure, let me correct a few of your opinions in regard to our gentle kinswoman and most gracious queen. She hath nobly enlarged my poor alimony. Look here ! to begin.

Elizabeth. What ! all golden pieces ? I have not ten groats in the world.

Mary. Be sure she will grant unto you plenteously. She hath condescended to advise me of her intent. Meanwhile I do entreat you will take home with you the purse you are stroking down, thinking about other things.

Elizabeth. Not I, not I, if it comes from such a creature.

Mary. You accept it from me.

Elizabeth. Then indeed unreservedly. Passing through your hands the soil has been wiped away. However, as I live, I will carefully wash every piece in it with soap and water. Do you believe they can lose anything of their weight thereby ?

Mary. Nothing material.

Elizabeth. I may reflect and cogitate upon it. I would not fain offer anybody light money.

Troth ! I fear the purse, although of chamois and double stitched, is insufficient to sustain the weight of the gold, which must be shaken violently on the road as I return. Dear sister Mary ! as you probably are not about to wear that head-tire, could you, commodiously to yourself, lend it me awhile, just to deposit a certain part of the moneys therein ? for the velvet is stout, and the Venetian netting close and stiff : I can hardly bend the threads. I shall have more leisure to admire its workmanship at home.

Mary. Elizabeth ! I see you are grown forgiving. In the commencement of our discourse I suggested a slight alteration of manner in speaking of our father. Do you pray for the repose of his soul morning and night ?

Elizabeth. The doubt is injurious.

Mary. Pardon me ! I feel it. But the voices of children, O Elizabeth ! come to the ear of God above all other voices. The best want intercession. Pray for him, Elizabeth ! pray for him.

Elizabeth. Why not ? He did indeed, but he was in a

passion, order my mother up the three black stairs, and he
left her pretty head on the landing; but I bear him no
malice for it.

Mary. Malice ! The baneful word hath shot up from hell
in many places, but never between child and parent. In
the space of that one span, on that single sod from Paradise,
the serpent never trailed. Husband and wife were severed
by him, then again clashed together : brother slew brother :
but parent and child stand where their Creator first placed
them, and drink at the only source of pure untroubled love.

Elizabeth. Beside, you know, being king, he had clearly
a right to do it, plea or no plea.

Mary. We will converse no longer on so dolorous a
subject.

Elizabeth. I will converse on it as long as such is my
pleasure.

Mary. Being my visitor, you command here.

Elizabeth. I command nowhere. I am blown about like
a leaf : I am yielding as a feather in a cushion, only one
among a million. But I tell you, honestly and plainly, I do
not approve of it anyhow ! It may have grown into a trick
and habit with him : no matter for that : in my view of the
business, it is not what a husband ought to do with a wife.
And, if she did . . . but she did not . . . and I say it.

Mary. It seems indeed severe.

Elizabeth. Yea, afore God, methinks it smacks a trifle of
the tart. ·

Mary. Our father was God's vicegerent. Probably it
is for the good of her soul, poor lady ! Better suffer
here than hereafter. We ought to kiss the rod, and be
thankful.

Elizabeth. Kiss the rod, forsooth. I have been constrained erewhile even unto that ; and no such a child
neither. But I would rather have kissed it fresh and fair,
with all its buds and knots upon it, than after it had
bestowed on me, in such a roundabout way, such a deal of
its embroidery and lace-work. I thank my father for all
that. I hope his soul lies easier than my skin did.

Mary. The wish is kind; but prayers would much help it. Our father of blessed memory, now (let us hope) among the saints, was somewhat sore in his visitations; but they tended heavenward.

Elizabeth. Yea, when he cursed and cuffed and kicked us.

Mary. He did kick, poor man!

Elizabeth. Kick! Fifty folks, young and old, have seen the marks his kicking left behind.

Mary. We should conceal all such his infirmities. They arose from an irritation in the foot, whereof he died.

Elizabeth. I only know I could hardly dance or ride for them; chiefly caught, as I was, fleeing from his wrath. He seldom vouchsafed to visit me: when he did, he pinched my ear so bitterly, I was fain to squeal. And then he said, I should turn out like my mother, calling me by such a name moreover as is heard but about the kennel; and even there it is never given to the young.

Mary. There was choler in him at certain times and seasons. Those who have much will, have their choler excited when opposite breath blows against it.

Elizabeth. Let them have will; let them have choler too, in God's name; but it is none the better, as gout is, for flying to hand or foot.

Mary. I have seen . . . now do, pray forgive me . . .

Elizabeth. Well, what have you seen?

Mary. My sweet little sister lift up the most delicate of all delicate white hands, and with their tiny narrow pink nails tear off ruffs and caps, and take sundry unerring aims at eyes and noses.

Elizabeth. Was that any impediment or hindrance to riding and dancing? I would always make people do their duty, and always will. Remember (for your memory seems accurate enough) that, whenever I scratched anybody's face, I permitted my hand to be kist by the offender within a day or two.

Mary. Undeniable.

Elizabeth. I may, peradventure, have been hasty in my

childhood : but all great hearts are warm ; all good ones are relenting. If, in combing my hair, the hussy lugged it, I obeyed God's command, and referred to the *lex talionis.* I have not too much of it ; and every soul on earth sees its beauty. A single one would be a public loss. Uncle Seymour . . . but what boots it ? there are others who can see perhaps as far as uncle Seymour.

Mary. I do remember his saying that he watched its growth as he would a melon's. And how fondly did those little sharp grey eyes of his look and wink when you blushed and chided his flattery.

Elizabeth. Never let any man dare to flatter me : I am above it. Only the weak and ugly want the refreshment of that perfumed fan. I take but my own ; and touch it who dares.

Really it is pleasant to see in what a pear-form fashion both purse and cowl are hanging. Faith ! they are heavy : I could hardly lift them from the back of the chair.

Mary. Let me call an attendant to carry them for you.

Elizabeth. Are you mad ? They are unsealed, and ill-tied : anyone could slip his hand in.

And so that . . . the word was well nigh out of my mouth . . . gave you all this gold.

Mary. For shame ! O for shame !

Elizabeth. I feel shame only for her. It turns my cheeks red . . . together with some anger upon it. But I can not keep my eyes off that book, if book it may be, on which the purse was lying.

Mary. Somewhat irreverently, God forgive me ! But it was sent at the same time by the same fair creature, with many kind words. It had always been kept in our father's bedroom closet, and was removed from Edward's by those unhappy men who superintended his education.

Elizabeth. She must have thought all those stones are garnets : to me they look like rubies, one and all. Yet, over so large a cover, they cannot all be rubies.

Mary. I believe they are, excepting the glory in the centre, which is composed of chrysolites. Our father was an excellent judge in jewellery, as in every thing else, and he spared no expenditure in objects of devotion.

Elizabeth. What creature could fail in devotion with an object such as that before the eyes ? Let me kiss it . . . partly for my Saviour's and partly for my father's sake.

Mary. How it comforts me, O Elizabeth, to see you thus press it to your bosom ! Its spirit, I am confident, has entered there. Disregard the pebbles : take it home : cherish it evermore. May there be virtue, as some think there is, even in the stones about it ! God bless you, strengthen you, lead you aright, and finally bring you to everlasting glory.

Elizabeth (going). The Popish puss !

LA FONTAINE AND DE LA ROCHEFOUCAULT.

La Fontaine. I am truly sensible of the honour I receive, M. de la Rochefoucault, in a visit from a personage so distinguished by his birth and by his genius. Pardon my ambition, if I confess to you that I have long and ardently wished for the good fortune, which I never could promise myself, of knowing you personally.

Rochefoucault. My dear M. de la Fontaine !

La Fontaine. Not *"de* la," not *"de* la." I am *La* Fontaine purely and simply.

Rochefoucault. The whole ; not derivative. You appear, in the midst of your purity, to have been educated at court, in the lap of the ladies. What was the last day (pardon !) I had the misfortune to miss you there ?

La Fontaine. I never go to court. They say one can not go without silk stockings ; and I have only thread : plenty of them indeed, thank God ! Yet, would you believe it ? Nanon, in putting a *solette* to the bottom of one, last week, sewed it so carelessly, she made a kind of cord across : and I verily believe it will lame me for life ; for I walked the whole morning upon it.

Rochefoucault. She ought to be whipt.

La Fontaine. I thought so too, and grew the warmer at being unable to find a wisp of osier or a roll of packthread in the house. Barely had I begun with my garter, when in came the bishop of Grasse, my old friend Godeau, and another lord, whose name he mentioned, and they both interceded for her so long and so touchingly, that at last I was fain to let her rise up and go. I never saw men look down on the erring and afflicted more compassionately. The bishop was quite concerned for me also. But the other, although he professed to feel even more, and said that it must surely be the pain of purgatory to me, took a pinch of snuff, opened his waistcoat, drew down his ruffles, and seemed rather more indifferent.

Rochefoucault. Providentially, in such moving scenes, the worst is soon over. But Godeau's friend was not too sensitive.

La Fontaine. Sensitive ! no more than if he had been educated at the butcher's or the Sorbonne.

Rochefoucault. I am afraid there are as many hard hearts under satin waistcoats as there are ugly visages under the same material in miniature cases.

La Fontaine. My lord, I could show you a miniature case which contains your humble servant, in which the painter has done what no tailor in his senses would do ; he has given me credit for a coat of violet silk, with silver frogs as large as tortoises. But I am loth to get up for it while the generous heart of this dog (if I mentioned his name he would jump up) places such confidence on my knee.

Rochefoucault. Pray do not move on any account ; above all, lest you should disturb that amiable grey cat, fast asleep in his innocence on your shoulder.

La Fontaine. Ah, rogue ! art thou there ? Why ! thou hast not licked my face this half-hour.

Rochefoucault. And more too, I should imagine. I do not judge from his somnolency, which, if he were President of the Parliament, could not be graver, but from his natural sagacity. Cats weigh practicabilities. What sort of tongue has he ?

La Fontaine. He has the roughest tongue and the tenderest heart of any cat in Paris. If you observe the colour of his coat, it is rather blue than grey ; a certain indication of goodness in these contemplative creatures.

Rochefoucault. We were talking of his tongue alone ; by which cats, like men, are flatterers.

La Fontaine. Ah ! you gentlemen of the court are much

mistaken in thinking that vices have so extensive a range. There are some of our vices, like some of our diseases, from which the quadrupeds are exempt ; and those, both diseases and vices, are the most discreditable.

Rochefoucault. I do not bear patiently any evil spoken of the court: for it must be acknowledged, by the most malicious, that the court is the purifier of the whole nation.

La Fontaine. I know little of the court, and less of the whole nation ; but how can this be ?

Rochefoucault. It collects all ramblers and gamblers ; all the market-men and market-women who deal in articles which God has thrown into their baskets, without any trouble on their part ; all the seducers and all who wish to be seduced ; all the duellists who erase their crimes with their swords, and sweat out their cowardice with daily practice ; all the nobles whose patents of nobility lie in gold snuff-boxes, or have worn Mechlin ruffles, or are deposited within the archives of knee-deep waistcoats ; all stock-jobbers and church-jobbers, the black-legged and the red-legged game, the flower of the *justaucorps*, the *robe*, and the *soutane.* If these were spread over the surface of France, instead of close compressure in the court or cabinet, they would corrupt the whole country in two years. As matters now stand, it will require a quarter of a century to effect it.

La Fontaine. Am I not right then in preferring my beasts to yours ? But if yours were loose, mine (as you prove to me) would be the last to suffer by it, poor dear creatures ! Speaking of cats, I would have avoided all personality that might be offensive to them : I would not exactly have said, in so many words, that, by their tongues, they are flatterers, like men. Language may take a turn advantageously in favour of our friends. True, we resemble all animals in something. I am quite ashamed and mortified that your lordship, or anybody, should have had the start of me in this reflection. When a cat flatters with his tongue he is not insincere: you may safely take it for a real kindness.

He is loyal, M. de la Rochefoucault! my word for him, he is loyal. Observe too, if you please, no cat ever licks you when he wants anything from you; so that there is nothing of baseness in such an act of adulation, if we must call it so. For my part, I am slow to designate by so foul a name, that (be it what it may) which is subsequent to a kindness. Cats ask plainly for what they want.

Rochefoucault. And, if they can not get it by protocols they get it by invasion and assault.

La Fontaine. No! no! usually they go elsewhere, and fondle those from whom they obtain it. In this I see no resemblance to invaders and conquerors. I draw no parallels: I would excite no heart-burnings between us and them. Let all have their due.

I do not like to lift this creature off, for it would waken him, else I could find out, by some subsequent action, the reason why he has not been on the alert to lick my cheek for so long a time.

Rochefoucault. Cats are wary and provident. He would not enter into any contest with you, however friendly. He only licks your face, I presume, while your beard is but a match for his tongue.

La Fontaine. Ha! you remind me. Indeed I did begin to think my beard was rather of the roughest; for yesterday Madame de Rambouillet sent me a plate of strawberries, the first of the season, and raised (would you believe it?) under glass. One of these strawberries was dropping from my lips, and I attempted to stop it. When I thought it had fallen to the ground, "Look for it, Nanon; pick it up and eat it," said I.

"Master!" cried the wench, "your beard has skewered and spitted it." "Honest girl," I answered, "come, cull it from the bed of its adoption."

I had resolved to shave myself this morning: but our wisest and best resolutions too often come to nothing, poor mortals!

Rochefoucault. We often do very well everything but the only thing we hope to do best of all; and our projects often drop from us by their weight. A little while ago your friend Molière exhibited a remarkable proof of it.

La Fontaine. Ah, poor Molière! the best man in the world; but flighty, negligent, thoughtless. He throws himself into other men, and does not remember where. The sight of an eagle, M. de la Rochefoucault, but the memory of a fly.

Rochefoucault. I will give you an example : but perhaps it is already known to you. · ·

La Fontaine. Likely enough. We have each so many friends, neither of us can trip but the other is invited to the laugh. Well; I am sure he has no malice, and I hope I have none : but who can see his own faults?

Rochefoucault. He had brought out a new edition of his comedies.

La Fontaine. There will be fifty; there will be a hundred: nothing in our language, or in any, is so delightful, so graceful; I will add, so clear at once and so profound.

Rochefoucault. You are among the few who, seeing well his other qualities, see that Molière is also profound. In order to present the new edition to the Dauphin, he had put on a sky-blue velvet coat, powdered with fleur-de-lis. He laid the volume on his library table; and, resolving that none of the courtiers should have an opportunity of ridiculing him for anything like absence of mind, he returned to his bedroom, which, as may often be the case · in the economy of poets, is also his dressing-room. Here he surveyed himself in his mirror, as well as the creeks and lagoons in it would permit.

La Fontaine. I do assure you, from my own observation, M. de la Rochefoucault, that his mirror is a splendid one. I should take it to be nearly three feet high, reckoning the frame, with the Cupid above and the elephant under. I suspected it was the present of some great lady; and indeed I have since heard as much.

Rochefoucault. Perhaps then the whole story may be quite as fabulous as the part of it which I have been relating.

La Fontaine. In that case, I may be able to set you right again.

Rochefoucault. He found his peruke a model of perfection; tight, yet easy; not an inch more on one side than on the other.   The black patch on the forehead . . .

La Fontaine. Black patch too! I would have given a fifteen-sous piece to have caught him with that black patch.

Rochefoucault. He found it lovely, marvellous, irresistible. Those on each cheek . . .

La Fontaine. Do you tell me he had one on each cheek?

Rochefoucault. Symmetrically.   The cravat was of its proper descent, and with its appropriate charge of the best Strasburg snuff upon it.   The waistcoat, for a moment, puzzled and perplexed him.   He was not quite sure whether the right number of buttons were in their holes; nor how many above, nor how many below, it was the fashion of the week to leave without occupation.   Such a piece of ignorance is enough to disgrace any courtier on earth.   He was in the act of striking his forehead with desperation; but he thought of the patch, fell on his knees, and thanked heaven for the intervention.

La Fontaine. Just like him! just like him! good soul!

Rochefoucault. The breeches . . . ah! those require attention: all proper: everything in its place.   Magnificent. The stockings rolled up, neither too loosely nor too negligently.   A picture!   The buckles in the shoes . . . all but one . . . soon set to rights . . . well thought of! And now the sword . . . ah, that cursed sword! it will bring at least one man to the ground if it has its own way much longer . . . up with it! up with it higher . . . *Allons!* we are out of danger.

La Fontaine. Delightful! I have him before my eyes. What simplicity! aye, what simplicity!

Rochefoucault. Now for hat.   Feather in?   Five at least. Bravo!

He took up hat and plumage, extended his arm to the full length, raised it a foot above his head, lowered it thereon, opened his fingers, and let them fall again at his side.

La Fontaine. Something of the comedian in that; aye, M. de la Rochefoucault? But, on the stage or off, all is natural in Molière.

Rochefoucault. Away he went: he reached the palace, stood before the Dauphin . . . O consternation! O despair! "Morbleau! bête que je suis," exclaimed the hapless man, "le livre, où donc est-il?" You are forcibly struck, I perceive, by this adventure of your friend.

La Fontaine. Strange coincidence! quite unaccountable! There are agents at work in our dreams, M. de la Rochefoucault, which we shall never see out of them, on this side the grave. [*To himself.*] Sky-blue? no. Fleurs-de-lis? bah! bah! Patches? I never wore one in my life.

Rochefoucault. It well becomes your character for generosity, M. la Fontaine, to look grave, and ponder, and ejaculate, on a friend's untoward accident, instead of laughing, as those who little know you, might expect. I beg your pardon for relating the occurrence.

La Fontaine. Right or wrong, I can not help laughing any longer. Comical, by my faith! above the tip-top of comedy. Excuse my flashes and dashes and rushes of merriment. Incontrollable! incontrollable! Indeed the laughter is immoderate. And you all the while are sitting as grave as a judge; I mean a criminal one; who has nothing to do but to keep up his popularity by sending his rogues to the gallows. The civil indeed have much weighty matter on their minds: they must displease one party: and sometimes a doubt arises whether the fairer hand or the fuller shall turn the balance.

Rochefoucault. I congratulate you on the return of your gravity and composure.

La Fontaine. Seriously now: all my lifetime I have been the plaything of dreams. Sometimes they have taken such possession of me, that nobody could persuade me afterward they were other than real events. Some are very oppressive, very painful, M. de la Rochefoucault! I have never been able, altogether, to disembarrass my head of the most wonderful vision that ever took possession of any man's.   There are some truly important differences, but in many respects this laughable adventure of my innocent, honest friend Molière seemed to have befallen myself.   I can only account for it by having heard the tale when I was half-asleep.

Rochefoucault. Nothing more probable.

La Fontaine. You absolutely have relieved me from an incubus.

Rochefoucault. I do not yet see how.

La Fontaine. No longer ago than when you entered this chamber, I would have sworn that I myself had gone to the Louvre, that I myself had been commanded to attend the dauphin, that I myself had come into his presence,* had fallen on my knee, and cried, "Peste! où est donc le livre!"   Ah, M. de la Rochefoucault, permit me to embrace you: this is really to find a friend at court.

Rochefoucault. My visit is even more auspicious than I could have ventured to expect: it was chiefly for the purpose of asking your permission to make another at my return to Paris . . . I am forced to go into the country on some family affairs: but hearing that you have spoken favourably of my *Maxims*, I presume to express my satisfaction and delight at your good opinion.

La Fontaine. Pray, M. de la Rochefoucault, do me the favour to continue here a few minutes: I would gladly reason with you on some of your doctrines.

Rochefoucault. For the pleasure of hearing your sentiments on the topics I have treated, I will, although it is late, steal a few minutes from the court, of which I must take my leave on parting for the province.

La Fontaine. Are you quite certain that all your *Maxims* are true, or, what is of greater consequence, that they are all original?   I have lately read a treatise written by an Englishman, Mr. Hobbes; so loyal a man that, while others tell you kings are appointed by God, he tells you God is appointed by kings.

---

* This happened.

Rochefoucault. Ah I such are precisely the men we want. If he establishes this verity, the rest will follow.

La Fontaine. He does not seem to care so much about the rest. In his treatise I find the ground-plan of your chief positions.

Rochefoucault. I have indeed looked over his publication; and we agree on the natural depravity of man.

La Fontaine. Reconsider your expression. It appears to me that what is natural is not depraved : that depravity is deflection from nature. Let it pass : I can not, however, concede to you that the generality of men are naturally bad. Badness is accidental, like disease. We find more tempers good than bad, where proper care is taken in proper time.

Rochefoucault. Care is not nature.

La Fontaine. Nature is soon inoperative without it ; so soon indeed as to allow no opportunity for experiment or hypothesis. Life itself requires care, and more continually than tempers and morals do. The strongest body ceases to be a body in a few days without a supply of food. When we speak of men being naturally bad or good, we mean susceptible and retentive and communicative of them. In this case (and there can be no other true or ostensible one) I believe that the more are good ; and nearly in the same proportion as there are animals and plants produced healthy and vigorous than wayward and weakly. Strange is the opinion of Mr. Hobbes, that, when God hath poured so abundantly his benefits on other creatures, the only one capable of great good should be uniformly disposed to greater evil.

Rochefoucault. Yet Holy Writ, to which Hobbes would reluctantly appeal, countenances the supposition.

La Fontaine. The Jews, above all nations, were morose and splenetic. Nothing is holy to me that lessens in my view the beneficence of my Creator. If you could show him ungentle and unkind in a single instance, you would render myriads of men so, throughout the whole course of their lives, and those too among the most religious. The less that people talk about God, the better.   He has left us a design to fill up : he has placed the canvas, the colours, and the pencils, within reach ; his directing hand is over ours incessantly ; it is our business to follow it, and neither to turn round and argue with our master, nor to kiss and fondle him. We must mind our lesson, and not neglect our time : for the room is closed early, and the lights are suspended in another, where no one works.   If every man would do all the good he might within an hour's walk from his house, he would live the happier and the longer : for nothing is so conducive to longevity as the union of activity and content.   But, like children, we deviate from the road, however well we know it, and run into mire and puddles in despite of frown and ferule.

Rochefoucault. Go on, M. la Fontaine ! pray go on.   We are walking in the same labyrinth, always within call, always within sight of each other.   We set out at its two extremities, and shall meet at last.

La Fontaine. I doubt it.   From deficiency of care proceed many vices, both in men and children, and more still from care taken improperly.   M. Hobbes attributes not only the order and peace of society, but equity and moderation and every other virtue, to the coercion an restriction of the laws.   The laws, as now constituted, do a great deal of good ; they also do a great deal of mischief. They transfer more property from the right owner in six months than all the thieves of the kingdom do in twelve. What the thieves take they soon disseminate abroad again ; what the laws take they hoard.   The thief takes a part of your property : he who prosecutes the thief for you takes another part : he who condemns the thief goes to the tax-gatherer and takes the third.   Power has been hitherto occupied in no employment but in keeping down Wisdom. Perhaps the time may come when Wisdom shall exert her energy in repressing the sallies of Power.

Rochefoucault. I think it more probable that they will agree ; that they will call together their servants of all liveries, to collect what they can lay their hands upon ; and that meanwhile they will sit together like good housewives, making nets from our purses to cover the coop for us. If you would be plump and in feather, pick up your millet and be quiet in your darkness. Speculate on nothing here below, and I promise you a nosegay in Paradise.

La Fontaine. Believe me, I shall be most happy to receive it there at your hands, my lord duke.

The greater number of men, I am inclined to think, with all the defects of education, all the frauds committed on their credulity, all the advantages taken of their ignorance and supineness, are disposed, on most occasions, rather to virtue than to vice, rather to the kindly affections than the unkindly, rather to the social than the selfish.

Rochefoucault. Here we differ : and were my opinion the same as yours, my book would be little read and less commended.

La Fontaine. Why think so ?

Rochefoucault. For this reason. Every man likes to hear evil of all men : every man is delighted to take the air of the common, though not a soul will consent to stand within his own allotment. No inclosure-act ! no finger-posts ! You may call every creature under heaven fool and rogue, and your auditor will join with you heartily : hint to him the slightest of his own defects or foibles, and he draws the rapier. You and he are the judges of the world, but not its denizens.

La Fontaine. Mr. Hobbes has taken advantage of these weaknesses. In his dissertation he betrays the timidity and malice of his character. It must be granted he reasons well, according to the view he has taken of things ; but he has given no proof whatever that his view is a correct one. I will believe that it is, when I am persuaded that sickness is the natural state of the body, and health the unnatural. If you call him a sound philosopher, you may call a mummy a sound man. Its darkness, its hardness, its forced uprightness, and the place in which you find it, may commend it to you ; give me rather some weakness and peccability, with vital warmth and human sympathies. A shrewd reasoner is one thing, a sound philosopher is another. I admire your power and precision. Monks will admonish us how little the author of the *Maxims* knows of the world; and heads of colleges will cry out "a libel on human nature!" but when they hear your titles, and, above all, your credit at court, they will cast back cowl, and peruke, and lick your boots. You start with great advantages. Throwing off from a dukedom, you are sure of enjoying, if not the tongue of these puzzlers, the full cry of the more animating, and will certainly be as long-lived as the imperfection of our language will allow. I consider your *Maxims* as a broken ridge of hills, on the shady side of which you are fondest of taking your exercise : but the same ridge hath also a sunny one. You attribute (let me say it again) all actions to self-interest. Now, a sentiment of interest must be preceded by calculation, long or brief, right or erroneous. Tell me then in what region lies the origin of that pleasure which a family in the country feels on the arrival of an unexpected friend. I say a family in the country; because the sweetest souls, like the sweetest flowers, soon canker in cities, and no purity is rarer there than the purity of delight. If I may judge from the few examples I have been in a position to see, no earthly one can be greater. There are pleasures which lie near the surface, and which are blocked up by artificial ones, or are diverted by some mechanical scheme, or are confined by some stiff evergreen vista of low advantage. But these pleasures do occasionally burst forth in all their brightness ; and, if ever you shall by chance find one of them, you will sit by it, I hope, complacently and cheerfully, and turn toward it the kindliest aspect of your meditations.

Rochefoucault. Many, indeed most people, will differ from me. Nothing is quite the same to the intellect of any two men, much less of all. When one says to another, "I am entirely of your opinion," he uses in general an easy and indifferent phrase, believing in its accuracy, without examination, without thought. The nearest resemblance in opinions, if we could trace every line of it, would be found

greatly more divergent than the nearest in the human form
or countenance, and in the same proportion as the varieties
of mental qualities are more numerous and fine than of the
bodily. Hence I do not expect nor wish that my opinions
should in all cases be similar to those of others : but in
many I shall be gratified if, by just degrees and after a long
survey, those of others approximate to mine. Nor does
this my sentiment spring from a love of power, as in many
good men quite unconsciously, when they would make
proselytes, since I shall see few and converse with fewer of
them, and profit in no way by their adherence and favour ;
but it springs from a natural and a cultivated love of all
truths whatever, and from a certainty that these delivered
by me are conducive to the happiness and dignity of man.
You shake your head.

La Fontaine. Make it out.

Rochefoucault. I have pointed out to him at what passes
he hath deviated from his true interest, and where he hath
mistaken selfishness for generosity, coldness for judgment,
contraction of heart for policy, rank for merit, pomp for
dignity ; of all mistakes, the commonest and the greatest.
I am accused of paradox and distortion. On paradox I
shall only say, that every new moral truth has been called
so. Inexperienced and negligent observers see no difference in the operations of ravelling and unravelling : they
never come close enough : they despise plain work.

La Fontaine. The more we simplify things, the better we
descry their substances and qualities. A good writer will
not coil them up and press them into the narrowest possible
space, nor macerate them into such particles that nothing
shall be remaining of their natural contexture. You are
accused of this too, by such as have forgotten your title-
page, and who look for treatises where maxims only have
been promised. Some of them perhaps are spinning out
sermons and dissertations from the poorest paragraph in the
volume.

Rochefoucault. Let them copy and write as they please ;
against or for, modestly or impudently. I have hitherto

had no assailant who is not of too slender a make to be detained an hour in the stocks he has unwarily put his foot into. If you hear of any, do not tell of them. On the subjects of my remarks, had others thought as I do, my labour would have been spared me. I am ready to point out the road where I know it, to whosoever wants it; but I walk side by side with few or none.

La Fontaine. We usually like those roads which show us the fronts of our friends' houses and the pleasure-grounds about them, and the smooth garden-walks, and the trim espaliers, and look at them with more satisfaction than at the docks and nettles that are thrown in heaps behind. The *Offices* of Cicero are imperfect; yet who would not rather guide his children by them than by the line and compass of harder-handed guides; such as Hobbes for instance?

Rochefoucault. Imperfect as some gentlemen in hoods may call the *Offices*, no founder of a philosophical or of a religious sect has been able to add to them anything important.

La Fontaine. Pity! that Cicero carried with him no better authorities than reason and humanity. He neither could work miracles, nor damn you for disbelieving them. Had he lived fourscore years later, who knows but he might have been another Simon Peter, and have talked Hebrew as fluently as Latin, all at once! Who knows but we might have heard of his patrimony! who knows but our venerable popes might have claimed dominion from him, as descendant from the kings of Rome!

Rochefoucault. The hint, some centuries ago, would have made your fortune, and that saintly cat there would have kittened in a mitre.

La Fontaine. Alas! the hint could have done nothing: Cicero could not have lived later.

Rochefoucault. I warrant him. Nothing is easier to correct than chronology. There is not a lady in Paris, nor a jockey in Normandy, that is not eligible to a professor's chair in it. I have seen a man's ancestor, whom nobody ever saw before, spring back over twenty generations. Our Vatican Jupiters have as little respect for old Chronos as the Cretan had : they mutilate him when and where they think necessary, limp as he may by the operation.

La Fontaine. When I think, as you make me do, how ambitious men are, even those whose teeth are too loose (one would fancy) for a bite at so hard an apple as the devil of ambition offers them, I am inclined to believe that we are actuated not so much by selfishness as you represent it, but under another form, the love of power. Not to speak of territorial dominion or political office, and such other things as we usually class under its appurtenances, do we not desire an exclusive control over what is beautiful and lovely? the possession of pleasant fields, of well-situated houses, of cabinets, of images, of pictures, and indeed of many things pleasant to see but useless to possess ; even of rocks, of streams, and of fountains? These things, you will tell me, have their utility. True, but not to the wisher, nor does the idea of it enter his mind. Do not we wish that the object of our love should be devoted to us only , and that our children should love us better than their brothers and sisters, or even than the mother who bore them? Love would be arrayed in the purple robe of sovranty, mildly as he may resolve to exercise his power.

Rochefoucault. Many things which appear to be incontrovertible are such for their age only, and must yield to others which, in their age, are equally so. There are only a few points that are always above the waves. Plain truths, like plain dishes, are commended by everybody, and everybody leaves them whole. If it were not even more impertinent and presumptuous to praise a great writer in his presence than to censure him in his absence, I would venture to say that your prose, from the few specimens you have given of it, is equal to your verse. Yet, even were I the possessor of such a style as yours, I would never employ it to support my *Maxims.* You would think a writer very impudent and self-sufficient who should quote his own works : to defend them is doing more. We are the worst auxiliaries in the world to the opinions we have brought into the field. Our business is, to measure the ground, and to calculate the forces ; then let them try their strength. If the weak assails me, he thinks me weak ; if the strong, he thinks me strong. He is more likely to compute ill his own vigour than mine. At all events, I love inquiry, even when I myself sit down. And I am not offended in my walks if my visitor asks me whither does that alley lead. It proves that he is ready to go on with me ; that he sees some space before him; and that he believes there may be something worth looking after.

La Fontaine. You have been standing a long time, my lord duke : I must entreat you to be seated.

Rochefoucault. Excuse me, my dear M. la Fontaine ; I would much rather stand.

La Fontaine. Mercy on us ! have you been upon your legs ever since you rose to leave me ?

Rochefoucault. A change of position is agreeable : a friend always permits it.

La Fontaine. Sad doings ! sad oversight ! The other two chairs were sent yesterday evening to be scoured and mended. But that dog is the best-tempered dog ! an angel of a dog, I do assure you ; he would have gone down in a moment, at a word. I am quite ashamed of myself for such inattention. With your sentiments of friendship for me, why could you not have taken the liberty to shove him gently off, rather than give me this uneasiness ?

Rochefoucault. My true and kind friend ! we authors are too sedentary ; we are heartily glad of standing to converse, whenever we can do it without any restraint on our acquaintance.

La Fontaine. I must reprove that animal when he uncurls his body. He seems to be dreaming of Paradise and Houris. Ay, twitch thy ear, my child ! I wish at my heart there were as troublesome a fly about the other : God forgive me ! The rogue covers all my clean linen ! shirt and cravat ! what cares he !

Rochefoucault. Dogs are not very modest.

La Fontaine. Never say that, M. de la Rochefoucault! The most modest people upon earth! Look at a dog's eyes, and he half closes them, or gently turns them away, with a motion of the lips, which he licks languidly, and of the tail, which he stirs tremulously, begging your forbearance. I am neither blind nor indifferent to the defects of these good and generous creatures. They are subject to many such as men are subject to: among the rest, they disturb the neighbourhood in the discussion of their private causes; they quarrel and fight on small motives, such as a little bad food, or a little vain-glory, or the sex. But it must be something present or near that excites them; and they calculate not the extent of evil they may do or suffer.

Rochefoucault. Certainly not: how should dogs calculate?

La Fontaine. I know nothing of the process. I am unable to inform you how they leap over hedges and brooks, with exertion just sufficient, and no more. In regard to honour and a sense of dignity, let me tell you, a dog accepts the subsidies of his friends, but never claims them: a dog would not take the field to obtain power for a son, but would leave the son to obtain it by his own activity and prowess. He conducts his visitor or inmate out a-hunting, and makes a present of the game to him as freely as an emperor to an elector. Fond as he is of slumber, which is indeed one of the pleasantest and best things in the universe, particularly after dinner, he shakes it off as willingly as he would a gadfly, in order to defend his master from theft or violence. Let the robber or assailant speak as courteously as he may, he waives your diplomatical terms, gives his reasons in plain language, and makes war. I could say many other things to his advantage; but I never was malicious, and would rather let both parties plead for themselves; give me the dog, however.

Rochefoucault. Faith! I will give you both, and never boast of my largess in so doing.

La Fontaine. I trust I have removed from you the suspicion of selfishness in my client, and I feel it quite as easy to make a properer disposal of another ill attribute, namely cruelty, which we vainly try to shuffle off our own shoulders upon others, by employing the offensive and most unjust term, brutality. But to convince you of my impartiality, now I have defended the dog from the first obloquy, I will defend the man from the last, hoping to make you think better of each. What you attribute to cruelty, both while we are children and afterward, may be assigned, for the greater part, to curiosity. Cruelty tends to the extinction of life, the dissolution of matter, the imprisonment and sepulture of truth ; and if it were our ruling and chief propensity, the human race would have been extinguished in a few centuries after its appearance. Curiosity, in its primary sense, implies care and consideration.

Rochefoucault. Words often deflect from their primary sense. We find the most curious men the most idle and silly, the least observant and conservative.

La Fontaine. So we think ; because we see every hour the idly curious, and not the strenuously ; we see only the persons of the one set, and only the works of the other.

More is heard of cruelty than of curiosity, because while curiosity is silent both in itself and about its òbject, cruelty on most occasions is like the wind, boisterous in itself, and exciting a murmur and bustle in all the things it moves among. Added to which, many of the higher topics whereto our curiosity would turn, are intercepted from it by the policy of our guides and rulers ; while the principal ones on which cruelty is most active, are pointed to by the sceptre and the truncheon, and wealth and dignity are the rewards of their attainment. What perversion ! He who brings a bullock into a city for its sustenance is called a butcher, and nobody has the civility to take off the hat to him, although knowing him as perfectly as I know Matthieu le Mince, who served me with those fine kidneys you must have remarked in passing through the kitchen :

on the contrary, he who reduces the same city to famine is styled M. le General or M. le Merechal, and gentlemen like you, unprejudiced (as one would think) and upright, make room for him in the antechamber.

Rochefoucault. He obeys orders without the degrading influence of any passion.

La Fontaine. Then he commits a baseness the more, a cruelty the greater. He goes off at another man's setting, as ingloriously as a rat-trap : he produces the worst effects of fury, and feels none : a Cain unirritated by a brother's incense.

Rochefoucault. I would hide from you this little rapier, which, like the barber's pole, I have often thought too obtrusive in the streets.

La Fontaine. Never shall I think my countrymen half civilised while on the dress of a courtier is hung the instrument of a cut-throat. How deplorably feeble must be that honour which requires defending at every hour of the day !

Rochefoucault. Ingenious as you are, M. Fontaine, I do not believe that, on this subject, you could add anything to what you have spoken already ; but really, I do think one of the most instructive things in the world would be a dissertation on dress by you.

La Fontaine. Nothing can be devised more commodious than the dress in fashion. Perukes have fallen among us by the peculiar dispensation of Providence. As in all the regions of the globe the indigenous have given way to stronger creatures, so have they (partly at least) on the human head. At present the wren and the squirrel are dominant there. Whenever I have a mind for a filbert, I have only to shake my foretop. Improvement does not end in that quarter. I might forget to take my pinch of snuff when it would do me good, unless I saw a store of it on another's cravat. Furthermore, the slit in the coat behind tells in a moment what it was made for : a thing of which, in regard to ourselves, the best preachers have to remind us all our lives : then the central part of our habiliment has either its loop-hole or its portcullis in the opposite direction, still more demonstrative. All these are for very mundane purposes : but Religion and Humanity have whispered some· later utilities. We pray the more commodiously, and of course the more frequently, for rolling up a royal ell of stocking round about our knees : and our high-heeled shoes must surely have been worn by some angel, to save those insects which the flat-footed would have crushed to death.

Rochefoucault. Ah ! the good dog has awakened : he saw me and my rapier, and ran away. Of what breed is he ? for I know nothing of dogs.

La Fontaine. And write so well !

Rochefoucault. Is he a trufler ?

La Fontaine. No, not he ; but quite as innocent.

Rochefoucault. Something of the shepherd-dog, I suspect.

La Fontaine. Nor that neither ; although he fain would make you believe it. Indeed he is very like one : pointed nose, pointed ears, apparently stiff, but readily yielding ; long hair, particularly about the neck ; noble tail over his back, three curls deep, exceedingly pleasant to stroke down again ; straw-colour all above, white all below. He might take it ill if you looked for it ; but so it is, upon my word : an ermeline might envy it.

Rochefoucault. What are his pursuits ?

La Fontaine. As to pursuit and occupation, he is good for nothing. In fact, I like those dogs best . . . and those men too.

Rochefoucault. Send Nanon then for a pair of silk stockings, and mount my carriage with me : it stops at the Louvre.

ROMILLY AND WILBERFORCE.

Romilly. Indeed, sir, I can not but suspect that the agitation of this question on the abolition of the slave-trade is countenanced by Mr. Pitt chiefly to divert the attention of the people from crying grievances nearer home. Our paupers are increasing daily both in number and in wretchedness; our workhouses, our hospitals, and our jails are crowded and overflowing; our manufactories are almost as stifling as slave-ships, and more immoral; apprentices, milliners, dressmakers, work throughout the greater part of the night, and, at last disabled by toil, take the sorrowful refuge of the street. After so many have coldly repeated that vice leads to misery, is there no generous man who will proclaim aloud that misery leads to vice? We all see it every day: we warn the wretched too late: we are afraid of warning the affluent too soon: we are prodigal of reproaches that make the crushed heart bleed afresh: we think it indecorous to approach the obdurate one, and unsafe to touch it . . . barbarous and dastardly as we are.

Wilberforce. Postponing all these considerations, not immediately applicable to the subject on which, Mr. Romilly, I have taken the liberty to knock at your door, I must assure you that my friend Mr. Pitt is not only the most unbending and unchanging, but also the most sincere man living.

Romilly. It is happy when we can think so of any, especially of one in power.

Wilberforce. Do you doubt it?

Romilly. I never oppose, without reluctance, opinion to sentiment; or, when I can help it, a bad opinion to a good one.

Wilberforce. O! if you knew him as I do!

Romilly. The thing is impossible.

Wilberforce. Why so? I should be proud to introduce you.

Romilly. The pride would rest entirely apart from me. It may be that coarse metals are less flexible than finer; certain it is that they do not well cohere.

Wilberforce. But on this occasion you invariably vote together.

Romilly. In the House of Commons.

Wilberforce. It is there we must draw up our forces.

Romilly. Do you never doubt, however slightly, and only on one occasion, the fidelity of your leader?

Wilberforce. Leader! Mr. Romilly! leader! Humble as I am, the humblest, indeed, of that august assembly, on this question, on this alone, perhaps, yes, certainly on this alone, I am acknowledged, universally acknowledged, I know too well how unworthily, yet I do know, and God has given me strength and grace to declare it before men, that I, the weakest of his creatures, *there* am leader. It is I, a band of withy, who bind giants: it is I who keep together on this ground the two rival parties: it is I, a potter's vessel, who hold out across the Atlantic the cup of freedom and of fellowship.

Romilly. Certainly you have seconded with admirable zeal the indefatigable Clarkson. Those who run with spirit and celerity have no breath for words: the whole is expended in action.

Wilberforce. Just so with me. However, I can spare a speech of a few hours every session in expounding the vexations and evils of slavery, and in showing how opposite it is to Christianity.

Romilly. I am almost a believer in that doctrine.

Wilberforce. Almost?

Romilly. I should be entirely, if many of the most ortho-dox men in both Houses, including a great part of the bishops, had been assenters.

Wilberforce. Are they not?

Romilly. Apparently no. Otherwise they would never be absent when the question is discussed, nor would they abstain from a petition to the Crown, that a practice so dangerous to salvation, so certain to bring down a curse on the country, be, with all expedient speed, abolished.

Wilberforce. It is unnecessary for me to defend the conduct of my Right Reverend friends ; men of such piety as no other country hath exhibited ; but permit me to remark, Mr. Romilly, that you yourself betray a lukewarmness in the cause, when you talk of expedient speed. Expedient, indeed ! Gracious Jesu ! Ought such a crime to be tolerated for one hour ? Are there no lightnings in heaven. . .

Romilly. Probably there are : there were last summer. But I would rather see them purifying the air than scorching the earth before me. My good Mr. Wilberforce ! abstain, I beseech you, from a species of eloquence in which Mr. Sheridan and Mr. Pitt excel you, especially when it is late in the evening : at that season such men are usually the most pious. The lightnings of heaven fall as frequently on granaries as on slave-ships. It is better at all times to abstain from expostulating with God ; and more especially on the righteousness of his judgments and the delay of his vengeance.

Wilberforce. Mr. Romilly ! Mr. Romilly ! the royal psalmist——

Romilly. Was too often like other royal personages, and, with much power of doing evil, was desirous of much more. Whenever we are conscious of such propensities, it would be wiser and more religious to implore of God to pardon than to promote them.

Wilberforce. We must bow to authority in all things.

Romilly. So we hear : but we may be so much in the habit of bowing as at last to be unable to stand upright. Before we begin at all, it is useful to inquire what is authority. We are accustomed to mistake place and power for it. Now the Devil, on this earth at least, possesess as much power as the Deity, and more place. Unless he did, we tell a manifest lie in every prayer and supplication. For we declare that we are, and always have been, miserable sinners, and that there is no truth in us.

Wilberforce. Ah, my dear sir! you are no theologian, I see. Some of us, by the blessing of God, are under grace; and, once under grace, we are safe. But it is not on this business I visit you. Here we may differ; but on the Abolition we think alike.

Romilly. I am not quite sure of that.

Wilberforce. Indeed! Then, pray, my dear sir, correct your judgment.

Romilly. I have been doing it, to the best of my ability, all my life.

Wilberforce. If you had only clung to the Cross, you would have been sure and steadfast from your very childhood.

Romilly. Alas! I see but one cross remaining on earth, and it is that of the unrepentant thief. What thousands of the most venomous wasps and hornets swarm about it, and fight for its putrescencies! The blessed one was pulled down long ago, indeed soon after its erection, in the scuffle of those who would sell the splinters. Great fortunes are daily made by it, and it maintains as many clerks and treasurers as the South Sea. The money-changers in the Temple of old did at least give change: ours bag the money, and say *call to-morrow.*

Wilberforce. Unholy as the gains may be, we must not meddle with vested rights and ancient institutions.

Romilly. Then, worthy Mr. Wilberforce, let slavery continue; for certainly no institution is more ancient. In this also am I to correct my judgment?

Wilberforce. The fact is too true. You were erroneous there only where you differed from me on that subject, which I had examined attentively and minutely.

Romilly. Namely, the Abolition.

Wilberforce. Exactly so.

Romilly. The clearers of ground in the forests of America clear first the places round about the homestead. On this principle I would begin to emancipate and enlighten the suffering labourers in my own vicinity. Look at the draught-horses now passing under the window. The first quarter of their lives was given to their growth: plentiful food came before painful service. They are ignorant of our vices, insensible of our affections: ease is all in all to them; and while they want it most, and while it is most profitable or promissory to the master, they enjoy it.

Wilberforce. We then put blinkers before their eyes, that nothing may make them swerve on the road. Here is another act of humanity.

Romilly. If you attempt to put blinkers before the intellectual eye, you only increase its obliquity. Give as much clear-sightedness as possible, give reasonable leisure, or you never will conciliate affection to your institutions. Inflict on men the labour and privations of brutes, and you impress on them the brutal character: render them rationally happy, and they are already on the highway to heaven. No man rationally happy will barter the possession he enjoys for the most brilliant theory: but the unhappy will dream of daggers until he clutches them. If your friend Mr. Pitt wishes to retard the revolutionary movement, he will not attempt to put the fetter on the white man while you are taking it off the black: he will not bring forward a flogged soldiery to confront an enthusiastical one: he will not display to the vigorous sons of starving yeomen the sight of twenty farm-houses rising up from the ruins of one *château.* Peace is easier to retain than to recall.

Wilberforce. Well, Mr. Romilly! we are departing a little from the object of my visit: and, if we continue to digress, I am afraid you may not be so entirely at leisure to hear me repeat the speech I have prepared on the Abolition. Your room appears to be well adapted to my voice.

Romilly. Already I have had the benefit of your observations the three last sessions.

Wilberforce. You will hear me again, I confidently hope, with the same pleasure in a very crowded House.

Romilly. You represent a Riding in the county of York.

Wilberforce. I have that honour.

Romilly. To represent a county is not in itself an honour, but it offers opportunities of earning many.   Inform your constituents that the slavery in the West Indies is less cruel and pernicious than the slavery in their own parishes : that the condition of the Black is better on the whole than the condition of the pauper in England, and that his children are incomparably more comfortable and happy.

Wilberforce. Lord of mercy! do I hear this from a philanthropist?

Romilly. I venture to assert, you do, however deficient I may be in the means of showing it.   You might, in any Session of Parliament, obtain a majority of votes in favour of a bill to diminish the hours of a child's labour in factories.   Every country gentleman, every peer, would vote that none under his eighth year should be incarcerated in these pesthouses.

Wilberforce. O Sir! is such a word applicable?

Romilly. Precisely: although a pesthouse is usually the appellation of that building which excludes the malady and receives the endangered.   From eight years to twelve, I would prohibit a longer daily work than of six hours, with two hours between each three, for food and exercise. After the twelfth year the sexes should not be confounded.

Wilberforce. The first regulation would create much discontent among our wealthiest supporters; and even the parents would object to them.

Romilly. Two signal and sorrowful truths!   There are also two additional.   They who feel the least for others feel the most for themselves: and the parents who waste away their own strength in gin-shops are ready to waste their children's in factories.   If our inconsiderate war and our prodigal expenditure permitted the exercise of policy, we should bethink ourselves that manly hearts and sound bodies are the support of states, not creaking looms nor over-pressed cotton-bags in human shape.   We have no right to break down the sinews of the rising generation: we have no right to devote the children of the poor either to Belial or to Moloch.   I do care about the Blacks; I do care greatly and anxiously about them; but I would rather that slavery should exist for seven centuries longer in the West Indies, than for seven years longer in Lancashire and Yorkshire. If there be any sincerity in the heart of Mr. Pitt, why does he not order his dependants in both Houses (and nearly all are his dependants in both alike) to vote for your motion?

Wilberforce. He wishes us well: but he is aware that a compensation must be made to the masters of the slaves; and he has not money for it.

Romilly. Whose fault is that? He always has found money enough for extending the miseries of other nations and the corruption of his own. By his extravagance and the excess of taxation he is leading to that catastrophe which he avowed it was his object to prevent.

Wilberforce. God forbid!

Romilly. God has forbidden; but he does not mind that.

Wilberforce. You force me to say, Mr. Romilly, what I hope you will not think a personality. The French Revolution was brought about in great measure by the gentlemen of your profession.

Romilly. The people were rendered so extremely poor by the imposts, that there were few litigations in the courts of law. Hence the lawyers, who starved others until now, began to be starved in turn, and incited the people to revolution, that there might be crime and change of property, England has now taken the sins of the world upon her, and pays for all.

Wilberforce. Awful expression! Let us return to the Blacks. It is calculated that twenty millions are requisite to indemnify the slave-holders.

Romilly. Do you wonder then that he is evasive?

Wilberforce. I should wonder if a man of his integrity were so upon any occasion. But he has frankly told me that he does not see clearly at what time the measure may be expedient.

Romilly. Everything can be caculated, except the hour for the abolition of injustice. It is not always in our power to retrace our steps when we have committed it. Nay, sometimes is it requisite not only to go on with it, but even to add fresh. We waged a most unnecessary, a most impolitic, a most unjust war against France. Nothing else could have united her people: nothing else could have endangered or have interrupted our commerce. Having taken the American islands from our enemy, we should have exported from them the younger slaves into our own, taking care that the number of females be proportional to the number of males. We should have granted our protection to Brazil and Cuba, on condition that the traffic in African slaves immediately cease, and that everyone belonging to Spaniard or Portuguese, who had served fourteen years, should be free. Unhappily we ourselves can do little more at present for our own, without a grievous injustice to a large body of our fellow-subjects. We can however place adequate power in the hands of the civil and military governors, authorising them to grant any slave his freedom who shall be proved to have been cruelly treated by his master. What a curse is it upon us, that at present we neither can make peace nor abolish slavery! We can decree, and we ought instantly, that the importation and sale of slaves do cease at this very hour throughout the world. We can decree, and we ought instantly, that husband and wife be united, and separated no more. We can decree, and ought instantly, that children from seven to ten years of age be instructed one hour daily. But, as things are now constituted, I think I have no right to deprive a proprietor of his property, unless he has forfeited it by a violation of law. To repay me for my protection, and for granting him a monopoly during the war, I would stipulate with him, that whoever had served him fourteen years should be emancipated. He should also be obliged to maintain as many females as males, or nearly, and to set apart a plot of ground for every emancipated slave, enough for his support, on lease for life, at such a rent as those deputed by the governor may think reasonable. The proposition of granting twenty, or ten, or five millions to carry into execution the abolition of slavery, by way of indemnity to the slave-holders, is absurd. Abolish all duties of importation and exportation; that will be sufficient. The abolition of the slave-trade is greatly more important than the abolition of slavery in our islands. The traffic can be terminated at once; the servitude but gradually. It is in politics as in diet. They who have committed excesses can not become quite temperate at the first perception of their perilous situation. The consequences of a sudden change might be fatal.

Wilberforce. Religion teaches us that we should consent to no truce with Sin.

Romilly. We should enter into no engagements with her: but the union is easier than the divorce. There are materials which, being warped, are not to be set right again by a stroke of the hammer, but by temperance and time. Our system of slavery is in this condition. We have done wrong with impunity; we can not with impunity do right. We wound the state in stripping the individual.

Wilberforce. I would not strip him; I would grant him a fair and full indemnity.

Romilly. What! when all your property is mortgaged? When you are without a hope of redeeming it, and can hardly find wherewithal to pay the interest? If ever you attempt the undertaking, it can be only at the peace.

Wilberforce. I am sorry to find you so despondent.

Romilly. I am more despondent than I have yet appeared to be.

Wilberforce. With what reason?

Romilly. Hostilities having ceased, the people will be clamorous for the removal of many taxes; and some of the most productive will be remitted the first. In my opinion, unwise as was the war, and entered into for the gratification of an old madman, who never knew the difference between a battle and a review, and who chuckled at the idea of his subjects being *peppered* when they were *shot;* a war conducted by grasping men, outrageous at the extortion of their compliance, and at the alternative that either their

609

places or their principles must be surrendered ; we nevertheless ought to discharge the debt we contracted, and not to leave the burden for our children. If our affairs are as ill-conducted in peace as they are in war, it is greatly to be feared that we may injure the colonist more than we benefit the slave. We may even carry our imprudence so far as to restore to our enemies the lands we have conquered from them, cultivated by blacks.

Wilberforce. Impossible. Mr. Pitt has declared that peace is never to be signed without indemnity for the past, and security for the future. These are his very words.

Romilly. Not as a politician, but as an arithmetician, he knew when he uttered these words that they never could be accomplished. War is alike the parent and the child of evil. It would surpass your ingenuity, or Mr. Pitt's, to discover any whatsoever which does not arise from war, or follow war, or romp and revel in the midst of war. It begins in pride and malice, it continues in cruelty and rapine, it terminates in poverty and oppression. Our bishops, who pray for success in it, are much bolder men than our soldiers who engage in it bayonet to bayonet. For the soldier fights only against man, and under the command of man : the bishop fights against the command of God, and against God himself. Every hand lifted up in prayer for homicide, strikes him in the face.

Wilberforce. Mr. Romilly ! I entertain a due respect for you, as being eminent in your profession, a member of Parliament, a virtuous and (I hope) a religious man : you would however rise higher in my estimation if you reverenced your superiors.

Romilly. It must be a man immeasurably above me, both in virtue and intellect, whom, knowing my own deficiency, I could reverence. Seldom is it that I quote a verse or a sentiment, but there is in a poet, not very original, a thought so original that nobody seems ever to have applied it to himself or others :—

" Below the good how far ! how far above the great ! "

Wilberforce. There is only one half of it I would hear willingly. When men begin to think themselves above the great, social order is wofully deranged. I deplore the absence of that self-abasement on which is laid the foundation of all Christian virtues.

Romilly. Unless we respect ourselves, our respect for superiors is prone to servility. No man can be thrown by another from such a height as he can throw himself from. I never have observed that a tendency toward the powerful was a sufficient check to spiritual pride : and extremely few have I known, or heard of, who, tossing up their nostrils into the air and giving tongue that they have hit upon the trail to heaven, could distinguish humility from baseness. Mostly they dirty those they fawn on, and get kicked before they get fed.

Wilberforce. Christianity makes allowances for human infirmity.

Romilly. Christianity, as now practised by the highest of its professors, makes more infirmities than allowances. Can we believe in *their* belief who wallow in wealth and war? in theirs who vote subsidies for slaughter? who speed the slave-ship with their prayers? who bind and lacerate and stifle the helpless wretches they call men and brethren?

Wilberforce. Parliamentary steps must be taken before you can expect to mitigate the curses of war and slavery.

Romilly. By whom first should the steps be taken? Persuade the bishops, if you can, to raise their voices for the double abolition. Let them at least unite and join you in that which, apparently, you have most at heart. In order to effect it gradually, I am ready to subscribe my name to any society, of which the main object shall be the conversion of our spiritual lords to Christianity. The waters of Jordan, which were formerly used for bleaching, serve at present no other purpose than the setting of scarlet and purple.

Wilberforce. There is danger in touching the altar. We may overturn the table and bruise the chalice in attempting any restoration of the structure.

Romilly. Christianity is a plant which grows well from seed, but ill from cuttings: they who have grafted it on a wilding have sometimes succeeded; never they who (as we have) inoculated it on one cracked in the stem and oozing over with foul luxuriance. I do not deny that families and small communities have profited by secession from more corrupt religions: but as soon as ever cities and provinces have embraced the purer creed, ambitious men have always been ready to materialise the word of God and to raise houses and estates upon it.

Wilberforce. The prosperity of the labourers in Christ's vineyard has excited the envy of the ill-disposed.

Romilly. What prosperity?   Success in improving it?

Wilberforce. No, indeed, but their honest earnings.

Romilly. Did the master pay such earnings to those whose work was harder? or did he command, or will, that such should be paid on any future day?

Wilberforce. I am sorry, Mr. Romilly, that you question and quibble (pardon me the expression) just like those unhappy men, miscalled philosophers, who have brought down the vengeance of Heaven on France, Voltaire at the head of them.

Romilly. No, indeed; I never have sunned myself on the trim and short grass bordered by the papered pinks and powdered ranunculuses of Voltaire.   His pertness is amusing; but I thought it pleasanter to bathe in the deep wisdom of wit running up to its banks through the romantic scenery of Cervantes.

Wilberforce. Little better than infidelity.

Romilly. But not, as infidelity generally is, sterile and flimsy.   Christians themselves are all infidels in the sight of some other Christians; and they who come nearest to them are the most obnoxious.   Strange interpretation of "Love your neighbour!"   If there are grades of belief, there must also be grades of unbelief.   The worst of unbelief is that which regrets the goodness of our heavenly Father, and from which there springs in us a desire of breaking what we cannot bend, and of twisting wire after wire and tying knot after knot in his scourge. Christianity, as I understand it, lies not in belief but in action. That servant is a good servant who obeys the just orders of his master; not he who repeats his words, measures his stature, or traces his pedigree! On all occasions it is well to be a little more than tolerant; especially when a wiser and better man than ourselves thinks differently from us. Religious minds will find an additional reason for their humility, when they observe such excellent men as Borromeo and Fénelon adhering to the religion they were born in, amidst the discussions and commotions of every land around.

Wilberforce. My opinion is, that religion should be mixed up in all our institutions, and that it not only should be a part, but the main part of the state.

Romilly. I am unwilling to obtrude my sentiments on this question, and even to answer any. For I always have observed that the most religious men become the most impatient in the course of discussion, calling their opponents weak wavering sceptics, or obstinate reckless unbelievers. But since the constitution of our country is involved in it, together with its present defects and future meliorations, I must declare to you my conviction that even the best government and the best religion should be kept apart in their ministries.

In building a house, brick and lime are ingredients. Let the brick be imbedded in the lime reduced to mortar : but if you mix it in the composition of the brick, it swells and cracks and falls to pieces in the kiln.

Wilberforce. That is no argument.

*Romilly.** Arguments cease to be arguments the moment

* Parliament has been proved in our times, and indeed in most others, a slippery foundation for names, although a commodious one for fortunes. But Romilly went into public life with temperate and healthy aspirations. Providence, having blessed him with domestic peace, withheld him from political animosities. He knew that the sweetest fruits grow nearest the ground, and he waited for the higher to fall into his bosom, without an effort or a wish to seize on them. No man whosoever in our Parliamentary history has united in more perfect accordance and constancy pure virtue and lofty wisdom.

they come home. But this, I acknowledge, is only an illustration. To detain you no longer, Mr. Wilberforce, I give you my promise I will attend at the debate, and vote with you. Neither of us can live long enough to see the Africans secure from bondage, or from the violence of tribe against tribe, and from the myriads of other calamities that precede it. Europe is semi-barbarous at the present hour; and, even among the more civilised, one state is as suspicious of another as one Black is of another in the belligerents of Senegal and Gambia. For many years to come, no nation will unite with us in any work or project for the furtherance of our mutual well-being: little then can we expect that Honour, now totally lost sight of on the Continent, will be recognised in a character so novel as the Knight-errant of Humanity.

One more remark at parting; the only one by which in this business I can hope to serve you materially. Permit me to advise you, Mr. Wilberforce, to display as small a portion of historical research as you possibly can, consistently with your eloquence and enthusiasm.

Wilberforce. Why so, Mr. Romilly?

Romilly. Because it may counteract your benevolent intentions.

Wilberforce. Nothing shall counteract them.

Romilly. Are you aware to which of our sovereigns we must attribute the deadly curse of African slavery, inasmuch as our country is concerned in it?

Wilberforce. Certainly to none of our justly revered kings can so horrible a crime be imputed, although the royal power, according to the limitations of our constitution, may have been insufficient to repress it effectively.

Romilly. Queen Elizabeth equipped two vessels for her own sole profit, in which two vessels, escorted by the fleet under the command of Hawkins, were the first unhappy Blacks inveigled from their shores by Englishmen, and doomed to end their lives in servitude. Elizabeth was avaricious and cruel; but a small segment of her heart had a brief sunshine on it, darting obliquely. We are under a king notoriously more avaricious; one who passes without a shudder the gibbets his sign-manual has garnished; one who sees on the fields of the most disastrous battles, battles in which he ordered his people to fight his people, nothing else to be regretted than the loss of horses and saddles, of haversacks and jackets. If this insensate and insatiable man ever hears that Queen Elizabeth was a slave-dealer, he will assert the inalienable rights of the Crown, and swamp your motion.

LUCIAN AND TIMOTHEUS.

Timotheus. I am delighted, my cousin Lucian, to observe how popular are become your *Dialogues of the Dead.* Nothing can be so gratifying and satisfactory to a rightly disposed mind, as the subversion of imposture by the force of ridicule. It hath scattered the crowd of heathen gods as if a thunderbolt had fallen in the midst of them. Now, I am confident you never would have assailed the false religion, unless you were prepared for the reception of the true. For it hath always been an indication of rashness and precipitancy, to throw down an edifice before you have collected materials for reconstruction.

Lucian. Of all metaphors and remarks, I believe this of yours, my good cousin Timotheus, is the most trite, and pardon me if I add, the most untrue. Surely we ought to remove an error the instant we detect it, although it may be out of our competence to state and establish what is right. A lie should be exposed as soon as born: we are not to wait until a healthier child is begotten. Whatever is evil in any way should be abolished. The husbandman never hesitates to eradicate weeds, or to burn them up, because he may not happen at the time to carry a sack on his shoulder with wheat or barley in it. Even if no wheat or barley is to be sown in future, the weeding and burning are in themselves beneficial, and something better will spring up.

Timotheus. That is not so certain.

Lucian. Doubt it as you may, at least you will allow that the temporary absence of evil is an advantage.

Timotheus. I think, O Lucian, you would reason much better if you would come over to our belief.

Lucian. I was unaware that belief is an encourager and guide to reason.

Timotheus. Depend upon it, there can be no stability of truth, no elevation of genius, without an unwavering faith in our holy mysteries. Babes and sucklings who are blest with it, stand higher, intellectually as well as morally, than stiff unbelievers and proud sceptics.

Lucian. I do not wonder that so many are firm holders of this novel doctrine. It is pleasant to grow wise and virtuous at so small an expenditure of thought or time. This saying of yours is exactly what I heard spoken with angry gravity not long ago.

Timotheus. Angry! no wonder! for it is impossible to keep our patience when truths so incontrovertible are assailed. What was your answer?

Lucian. My answer was. If you talk in this manner, my honest friend, you will excite a spirit of ridicule in the gravest and most saturnine of men, who never had let a laugh out of their breasts before. Lie to *me*, and welcome; but beware lest your own heart take you to task for it, reminding you that both anger and falsehood are repre-hended by all religions, yours included.

Timotheus. Lucian! Lucian! you have always been called profane.

Lucian. For what? for having turned into ridicule the gods whom you have turned out of house and home, and are reducing to dust?

Timotheus. Well; but you are equally ready to turn into ridicule the true and holy.

Lucian. In other words, to turn myself into a fool. He who brings ridicule to bear against Truth, finds in his hand a blade without a hilt. The most sparkling and pointed flame of wit flickers and expires against the incombustible walls of her sanctuary.

Timotheus. Fine talking! Do you know, you have really been called an atheist?

Lucian. Yes, yes; I know it well. But, in fact, I believe there are almost as few atheists in the world as there are Christians.

Timotheus. How! as few? Most of Europe, most of Asia, most of Africa, is Christian.

Lucian. Show me five men in each who obey the commands of Christ, and I will show you five hundred in this very city who observe the dictates of Pythagoras. Every Pythagorean obeys his defunct philosopher; and almost every Christian disobeys his living God. Where is there one who practises the most important and the easiest of his commands, to abstain from strife? Men easily and perpetually find something new to quarrel about; but the objects of affection are limited in number, and grow up scantily and slowly. Even a small house is often too spacious for them, and there is a vacant seat at the table. Religious men themselves, when the Deity has bestowed on them everything they prayed for, discover, as a peculiar gift of Providence, some fault in the actions or opinions of a neighbour, and run it down, crying and shouting after it, with more alacrity and more clamour than boys would a leveret or a squirrel in the playground. Are our years and our intellects, and the word of God itself, given us for this, O Timotheus?

Timotheus. A certain latitude, a liberal construction . . .

Lucian. Ay, ay! These "liberal constructions" let loose all the worst passions into those "certain latitudes." The priests themselves, who ought to be the poorest, are the richest; who ought to be the most obedient, are the most refractory and rebellious. All trouble and all piety are vicarious. They send missionaries, at the cost of others, into foreign lands, to teach observances which they supersede at home. I have ridiculed the puppets of all features, all colours, all sizes, by which an impudent and audacious set of impostors have been gaining an easy livelihood these two thousand years.

Timotheus. Gently! gently! Ours have not been at it yet two hundred. We abolish all idolatry. We know that

Jupiter was not the father of gods and men : we know that Mars was not the Lord of Hosts : we know who is : we are quite at ease upon that question.

Lucian. Are you so fanatical, my good Timotheus, as to imagine that the Creator of the world cares a fig by what appellation you adore him ? whether you call him on one occasion Jupiter, on another Apollo ? I will not add Mars or Lord of Hosts ; for, wanting as I may be in piety, I am not, and never was, so impious as to call the Maker the Destroyer ; to call him Lord of Hosts who, according to your holiest of books, declared so lately and so plainly that he permits no hosts at all ; much less will he take the command of one against another. Would any man in his senses go down into the cellar, and seize first an amphora from the right, and then an amphora from the left, for the pleasure of breaking them in pieces, and of letting out the wine he had taken the trouble to put in ? We are not contented with attributing to the gods our own infirmities ; we make them even more wayward, even more passionate, even more exigent and more malignant : and then some of us try to coax and cajole them, and others run away from them outright.

Timotheus. No wonder : but only in regard to yours : and even those are types.

Lucian. There are honest men who occupy their lives in discovering types for all things.

Timotheus. Truly and rationally thou speakest now. Honest men and wise men above their fellows are they, and the greatest of all discoverers. There are many types above thy reach, O Lucian !

Lucian. And one which my mind, and perhaps yours also, can comprehend. There is in Italy, I hear, on the border of a quiet and beautiful lake,* a temple dedicated to Diana ; the priests of which temple have murdered each his predecessor for unrecorded ages.

Timotheus. What of that ? They were idolaters.

---

* The lake of Nemi.

Lucian. They made the type, however : take it home with you, and hang it up in your temple.

Timotheus. Why ! you seem to have forgotten on a sudden that I am a Christian : you are talking of the heathens.

Lucian. True ! true ! I am near upon eighty years of age, and to my poor eyesight one thing looks very like another.

Timotheus. You are too indifferent.

Lucian. No indeed. I love those best who quarrel least, and who bring into public use the most civility and good humour.

Timotheus. Our holy religion inculcates this duty especially.

Lucian. Such being the case, a pleasant story will not be thrown away upon you. Xenophanes, my townsman of Samosata, was resolved to buy a new horse : he had tried him, and liked him well enough. I asked him why he wished to dispose of his old one, knowing how sure-footed he was, how easy in his paces, and how quiet in his pasture. "Very true, O Lucian," said he; "the horse is a clever horse; noble eye, beautiful figure, stately step; rather too fond of neighing and of shuffling a little in the vicinity of a mare; but tractable and good tempered." "I would not have parted with him then," said I. "The fact is," replied he, "my grandfather, whom I am about to visit, likes no horses but what are *Saturnised*. To-morrow I begin my journey : come and see me set out." I went at the hour appointed. The new purchase looked quiet and demure; but *he* also pricked up his ears, and gave sundry other tokens of equinity, when the more interesting part of his fellow-creatures came near him. As the morning oats began to operate, he grew more and more unruly, and snapped at one friend of Xenophanes, and sidled against another, and gave a kick at a third. "All in play ! all in play !" said Xenophanes ; "his nature is more of a lamb's than a horse's." However, these mute salutations being over, away went Xenophanes. In the evening, when my lamp had just been replenished for the commencement of my studies, my friend came in striding as if he were still across the saddle. "I am apprehensive, O Xenophanes," said I, "your new acquisition has disappointed you." "Not in the least," answered he. "I do assure you, O Lucian! he is the very horse I was looking out for." On my requesting him to be seated, he no more thought of doing so than if it had been in the presence of the Persian king. I then handed my lamp to him, telling him (as was true) it contained all the oil I had in the house, and protesting I should be happier to finish my *Dialogue* in the morning. He took the lamp into my bedroom, and appeared to be much refreshed on his return. Nevertheless, he treated his chair with great delicacy and circumspection, and evidently was afraid of breaking it by too sudden a descent. I did not revert to the horse: but he went on of his own accord. "I declare to you, O Lucian! it is impossible for me to be mistaken in a palfrey. My new one is the only one in Samosata that could carry me at one stretch to my grand father's." "But *has* he?" said I, timidly. "No; he has not yet," answered my friend. "To-morrow, then, I am afraid, we really must lose you." "No," said he; "the horse does trot hard: but he is the better for that: I shall soon get used to him." In fine, my worthy friend deferred his visit to his grandfather: his rides were neither long nor frequent: he was ashamed to part with his purchase, boasted of him everywhere, and, humane as he is by nature, could almost have broken on the cross the quiet contented owner of old Bucephalus.

Timotheus. Am I to understand by this, O cousin Lucian, that I ought to be contented with the impurities of paganism?

Lucian. Unless you are very unreasonable. A moderate man finds plenty in it.

Timotheus. We abominate the Deities who patronise them, and we hurl down the images of the monsters.

Lucian. Sweet cousin! be tenderer to my feelings. In such a tempest as this, my spark of piety may be blown out. Hold your hand cautiously before it, until I can find

my way.   Believe me, no Deities (out of their own houses)
patronise immorality; none patronise unruly passions, least
of all the fierce and ferocious.   In my opinion, you are
wrong in throwing down the images of those among them
who look on you benignly: the others I give up to your
discretion.   But I think it impossible to stand habitually
in the presence of a sweet and open countenance, graven
or depicted, without in some degree partaking of the
character it expresses.   Never tell any man that he can
derive no good, in his devotions, from this or from that:
abolish neither hope nor gratitude.

Timotheus. God is offended at vain efforts to represent
him.

Lucian. No such thing, my dear Timotheus.   If you
knew him at all, you would not talk of him so irreverently.
He is pleased, I am convinced, at every effort to resemble
him, at every wish to remind both ourselves and others of
his benefits.   You can not think so often of him without
an effigy.

Timotheus. What likeness is there in the perishable to
the unperishable?

Lucian. I see no reason why there may not be a
similitude.   All that the senses can comprehend may be
represented by any material; clay or fig-tree, bronze or
ivory, porphyry or gold.   Indeed I have a faint remembrance that, according to your sacred volumes, man was
made by God after his own image.   If so, man's intellectual
powers are worthily exercised in attempting to collect all
that is beautiful, serene, and dignified, and to bring him
back to earth again by showing him the noblest of his
gifts, the work most like his own.   Surely he can not hate
or abandon those who thus cherish his memory, and thus
implore his regard.   Perishable and imperfect is everything
human: but in these very qualities I find the best reason
for striving to attain what is least so.   Would not any
father be gratified by seeing his child attempt to delineate
his features?   And would not the gratification be rather
increased than diminished by his incapacity?   How long

shall the narrow mind of man stand between goodness and omnipotence ? Perhaps the effigy of your ancestor Isknos is unlike him; whether it is or no, you can not tell; but you keep it in your hall, and would be angry if anybody broke it to pieces or defaced it. Be quite sure there are many who think as much of their gods as you think of your ancestor Isknos, and who see in their images as good a likeness. Let men have their own way, especially their way to the temples. It is easier to drive them out of one road than into another. Our judicious and good-humoured Trajan has found it necessary on many occasions to chastise the law-breakers of your sect, indifferent as he is what gods are worshipped, so long as their followers are orderly and decorous. The fiercest of the Dacians never knocked off Jupiter's beard, or broke an arm off Venus; and the emperor will hardly tolerate in those who have received a liberal education what he would punish in barbarians. Do not wear out his patience : try rather to imitate his equity, his equanimity, and forbearance.

Timotheus. I have been listening to you with much attention, O Lucian! for I seldom have heard you speak with such gravity. And yet, O cousin Lucian! I really do find in you a sad deficiency of that wisdom which alone is of any value. You talk of Trajan ! what is Trajan?

Lucian. A beneficent citizen, an impartial judge, a sagacious ruler; the comrade of every brave soldier, the friend and associate of every man eminent in genius, throughout his empire, the empire of the world. All arts, all sciences, all philosophies, all religions, are protected by him. Wherefore his name will flourish, when the proudest of these have perished in the land of Egypt. Philosophies and religions will strive, struggle, and suffocate one another. Priesthoods, I know not how many, are quarrelling and scuffling in the street at this instant, all calling on Trajan to come and knock an antagonist on the head ; and the most peaceful of them, as it wishes to be thought, proclaiming him an infidel for turning a deaf ear to its imprecations.

Mankind was never so happy as under his guidance ; and he has nothing now to do but to put down the battles of the gods. If they must fight it out, he will insist on our neutrality.

Timotheus. He has no authority and no influence over us in matters of faith. A wise and upright man, whose serious thoughts lead him forward to religion, will never be turned aside from it by any worldly consideration or any human force.

Lucian. True : but mankind is composed not entirely of the upright and the wise. I suspect that we may find some, here and there, who are rather too fond of novelties in the furniture of temples ; and I have observed that new sects are apt to warp, crack, and split, under the heat they generate. Our homely old religion has run into fewer quarrels, ever since the Centaurs and Lapiths (whose controversy was on a subject quite comprehensible), than yours has engendered in twenty years.

Timotheus. We shall obviate that inconvenience by electing a supreme Pontiff to decide all differences. It has been seriously thought about long ago ; and latterly we have been making out an ideal series down to the present day, in order that our successors in the ministry may have stepping-stones up to the fountain-head. At first the disseminators of our doctrines were equal in their commission ; we do not approve of this any longer, for reasons of our own.

Lucian. You may shut, one after another, all our other temples, but, I plainly see, you will never shut the temple of Janus. The Roman empire will never lose its pugnacious character while your sect exists. The only danger is, lest the fever rage internally and consume the vitals. If you sincerely wish your religion to be long-lived, maintain in it the spirit of its constitution, and keep it patient, humble, abstemious, domestic, and zealous only in the services of humanity. Whenever the higher of your priesthood shall attain the riches they are aiming at, the people will envy their possessions and revolt from their impostures. Do not let them seize upon the palace, and shove their God again into the manger.

Timotheus. Lucian ! Lucian ! I call this impiety.

Lucian. So do I, and shudder at its consequences. Caverns which at first look inviting, the roof at the aperture green with overhanging ferns and clinging mosses, then glittering with native gems and with water as sparkling and pellucid, freshening the air all around ; these caverns grow darker and closer, until you find yourself among animals that shun the daylight, adhering to the walls, hissing along the bottom, flapping, screeching, gaping, glaring, making you shrink at the sounds, and sicken at the smells, and afraid to advance or retreat.

Timotheus. To what can this refer ? Our caverns open on verdure, and terminate in veins of gold.

Lucian. Veins of gold, my good Timotheus, such as your excavations have opened and are opening, in the spirit of avarice and ambition, will be washed (or as you would say, *purified*) in streams of blood. Arrogance, intolerance, resistance to authority and contempt of law, distinguish your aspiring sectarians from the other subjects of the empire.

Timotheus. Blindness hath often a calm and composed countenance ; but, my cousin Lucian ! it usually hath also the advantage of a cautious and a measured step. It hath pleased God to blind you, like all the other adversaries of our faith ; but he has given you no staff to lean upon. You object against us the very vices from which we are peculiarly exempt.

Lucian. Then it is all a story, a fable, a fabrication, about one of your earlier leaders cutting off with his sword a servant's ear ? If the accusation is true, the offence is heavy. For not only was the wounded man innocent of any provocation, but he is represented as being in the service of the High Priest at Jerusalem. Moreover, from the direction and violence of the blow, it is evident that his life was aimed at. According to law, you know, my dear cousin, all the party might have been condemned

610

to death, as accessaries to an attempt at murder. I am unwilling to think so unfavourably of your sect; nor indeed do I see the possibility that, in such an outrage, the principal could be pardoned. For any man but a soldier to go about armed is against the Roman law, which, on that head, as on many others, is borrowed from the Athenian; and it is incredible that in any civilised country so barbarous a practice can be tolerated. Travellers do indeed relate that, in certain parts of India, there are princes at whose courts even civilians are armed. But *traveller* has occasionally the same signification as *liar*, and *India* as *fable.* However, if the practice really does exist in that remote and rarely visited country, it must be in some region of it very for beyond the Indus or the Ganges: for the nations situated between those rivers are, and were in the reign of Alexander, and some thousand years before his birth, as civilised as the Europeans; nay, incomparably more courteous, more industrious, and more pacific; the three grand criterions.

But answer my question: is there any foundation for so mischievous a report?

Timotheus. There was indeed, so to say, an ear, or something of the kind, abscinded; probably by mistake. But High Priests' servants are propense to follow the swaggering gait of their masters, and to carry things with a high hand, in such wise as to excite the choler of the most quiet. If you knew the character of the eminently holy man who punished the atrocious insolence of that bloody-minded wretch, you would be sparing of your animadversions. We take him for our model.

Lucian. I see you do.

Timotheus. We proclaim him Prince of the Apostles.

Lucian. I am the last in the world to question his princely qualifications; but, if I might advise you, it should be to follow in preference him whom you acknowledge to be an unerring guide; who delivered to you his ordinances with his own hand, equitable, plain, explicit, compendious, and complete; who committed no violence, who countenanced no injustice, whose compassion was without weakness, whose love was without frailty, whose life was led in humility, in purity, in beneficence, and, at the end, laid down in obedience to his father's will.

Timotheus. Ah, Lucian! what strangely imperfect notions! all that is little.

Lucian. Enough to follow.

Timotheus. Not enough to compel others. I did indeed hope, O Lucian! that you would again come forward with the irresistible arrows of your wit, and unite with us against our adversaries. By what you have just spoken, I doubt no longer that you approve of the doctrines inculcated by the blessed founder of our religion.

Lucian. To the best of my understanding.

Timotheus. So ardent is my desire for the salvation of your precious soul, O my cousin! that I would devote many hours of every day to disputation with you on the principal points of our Christian controversy.

Lucian. Many thanks, my kind Timotheus! But I think the blessed founder of your religion very strictly forbade that there should be *any* points of controversy. Not only has he prohibited them on the doctrines he delivered, but on everything else. Some of the most obstinate might never have doubted of his divinity, if the conduct of his followers had not repelled them from the belief of it. How can they imagine you sincere when they see you disobedient? It is in vain for you to protest that you worship the God of Peace, when you are found daily in the courts and market-places with clenched fists and bloody noses. I acknowledge the full value of your offer; but really I am as anxious for the salvation of your precious time as you appear to be for the salvation of my precious soul, particularly since I am come to the conclusion that souls can not be lost, and that time can.

Timotheus. We mean by *salvation* exemption from eternal torments.

Lucian. Among all my old gods and their children, morose as some of the senior are, and mischievous as are some of the junior, I have never represented the worst of them as capable of inflicting such atrocity. Passionate and capricious and unjust are several of them; but a skin stripped off the shoulder, and a liver tossed to a vulture, are among the worst of their inflictions.

Timotheus. This is scoffing.

Lucian. Nobody but an honest man has a right to scoff at anything.

Timotheus. And yet people of a very different cast are usually those who scoff the most.

Lucian. We are apt to push forward at that which we are without : the low-born at titles and distinctions, the silly at wit, the knave at the semblance of probity. But I was about to remark, that an honest man may fairly scoff at all philosophies and religions which are proud, ambitious, intemperate, and contradictory. The thing most adverse to the spirit and essence of them all is falsehood. It is the business of the philosophical to seek truth : it is the office of the religious to worship her; under what name is unimportant. The falsehood that the tongue commits is slight in comparison with what is conceived by the heart, and executed by the whole man, throughout life. If, professing love and charity to the human race at large, I quarrel day after day with my next neighbour; if, professing that the rich can never see God, I spend in the luxuries of my household a talent monthly; if, professing to place so much confidence in his word, that, in regard to worldly weal, I need take no care for to-morrow, I accumulate stores even beyond what would be necessary, though I quite distrusted both his providence and his veracity; if, professing that "he who giveth to the poor lendeth to the Lord," I question the Lord's security, and haggle with him about the amount of the loan; if, professing that I am their steward, I keep ninety-nine parts in the hundred as the emolument of my stewardship; how, when God hates liars and punishes defrauders, shall I, and other such thieves and hypocrites, fare hereafter ?

Timotheus. Let us hope there are few of them.

Lucian. We can not hope against what is: we may, however, hope that in future these will be fewer; but never while the overseers of a priesthood look for offices out of it, taking the lead in politics, in debate, and strife. Such men bring to ruin all religion, but their own first, and raise unbelievers not only in divine providence, but in human faith.

Timotheus. If they leave the altar for the market-place, the sanctuary for the senate-house, and agitate party questions instead of Christian verities, everlasting punishments await them.

Lucian. Everlasting?

Timotheus. Certainly : at the very least.   I rank it next to heresy in the catalogue of sins; and the church supports my opinion.

Lucian. I have no measure for ascertaining the distance between the opinions and practices of men; I only know that they stand widely apart in all countries on the most important occasions; but this newly-hatched word *heresy*, alighting on my ear, makes me rub it.   A beneficent God descends on earth in the human form, to redeem us from the slavery of sin, from the penalty of our passions : can you imagine he will punish an error in opinion, or even an obstinacy in unbelief, with everlasting torments? Supposing it highly criminal to refuse to weigh a string of arguments, or to cross-question a herd of witnesses, on a subject which no experience has warranted and no sagacity can comprehend; supposing it highly criminal to be contented with the religion which our parents taught us, which they bequeathed to us as the most precious of possessions, and which it would have broken their hearts if they had foreseen we should cast aside; yet are eternal pains the just retribution of what at worst is but indifference and supineness ?

Timotheus. Our religion has clearly this advantage over yours : it teaches us to regulate our passions.

Lucian. Rather say it *tells* us.   I believe all religions do the same; some indeed more emphatically and primarily than others; but *that* indeed would be incontestably of divine origin, and acknowledged at once by the most sceptical, which should thoroughly teach it. Now, my friend Timotheus, I think you are about seventy-five years of age.

Timotheus. Nigh upon it.

Lucian. Seventy-five years, according to my calculation, are equivalent to seventy-five gods and goddesses in regulating our passions for us, if we speak of the amatory, which are always thought in every stage of life the least to be pardoned.

Timotheus. Execrable !

Lucian. I am afraid the sourest hang longest on the tree. Mimnermus says :—

> In early youth we often sigh
> Because our pulses beat so high ;
> All this we conquer, and at last
> We sigh that we are grown so chaste.

Timotheus. Swine !

Lucian. No animal sighs oftener or louder. But, my dear cousin, the quiet swine is less troublesome and less odious than the grumbling and growling and fierce hyæna, which will not let the dead rest in their graves. We may be merry with the follies and even the vices of men, without doing or wishing them harm ; punishment should come from the magistrate, not from us. If we are to give pain to anyone because he thinks differently from us, we ought to begin by inflicting a few smart stripes on ourselves ; for both upon light and upon grave occasions, if we have thought much and often, our opinions must have varied. We are always fond of seizing and managing what appertains to others. In the savage state all belongs to all. Our neighbours the Arabs, who stand between barbarism and civilisation, waylay travellers, and plunder their equipage and their gold. The wilier marauders in Alexandria start up from under the shadow of temples, force us to change our habiliments for theirs, and strangle us with fingers dipped in holy water if we say they sit uneasily.

Timotheus. This is not the right view of things.

Lucian. That is never the right view which lets in too much light. About two centuries have elapsed since your religion was founded. Show me the pride it has humbled; show me the cruelty it has mitigated; show me the lust it has extinguished or repressed. I have now been living ten years in Alexandria; and you never will accuse me, I think, of any undue partiality for the system in which I was educated; yet, from all my observation, I find no priest or elder, in your community, wise, tranquil, firm, and sedate as Epicurus, and Carneades, and Zeno, and Epictetus; or indeed in the same degree as some who were often called forth into political and military life; Epaminondas, for instance, and Phocion.

Timotheus. I pity them from my soul : they were ignorant of the truth : they are lost, my cousin ! take my word for it, they are lost men.

Lucian. Unhappily, they are. I wish we had them back again; or that, since we have lost them, we could at least find among us the virtues they left for our example.

Timotheus. Alas, my poor cousin ! you too are blind; you do not understand the plainest words, nor comprehend those verities which are the most evident and palpable. Virtues ! if the poor wretches had any, they were false ones.

Lucian. Scarcely ever has there been a politician, in any free state, without much falsehood and duplicity. I have named the most illustrious exceptions. Slender and irregular lines of a darker colour run along the bright blade that decides the fate of nations, and may indeed be necessary to the perfection of its temper. The great warrior has usually his darker lines of character, necessary (it may be) to constitute his greatness. No two men possess the same quantity of the same virtues, if they have many or much. We want some which do not far outstep us, and which we may follow with the hope of reaching; we want others to elevate, and others to defend us. The order of things would be less beautiful without this variety.

Without the ebb and flow of our passions, but guided and moderated by a beneficent light above, the ocean of life would stagnate; and zeal, devotion, eloquence, would become dead carcases, collapsing and wasting on unprofitable sands. The vices of some men cause the virtues of others, as corruption is the parent of fertility.

Timotheus. O my cousin! this doctrine is diabolical.

Lucian. What is it?

Timotheus. Diabolical; a strong expression in daily use among us. We turn it a little from its origin.

Lucian. Timotheus, I love to sit by the side of a clear water, although there is nothing in it but naked stones. Do not take the trouble to muddy the stream of language for my benefit; I am not about to fish in it.

Timotheus. Well, we will speak about things which come nearer to your apprehension. I only wish you were somewhat less indifferent in your choice between the true and the false.

Lucian. We take it for granted that what is not true must be false.

Timotheus. Surely we do.

Lucian. This is erroneous.

Timotheus. Are you grown captious? Pray explain.

Lucian. What is not true, I need not say, must be untrue; but that alone is false which is intended to deceive. A witness may be mistaken, yet you would not call him a false witness unless he asserted what he knew to be false.

Timotheus. Quibbles upon words!

Lucian. On words, on quibbles, if you please to call distinctions so, rests the axis of the intellectual world. A winged word hath stuck ineradicably in a million hearts, and envenomed every hour throughout their hard pulsation. On a winged word hath hung the destiny of nations. On a winged word hath human wisdom been willing to cast the immortal soul, and to leave it dependent for all its future happiness. It is because a word is unsusceptible of explanation, or because they who employed it were impatient of any, that enormous evils have prevailed, not only against our common sense, but against our common humanity. Hence the most pernicious of absurdities, far exceeding in folly and mischief the worship of three score gods; namely, that an implicit faith in what outrages our reason, which we know is God's gift, and bestowed on us for our guidance, that this weak, blind, stupid· faith is surer of his favour than the constant practice of every human virtue. They at whose hands one prodigious lie, such as this, hath been accepted, may reckon on their influence in the dissemination of many smaller, and may turn them easily to their own account. Be sure they will do it sooner or later. The fly floats on the surface for a while, but up springs the fish at last and swallows it.

Timotheus. Was ever man so unjust as you are? The abominable old priesthoods are avaricious and luxurious: ours is willing to stand or fall by maintaining its ordinances of fellowship and frugality. Point out to me a priest of our religion whom you could, by any temptation or entreaty, so far mislead, that he shall reserve for his own consumption one loaf, one plate of lentils, while another poor Christian hungers. In the meanwhile the priests of Isis are proud and wealthy, and admit none of the indigent to their tables. And now, to tell you the whole truth, my cousin Lucian, I come to you this morning to propose that we should lay our heads together and compose a merry dialogue on these said priests of Isis. What say you?

Lucian. These said priests of Isis have already been with me, several times, on a similar business in regard to yours.

Timotheus. Malicious wretches!

Lucian. Beside, they have attempted to persuade me that your religion is borrowed from theirs, altering a name a little, and laying the scene of action in a corner, in the midst of obscurity and ruins.

Timotheus. The wicked dogs! the hellish liars! We have nothing in common with such vile impostors. Are they not ashamed of taking such unfair means of lowering us in the estimation of our fellow-citizens? And so, they artfully came to you, craving any spare jibe to throw against us ! They lie open to these weapons ; we do not : we stand above the malignity, above the strength, of man. You would do justly in turning their own devices against them : it would be amusing to see how they would look. If you refuse me, I am resolved to write a *Dialogue of the Dead*, myself, and to introduce these hypocrites in it.

Lucian. Consider well first, my good Timotheus, whether you can do any such thing with propriety; I mean to say judiciously in regard to composition.

Timotheus. I always thought you generous and open-hearted, and quite inaccessible to jealousy.

Lucian. Let nobody ever profess himself so much as that : for, although he may be insensible of the disease, it lurks within him, and only waits its season to break out. But really, my cousin, at present I feel no symptoms : and, to prove that I am ingenuous and sincere with you, these are my reasons for dissuasion. We believers in the Homeric family of gods and goddesses, believe also in the locality of Tartarus and Elysium. We entertain no doubt whatever that the passions of men and demigods and gods are nearly the same above-ground and below ; and that Achilles would dispatch his spear through the body of any shade who would lead Briseis too far among the myrtles, or attempt to throw the halter over the ears of any chariot-horse belonging to him in the meads of asphodel. We admit no doubt of these verities, delivered down to us from the ages when Theseus and Hercules had descended into Hades itself. Instead of a few stadions in a cavern, with a bank and a bower at the end of it, under a very small portion of our diminutive Hellas, you Christians possess the whole cavity of the earth for punishment, and the whole convex of the sky for felicity.

Timotheus. Our passions are burnt out amid the fires of purification, and our intellects are elevated to the enjoyment of perfect intelligence.

Lucian. How silly then and incongruous would it be, not to say how impious, to represent your people as no better and no wiser than they were before, and discoursing on subjects which no longer can or ought to concern them. Christians must think that your *Dialogue of the Dead* no less irreligious than their opponents think mine, and infinitely more absurd. If indeed you are resolved on this form of composition, there is no topic which may not, with equal facility, be discussed on earth ; and you may intersperse as much ridicule as you please, without any fear of censure for inconsistency or irreverence. Hitherto such writers have confined their view mostly to speculative points, sophistic reasonings, and sarcastic interpellations.

Timotheus. Ha ! you are always fond of throwing a little pebble at the lofty Plato, whom we, on the contrary, are ready to receive (in a manner) as one of ourselves.

Lucian. To throw pebbles is a very uncertain way of showing where lie defects. Whenever I have mentioned him seriously, I have brought forward, not accusations, but passages from his writings, such as no philosopher or scholar or moralist can defend.

Timotheus. His doctrines are too abstruse and too sublime or you.

Lucian. Solon, Anaxagoras, and Epicurus, are more sublime, if truth is sublimity.

Timotheus. Truth is, indeed ; for God is truth.

Lucian. We are upon earth to learn what can be learnt upon earth, and not to speculate on what never can be. This you, O Timotheus, may call philosophy : to me it appears the idlest of curiosity ; for every other kind may teach us something, and may lead to more beyond. Let men learn what benefits men ; above all things, to contract their wishes, to calm their passions, and, more especially, to dispel their fears. Now these are to be dispelled, not by collecting clouds, but by piercing and scattering them. In the dark we may imagine depths and heights immeasurable, which, if a torch be carried right before us, we find it easy to leap across. Much of what we call sublime is only the residue of infancy, and the worst of it.

The philosophers I quoted are too capacious for schools

and systems. Without noise, without ostentation, without mystery, not quarrelsome, not captious, not frivolous, their lives were commentaries on their doctrines. Never evaporating into mist, never stagnating into mire, their limpid and broad morality runs parallel with the lofty summits of their genius.

Timotheus. Genius! was ever genius like Plato's?

Lucian. The most admired of his *Dialogues*, his *Banquet*, is beset with such puerilities, deformed with such pedantry, and disgraced with such impurity, that none but the thickest beards, and chiefly of the philosophers and the satyrs, should bend over it. On a former occasion he has given us a specimen of history, than which nothing in our language is worse : here he gives us one of poetry, in honour of Love, for which the god has taken ample vengeance on him, by perverting his taste and feelings. The grossest of all the absurdities in this dialogue is, attributing to Aristophanes, so much of a scoffer and so little of a visionary, the silly notion of male and female having been originally complete in one person, and walking circuitously. He may be joking : who knows?

Timotheus. Forbear! forbear! do not call this notion a silly one: he took it from our Holy Scriptures, but perverted it somewhat. Woman was made from man's rib, and did not require to be cut asunder all the way down : this is no proof of bad reasoning, but merely of misinterpretation.

Lucian. If you would rather have bad reasoning, I will adduce a little of it. Farther on, he wishes to extol the wisdom of Agathon by attributing to him such a sentence as this :—

" It is evident that Love is the most beautiful of the gods, *because* he is the youngest of them."

Now, even on earth, the youngest is not always the most beautiful ; how infinitely less cogent, then, is the argument when we come to speak of the Immortals, with whom age can have no concern! There was a time when Vulcan was the youngest of the gods : was he, also, at that time, and

for that reason, the most beautiful ?   Your philosopher tells
us, moreover, that " Love is of all deities the most *liquid ;*
else he never could fold himself about everything, and flow
into and out of men's souls."

The three last sentences of Agathon's rhapsody are very
harmonious, and exhibit the finest specimen of Plato's
style ; but we, accustomed as we are to hear him lauded for
his poetical diction, should hold that poem a very indifferent
one which left on the mind so superficial an impression.
The garden of Academus is flowery without fragrance, and
dazzling without warmth : I am ready to dream away an
hour in it after dinner, but I think it unsalutary for a
night's repose.   So satisfied was Plato with his *Banquet*,
that he says of himself, in the person of Socrates, " How
can I or anyone but find it difficult to speak after a discourse so eloquent ?   It would have been wonderful if the
brilliancy of the sentences at the end of it, and the choice
of expression throughout, had not astonished all the
auditors.   I, who can never say anything nearly so beautiful, would if possible have made my escape, and have fairly
run off for shame."   He had indeed much better run off
before he made so wretched a pun on the name of Gorgias.
" I dreaded," says he, " lest Agathon, *measuring my discourse by the head of the eloquent Gorgias, should turn me to
stone* for inability of utterance."

Was there ever joke more frigid ?   What painful twisting
of unelastic stuff !   If Socrates was the wisest man in the
world, it would require another oracle to persuade us, after
this, that he was the wittiest.   But surely a small share of
common sense would have made him abstain from hazard-
ing such failures.   He falls on his face in very flat and very
dry ground ; and, when he gets up again, his quibbles are
well-nigh as tedious as his witticisms.   However, he has
the presence of mind to throw them on the shoulders of
Diotima, whom he calls a prophetess, and who, ten years
before the Plague broke out in Athens, obtained from the
gods (he tells us) that delay.   Ah ! the gods were doubly
mischievous : they sent her first.   Read her words, my

cousin, as delivered by Socrates; and if they have another Plague in store for us, you may avert it by such an act of expiation.

Timotheus. The world will have ended before ten years are over.

Lucian. Indeed !

Timotheus. It has been pronounced.

Lucian. How the threads of belief and unbelief run woven close together in the whole web of human life ! Come, come; take courage; you will have time for your *Dialogue.* Enlarge the circle; enrich it with a variety of matter, enliven it with a multitude of characters, occupy the intellect of the thoughtful, the imagination of the lively; spread the board with solid viands, delicate rarities, and sparkling wines; and throw, along the whole extent of it, geniality and festal crowns.

Timotheus. What writer of dialogues hath ever done this, or undertaken, or conceived, or hoped it ?

Lucian. None whatever; yet surely you yourself may, when even your babes and sucklings are endowed with abilities incomparably greater than our niggardly old gods have bestowed on the very best of us.

Timotheus. I wish, my dear Lucian, you would let our babes and sucklings lie quiet, and say no more about them : as for your gods, I leave them at your mercy. Do not impose on me the performance of a task in which Plato himself, if he had attempted it, would have failed.

Lucian. No man ever detected false reasoning with more quickness; but unluckily he called in Wit at the exposure; and Wit, I am sorry to say, held the lowest place in his household. He sadly mistook the qualities of his mind in attempting the facetious; or, rather, he fancied he possessed one quality more than belonged to him. But, if he himself had not been a worse quibbler than any whose writings are come down to us, we might have been gratified by the exposure of wonderful acuteness wretchedly applied. It is no small service to the community to turn into ridicule the grave impostors, who are contending which of them shall guide and govern us, whether in politics or religion. There are always a few who will take the trouble to walk down among the sea-weeds and slippery stones, for the sake of showing their credulous fellow-citizens that skins filled with sand, and set upright at the forecastle, are neither men nor merchandise.

Timotheus. I can bring to mind, O Lucian, no writer possessing so great a variety of wit as you.

Lucian. No man ever possessed any variety of this gift ; and the holder is not allowed to exchange the quality for another. Banter (and such is Plato's) never grows large, never sheds its bristles, and never do they soften into the humorous or the facetious.

Timotheus. I agree with you that banter is the worst species of wit. We have indeed no correct idea what persons those really were whom Plato drags by the ears, to undergo slow torture under Socrates. One sophist, I must allow, is precisely like another : no discrimination of character, none of manner, none of language.

Lucian. He wanted the fancy and fertility of Aristophanes.

Timotheus. Otherwise, his mind was more elevated and more poetical.

Lucian. Pardon me if I venture to express my dissent in both particulars. Knowledge of the human heart, and discrimination of character, are requisites of the poet. Few ever have possessed them in an equal degree with Aristophanes : Plato has given no indication of either.

Timotheus. But consider his imagination.

Lucian. On what does it rest? He is nowhere so imaginative as in his *Polity.* Nor is there any state in the world that is, or would be, governed by it. One day you may find him at his counter in the midst of old-fashioned toys, which crack and crumble under his fingers while he exhibits and recommends them ; another day, while he is sitting on a goat's bladder, I may discover his bald head · surmounting an enormous mass of loose chaff and uncleanly feathers, which he would persuade you is the pleasantest and healthiest of beds, and that dreams descend on it from the gods.

" Open your mouth, and shut your eyes, and see what Zeus shall send you,"

says Aristophanes in his favourite metre. In this helpless condition of closed optics and hanging jaw, we find the followers of Plato. It is by shutting their eyes that they see, and by opening their mouths that they apprehend. Like certain broad-muzzled dogs, all stand equally stiff and staunch, although few scent the game, and their lips wag, and water, at whatever distance from the net. We must leave them with their hands hanging down before them, confident that they are wiser than we are, were it only for this attitude of humility. It is amusing to see them in it before the tall, well-robed Athenian, while he mis-spells the charms, and plays clumsily the tricks, he acquired from the conjurors here in Egypt. I wish you better success with the same materials. But in my opinion all philosophers should speak clearly. The highest things are the purest and brightest ; and the best writers are those who render them the most intelligible to the world below. In the arts and sciences, and particularly in music and metaphysics, this is difficult : but the subjects not being such as lie within the range of the community, I lay little stress upon them, and wish authors to deal with them as they best may, only beseeching that they recompense us, by bringing within our comprehension the other things with which they are entrusted for us. The followers of Plato fly off indignantly from any such proposal. If I ask them the meaning of some obscure passage, they answer that I am unprepared and unfitted for it, and that his mind is so far above mine, I can not grasp it. I look up into the faces of these worthy men, who mingle so much commiseration with so much calmness, and wonder at seeing them look no less vacant than my own.

Timotheus. You have acknowledged his eloquence, while you derided his philosophy and repudiated his morals.

Lucian. Certainly there was never so much eloquence with so little animation. When he has heated his oven, he forgets to put the bread into it; instead of which, he throws in another bundle of faggots. His words and sentences are often too large for the place they occupy. If a water-melon is not to be placed in an oyster-shell, neither is a grain of millet in a golden salver. At high festivals a full band may enter : ordinary conversation goes on better without it.

Timotheus. There is something so spiritual about him, that many of us Christians are firmly of opinion he must have been partially enlightened from above.

Lucian. I hope and believe we all are. His entire works are in our library. Do me the favour to point out to me a few of those passages where in poetry he approaches the spirit of Aristophanes, or where in morals he comes up to Epictetus.

Timotheus. It is useless to attempt it if you carry your prejudices with you. Beside, my dear cousin, I would not offend you, but really your mind has no point about it which could be brought to contact or affinity with Plato's.

Lucian. In the universality of his genius there must surely be some atom coincident with another in mine. You acknowledge, as everybody must do, that his wit is the heaviest and lowest : pray, is the specimen he has given us of history at all better ?

Timotheus. I would rather look to the loftiness of·his mind, and the genius that sustains him.

Lucian. So would I. Magnificent words, and the pomp and procession of stately sentences, may accompany genius, but are not always nor frequently called out by it. The voice ought not to be perpetually nor much elevated in the ethic and didactic, nor to roll sonorously, as if it issued from a mask in the theatre. The horses in the plain under Troy are not always kicking and neighing ; nor is the dust always raised in whirlwinds on the banks of Simois and Scamander ; nor are the rampires always in a blaze. Hector has lowered his helmet to the infant of Andromache, and Achilles to the embraces of Briseis. I do not blame the prose-writer who opens his bosom occasionally to a breath of poetry; neither, on the contrary, can I praise the gait of that pedestrian who lifts up his legs as high on a bare heath as in a corn-field.   Be authority as old and obstinate as it may, never let it persuade you that a man is the stronger for being unable to keep himself on the ground, or the weaker for breathing quietly and softly on ordinary occasions.   Tell me, over and over, that you find every great quality in Plato : let me only once ask you in return, whether he ever is ardent and energetic, whether he wins the affections, whether he agitates the heart.   Finding him deficient in every one of these faculties, I think his disciples have extolled him too highly.   Where power is absent, we may find the robes of genius, but we miss the throne.   He would acquit a slave who killed another in self-defence, but if he killed any free man, even in self-defence, he was not only to be punished with death, but to undergo the cruel death of a parricide.   This effeminate philosopher was more severe than the manly Demosthenes, who quotes a law against the striking of a slave : and Diogenes, when one ran away from him, remarked that it would be horrible if Diogenes could not do without a slave, when a slave could do without Diogenes?

Timotheus. Surely the allegories of Plato are evidences of his genius.

Lucian. A great poet in the hours of his idleness may indulge in allegory : but the highest poetical character will never rest on so unsubstantial a foundation.   The poet must take man from God's hands, must look into every fibre of his heart and brain, must be able to take the magnificent work to pieces, and to reconstruct it.   When this labour is completed, let him throw himself composedly on the earth, and care little how many of its ephemeral insects creep over him.   In regard to these allegories of Plato, about which I have heard so much, pray what and where are they?   You hesitate, my fair cousin Timotheus!   Employ one morning in transcribing them, and another in noting all the passages which are of practical utility in the

commerce of social life, or purify our affections at home, or
excite and elevate our enthusiasm in the prosperity and
glory of our country.   Useful books, moral books, instructive
books are easily composed : and surely so great a writer
should present them to us without blot or blemish : I find
among his many volumes no copy of a similar composition.
My enthusiasm is not easily raised indeed ; yet such a
whirlwind of a poet must carry it away with him ; nevertheless, here I stand, calm and collected, not a hair of my
beard in commotion.   Declamation will find its echo in
vacant places : it beats ineffectually on the well-furnished
mind.   Give me proof; bring the work; show the passages ;
convince, confound, overwhelm me.

Timotheus. I may do that another time with Plato.
And yet, what effect can I hope to produce on an unhappy
man who doubts even that the world is on the point of
extinction ?

Lucian. Are there many of your association who believe
that this catastrophe is so near at hand ?

Timotheus. We all believe it ; or rather, we all are certain
of it.

Lucian. How so?   Have you observed any fracture in
the disc of the sun ?   Are any of the stars loosened in
their orbits ?   Has the beautiful light of Venus ceased
to pant in the heavens, or has the belt of Orion lost its
gems !

Timotheus. O for shame !

Lucian. Rather should I be ashamed of indifference on
so important an occasion.

Timotheus. We know the fact by surer signs.

Lucian. These, if you could vouch for them, would be
sure enough for me.   The least of them would make me
sweat as profusely as if I stood up to the neck in the hot
preparation of a mummy.   Surely no wise or benevolent
philosopher could ever have uttered what he knew or
believed might be distorted into any such interpretation.
For if men are persuaded that they and their works are so
soon about to perish, what provident care are they likely to

take in the education and welfare of their families? What sciences will they improve, what learning will they cultivate, what monuments of past ages will they be studious to preserve, who are certain that there can be no future ones? Poetry will be censured as rank profaneness, eloquence will be converted into howls and execrations, statuary will exhibit only Midases and Ixions, and all the colours of painting will be mixed together to produce one grand conflagration: *flammantia mœnia mundi.*

Timotheus. Do not quote an atheist; especially in Latin. I hate the language; the Romans are beginning to differ from us already.

Lucian. Ah! you will soon split into smaller fractions. But pardon me my unusual fault of quoting. Before I let fall a quotation I must be taken by surprise. I seldom do it in conversation, seldomer in composition; for it mars the beauty and unity of style, especially when it invades it from a foreign tongue. A quoter is either ostentatious of his acquirements or doubtful of his cause. And moreover, he never walks gracefully who leans upon the shoulder of another, however gracefully that other may walk. Herodotus, Plato, Aristoteles, Demosthenes, are no quoters. Thucydides, twice or thrice, inserts a few sentences of Pericles: but Thucydides is an emanation of Pericles, somewhat less clear indeed, being lower, although at no great distance from that purest and most pellucid source. The best of the Romans, I agree with you, are remote from such originals, if not in power of mind, or in acuteness of remark, or in sobriety of judgment, yet in the graces of composition. While I admired, with a species of awe such as not Homer himself ever impressed me with, the majesty and sanctimony of Livy, I have been informed by learned Romans that in the structure of his sentences he is often inharmonious, and sometimes uncouth. I can imagine such uncouthness in the goddess of battles, confident of power and victory, when part of her hair is waving round the helmet, loosened by the rapidity of her descent or the vibration of her spear. Composition may be too adorned even for beauty. In painting it is often requisite to cover a bright colour with one less bright; and, in language, to relieve the ear from the tension of high notes, even at the cost of a discord. There are urns of which the borders are too prominent and too decorated for use, and which appear to be brought out chiefly for state, at grand carousals. The author who imitates the artificers of these, shall never have my custom.

Timotheus. I think you judge rightly: but I do not understand languages : I only understand religion.

Lucian. He must be a most accomplished, a most extraordinary man, who comprehends them both together. We do not even talk clearly when we are walking in the dark.

Timotheus. Thou art not merely walking in the dark, but fast asleep.

Lucian. And thou, my cousin, wouldst kindly awaken me with a red-hot poker. I have but a few paces to go along the corridor of life: prythee let me turn into my bed again and lie quiet. Never was any man less an enemy to religion than I am, whatever may be said to the contrary: and you shall judge of me by the soundness of my advice. If your leaders are in earnest, as many think, do persuade them to abstain from quarrelsomeness and contention, and not to declare it necessary that there should perpetually be a religious as well as a political war between east and west. No honest and considerate man will believe in their doctrines, who, inculcating peace and good-will, continue all the time to assail their fellow-citizens with the utmost rancour at every divergency of opinion, and, forbidding the indulgence of the kindlier affections, exercise at full stretch the fiercer. This is certain : if they obey any commander, they will never sound a charge when his order is to sound a retreat : if they acknowledge any magistrate, they will never tear down the tablet of his edicts.

Timotheus. We have what is all-sufficient.

Lucian. I see you have.

Timotheus. You have ridiculed all religion and all philosophy.

Lucian. I have found but little of either. I have cracked many a nut, and have come only to dust or maggots.

Timotheus. To say nothing of the saints, are all philosophers fools or impostors? And, because you can not rise to the ethereal heights of Plato, nor comprehend the real magnitude of a man so much above you, must he be a dwarf?

Lucian. The best sight is not that which sees best in the dark or the twilight; for no objects are then visible in their true colours and just proportions; but it is that which presents to us things as they are, and indicates what is within our reach and what is beyond it. Never were any three writers, of high celebrity, so little understood in the main character, as Plato, Diogenes, and Epicurus. Plato is a perfect master of logic and rhetoric; and whenever he errs in either, as I have proved to you he does occasionally, he errs through perverseness, not through unwariness. His language often settles into clear and most beautiful prose, often takes an imperfect and incoherent shape of poetry, and often, cloud against cloud, bursts with a vehement detonation in the air. Diogenes was hated both by the vulgar and the philosophers. By the philosophers, because he exposed their ignorance, ridiculed their jealousies, and rebuked their pride: by the vulgar, because they never can endure a man apparently of their own class who avoids their society and partakes in none of their humours, prejudices, and animosities. What right has he to be greater or better than they are? he who wears older clothes, who eats staler fish, and possesses no vote to imprison or banish anybody. I am now ashamed that I mingled in the rabble, and that I could not resist the childish mischief of smoking him in his tub. He was the wisest man of his time, not excepting Aristoteles; for he knew that he was greater than Philip or Alexander. Aristoteles did not know that he himself was, or, knowing it, did not act up to his knowledge; and here is a deficiency of wisdom.

Timotheus. Whether you did or did not strike the cask,

Diogenes would have closed his eyes equally. He would never have come forth and seen the truth, had it shone upon the world in that day. But, intractable as was this recluse, Epicurus, I fear, is quite as lamentable. What horrible doctrines !

Lucian. Enjoy, said he, the pleasant walks where you are : repose, and eat gratefully the fruit that falls into your bosom : do not weary your feet with an excursion, at the end whereof you will find no resting-place : reject not the odour of roses for the fumes of pitch and sulphur. What horrible doctrines !

Timotheus. Speak seriously. He was much too bad for ridicule.

Lucian. I will then speak as you desire me, seriously. His smile was so unaffected and so graceful, that I should have thought it very injudicious to set my laugh against it. No philosopher ever lived with such uniform purity, such abstinence from censoriousness, from controversy, from jealousy, and from arrogance.

Timotheus. Ah, poor mortal ! I pity him, as far as may be ; he is in hell : it would be wicked to wish him out : we are not to murmur against the all-wise dispensations.

Lucian. I am sure he would not ; and it is therefore I hope he is more comfortable than you believe.

Timotheus. Never have I defiled my fingers, and never will I defile them, by turning over his writings. But in regard to Plato, I can have no objection to take your advice.

Lucian. He will reward your assiduity : but he will assist you very little if you consult him principally (and eloquence for this should principally be consulted) to strengthen your humanity. Grandiloquent and sonorous, his lungs seem to play the better for the absence of the heart. His imagination is the most conspicuous, buoyed up by swelling billows over unsounded depths. There are his mild thunders, there are his glowing clouds, his traversing coruscations, and his shooting stars. More of true wisdom, more of trustworthy manliness, more of promptitude and power to keep you steady and straightforward on the perilous road of life, may be found in the little manual of Epictetus, which I could write in the palm of my left-hand, than there is in all the rolling and redundant volumes of this mighty rhetorician, which you may begin to transcribe on the summit of the great Pyramid, carry down over the Sphynx at the bottom, and continue on the sands half-way to Memphis.   And indeed the materials are appropriate ; one part being far above our sight, and the other on what, by the most befitting epithet, Homer calls the *no-corn-bearing.*

Timotheus. There are many who will stand against you on this ground.

Lucian. With what perfect ease and fluency do some of the dullest men in existence toss over and discuss the most elaborate of all works !   How many myriads of such creatures would be insufficient to furnish intellect enough for any single paragraph in them !   Yet '*we think this,*' '*we advise that,*' are expressions now become so customary, that it would be difficult to turn them into ridicule.   We must pull the creatures out while they are in the very act, and show who and what they are.   One of these fellows said to Caius Fuscus in my hearing, that there was a time when it was permitted him to doubt occasionally on particular points of criticism, but that the time was now over.

Timotheus. And what did you think of such arrogance ? What did you reply to such impertinence ?

Lucian. Let me answer one question at a time.   First : I thought him a legitimate fool, of the purest breed. Secondly : I promised him I would always be contented with the judgment he had rejected, leaving him and his friends in the enjoyment of the rest.

Timotheus. And what said he ?

Lucian. I forget.   He seemed pleased at my acknowledgment of his discrimination, at my deference and delicacy. He wished, however, I had studied Plato, Xenophon, and Cicero, more attentively ; without which preparatory discipline, no two persons could be introduced advantageously into a dialogue.   I agreed with him on this position, remarking that we ourselves were at that very time giving our sentence on the fact. He suggested a slight mistake on my side, and expressed a wish that he were conversing with a writer able to sustain the opposite part. With his experience and skill in rhetoric, his long habitude of composition, his knowledge of life, of morals, and of character, he should be less verbose than Cicero, less gorgeous than Plato, and less trimly attired than Xenophon.

Timotheus. If he spoke in that manner, he might indeed be ridiculed for conceitedness and presumption, but his language is not altogether a fool's.

Lucian. I deliver his sentiments, not his words : for who would read, or who would listen to me, if such fell from me as from him? Poetry has its probabilities, so has prose : when people cry out against the representation of a dullard, *Could he have spoken all that?* 'Certainly no,' is the reply : neither did Priam implore, in harmonious verse, the pity of Achilles. We say only what might be said, when great postulates are conceded.

Timotheus. We will pretermit these absurd and silly men : but, cousin Lucian! cousin Lucian! the name of Plato will be durable as that of Sesostris.

Lucian. So will the pebbles and bricks which gangs of slaves erected into a pyramid. I do not hold Sesostris in much higher estimation than those quieter lumps of matter. They, O Timotheus, who survive the wreck of ages, are by no means, as a body, the worthiest of our admiration. It is in these wrecks, as in those at sea, the best things are not always saved. Hen-coops and empty barrels bob upon the surface, under a serene and smiling sky, when the graven or depicted images of the gods are scattered on invisible rocks, and when those who most resemble them in knowledge and beneficence are devoured by cold monsters below.

Timotheus. You now talk reasonably, seriously, almost religiously. Do you ever pray?

Lucian. I do. It was no longer than five years ago that I was deprived by death of my dog Melanops. He had uniformly led an innocent life; for I never would let him walk out with me, lest he should bring home in his mouth the remnant of some god or other, and at last get bitten or stung by one. I reminded Anubis of this : and moreover I told him, what he ought to be aware of, that Melanops did honour to his relationship.

Timotheus. I can not ever call it piety to pray for dumb and dead beasts.

Lucian. Timotheus! Timotheus! have you no heart? have you no dog? do you always pray only for yourself?

Timotheus. We do not believe that dogs can live again.

Lucian. More shame for you! If they enjoy and suffer, if they hope and fear, if calamities and wrongs befall them, such as agitate their hearts and excite their apprehensions ; if they possess the option of being grateful or malicious, and choose the worthier ; if they exercise the same sound judgment on many other occasions, some for their own benefit and some for the benefit of their masters, they have as good a chance of a future life, and a better chance of a happy one, than half the priests of all the religions in the world. Wherever there is the choice of doing well or ill, and that choice (often against a first impulse) decides for well, there must not only be a soul of the same nature as man's, although of less compass and comprehension, but, being of the same nature, the same immortality must appertain to it ; for spirit, like body, may change, but can not be annihilated.

It was among the prejudices of former times that pigs are uncleanly animals, and fond of wallowing in the mire for mire's sake. Philosophy has now discovered, that when they roll in mud and ordure, it is only from an excessive love of cleanliness, and a vehement desire to rid themselves of scabs and vermin. Unfortunately, doubts keep pace with discoveries. They are like warts, of which the blood that springs from a great one extirpated, makes twenty little ones.

Timotheus. The Hydra would be a more noble simile.

Lucian. I was indeed about to illustrate my position by the old Hydra, so ready at hand and so tractable; but I will never take hold of a hydra, when a wart will serve my turn.

Timotheus. Continue then.

Lucian. Even children are now taught, in despite of Æsop, that animals never spoke. The uttermost that can be advanced with any show of confidence is, that if they spoke at all, they spoke in unknown tongues. Supposing the fact, is this a reason why they should not be respected ? Quite the contrary. If the tongues were unknown, it tends to demonstrate *our* ignorance, not *theirs*. If we could not understand them, while they possessed the gift, here is no proof that they did not speak to the purpose, but only that it was not to *our* purpose ; which may likewise be said with equal certainty of the wisest men that ever existed. How little have we learned from them, for the conduct of life or the avoidance of calamity ! Unknown tongues, indeed ! yes, so are all tongues to the vulgar and the negligent.

Timotheus. It comforts me to hear you talk in this manner, without a glance at our gifts and privileges.

Lucian. I am less incredulous than you suppose, my cousin ! Indeed I have been giving you what ought to be a sufficient proof of it.

Timotheus. You have spoken with becoming gravity, I must confess.

Lucian. Let me then submit to your judgment some fragments of history which have lately fallen into my hands. There is among them a *Hymn,* of which the metre is so incondite, and the phraseology so ancient, that the grammarians have attributed it to Linus. But the Hymn will interest you less, and is less to our purpose, than the tradition ; by which it appears that certain priests of high antiquity were of the brute creation.

Timotheus. No better, any of them.

Lucian. Now you have polished the palms of your hands. I will commence my narrative from the manuscript.

Timotheus. Pray do.

Lucian. There existed in the city of Nephosis a fraternity of priests, reverenced by the appellation of *Gasteres.* It is reported that they were not always of their present form, but were birds, aquatic and migratory, a species of cormorant. The poet Linus, who lived nearer the transformation (if there indeed was any), sings thus, in his Hymn to Zeus :—

"Thy power is manifest, O Zeus! in the Gasteres. Wild birds were they, strong of talon, clanging of wing, and clamorous of gullet. Wild birds, O Zeus! wild birds; now cropping the tender grass by the river of Adonis, and breaking the nascent reed at the root, and depasturing the sweet nymphæa; now again picking up serpents and other creeping things on each hand of old Ægyptos, whose head is hidden in the clouds.

"O that Mnemosyne would command the staidest of her three daughters to stand and sing before me! to sing clearly and strongly. How before thy throne, Saturnian! sharp voices arose, even the voices of Heré and of thy children. How they cried out that innumerable mortal men, various-tongued, kid-roasters in tent and tabernacle, devising in their many-turning hearts and thoughtful minds how to fabricate well-rounded spits of beech-tree, how such men, having been changed into brute animals, it behoved thee to trim the balance, and in thy wisdom to change sundry brute animals into men; in order that they might pour out flame-coloured wine unto thee, and sprinkle the white flower of the sea upon the thighs of many bulls, to pleasure thee. Then didst thou, O storm-driver! overshadow far lands with thy dark eyebrows, looking down on them, to accomplish thy will. And then didst thou behold the Gasteres, fat, tall, prominent-crested, purple-legged, dædal-plumed, white and black, changeable in colour as Iris. And lo! thou didst will it, and they were men."

Timotheus. No doubt whatever can be entertained of this Hymn's antiquity. But what farther says the historian?

Lucian. I will read on, to gratify you.

"It is recorded that this ancient order of a most lordly priesthood went through many changes of customs and ceremonies, which indeed they were always ready to accommodate to the maintenance of their authority and the enjoyment of their riches. It is recorded that, in the beginning, they kept various tame animals, and some wild ones, within the precincts of the temple : nevertheless, after a time, they applied to their own uses everything they could lay their hands on, whatever might have been the vow of those who came forward with the offering. And when it was expected of them to make sacrifices, they not only would make none, but declared it an act of impiety to expect it. Some of the people, who feared the Immortals, were dismayed and indignant at this backwardness ; and the discontent at last grew universal. Whereupon, the two chief priests held a long conference together, and agreed that something must be done to pacify the multitude. But it was not until the greater of them, acknowledging his despondency, called on the gods to answer for him that his grief was only because he never could abide bad precedents : and the other, on his side, protested that he was overruled by his superior, and moreover had a serious objection (founded on principle) to be knocked on the head. Meanwhile the elder was looking down on the folds of his robe, in deep melancholy. After long consideration, he sprang upon his feet, pushing his chair behind him, and said, 'Well, it is grown old, and was always too long for me : I am resolved to cut off a finger's breadth.'

"'Having, in your wisdom and piety, well contemplated the bad precedent,' said the other, with much consternation in his countenance at seeing so elastic a spring in a heel by no means bearing any resemblance to a stag's ... 'I have, I have,' replied the other, interrupting him ; 'say no more ; I am sick at heart ; you must do the same.'

"'A cursed dog has torn a hole in mine,' answered the other, 'and, if I cut anywhere about it, I only make bad worse. In regard to its length, I wish it were as long again.' 'Brother ! brother ! never be worldly-minded,' said the senior. 'Follow my example : snip off it not a finger's breadth, half a finger's breadth.'

"'But,' expostulated the other, 'will that satisfy the gods ?' 'Who talked about them ?' placidly said the senior. 'It is very unbecoming to have them always in our mouths : surely there are appointed times for them. Let us be contented with laying the snippings on the altar, and thus showing the people our piety and condescension. They, and the gods also, will be just as well satisfied, as if we offered up a buttock of beef, with a bushel of salt and the same quantity of wheaten flour on it.'

"'Well, if that will do . . . and you know best,' replied the other, 'so be it.' Saying which words, he carefully and considerately snipped off as much in proportion (for he was shorter by an inch) as the elder had done, yet leaving on his shoulders quite enough of materials to make handsome cloaks for seven or eight stout-built generals. Away they both went, arm-in-arm, and then holding up their skirts a great deal higher than was necessary, told the gods what they two had been doing for them and their glory. About the court of the temple the sacred swine were lying in indolent composure : seeing which, the brotherly twain began to commune with themselves afresh : and the senior said repentantly, 'What fools we have been! The populace will laugh outright at the curtailment of our vestures, but would gladly have seen these animals eat daily a quarter less of the lentils.' The words were spoken so earnestly and emphatically that they were overheard by the quadrupeds. Suddenly there was a rising of all the principal ones in the sacred inclosure : and many that were in the streets took up, each according to his temperament and condition, the gravest or shrillest tone of reprobation. The thinner and therefore the more desperate of the creatures, pushing their snouts under the curtailed habiliments of the high priests, assailed them with ridicule and reproach. For it had pleased the gods to work a miracle in their behoof, and they became as loquacious as those who governed them, and who were appointed to speak in the high places. 'Let the worst come to the worst, we at least have our tails to our hams,' said they. 'For how long?' whined others, piteously : others incessantly ejaculated tremendous imprecations : others, more serious and

sedate, groaned inwardly; and, although under their hearts
there lay a huge mass of indigestible sourness ready to
rise up against the chief priests, they ventured no farther
than expostulation.   'We shall lose our voices,' said they,
'if we lose our complement of lentils; and then, most
reverend lords, what will ye do for choristers?'   Finally,
one of grand dimensions, who seemed almost half-human,
imposed silence on every debater.   He lay stretched out
apart from his brethren, covering with his side the greater
portion of a noble dunghill, and all its verdure native and
imported.   He crashed a few measures of peascods to cool
his tusks; then turned his pleasurable longitudinal eyes
far toward the outer extremities of their sockets, and leered
fixedly and sarcastically at the high priests, showing every
tooth in each jaw.   Other men might have feared them;
the high priests envied them, seeing what order they were
in, and what exploits they were capable of.   A great painter,
who flourished many olympiads ago, has, in his volume
entitled the *Canon*, defined the line of beauty!   It was
here in its perfection: it followed with winning obsequiousness every member, but delighted more especially to swim
along that placid and pliant curvature on which Nature had
ranged the implements of mastication.   Pawing with his
cloven hoof, he suddenly changed his countenance from the
contemplative to the wrathful.   At one effort he rose up
to his whole length, breadth, and height: and they who
had never seen him in earnest, nor separate from the
common swine of the inclosure, with which he was in
the habit of husking what was thrown to him, could
form no idea what a prodigious beast he was.   Terrible
were the expressions of choler and comminations which
burst forth from his fulminating tusks.   Erimanthus would
have hidden his puny offspring before them; and Hercules
would have paused at the encounter.   Thrice he called
aloud to the high priests: thrice he swore in their own
sacred language that they were a couple of thieves and
impostors: thrice he imprecated the worst maledictions
on his own head if they had not violated the holiest of their

vows, and were not ready even to sell their gods. A tremor ran throughout the whole body of the united swine; so awful was the adjuration! Even the Gasteres themselves in some sort shuddered, not perhaps altogether at the solemn tone of its impiety; for they had much experience in these matters. But among them was a Gaster who was calmer than the swearer, and more prudent and conciliating than those he swore against. Hearing this objurgation, he went blandly up to the sacred porker, and, lifting the flap of his right ear between forefinger and thumb with all delicacy and gentleness, thus whispered into it: 'You do not in your heart believe that any of us are such fools as to sell our gods, at least while we have such a reserve to fall back upon.'

"'Are we to be devoured?' cried the noble porker, twitching his ear indignantly from under the hand of the monitor. 'Hush!' said he, laying it again, most soothingly, rather farther from the tusks: 'hush! sweet friend! Devoured? O certainly not: that is to say, not *all*: or, if all, not all at once. Indeed the holy men my brethren may perhaps be contented with taking a little blood from each of you, entirely for the advantage of your health and activity, and merely to compose a few slender black-puddings for the inferior monsters of the temple, who latterly are grown very exacting, and either are, or pretend to be, hungry after they have eaten a whole handful of acorns, swallowing I am ashamed to say what a quantity of water to wash them down. We do not grudge them it, as they well know: but they appear to have forgotten how recently no inconsiderable portion of this bounty has been conferred. If we, as they object to us, eat more, they ought to be aware that it is by no means for our gratification, since we have abjured it before the gods, but to maintain the dignity of the priesthood, and to exhibit the beauty and utility of subordination.'

"The noble porker had beaten time with his muscular tail at many of these periods; but again his heart panted visibly, and he could bear no more.

"'All this for our good! for our activity! for our health! Let us alone : we have health enough ; we want no activity. Let us alone, I say again, or by the Immortals ! . . .' 'Peace, my son! Your breath is valuable : evidently you have but little to spare : and what mortal knows how soon the gods may demand the last of it ? '

"At the beginning of this exhortation, the worthy high priest had somewhat repressed the ebullient choler of his refractory and pertinacious disciple, by applying his flat soft palm to the signet-formed extremity of the snout.

"'We are ready to hear complaints at all times,' added he, 'and to redress any grievance at our own. But beyond a doubt, if you continue to raise your abominable outcries, some of the people are likely to hit upon two discoveries : first, that your lentils would be sufficient to make daily for every poor family a good wholesome porridge ; and secondly, that your flesh, properly cured, might hang up nicely against the forthcoming bean-season.' Pondering these mighty words, the noble porker kept his eyes fixed upon him for some instants, then leaned forward dejectedly, then tucked one foot under him, then another, cautious to descend with dignity. At last he grunted (it must for ever be ambiguous whether with despondency or with resignation), pushed his wedgy snout far within the straw subjacent, and sank into that repose which is granted to the just."

Timotheus. Cousin ! there are glimmerings of truth and wisdom in sundry parts of this discourse, not unlike little broken shells entangled in dark masses of sea-weed. But I would rather you had continued to adduce fresh arguments to demonstrate the beneficence of the Deity, proving (if you could) that our horses and dogs, faithful servants and companions to us, and often treated cruelly, may recognise us hereafter, and we them. We have no authority for any such belief.

Lucian. We have authority for thinking and doing whatever is humane. Speaking of humanity, it now occurs to me, I have heard a report that some well-intentioned men of your religion so interpret the words or wishes of its founder, they would abolish slavery throughout the empire.

Timotheus. Such deductions have been drawn indeed from our Master's doctrine : but the saner part of us receive it metaphorically, and would only set men free from the bonds of sin.   For if domestic slaves were manumitted, we should neither have a dinner dressed nor a bed made, unless by our own children : and as to labour in the fields, who would cultivate them in this hot climate?   We must import slaves from Æthiopia and elsewhere, wheresoever they can be procured : but the hardship lies not on them ; it lies on us, and bears heavily ; for we must first buy them with our money, and then feed them; and not only must we maintain them while they are hale and hearty and can serve us, but likewise in sickness and (unless we can sell them for a trifle) in decrepitude.   Do not imagine, my cousin, that we are no better than enthusiasts, visionaries, subverters of order, and ready to roll society down into one flat surface.

Lucian. I thought you were maligned : I said so.

Timotheus. When the subject was discussed in our congregation, the meaner part of the people were much in favour of the abolition : but the chief priests and ministers absented themselves, and gave no vote at all, deeming it secular, and saying that in such matters the laws and customs of the country ought to be observed.

Lucian. Several of these chief priests and ministers are robed in purple and fine linen, and fare sumptuously every day.

Timotheus. I have hopes of you now.

Lucian. Why so suddenly?

Timotheus. Because you have repeated those blessed words, which are only to be found in our scriptures.

Lucian. There indeed I found them.   But I also found in the same volume words of the same speaker, declaring that the rich shall never see his face in heaven.

Timotheus. He does not always mean what you think he does.

Lucian. How is this? Did he then direct his discourses to none but men more intelligent than I am?

Timotheus. Unless he gave you understanding for the occasion, they might mislead you.

Lucian. Indeed!

Timotheus. Unquestionably. For instance, he tells us to take no heed of to-morrow : he tells us to share equally all our wordly goods: but we know that we can not be respected unless we bestow due care on our possessions, and that not only the vulgar but the well-educated esteem us in proportion to the gifts of fortune.

Lucian. The eclectic philosophy is most flourishing among you Christians. You take whatever suits your appetites, and reject the rest.

Timotheus. We are not half so rich as the priests of Isis. Give us their possessions; and we will not sit idle as they do, but be able and ready to do incalculable good to our fellow-creatures.

Lucian. I have never seen great possessions excite to great alacrity. Usually they enfeeble the sympathies, and often overlie and smother them.

Timotheus. Our religion is founded less on sympathies than on miracles. Cousin! you smile most when you ought to be most serious.

Lucian. I was smiling at the thought of one whom I would recommend to your especial notice, as soon as you disinherit the priests of Isis. He may perhaps be refractory; for he pretends (the knave!) to work miracles.

Timotheus. Impostor! who is he?

Lucian. Aulus of Pelusium. Idle and dissolute, he never gained anything honestly but a scourging, if indeed he ever made, what he long merited, this acquisition. Unable to run into debt where he was known, he came over to Alexandria.

Timotheus. I know him : I know him well. Here, of his own accord, he has betaken himself to a new and regular life.

Lucian. He will presently wear it out, or make it sit

easier on his shoulders.   My metaphor brings me to my
story.   Having nothing to carry with him beside an empty
valise, he resolved on filling it with something, however
worthless, lest, seeing his utter destitution, and hopeless of
payment, a receiver of lodgers should refuse to admit him
into the hostelry.   Accordingly, he went to a tailor's, and
began to joke about his poverty.   Nothing is more apt to
bring people into good-humour : for, if they are poor themselves, they enjoy the pleasure of discovering that others
are no better off; and, if not poor, there is the consciousness of superiority.

"The favour I am about to ask of a man so wealthy and
so liberal as you are," said Aulus, "is extremely small: you
can materially serve me, without the slightest loss, hazard,
or inconvenience.   In few words, my valise is empty : and
to some ears an empty valise is louder and more discordant
than a bagpipe : I can not say I like the sound of it myself.
Give me all the shreds and snippings you can spare me.
They will feel like clothes ; not exactly so to me and my
person, but to those who are inquisitive, and who may be
importunate."

The tailor laughed, and distended both arms of Aulus
with his munificence.   Soon was the valise well filled and
rammed down.   Plenty of boys were in readiness to carry
it to the boat.   Aulus waved them off, looking at some
angrily, at others suspiciously.   Boarding the skiff, he
lowered his treasure with care and caution, staggering a
little at the weight, and shaking it gently on deck, with his
ear against it : and then, finding all safe and compact, he
sat on it ; but as tenderly as a pullet on her first eggs.
When he was landed, his care was even greater, and whoever came near him was warned off with loud vociferations.
Anxiously as the other passengers were invited by the inn-
keepers to give their houses the preference, Aulus was
importuned most : the others were only beset ; he was
borne off in triumphant captivity.   He ordered a bedroom,
and carried his valise with him ; he ordered a bath, and
carried with him his valise.   He started up from the

company at dinner, struck his forehead, and cried out, "Where is my valise?" "We are honest men here," replied the host. "You have left it, sir, in your chamber: where else indeed should you leave it?"

"Honesty is seated on your brow," exclaimed Aulus; "but there are few to be trusted in the world we live in. I now believe I can eat." And he gave a sure token of the belief that was in him, not without a start now and then and a finger at his ear, as if he heard somebody walking in the direction of his bed-chamber. Now began his first miracle: for now he contrived to pick up, from time to time, a little money. In the presence of his host and fellow-lodgers, he threw a few obols, negligently and indifferently, among the beggars. "These poor creatures," said he, "know a new comer as well as the gnats do: in one half-hour I am half-ruined by them; and this daily."

Nearly a month had elapsed since his arrival, and no account of board and lodging had been delivered or called for. Suspicion at length arose in the host whether he really was rich. When another man's honesty is doubted, the doubter's is sometimes in jeopardy. The host was tempted to unsew the valise. To his amazement and horror he found only shreds within it. However, he was determined to be cautious, and to consult his wife, who, although a Christian like Aulus, and much edified by his discourses, might dissent from him in regard to a community of goods, at least in her own household, and might defy him to prove by any authority that the doctrine was meant for inn-keepers. Aulus, on his return in the evening, found out that his valise had been opened. He hurried back, threw its contents into the canal, and, borrowing an old cloak, he tucked it up under his dress, and returned. Nobody had seen him enter or come back again, nor was it immediately that his host or hostess were willing to appear. But, after he had called them loudly for some time, they entered his apartment: and he thus addressed the woman:—

"O Eucharis! no words are requsite to convince you (firm as you are in the faith) of eternal verities, however mysterious. But your unhappy husband has betrayed his incredulity in regard to the most awful. If my prayers, offered up in our holy temples all day long, have been heard, and that they have been heard I feel within me the blessed certainty, something miraculous has been vouchsafed for the conversion of this miserable sinner. Until the present hour, the valise before you was filled with precious relics from the apparel of saints and martyrs, fresh as when on them." "True, by Jove!" said the husband to himself. "Within the present hour," continued Aulus, "they are united into one raiment, signifying our own union, our own restoration."

He drew forth the cloak, and fell on his face. Eucharis fell also, and kissed the saintly head prostrate before her. The host's eyes were opened, and he bewailed his hardness of heart. Aulus is now occupied in strengthening his faith, not without an occasional support to the wife's: all three live together in unity.

Timotheus. And do you make a joke even of this? Will you never cease from the habitude?

Lucian. Too soon. The farther we descend into the vale of years, the fewer illusions accompany us: we have little inclination, little time, for jocularity and laughter. Light things are easily detached from us, and we shake off heavier as we can. Instead of levity, we are liable to moroseness: for always near the grave there are more briars than flowers, unless we plant them ourselves, or our friends supply them.

Timotheus. Thinking thus, do you continue to dissemble or to distort the truth? The shreds are become a cable for the faithful. That they were miraculously turned into one entire garment who shall gainsay? How many hath it already clothed with righteousness? Happy men, casting their doubts away before it! Who knows, O cousin Lucian, but on some future day you yourself will invoke the merciful interposition of Aulus!

Lucian. Possibly: for if ever I fall among thieves, nobody is likelier to be at the head of them.

Timotheus. Uncharitable man! how suspicious! how ungenerous! how hardened in unbelief! Reason is a bladder on which you may paddle like a child as you swim in summer waters: but, when the winds rise and the waves roughen, it slips from under you, and you sink; yes, O Lucian, you sink into a gulf whence you never can emerge.

Lucian. I deem those the wisest who exert the soonest their own manly strength, now with the stream and now against it, enjoying the exercise in fine weather, venturing out in foul, if need be, yet avoiding not only rocks and whirlpools, but also shallows. In such a light, my cousin, I look on your dispensations. I shut them out as we shut out winds blowing from the desert; hot, debilitating, oppressive, laden with impalpable sands and pungent salts, and inflicting an incurable blindness.

Timotheus. Well, cousin Lucian! I can bear all you say while you are not witty. Let me bid you farewell in this happy interval.

Lucian. Is it not serious and sad, O my cousin, that what the Deity hath willed to lie incomprehensible in his mysteries, we should fall upon with tooth and nail, and ferociously growl over, or ignorantly dissect?

Timotheus. Ho! now you come to be serious and sad, there are hopes of you. Truth always begins or ends so.

Lucian. Undoubtedly. But I think it more reverential to abstain from that which, with whatever effort, I should never understand.

Timotheus. You are lukewarm, my cousin, you are lukewarm. A most dangerous state.

Lucian. For milk to continue in, not for men. I would not fain be frozen or scalded.

Timotheus. Alas! you are blind, my sweet cousin!

Lucian. Well; do not open my eyes with pincers, nor compose for them a collyrium of spurge.

May not men eat and drink and talk together, and perform in relation one to another all the duties of social life, whose opinions are different on things immediately under their eyes? If they can and do, surely they may as easily on things equally above the comprehension of each party. The wisest and most virtuous man in the whole extent of the Roman empire is Plutarch of Cheronæa : yet Plutarch holds a firm belief in the existence of I know not how many gods, every one of whom has committed notorious misdemeanours. The nearest to the Cheronæan in virtue and wisdom is Trajan, who holds all the gods dog-cheap. These two men are friends. If either of them were influenced by your religion, as inculcated and practised by the priesthood, he would be the enemy of the other, and wisdom and virtue would plead for the delinquent in vain. When your religion had existed, as you tell us, about a century, Caius Cæcilius,* of Novum Comum, was Proconsul in Bithynia. Trajan, the mildest and most equitable of mankind, desirous to remove from them, as far as might be, the hatred and invectives of those whose old religion was assailed by them, applied to Cæcilius for information on their behaviour as good citizens. The reply of Cæcilius was favourable. Had Trajan applied to the most eminent and authoritative of the sect, they would certainly have brought into jeopardy all who differed in one tittle from any point of their doctrine or discipline. For the thorny and bitter aloe of dissension required less than a century to flower on the steps of your temple.

Timotheus. You are already half a Christian, in exposing to the world the vanities both of philosophy and of power.

Lucian. I have done no such thing : I have exposed the vanities of the philosophising and the powerful. Philosophy is admirable ; and Power may be glorious : the one conduces to truth, the other has nearly all the means of conferring peace and happiness, but it usually, and indeed almost always, takes a contrary direction. I have ridiculed the futility of speculative minds, only when they would pave the clouds instead of the streets. To see distant things better than near is a certain proof of a defective sight. The people I have held in derision never turn their eyes to what they can see, but direct them continually where

* The younger Pliny.

nothing is to be seen. And this, by their disciples, is called the sublimity of speculation! There is little merit acquired, or force exhibited, in blowing off a feather that would settle on my nose : and this is all I have done in regard to the philosophers : but I claim for myself the approbation of humanity, in having shown the true dimensions of the great. The highest of them are no higher than my tunic; but they are high enough to trample on the necks of those wretches who throw themselves on the ground before them.

Timotheus. Was Alexander of Macedon no higher?

Lucian. What region of the earth, what city, what theatre, what library, what private study, hath he enlightened? If you are silent, I may well be. It is neither my philosophy nor your religion which casts the blood and bones of men in their faces, and insists on the most reverence for those who have made the most unhappy. If the Romans scourged by the hands of children the schoolmaster who would have betrayed them, how greatly more deserving of flagellation, from the same quarter, are those hundreds of pedagogues who deliver up the intellects of youth to such immoral revellers and mad murderers! They would punish a thirsty child for purloining a bunch of grapes from a vineyard, and the same men on the same day would insist on his reverence for the subverter of Tyre, the plunderer of Babylon, and the incendiary of Persepolis. And are these men teachers? are these men philosophers? are these men priests? Of all the curses that ever afflicted the earth, I think Alexander was the worst. Never was he in so little mischief as when he was murdering his friends.

Timotheus. Yet he built this very city; a noble and opulent one when Rome was of hurdles and rushes.

Lucian. He built it! I wish, O Timotheus! he had been as well employed as the stone-cutters or the plasterers. No, no: the wisest of architects planned the most beautiful and commodious of cities, by which, under a rational government and equitable laws, Africa might have been civilised to the centre, and the palm have extended her conquests through the remotest desert. Instead of which, a dozen of Macedonian thieves rifled a dying drunkard and murdered his children. In process of time, another drunkard reeled hitherward from Rome, made an easy mistake in mistaking a palace for a brothel, permitted a stripling boy to beat him soundly, and a serpent to receive the last caresses of his paramour.

Shame upon historians and pedagogues for exciting the worst passions of youth by the display of such false glories! If your religion hath any truth or influence, her professors will extinguish the promontory lights, which only allure to breakers. They will be assiduous in teaching the young and ardent that great abilities do not constitute great men, without the right and unremitting application of them; and that, in the sight of Humanity and Wisdom, it is better to erect one cottage than to demolish a hundred cities. Down to the present day we have been taught little else than falsehood. We have been told to do this thing and that: we have been told we shall be punished unless we do: but at the same time we are shown by the finger that prosperity and glory, and the esteem of all about us, rest upon other and very different foundations. Now, do the ears or the eyes seduce the most easily and lead the most directly to the heart? But both eyes and ears are won over, and alike are persuaded to corrupt us.

Timotheus. Cousin Lucian, I was leaving you with the strangest of all notions in my head. I began to think for a moment that you doubted my sincerity in the religion I profess; and that a man of your admirable good sense, and at your advanced age, could reject that only sustenance which supports us through the grave into eternal life.

Lucian. I am the most docile and practicable of men, and never reject what people set before me: for if it is bread, it is good for my own use; if bone or bran, it will do for my dog or mule. But, although you know my weakness and facility, it is unfair to expect I should have admitted at once what the followers, and personal friends of your Master, for a long time hesitated to receive. I remember to have read in one of the early commentators, that his disciples themselves* could not swallow the miracle of the loaves ; and one who wrote more recently says, that even his brethren did not believe† in him.

Timotheus. Yet, finally, when they have looked over each other's accounts, they cast them up, and make them all tally in the main sum ; and if one omits an article, the next supplies its place with a commodity of the same value. What would you have ? But it is of little use to argue on religion with a man who, professing his readiness to believe, and even his credulity, yet disbelieves in miracles.

Lucian. I should be obstinate and perverse if I disbelieved in the existence of a thing for no better reason than because I never saw it, and can not understand its operations. Do you believe, O Timotheus, that Perictione, the mother of Plato, became his mother by the sole agency of Apollo's divine spirit, under the phantasm of that god ?

Timotheus. I indeed believe such absurdities !

Lucian. You touch me on a vital part if you call an absurdity the religion or philosophy in which I was educated. Anaxalides, and Clearagus, and Speusippus, his own nephew, assert it. Who should know better than they ?

Timotheus. Where are their proofs ?

Lucian. I would not be so indelicate as to require them on such an occasion. A short time ago I conversed with an old centurion, who was in service by the side of Vespasian, when Titus, and many officers and soldiers of the army, and many captives, were present, and who saw one Eleazar put a ring to the nostril of a demoniac (as the patient was called) and draw the demon out of it.

Timotheus. And do you pretend to believe this nonsense?

Lucian. I only believe that Vespasian and Titus had nothing to gain or accomplish by the miracle ; and that Eleazar, if he had been detected in a trick by two

* *Mark* vi.   † *John* vii.

acute men and several thousand enemies, had nothing to look forward to but a cross—the only piece of upholstery for which Judea seems to have either wood or workmen, and which are as common in that country as direction-posts are in any other.

Timotheus. The Jews are a stiff-necked people.

Lucian. On such occasions, no doubt.

Timotheus. Would you, O Lucian, be classed among the atheists, like Epicurus?

Lucian. It lies not at my discretion what name shall be given me at present or hereafter, any more than it did at my birth.   But I wonder at the ignorance and precipitancy of those who call Epicurus an atheist.   He saw on the same earth with himself a great variety of inferior creatures, some possessing more sensibility and more thoughtfulness than others.   Analogy would lead so contemplative a reasoner to the conclusion that if many were inferior and in sight, others might be superior and out of sight.   He never disbelieved in the existence of the gods ; he only disbelieved that they troubled their heads with our concerns.   Have they none of their own?   If they are happy, does their happiness depend on us, comparatively so imbecile and vile?   He believed, as nearly all nations do, in different ranks and orders of superhuman beings ; and perhaps he thought (but I never was in his confidence or counsels) that the higher were rather in communication with the next to them in intellectual faculties, than with the most remote. To me the suggestion appears by no means irrational, that, if we are managed or cared for at all by beings wiser than ourselves (which in truth would be no sign of any great wisdom in them), it can only be by such as are very far from perfection, and who indulge us in the commission of innumerable faults and follies, for their own speculation or amusement.

Timotheus. There is only one such ; and he is the Devil.

Lucian. If he delights in our wickedness, which you believe, he must be incomparably the happiest of beings, which you do not believe.   No god of Epicurus rests his elbow on his arm-chair with less energetic exertion or dis-composure.

Timotheus. We lead holier and purer lives than such ignorant mortals as are not living under Grace.

Lucian. I also live under Grace, O Timotheus! and I venerate her for the pleasures I have received at her hands. I do not believe she has quite deserted me. If my gray hairs are unattractive to her, and if the trace of her fingers is lost in the wrinkles of my forehead, still I sometimes am told it is discernible even on the latest and coldest of my writings.

Timotheus. You are wilful in misapprehension. The Grace of which I speak is adverse to pleasure and impurity.

Lucian. Rightly do you separate impurity and pleasure, which indeed soon fly asunder when the improvident would unite them. But never believe that tenderness of heart signifies corruption of morals, if you happen to find it (which indeed is unlikely) in the direction you have taken; on the contrary, no two qualities are oftener found together, on mind as on matter, than hardness and lubricity.

Believe me, cousin Timotheus, when we come to eighty years of age we are all Essenes. In our kingdom of heaven there is no marrying or giving in marriage; and austerity in ourselves, when Nature holds over us the sharp instrument with which Jupiter operated on Saturn, makes us austere to others. But how happens it that you, both old and young, break every bond which connected you anciently with the Essenes? Not only do you marry (a height of wisdom to which I never have attained, although in others I commend it), but you never share your substance with the poorest of your community, as they did, nor live simply and frugally, nor purchase nor employ slaves, nor refuse rank and offices in the state, nor abstain from litigation, nor abominate and execrate the wounds and cruelties of war. The Essenes did all this, and greatly more, if Josephus and Philo, whose political and religious tenets are opposite to theirs, are credible and trustworthy.

Timotheus. Doubtless you would also wish us to retire into the desert, and eschew the conversation of mankind.

Lucian. No, indeed; but I would wish the greater part of your people to eschew mine, for they bring all the worst of the desert with them whenever they enter; its smothering heats, its blinding sands, its sweeping suffocation. Return to the pure spirit of the Essenes, without their asceticism; cease from controversy, and drop party designations. If you will not do this, do less, and be merely what you profess to be, which is quite enough for an honest, a virtuous, and a religious man.

Timotheus. Cousin Lucian, I did not come hither to receive a lecture from you.

Lucian. I have often given a dinner to a friend who did not come to dine with me.

Timotheus. Then, I trust, you gave him something better for dinner than bay-salt and dandelions. If you will not assist us in nettling our enemies a little for their absurdities and impositions, let me entreat you, however, to let us alone, and to make no remarks on us. I myself run into no extravagances, like the Essenes, washing and fasting, and retiring into solitude. I am not called to them; when I am, I go.

Lucian. I am apprehensive the Lord may afflict you with deafness in that ear.

Timotheus. Nevertheless, I am indifferent to the world, and all things in it. This, I trust, you will acknowledge to be true religion and true philosophy.

Lucian. That is not philosophy which betrays an indifference to those for whose benefit philosophy was designed; and those are the whole human race. But I hold it to be the most unphilosophical thing in the world to call away men from useful occupations and mutual help, to profitless speculations and acrid controversies. Censurable enough, and contemptible too, is that supercilious philosopher, sneeringly sedate, who narrates in full and flowing periods the persecutions and tortures of a fellow-man, led astray by his credulity, and ready to die in the assertion of what in his soul he believes to be the truth. But hardly less censurable, hardly less contemptible, is the tranquilly arrogant sectarian, who denies that wisdom or honesty can exist beyond the limits of his own ill-lighted chamber.

Timotheus. What! is he sanguinary?

Lucian. Whenever he can be, he is ; and he always has it in his power to be even worse than that, for he refuses his custom to the industrious and honest shopkeeper who has been taught to think differently from himself in matters which he has had no leisure to study, and by which, if he had enjoyed that leisure, he would have been a less industrious and a less expert artificer.

Timotheus. We can not countenance those hard-hearted men who refuse to hear the word of the Lord.

Lucian. The hard-hearted knowing this of the tender-hearted, and receiving the declaration from their own lips, will refuse to hear the word of the Lord all their lives.

Timotheus. Well, well ; it can not be helped. I see, cousin, my hopes of obtaining a little of your assistance in your own pleasant way are disappointed ; but it is something to have conceived a better hope of saving your soul, from your readiness to acknowledge your belief in miracles.

Lucian. Miracles have existed in all ages and in all religions. Witnesses to some of them have been numerous ; to others of them fewer. Occasionally the witnesses have been disinterested in the result.

Timotheus. Now indeed you speak truly and wisely.

Lucian. But sometimes the most honest and the most quiescent have either been unable or unwilling to push themselves so forward as to see clearly and distinctly the whole of the operation ; and have listened to some knave who felt a pleasure in deluding their credulity, or some other who himself was either an enthusiast or a dupe. It also may have happened in the ancient religions, of Egypt for instance, or of India, or even of Greece, that narratives have been attributed to authors who never heard of them ; and have been circulated by honest men who firmly believed them; by half-honest, who indulged their vanity in becoming members of a novel and bustling society; and by utterly dishonest, who, having no other means of rising above the shoulders of the vulgar, threw dust into their eyes and made them stoop.

Timotheus. Ha! the rogues! It is nearly all over with them.

Lucian. Let us hope so. Parthenius and the Roman poet Ovidius Naso, have related the transformations of sundry men, women, and gods.

Timotheus. Idleness! Idleness! I never read such lying authors.

Lucian. I myself have seen enough to incline me toward a belief in them.

Timotheus. You? Why! you have always been thought an utter infidel; and now you are running, hot and heedless as any mad dog, to the opposite extreme!

Lucian. I have lived to see, not indeed one man, but certainly one animal turned into another; nay, great numbers. I have seen sheep with the most placid faces in the morning, one nibbling the tender herb with all its dew upon it; another, negligent of its own sustenance, and giving it copiously to the tottering lamb aside it.

Timotheus. How pretty! half poetical!

Lucian. In the heat of the day I saw the very same sheep tearing off each other's fleeces with long teeth and longer claws, and imitating so admirably the howl of wolves, that at last the wolves came down on them in a body, and lent their best assistance at the general devouring. What is more remarkable, the people of the villages seemed to enjoy the sport; and, instead of attacking the wolves, waited until they had filled their stomachs, ate the little that was left, said piously and from the bottom of their hearts what you call *grace,* and went home singing and piping.

MELANCTHON AND CALVIN.

Calvin. Are you sure, O Melancthon ! that you yourself are among the elect ?

Melancthon. My dear brother ! so please it God, I would rather be among the many.

Calvin. Of the damned ?

Melancthon. Alas ! no. But I am inclined to believe that the many will be saved and will be happy, since Christ came into the world for the redemption of sinners.

Calvin. Hath not our Saviour said explicitly, that many are called, but few chosen.

Melancthon. Our Saviour ? hath he said it ?

Calvin. Hath he, forsooth ! Where is your New Testament ?

Melancthon. In my heart.

Calvin. Without this page, however.

Melancthon. When we are wiser and more docile, that is, when we are above the jars and turmoils and disputations of the world, our Saviour will vouchsafe to interpret what, through the fumes of our intemperate vanity, is now indistinct or dark. He will plead for us before no inexorable judge. He came to remit the sins of man ; not the sins of a few, but of many ; not the sins of many, but of all.

Calvin. What ! of the benighted heathen too ? of the pagan ? of the idolater ?

Melancthon. I hope so ; but I dare not say it.

Calvin. You would include even the negligent, the indifferent, the sceptic, the unbeliever.

Melancthon. Pitying them for a want of happiness in a want of faith. They are my brethren : they are God's children. He will pardon the presumption of my wishes for their welfare; my sorrow that they have fallen, some through their blindness, others through their deafness, others through their terror, others through their anger, peradventure at the loud denunciations of unforgiving man. If I would forgive a brother, may not he, who is immeasurably better and more merciful, have pity on a child? He came on earth to take our nature upon him: will he punish, will he reprehend us, for an attempt to take as much as may be of his upon ourselves?

Calvin. There is no bearing any such fallacies.

Melancthon. Is it harder to bear these fallacies (as they appear to you, and perhaps are, for we all are fallible, and many even of our best thoughts are fallacies), is it harder, O my friend, to bear these, than to believe in the eternal punishment of the erroneous?

Calvin. Erroneous, indeed! Have they not the Book of Life, now at last laid open before them, for their guidance?

Melancthon. No, indeed; they have only two or three places, dog-eared and bedaubed, which they are commanded to look into and study. These are so uninviting, that many close again the volume of salvation, clasp it tight, and throw it back in our faces. I would rather show a man green fields than gibbets: and if I called him to enter the service of a plenteous house and powerful master, he may not be rendered the more willing to enter it by my pointing out to him the stocks in the gateway, and telling him that nine-tenths of the household, however orderly, must occupy that position. The book of *good news* under your interpretation, tells people not only that they may go and be damned, but that unless they are lucky, they must inevitably. Again it informs another set of inquirers that if once they have been under what they feel to be the influence of grace, they never can relapse. All must go well who have once gone well: and a name once written in the list of favourites can never be erased.

Calvin. This is certain.

Melancthon. Let us hope then, and in holy confidence let us believe, that the book is large and voluminous; that it begins at an early date of man's existence; and that amid the agitation of inquiry, it comprehends the humble and submissive doubter. For doubt itself, between the richest patrimony and utter destitution, is quite sufficiently painful: and surely it is a hardship to be turned over into a criminal court for having lost in a civil one. But if all who have once gone right can never go astray, how happens it that so large a part of the angels fell off from their allegiance? They were purer and wiser than we are, and had the advantage of seeing God face to face. They were the ministers of his power; they knew its extent; yet they defied it. If we err, it is in relying too confidently on his mercies; not in questioning his omnipotence. If our hopes forsake us, if the bonds of sin bruise and corrode us, so that we can not walk upright, there is, in the midst of these calamities, no proof that we are utterly lost. Danger far greater is there in the presumption of an especial favour, which men incomparably better than ourselves can never have deserved. Let us pray, O Calvin, that we may hereafter be happier than our contentions and animosities will permit us to be at present; and that our opponents, whether now in the right or in the wrong, may come at last where all error ceases.

Calvin. I am uncertain whether such a wish is rational: and I doubt more whether it is religious. God hath willed them to walk in their blindness. To hope against it seems like repining at his unalterable decree; a weak indulgence in an unpermitted desire; an unholy entreaty of the heart that He will forego his vengeance, and abrogate the law that was from the beginning. Of one thing I am certain: we must lop off the unsound.

Melancthon. What a curse hath metaphor been to religion! It is the wedge that holds asunder the two great portions of the Christian world. We hear of nothing so commonly as fire and sword. And here indeed what was metaphor is converted into substance and applied to practice. The unsoundness of doctrine is not cut off nor cauterised; the professor is. The head falls on the scaffold, or fire surrounds the stake, because a doctrine is bloodless and incombustible. Fierce outrageous animals, for want of the man who has escaped them, lacerate and trample his cloak or bonnet. This, although the work of brutes, is not half so brutal as the practice of theologians, seizing the man himself, instead of bonnet or cloak.

Calvin. We must leave such matters to the magistrate.

Melancthon. Let us instruct the magistrate in his duty; this is ours. Unless we can teach humanity, we may resign the charge of religion. For fifteen centuries, Christianity has been conveyed into many houses, in many cities, in many regions, but always through slender pipes; and never yet into any great reservoir in any part of the earth. Its principal ordinances have never been observed in the polity of any state whatever. Abstinence from spoliation, from oppression, from bloodshed, has never been inculcated by the chief priests of any. These two facts excite the doubts of many in regard to a divine origin and a divine protection. Wherefore it behoves us the more especially to preach forbearance. If the people are tolerant one toward another in the same country, they will become tolerant in time toward those whom rivers or seas have separated from them. For surely it is strange and wonderful that nations which are near enough for hostility should never be near enough for concord. This arises from bad government; and bad government arises from a negligent choice of counsellors by the prince, usually led or terrified by a corrupt, ambitious, wealthy (and therefore unchristian) priesthood. While their wealth lay beyond the visible horizon, they tarried at the cottage, instead of pricking on for the palace.

Calvin. By the grace and help of God we will turn them back again to their quiet and wholesome resting-place, before the people lay a rough hand upon the silk.

But you evaded my argument on predestination.

Melancthon. Our blessed Lord himself, in his last hours, ventured to express a wish before his heavenly Father, that the bitter cup might pass away from him. I humbly dare to implore that a cup much bitterer may be removed from the great body of mankind; a cup containing the poison of eternal punishment, where agony succeeds to agony, but never death.

Calvin. I come armed with the Gospel.

Melancthon. Tremendous weapon! as we have seen it through many ages, if man wields it against man; but like the fabled spear of old mythology, endued with the faculty of healing the saddest wound its most violent wielder can inflict. Obscured and rusting with the blood upon it, let us hasten to take it up again, and apply it, as best we may, to its appointed uses.

The life of our Saviour is the simplest exposition of his words. Strife is what he both discountenanced and forbade. We ourselves are right-minded, each of us all : and others are right-minded in proportion as they agree with us, chiefly in matters which we insist are well worthy of our adherence, but which whosoever refuses to embrace displays a factious and unchristian spirit. These for the most part are matters which neither they nor we understand, and which, if we did understand them, would little profit us. The weak will be supported by the strong, if they can ; if they can not, they are ready to be supported even by the weaker, and cry out against the strong, as arrogant or negligent, or deaf or blind ; at last even their strength is questioned, and the more if, while there is fury all around them, they are quiet.

I remember no discussion on religion in which religion was not a sufferer by it, if mutual forbearance, and belief in another's good motives and intentions, are (as I must always think they are) its proper and necessary appurtenances.

Calvin. Would you never make inquiries?

Melancthon. Yes ; and as deep as possible ; but into my own heart, for that belongs to me ; and God hath entrusted it most especially to my own superintendence.

Calvin. We must also keep others from going astray, by showing them the right road, and, if they are obstinate in resistance, then by coercing and chastising them through the magistrate.

Melancthon. It is sorrowful to dream that we are scourges in God's hand, and that he appoints 'for us no better work than lacerating one another. I am no enemy to inquiry, where I see abuses, and where I suspect falsehood. The Romanists, our great oppressors, think it presumptuous to search into things abstruse; and let us do them the justice to acknowledge that, if it is a fault, it is one which they never commit. But surely we are kept sufficiently in the dark by the infirmity of our nature : no need to creep into a corner and put our hands before our eyes. To throw away or turn aside from God's best gifts is verily a curious sign of obedience and submission. He not only hath given us a garden to walk in, but he hath planted it also for us, and he wills us to know the nature and properties of everything that grows up within it. Unless we look into them and handle them and register them, how shall we discover this to be salutary, that to be poisonous; this annual, that perennial?

Calvin. Here we coincide; and I am pleased to find in you less apathy than I expected. It becomes us, moreover, to denounce God's vengeance on a sinful world.

Melancthon. Is it not better and pleasanter to show the wanderer by what course of life it may be avoided? is it not better and pleasanter to enlarge on God's promises of salvation, than to insist on his denunciations of wrath? is it not better and pleasanter to lead the wretched up to his mercy-seat, than to hurl them by thousands under his fiery chariot?

Calvin. We have no option. By our heavenly Father many are called, but few are chosen.

Melancthon. There is scarcely a text in the Holy Scriptures to which there is not an opposite text, written in characters equally large and legible; and there has usually been a sword laid upon each. Even the weakest disputant is made so conceited by what he calls religion, as to think himself wiser than the wisest who thinks differently from him; and he becomes so ferocious by what he calls holding it fast, that he appears to me as if he held it fast much in the same manner as a terrier holds a rat, and you have about as much trouble in getting it from between his incisors. When at last it does come out, it is mangled, distorted, and extinct.

Calvin. M. Melancthon! you have taken a very perverse view of the subject. Such language as yours would extinguish that zeal which is to enlighten the nations, and to consume the tares by which they are overrun.

Melancthon. The tares and the corn are so intermingled throughout the wide plain which our God hath given us to cultivate, that I would rather turn the patient and humble into it to weed it carefully, than a thresher who would thresh wheat and tare together before the grain is ripened, or who would carry fire into the furrows when it is.

Calvin. Yet even the most gentle, and of the gentler sex, are inflamed with a holy zeal in the propagation of the faith.

Melancthon. I do not censure them for their earnestness in maintaining truth. We not only owe our birth to them, but also the better part of our education; and if we were not divided after their first lesson, we should continue to live in a widening circle of brothers and sisters all our lives. After our infancy and removal from home, the use of the rod is the principal thing we learn of our alien preceptors; and, catching their dictatorial language, we soon begin to exercise their instrument of enforcing it, and swing it right and left, even after we are paralysed by age, and until Death's hand strikes it out of ours. I am sorry you have cited the gentler part of the creation to appear before you, obliged as I am to bear witness that I myself have known a few specimens of the fair sex become a shade less fair, among the perplexities of religion. Indeed I am credibly informed that certain of them have lost their patience, running up and down in the dust where many roads diverge. This surely is not walking humbly with their God, nor walking with him at all; for those who walk with him are always readier to hear *His* voice than their own, and to admit that it is more persuasive. But at last the zealot is so infatuated, by the serious mockeries he imitates and repeats, that he really takes his own voice for God's. Is it not wonderful that the words of eternal life should have hitherto produced only eternal litigation ; and that, in our progress heavenward, we should think it expedient to plant unthrifty thorns over bitter wells of blood in the wilderness we leave behind us ?

Calvin. It appears to me that you are inclined to tolerate even the rank idolatry of our persecutors.   Shame ! shame !

Melancthon. Greater shame if I tolerated it within my own dark heart, and waved before it the foul incense of self-love.

Calvin. I do not understand you.   What I do under- stand is this, and deny it at your peril . . . I mean at the peril of your salvation . . . that God is a jealous God : he himself declares it.

Melancthon. We are in the habit of considering the God of Nature as a jealous God, and idolatry as an enormous evil : an evil which is about to come back into the world, and to subdue or seduce once more our strongest and most sublime affections.   Why do you lift up your eyes and hands ?

Calvin. An evil *about* to come back ! *about* to come ! Do we not find it in high places ?

Melancthon. We do indeed, and always shall, while there are any high places upon earth.   Thither will men creep, and there fall prostrate.

Calvin. Against idolatry we still implore the Almighty that he will incline our hearts to keep his law.

Melancthon. The Jewish law ; the Jewish idolatry.   You fear the approach of this, and do not suspect the presence of a worse.

Calvin. A worse than that which the living God hath denounced ?

Melancthon. Even so.

Calvin. Would it not offend, would it not wound to the quick, a mere human creature, to be likened to a piece of metal or stone, a calf or monkey ?

Melancthon. A mere human creature might be angry ; because his influence among his neighbours arises in great measure from the light in which he appears to them ; and this light does not emanate from himself, but may be thrown on him by any hand that is expert at mischief: beside, the likeness of such animals to him could never be suggested by reverence or esteem, nor be regarded as a type of any virtue. The mere human creature, such as human creatures for the most part are, would be angry; because he has nothing which he can oppose to ridicule but resentment.

Calvin. I am in consternation at your lukewarmness. If you treat idolaters thus lightly, what hope can I entertain of discussing with you the doctrine of grace and predestination.

Melancthon. Entertain no such hope at all. Wherever I find in the Holy Scriptures a disputable doctrine, I interpret it as judges do, in favour of the culprit: such is man: the benevolent judge is God. But in regard to idolatry, I see more criminals who are guilty of it than you do. I go beyond the stone-quarry and the pasture, beyond the graven image and the ox-stall. If we bow before the distant image of good, while there exists within our reach one solitary object of substantial sorrow, which sorrow our efforts can remove, we are guilty (I pronounce it) of idolatry: we prefer the intangible effigy to the living form. Surely we neglect the service of our Maker if we neglect his children. He left us in the chamber with them, to take care of them, to feed them, to admonish them, and occasionally to amuse them: instead of which, after a warning not to run into the fire, we slam the door behind us in their faces, and run eagerly downstairs to dispute and quarrel with our fellows of the household who are about their business. The wickedness of idolatry does not consist in any inadequate representation of the Deity, for whether our hands or our hearts represent him, the representation is almost alike inadequate. Every man does what he hopes and believes will be most pleasing to his God; and God, in his wisdom and mercy, will not punish gratitude in its error.

Calvin. How do you know that?

Melancthon. Because I know his loving-kindness, and experience it daily.

Calvin. If men blindly and wilfully run into error when God hath shown the right way, he will visit it on their souls.

Melancthon. He will observe from the serenity of heaven, a serenity emanating from his presence, that there is scarcely any work of his creation on earth which hath not excited, in some people or other, a remembrance, an admiration, a symbol, of his power. The evil of idolatry is this. Rival nations have raised up rival deities: war hath been denounced in the name of Heaven: men have been murdered for the love of God: and such impiety hath darkened all the regions of the world, that the Lord of all things hath been invoked by all simultaneously as the Lord of Hosts. This is the only invocation in which men of every creed are united: an invocation to which Satan, bent on the perdition of the human race, might have listened from the fallen angels.

Calvin. We can not hope to purify men's hearts until we lead them away from the abomination of Babylon: nor will they be led away from it until we reduce the images to dust. So long as they stand, the eye will hanker after them, and the spirit be corrupt.

Melancthon. And long afterward, I sadly fear. We attribute to the weakest of men the appellations and powers of Deity: we fall down before them: we call the impious and cruel by the title of *gracious* and *most religious:* and, even in the house of God himself, and before his very altar, we split his Divine Majesty asunder, and offer the largest part to the most corrupt and most corrupting of his creatures.

Calvin. Not *we*, M. Melancthon. I will preach, I will exist, in no land of such abomination.

Melancthon. So far, well: but religion demands more. Our reformers knock off the head from Jupiter: thunderbolt and sceptre stand. The attractive, the impressive, the august, they would annihilate, leaving men nothing but their sordid fears of vindictive punishment, and their impious doubts of our Saviour's promises.

Calvin. We should teach men to retain for ever the fear of God before their eyes, never to cease from the apprehension of His wrath, to be well aware that He often afflicts when He is farthest from wrath, and that such infliction is a benefit bestowed by Him.

Melancthon. What! if only a few are to be saved when the infliction is over?

Calvin. It becometh not us to repine at the number of vessels which the supremely wise artificer forms, breaks, and casts away, or at the paucity it pleaseth him to preserve. The ways of Providence are inscrutable.

Melancthon. Some of them are, and some of them are not; and in these it seems to be his design that we should see and adore his wisdom. We fancy that all our inflictions are sent us directly and immediately from above: sometimes we think it in piety and contrition, but oftener in moroseness and discontent. It would, however, be well if we attempted to trace the causes of them. We should probably find their origin in some region of the heart which we never had well explored, or in which we had secretly deposited our worst indulgences. The clouds that intercept the heavens from us, come not from the heavens, but from the earth.

Why should we scribble our own devices over the Book of God, erasing the plainest words, and rendering the Holy Scriptures a worthless palimpsest? Can not we agree to show the nations of the world that the whole of Christianity is practicable, although the better parts never have been practised, no, not even by the priesthood, in any single one of them. Bishops, confessors, saints, martyrs, have never denounced to king or people, nor ever have attempted to delay or mitigate, the most accursed of crimes, the crime of Cain, the crime indeed whereof Cain's was only a germ, the crime of fratricide, war, war, devastating, depopulating, soul-slaughtering, heaven-defying war. Alas! the gentle call of mercy sounds feebly, and soon dies away, leaving no trace on the memory: but the swelling cries of vengeance, in which we believe we imitate the voice of Heaven, run and reverberate in loud peals and multiplied echoes along the whole vault of the brain.   All the man is shaken by them ; and he shakes all the earth.

Calvin ! I beseech you, do you who guide and govern so many, do you (whatever others may) spare your brethren. Doubtful as I am of lighter texts, blown backward and forward at the opening of opposite windows, I am convinced and certain of one grand immovable verity.   It sounds strange ; it sounds contradictory.

Calvin. I am curious to hear it.

Melancthon. You shall.   This is the tenet.   There is nothing on earth divine beside humanity.

www.ingramcontent.com/pod-product-compliance
Lightning Source LLC
Chambersburg PA
CBHW020939030726
47496CB00005B/1256